A MOTHER'S BETRAYAL

LOUISE GUY

B

First published in Great Britain in 2024 by Boldwood Books Ltd.

Copyright © Louise Guy, 2024

Cover Design by Becky Glibbery

Cover Illustration: Shutterstock

A CIP catalogue record for this book is available from the British Library.

Paperback ISBN 978-1-83533-147-7

Large Print ISBN 978-1-83533-146-0

Hardback ISBN 978-1-83533-148-4

Ebook ISBN 978-1-83533-145-3

Kindle ISBN 978-1-83533-144-6

Audio CD ISBN 978-1-83533-153-8

MP3 CD ISBN 978-1-83533-152-1

Digital audio download ISBN 978-1-83533-150-7

Boldwood Books Ltd
23 Bowerdean Street
London SW6 3TN
www.boldwoodbooks.com

To all the wonderful mothers – especially mine – who nurture, inspire and support unconditionally.

PROLOGUE

THIRTY-TWO YEARS EARLIER

As the towering gum trees cast their late-afternoon shadow across the park, Julia looked up from the crisp white pages of the journal she'd purchased the previous day. A smile tugged at her lips as she observed Arabella and Florence, her four-year-old identical twins, playing on the swings. Their carefree laughter echoed through the air, a testament to the unbreakable bond they shared.

'Higher, Flo! Push me higher!' Arabella giggled, her little body swaying back and forth with delight.

Florence obliged by giving her sister's swing a vigorous push. 'Hold on tight, Ari!'

Julia's smile widened. She'd always dreamed of having children, but twins and their incredible bond wasn't something she'd imagined she'd get to witness first-hand. They were two little girls, but often seemed to think and act as one. Julia wasn't sure if she found their development fascinating because of her background as a neuroscientist, or whether she would have felt this way regardless of the fact that she specialised in the study of cognitive function and how it affected human behaviour.

She turned her attention back to her journal, carefully dating the first entry of what she intended to be an ongoing documenta-tion of her twins. She was deep in her own thoughts when a sudden shriek jarred her from them. She looked up as Arabella tumbled backwards off the swing. The painful impact of her head meeting the rubber matting was followed by heart-wrenching cries.

Julia's journal slipped from her hands to the ground as panic gripped her and she raced towards her daughters.

Florence's cries were as loud as Arabella's with words mixing with her tears. 'I'm sorry. I'm sorry. I'm sorry.'

'It's okay, Florence,' Julia assured her, taking Arabella into her arms, as she checked her head where a lump was beginning to form. 'You were having fun. It wasn't your fault. Try and stop crying so we can look after Arabella.'

Florence's lip trembled as she did her best to calm herself.

Julia held Arabella close, stroking her back. 'You're fine, darling. We'll get you home and put some ice on the lump.' *And monitor you for concussion.*

She reached her other arm out and pulled Florence to her, her heart aching as she shared her daughter's pain. Even at four, poor Florence would blame herself for the accident and spend days trying to make it up to Arabella. The irony being that Arabella adored Florence to the point she was unlikely to ever blame her for anything.

Julia's internal thoughts raced, and she found it almost hard to breathe as an overwhelming sense of protectiveness seemed to crush her. She knew she couldn't shield them from every minor mishap, but in a moment of clarity, she knew that she would go to any length to ensure her daughters' happiness... *any length at all.*

1

CURRENT DAY

Ari grinned and waved as she pulled up outside Flo's house where her sister and nephew were waiting for her.

Kayden flung open the back door of the Lexus and jumped in. 'Hi, Aunty A.'

'Hey, buddy, how's your day been?'

'Great,' he said as he strapped himself in. 'Are we Abba-ing tonight?'

Ari laughed. 'Of course. I can't imagine a car trip without a little bit of "Waterloo", can you?'

'Hey,' Flo said, carefully placing a gorgeous bouquet of yellow tulips on the back seat next to Kayden before joining Ari in the front. 'Thanks for picking us up. It's not exactly on your way.' She reached over and hugged her sister.

'You're welcome. And it doesn't need to be on my way if I get to spend time with my two favourite people.' Ari squeezed her tight before indicating and pulling back into the road. 'You ready for the grand birthday extravaganza?'

Flo rolled her green eyes and gave a theatrical sigh. 'Oh, you know me, Sis. I live for these family gatherings.'

'No comment,' Ari said, a smile playing on her lips. 'Now, I must say, you do look rather beautiful tonight. Love the highlights.'

A groan came from the back seat, causing them both to laugh.

'You say that every time, Aunty A. Mum looks exactly the same as you. That's how it works when you're identical twins.'

'Yes.' Ari winked at Flo. 'Beautiful. And we're not *exactly* the same. My hair's long and without the highlights, and darker than your mum's. And we're wearing different clothes. I'm in my silly work suit and your mum looks lovely and relaxed. I wish I'd had time to throw on something more comfortable. Now, let's get the important things underway.' She turned up the music she'd cued earlier for the Abba singalong.

On the day they'd turned eighteen, and were eligible, Ari and Flo had both passed their driving licences. They'd spent the rest of the day driving their grandmother's old VW Golf around town and blasting Abba at top volume for no other reason than the car had an old CD player and one Abba disc. They'd stopped for lunch and for a walk along the beach at Brighton, before returning home for a celebratory dinner with their parents and grandmother. It had been wonderful day with Flo often referencing it as one of the best days of her life. 'I now play Abba anytime I'm sad,' she'd confided in Ari years later. 'It brings our eighteenth back and how excited we were. I think I felt pure joy that day. We'd finished school, we had our licences, and it was the start of being adults. Weirdly, Abba was part of that. The music and the feeling of that day made me feel like I could tackle anything.'

Since that day, Abba remained a favourite, and was an essential warm-up on occasions when Ari and Flo were summoned to spend time with their mother. 'It'll get us in the mood,' Ari would say.

'We'll be able to tackle anything,' Flo would reply, neither of them believing this, but always enjoying the light-hearted mood they'd at least start the visits in.

Now, as the music blasted while they travelled along the busy streets from Box Hill to South Yarra, they all joined in at the tops of their voices as the final line was sung.

Ari reached across and squeezed Flo's hand. 'Can you tackle anything?'

Flo nodded, a wide smile on her lips. 'Right at this moment, yes. Not so sure if that's likely to be the same answer once we reach South Yarra.'

Ari gave Flo's hand another squeeze before placing her hand back on the steering wheel.

'Can I watch my iPad the rest of the way?' Kayden asked. 'There's some important soccer on.'

Flo took the device from the bag she had by her feet and handed it, with his headphones, back to him. 'We'll be there in about ten minutes, so you won't have much time.'

Kayden rushed to put his headphones on and start up the device.

'Still soccer-obsessed?' Ari asked.

Flo nodded. 'Which is good because he's outside kicking a ball at every possible minute. That should keep Mum happy at least. She can't complain he's not getting enough fresh air.'

'Shh,' Ari said putting a finger to her lips. 'No spoiling the car trip. "Mum talk" waits until we enter the "Mum zone". Until then, more Abba-ing.'

Flo laughed as Ari turned up the music and 'Take a Chance on Me' filled the car.

One and a half songs later, Ari pulled into the driveway of their parents' South Yarra home, killed the engine and turned to face her twin sister. She grinned. 'You can *tackle anything*, remember?'

Flo pulled a face that suggested that was very unlikely.

'*No need to look so enthusiastic, Florence.*' Ari enunciated her words in a perfect imitation of their mother's disapproving tone.

Flo closed her eyes momentarily, took a deep breath and then reopened them. 'I know I shouldn't say it. I should be ready to tackle anything, but I'm not in the mood for this. Work's been hectic the last few weeks, and even though I finally had a weekend off, I could do without the examination of everything Kayden or I've done. She's probably got a list of complaints, and I can guarantee they'll all be directed at me. I'm sure she won't be happy with the fact I'm wearing jeans for a start.'

Ari glanced in the rear-vision mirror. Her six-year-old nephew was deep in concentration, headphones on, iPad in his hands. 'It's Mum's birthday, so we don't have much choice. Ignore any criticisms. I, for one, love those jeans. I should have thrown a change of clothes in, but coming straight from work means the suit I'm afraid. If you need to, use Kayden as an excuse to leave early. Or I'll come up with a work-related emergency.' She glanced at her watch. 'It's six-thirty. Let's aim for an eight-thirty departure. Nine at the latest.'

Flo laughed. 'Your scheduling used to drive me mad, but right now, it sounds good.'

As they waited for the front door to be opened, Ari couldn't help but cringe at the instructions Flo was giving her son.

'Pass the flowers to Grandma, okay, and wish her a happy birthday. They're her favourites, so she shouldn't have any reason to complain about them. And only give her a hug if she hugs you first. And if she asks you questions, answer them politely, but don't tell her too much. Yes and no is fine.'

'Flo! I think Kayden can handle himself. Mum's not that bad.' Well, she probably was that bad, but it seemed wrong to be giving Kayden such extensive instruction. Ari could only imagine what else Flo had said to him about his grandmother.

Flo opened her mouth, about to object as the front door opened. She shut it again and plastered on a smile as their father appeared, the edges of his eyes crinkling in delight as his tall, broad frame filled the doorway.

'Girls,' he said, pulling them to him. He quickly released them and turned to Kayden. 'And then, of course, my favourite person on the planet.'

Kayden squealed as Mike drew him into a bear hug.

'How are you, buddy? Kicking lots of goals?'

'Yep. Scored two at the game after school today. It would have been more, but I was tired, so I sat out for half. One of my goals was from the edge of the box, and the other from the penalty area. Our team won ten to three.'

'Wow, ten to three. That's a lot of goals. Sounds like you grade-one kids could teach the pros something. Sometimes they don't get any goals for an entire match.' Mike ruffled his grandson's sandy hair as he let him out of his embrace. 'Now come on in. Grandma's by the fire with a glass of bubbles, and I've got a few things to finish in the kitchen.'

'We'll help you,' Flo said without hesitation.

Mike shook his head and steered her down the corridor. 'No, you won't. You'll make an effort with your mum for her birthday.'

Ari snorted and quickly coughed to hide it. It wasn't her and Flo that needed to make the effort.

Her father gave her a warning look. 'You know, whether she shows it or not, she struggles on her birthday. Today's a day to give her a break. The fact that she took an annual leave day from work to spend it with us says a lot.'

Ari was quickly subdued. She had forgotten the significance of the date.

'Be extra nice,' her father added. 'She won't tell me what's going on, but she's had a stressful week at work. Someone's causing some issues for her.'

This piqued Ari's interest. 'Really? She never usually talks about anything to do with work. What kind of issues?'

'She wouldn't elaborate,' Mike said, 'but it must be pretty bad if she's even mentioned it. Everything is usually confidential. It's the most detail she's shared in the thirty years she's worked there.'

'We'll be nice,' Flo muttered under her breath as they reached the entrance to the lounge room.

'Grandma,' Kayden said, a genuine smile on his lips as he entered the cosy lounge room. 'Happy birthday.' He held out the flowers. 'Mummy said they're your favourite.'

Julia placed her champagne flute on the side table next to her and rose from the chair. Her short, ash-brown hair looked as if it had been recently coloured and styled, and as usual, her make-up was flawless, with her eyeshadow skilfully applied to accentuate her unusual grey eyes. Ari couldn't remember ever seeing her mother look anything but perfect.

'Thank you, Kayden and girls,' she said, 'that's sweet of you. And yes, Kayden, majestic tulips are my favourite. Perhaps not this colour, but that's neither here nor there.'

Kayden turned to Flo and Ari with a beaming smile. 'See, Grandma loves them. They're pretty, so why would she complain—'

'Happy birthday, Mum,' Flo said, cutting her son off. 'Would you like me to put the tulips in water?'

'No, let's leave them as they are for now to enjoy tonight, and then you can take them with you. I'm off to Canberra in the morning, so there isn't much point having them here.' She gave a little laugh. 'Your father is hardly going to appreciate them.'

Flo's cheeks coloured. 'I didn't think.'

Julia patted her arm. 'That's okay, Florence, you rarely do.' She grimaced as she looked more closely at Flo.

Ari held her breath, waiting for her mother's usual comments about Flo's clothes being too casual and not as stylish as Ari's, and questioning why her daughter always wore her hair short rather than long like Ari did. If she was in hospital scrubs most of the day, Ari would quite likely opt for a stylish, easy-to-manage haircut like Flo's. She knew Flo hated these comparisons, as did she. If anything, she'd always been grateful that Flo had an individual sense of style as it made it easier for friends and family to tell them apart. But, surprisingly, other than the disapproving look, tonight their mother didn't go down that track.

'Now, let's see about some drinks for everyone,' Julia said. 'And Kayden, why don't you come and sit beside me and tell me your news.'

'I have lots of soccer news,' Kayden said.

'School news first,' Julia replied as they sat down on the couch. 'And then I'd love to hear your soccer news after dinner.'

'Really?' Kayden's eyes widened.

Julia nodded. 'Of course. Now, what reading level are you at? I hope you're almost ready to move to independent reading and that you've spent time this weekend with a book.'

'Three soccer books,' Kayden said proudly. 'I can read quite a lot of the words myself.'

Ari caught Flo's gaze and winked. She imagined Flo was on edge waiting for some kind of criticism from their mother.

Julia patted Kayden's knee. 'That's wonderful. You know, the key to reading is finding books about things you like. There's a lovely bookshop near my work in Canberra. I'll drop in during the week and see if they have any soccer books.'

Ari almost laughed at the shock on Flo's face.

'Thank you,' Kayden said, leaning in and hugging Julia.

'Drinks?'

Their father walked into the room with a tray housing a bottle of Bollinger, their mother's favourite champagne, champagne flutes and a glass of orange juice. 'Fresh,' he said to Flo before she had a chance to object to a sugary drink. 'Squeezed them myself.'

'The tree's loaded with them,' Julia said. 'Take some home with you if you like.'

'Hon,' Mike said, 'your mother called. The painkillers haven't touched her migraine. She sent her apologies. She said she'll call you later tomorrow for a chat and take you out for lunch when you're back from Canberra.'

'Gigi's not coming?' Kayden's disappointment mirrored Ari's own feelings. She'd been looking forward to seeing her grandmother.

'Not tonight, buddy,' Mike said. 'Now, how about you come through to the kitchen with me and give me a hand?' He winked at Kayden, and Kayden grinned. Everyone, except Julia, knew this was code for watching more soccer.

'Even all these years later, it has to be a hard day for Gigi,' Flo said. 'And for you, of course,' she added, looking to her mother.

Julia nodded. 'I don't think she ever fully recovered. But you know, she did her best to make sure her sadness didn't ruin my birthdays moving forward. If anything, she went over the top to ensure that everyone was smiling and happy. I've always felt bad for Dad that my birthday clouded what should have been a day of remembrance for him.'

'Did you ever tell Gigi that?' Ari asked.

Julia nodded. 'She was quick to dismiss it. Said she remembered him every day, and he would have hated to think my birthdays were a sad day every year rather than a day of celebration.'

'It might have made it easier to concentrate on you than relive the day of the car accident,' Flo said.

'Possibly. I'll never forget that afternoon.' Julia's eyes clouded with a faraway look. 'My cake was ready, and we were about to light the candles when the police knocked on the door. We never did end up lighting them. Turning eight was not a good day, and to be honest, is probably why I've never enjoyed birthdays or birthday cakes.'

Ari was surprised to hear her mother open up. Other than knowing their grandfather was killed in a car accident, she barely spoke about him, and while Ari was aware that her mother had never seemed particularly enthusiastic about birthdays or cakes, it was only now that she realised how difficult this day must be.

'I hope Gigi's doing okay,' Flo said. 'It's sad that she never found someone else. It's a lot of years to be on your own. Did she ever show any interest in anyone?'

'I asked her once, and she said that her heart belonged to my father and she'd never betray him, not even in death.'

'Oh, Gigi,' Ari said. 'That's so beautiful and yet so sad.'

'Gigi,' Julia tutted. 'Why you can't all call her by her actual name or Grandma, I'll never know. I should have insisted when Flo came up with the ridiculous nickname that it be banned on the spot.'

'Flo was two,' Ari reminded her, choosing to go along with her mother's not-so-subtle attempt at changing the subject. 'Genevieve isn't exactly an easy name for a two-year-old to pronounce and Gigi loves it. She's always said she never wanted to be called Grandma, and this works for all of us. I couldn't imagine calling her anything else now. She's Gigi.'

Julia sighed. 'You're probably right. The traditional names don't really fit her personality, do they? Now...' Julia turned to Ari.

'Let's move on to more important matters. What press has been organised following the awards ceremony on Wednesday night?'

Ari spluttered on her drink. 'Press? I haven't even won the award yet.'

'Is there any reason you won't win?'

'The other finalists for a start. I have no control over whether I win.' And if she was honest, she couldn't care if she won or not. A year ago, she would have been ecstatic to be nominated, but in the last few months, something had changed. She half wondered if she was entering menopause early. Although at thirty-six, it was probably unlikely. At least it might explain why she was feeling so restless and unenthusiastic about work and life.

'You had full control,' Julia said. 'Every case and every decision you've made in the past year was under your control. You've run a perfect race. You *will* win.'

Ari stared at her mother. It was hard to know whether the words were meant as a compliment or a threat. 'It's just an award, Mum.'

'It isn't *just* an award, Arabella. It's recognition by your peers and leaders in the legal field. It's important. How you dress is too. I hope you're planning to wear my black Chanel we had adjusted a few months ago? It makes the perfect statement. Intelligent, successful and, of course, beautiful.'

Ari nodded, not wanting to pursue the award discussion any further. She searched her mind frantically for a change of subject. She turned to her sister. 'Have you told Mum about your promotion opportunity?'

Daggers shot from Flo's eyes.

Ari grimaced. Of course, Flo hadn't told their mother, and now Flo would kill her.

'Dinner.' Their father appeared in the doorway. 'Bring your drinks, and we'll top them up, or you might prefer wine.'

Ari stood; mouthing 'sorry' to Flo. Flo shook her head in the familiar *Why would you do that?* way Ari had seen many times over their lifetime before draining her champagne glass and following their father out of the living room. If she wasn't driving, Ari would have loved to have done the same.

2

Flo gratefully accepted a drink top-up from her father and racked her brain for a topic to change the conversation to. She didn't want to discuss the ER nurse manager position with her mother.

'Let's raise our glasses,' her father said once everyone was seated with plates overloaded with roast lamb, Mike's famous crispy roast potatoes and a range of vegetables. Flo had to hand it to her father – he was an exceptional cook, and she was grateful he'd given Kayden a manageable amount of food. Her mother had the habit of piling the plate full of the vegetables Kayden didn't like – broccoli in particular – and then making a big deal out of him not eating it.

'To my darling Julia, happy sixty-sixth birthday.'

They raised their glasses. 'To Mum,' Ari and Flo both said.

'Grandma,' Kayden added, his glass in the air.

'Try not to spill that, Kayden,' Julia said, as Kayden's glass tipped at a precarious angle.

Mike cleared his throat. 'Now, you'll have to catch me up on the news. Kayden and I were busy chatting in the kitchen.' He winked at his grandson. 'So, I couldn't eavesdrop.'

'Flo was about to tell us about a promotion she's been offered,' Julia said.

'Actually, I was about to ask you about your work,' Flo said. 'Are they going to expect you to retire anytime soon? Sixty-six is past retirement age. Isn't it sixty-five?'

'No, there's no official retirement age these days. You're expected to work right up to having one foot, if not both, in the grave.'

'But surely, with what you do, there'd be an age they'd want you to move on?' Ari said.

Julia put down her knife and fork and considered the question. 'I don't see why. I've worked in the area for over thirty years, and I'm completely up to date with all new technology and processes. If anything, my extensive background in neuroscience would be a huge loss to the department.'

'The secret department,' Kayden said, pushing a potato around his plate. He looked up at Julia. 'What do you do for a job, Grandma? Mum said you're something important, that thing you just said, a neuro something and your work is top secret. Are you a spy?'

Julia smiled. 'No, not a spy, and yes, you're right I'm a neuroscientist. I spend most of my day doing research, collecting data and all sorts of things to do with our brains and human behaviour.'

'Then it's not secret?'

'What a neuroscientist does isn't a secret,' Julia said, 'but working for the Bureau of Strategic Intelligence means that the details of my work must be kept confidential, which is a big word for secret. We do a lot of work with the Australian military, and they don't always want to share what we're doing with other countries.'

'I think I'll still tell my friends that you're a spy,' Kayden said. 'They'll think it's cool that my grandma is a spy.'

A small smile played on Julia's lips. 'I never thought I'd be cool with the six-year-old crowd.'

'Dad mentioned you were having some trouble with someone,' Flo said. 'Is there anything we can do to help?'

Julia raised an eyebrow at her husband. 'Why on earth would you share that with them? You know I don't like to worry the girls.'

'He didn't tell us anything,' Ari said. 'Only to be a bit nicer than usual, as you've had a rough week.'

Julia's face softened. 'Oh.' She turned to her husband. 'Sorry, hon. I'm a bit on edge, but issues with a colleague aren't something I want to discuss. What I can share with you is that I'm finally being published in some scientific journals. It's nothing that will probably interest you, but it's nice to know that my work's being recognised by external parties.'

'What's the topic?' Ari asked.

'I can't tell you until publication's confirmed.'

'Geez,' Flo said. 'You never tell us anything about work, and now you dangle a carrot in front of us.'

The exuberant laugh that escaped Julia's lips was both startling and delightful. It was something Ari loved about her mother. She was so serious at times. So focused on work and success, but then she'd laugh, and it was impossible not to join her. 'I didn't realise you were so interested,' Julia said.

'Of course we are,' Ari said. 'We'd love to hear some details of what you're working on. You've kept it all secret for so many years.'

'That's an exaggeration. I work for the Bureau of Strategic Intelligence. Lots of research and lab work. That's not a secret. I just can't give you any details of exactly what I'm doing or why. If the articles are published they're not going to reveal any national secrets; nothing's changed there. Like I said, we need to wait until the articles are confirmed to be published. Topic closed. Now, back to you, Florence. Tell us about the promotion.'

'It's not a promotion,' Flo said, knowing that *topic closed* meant exactly that. 'The ER nurse manager role has become available, and I'm being encouraged to apply.'

'That's fantastic,' Mike said. 'Congratulations.'

Flo smiled. 'I haven't applied yet, Dad.'

'Nurse manager?' Julia said. 'That would be a lot more responsibility, wouldn't it?'

Flo nodded. 'Yes. It's a good opportunity, but I'm not sure I'm quite at that level yet. I'd need to do some management courses.'

Julia tutted. 'It's too much, Flo. You've got Kayden to look after, and you're still struggling with your nursing duties from time to time. Until you're on top of them, you shouldn't be in a management position.'

'Mum!' Ari said. 'That's hardly supportive, and what do you mean Flo's struggling? She's an excellent nurse.'

'Really? Well, what about the elderly gentleman a month or so ago? They nearly amputated the wrong leg, for God's sake.'

'That wasn't my fault,' Flo said. 'I wasn't the one who marked up the wrong leg! That was one of the contract nurses. And why he didn't speak up at the time is beyond me.'

'But you didn't correct it,' Julia said. 'That poor man nearly lost a good leg.'

'I wasn't even in the room,' Flo said. 'He wasn't my patient. I told Gigi that story because...' heat rose up her cheeks '...as awful as it *nearly* was, I knew it would make her laugh. She wasn't supposed to share the details.'

'Well, she did,' Julia said, 'and I guess it concerns me. Would you have picked up on it if you'd been in charge? Would you have even considered that the contract nurse might have got it wrong and checked? You're the only one who can answer that, Flo. I just want to make sure you're honest with yourself about your capabilities. But don't let me stop you from applying. It will be a good experience, and if you don't get it, hopefully they'll give feedback so you'll know what parts of your game to lift for next time.'

Flo speared a piece of cauliflower with her fork.

'Kayden,' Julia said. 'You haven't eaten much. Are you feeling alright?'

Flo turned to her son. His meal looked untouched, which was unlike him. He loved his grandfather's roasts.

'I'm not hungry,' Kayden said.

'Did you fill up on biscuits after soccer?' Flo asked. 'I did say you could only have two.'

Kayden shook his head. 'I didn't have anything after soccer.' He turned to Flo. 'I don't feel good.'

'He's pale,' Ari said.

'Can he lie down somewhere?' Flo asked her father.

'Of course,' Mike said, starting to stand.

'No, stay here, Mike,' Julia said. 'Florence can get him sorted. Use the spare room. The bed's made up if he wants to go to sleep.'

Flo took Kayden through to the spare room and sat him on the bed. She put a hand on his chest; he was a little warm.

'I'm tired,' Kayden said. 'That's all.'

'Let's tuck you in then. Do you want your iPad? You can watch something if you like.'

Kayden nodded, and Flo went back out to the kitchen and got his backpack before returning to the bedroom. She handed him the iPad and then realised his lunchbox was still in the bag.

'This is full,' she said, lifting it from the bag. 'Didn't you eat your lunch?'

'I ate the biscuits and cheese, but I wasn't hungry after that.'

'Or were you too busy rushing off to play soccer?' Flo smiled at her son but couldn't push away a mild feeling of concern. He hadn't eaten much over the last few days now that she gave it more thought. Kayden rarely got sick, and not eating was practically unheard of. 'Get some rest, okay? We'll finish dinner and then go home.'

He nodded and turned on his iPad.

Flo left Kayden and hesitated outside the dining room. She hoped he wasn't coming down with anything. She couldn't afford to take time off work. She'd already used most of her sick days for the year, and with bills piling up, taking unpaid leave was not ideal. She sighed. This single-parent gig might have been her choice, but at times, it certainly wasn't easy.

* * *

'Is he okay?' Ari asked as Flo took her seat back at the table.

Flo nodded. 'There are a few things going around at school, but hopefully, he's not coming down with anything. He's tired and hasn't eaten much today or the last few days. I'm hoping a good night's sleep will set him right. We might head off after dinner if no one minds.'

'Of course,' Julia said. 'I have to pack for the trip tomorrow.' She turned to Ari. 'I don't suppose you could take me to the airport in the morning?'

Ari stared at her mother. She'd been commuting every other week to Canberra since Ari and Flo were young children, and never once had she asked for a lift.

'My car's being serviced, and your father's playing golf,' Julia explained. 'I wouldn't normally ask. If you're too busy, I can get a taxi or an Uber.'

'I thought that's how you usually got to the airport,' Flo said.

Ari had thought the same.

'As I said,' Julia repeated, 'if you're too busy…'

'No, that's fine,' Ari said. Concern washed over her. Was her mother ill? Dying? It was an extreme conclusion to draw, but it was such an odd request from her ever-so-independent mother she couldn't think of any other reason. 'What time do you need to be there?'

'Eight-thirty, for a nine-thirty flight. If you could pick me up at seven, it would be perfect. The traffic can be heavy at that time of the morning.'

'I'm happy to cancel my golf,' Mike said.

'No need. Ari will take me. It'll be a nice opportunity to spend some time on our own.'

'Speaking of golf,' Mike said, 'did you tell Ari who I bumped into during the week?'

Julia cleared her throat. 'No, and as I told you when you told me, I thought it best not to mention.'

'Don't be silly. The girls will want to hear.'

'Of course, we'd love to know,' Ari said. 'Not that I think I know anyone who plays golf. The last time I even went to a course would have been when Ben and I were still together.'

Julia took a sip from her wine glass, not meeting Ari's gaze.

'Mum?'

She put down her drink and sighed. 'Fine, I suggested your father keep it to himself as I don't think it's of any benefit for you to know this.' She looked pointedly at Mike. 'You tell them if you think it's a good idea.'

Mike hesitated.

'Come on, Dad,' Ari said. 'We're intrigued now.'

'I'm not sure why your mum thinks this is an issue, but it was Ben who I saw at the course on Saturday. I believe he's a member there now.'

'Ben? But he lives in London,' Ari said. She looked to Flo for confirmation, appreciating the empathetic concern that flashed across her sister's face. 'Doesn't he?'

Flo nodded. 'That's what his mum told me when I bumped

into her that time. But that was years ago. He could have moved around a lot since then.'

'Have you not spoken to him, Ari?' Julia asked. 'After all, you were married to the man for seven years.'

'The last time I saw Ben was the night he walked out. Our lawyers then dealt with everything.'

'Walked out?' Flo said. 'Didn't you ask him to leave? I thought you were the one who ended it.'

'Does it matter what happened?' Ari glanced at Flo. It made her feel better to say he walked out, even if that wasn't quite the case. It was a conversation she didn't want to have again. Flo had been devastated when Ari told her she was ending her marriage to Ben. Ben had been in their lives for ten years, and to Flo, he'd been like a big brother. The protective big brother they'd never had.

Flo had tried to convince her to reconsider, but it was no good. Work had been Ari's focus back then, and Ben couldn't understand that. She felt he wasn't supportive, and Ari knew she needed to end it for both their sakes. He was also pushing for kids, which Ari had made clear before they'd married was not something she ever wanted. She had to admit she did feel a little guilty she'd used that as one of her reasons for ending the marriage when she'd explained everything to Flo. Except she hadn't been entirely honest, reversing the situation for Flo's benefit. *He never wants to have kids, Flo. Even if we could get past the other issues, how do we get past that?* It had finally got Flo off her back about trying to reconcile with Ben.

About a year after he moved out, Flo had bumped into Ben's mother, who'd initially mistaken her for Ari, and learned that he was moving to London for work. When she'd shared this information with Ari, it had been a relief. While she'd wanted out of the relationship, she didn't want to bump into him or hear through friends how she'd broken his heart. It got him far away from the entire family and gave everyone a chance to move on.

'So how was he?' Ari asked her father.

'Not great,' Mike said. 'He's come back to be closer to his parents.'

'Really? That's surprising. He was never that close to them.'

'Things change,' Mike said. 'He's had a rough time the past few years. Widowed, apparently.'

'Widowed? He got remarried?' Ari wasn't sure why it was such a shock to hear that. Perhaps because in the seven years since they'd been divorced, she'd hardly been on a date because she'd been so preoccupied with work. To think of being married again was completely foreign to her.

Mike nodded. 'Yes, but unfortunately, she was diagnosed with pancreatic cancer and only lasted eighteen months from diagnosis.'

'That's awful,' Flo said.

'Very sad,' Julia added. 'And particularly hard with a toddler in tow.'

'They had a child?' Flo asked. 'But I thought he didn't want children?' She turned to Ari. 'It was one of the reasons you divorced, wasn't it?'

Ari nodded, deciding not to correct Flo as to who hadn't wanted children. 'How old is his child?'

'She's four,' Mike said. 'His wife was also Australian, and as both sets of grandparents are here, he decided to move back with his daughter. Bit of built-in babysitting, I guess. I don't imagine he'd be playing golf without their backup.'

Ari sipped her drink, digesting this information. It was strange to be talking about Ben now and to learn that he'd gone on and had a whole other life since she'd last thought of him. Was it bad that she'd hardly given him a thought once their divorce had been finalised? There'd been a couple of occasions where she'd bumped into acquaintances who hadn't heard they'd split in the few months after Ben had moved out. And there was the one night with Ben's best friend, Sean, that she'd do anything to take back, but other than hearing Ben had moved to London, she'd barely given him a thought.

'You okay, love?'

Her father's words broke into her thoughts, causing her to look up and realise he was talking to Flo, not her. Flo did look quite pale.

'Maybe you should go home? Have a good night's sleep and Kayden too,' Julia suggested. 'Ari's got her awards night coming up and I have a busy week ahead of me. I don't think any of us can afford to get sick right now.'

'What about dessert?' Mike said. 'It's my famous blueberry cheesecake, and we need to sing "Happy Birthday".'

'Cut them some slices to take,' Julia instructed. 'It's been a lovely evening, but with people feeling unwell and me still to pack, we should call it a night. They'll probably make a fuss at work tomorrow and sing "Happy Birthday", so don't worry, I won't be able to avoid that.' She pushed her chair back from the table. 'See you at seven, Arabella?'

Ari nodded and began to gather the dirty dishes to take through to the kitchen. Once her mother left the room, she turned to Flo. 'You don't look great. Why don't you get Kayden sorted, and we can get going. Dad and I can do the dishes while you get organised.'

'Thanks,' Flo said. 'And sorry about tonight, Dad. I wouldn't have come if I thought we were getting sick.'

'No problem at all,' Mike said. 'You get yourselves better. I think it suits your mother anyway. She wasn't all that keen on doing anything for her birthday.'

'Does that worry you?' Ari asked a few moments later as she started stacking the dishes in the dishwasher.

'Does what worry me?' Mike looked up from the container he was filling with leftovers.

'That Mum didn't want to celebrate with us and, by the looks of it, can't wait to get back to Canberra?'

'It's what she's like, especially around her birthday,' Mike said. 'Don't forget, she's dealing with the anniversary of her father's death too. I know she doesn't say much, but it really affected her as a kid and still does. And she did want to be with us, or she would have gone back to Canberra early this morning and not taken the day off.'

Ari nodded. She was aware that her mother had shielded her and Flo throughout their lives, choosing not to discuss the harder parts of life. 'Do you miss her when she's away?'

'Of course, but I'm used to it too. She's been away every other week for over thirty years. It'll be an adjustment for both of us when she eventually retires and is home full-time.' He gave a little laugh. 'As much as I love it when she's here, I quite enjoy my bachelor weeks too.'

* * *

Flo found herself tuning out Ari's conversation as her sister drove her and Kayden home. She should have driven her own car. It was nice of Ari to offer, but it was too far out of her way. Flo and Kayden lived in Box Hill, thirty minutes from their parents' South Yarra home and in the opposite direction from Ari's CBD apartment.

'You okay?' Ari said, squeezing Flo's leg. 'You're quiet.'

'Just feeling a bit off,' Flo said. 'Guess Kayden's given me something. He might have picked up a virus from school.'

'I felt a bit sorry for Mum tonight,' Ari said.

Flo turned to face Ari, her anger rising. 'Why would you feel sorry for her? She's so horrible. Telling me I'm not good enough for a promotion. Who says things like that?'

Ari flinched. 'Sorry, I was thinking about earlier in the night. Of course, you're more than capable. Make sure you ignore her and apply. What I meant was her revealing why she doesn't enjoy birthdays or cakes. It makes a lot of sense. Imagine if we'd lost Dad when we were eight. We would have had each other at least, but Mum was an only child. She only had Gigi, and she was probably a mess.'

'It would have been difficult,' Flo agreed. 'But it doesn't excuse her behaviour now.' Flo closed her eyes. Her stomach had started to churn, and she really did feel unwell.

'Flo?'

'Can you stop?' Flo asked. 'I think I need to be sick.'

Ari indicated, and pulled the car to a stop.

Flo pushed open the door with only seconds to spare as the contents of her stomach expelled onto the kerb. She closed her eyes as her stomach spasmed, and she heaved again. She'd like to believe she'd caught something from Kayden, but she was painfully aware that these symptoms ran far deeper than any virus – they were rooted in a secret she'd harboured for years.

3

The next morning, Ari was in her apartment block gym at five. She had to be showered, dressed and back in South Yarra by seven to pick up her mother, which gave her forty-five minutes for a quick workout. She yawned as she picked up the pace on the treadmill. While she'd arrived home earlier than expected the previous night, she'd struggled to get to sleep. Having hardly given Ben a thought in the past seven years, overnight she'd thought of nothing else.

She increased the pace of the treadmill to a jog, trying to work out why the conversation around Ben had affected her. She didn't miss him, but hearing he'd remarried and had a child had stirred something up in her. If she was being honest, she'd admit to a slight feeling of jealousy, but she quickly pushed that away. She didn't want Ben back. They'd drifted apart quickly after marrying and with him longing for kids and her not wanting them, in hindsight, they should never have married. Ari sighed, increasing the pace so that she was now running. It probably had nothing to do with Ben but rather this restless feeling she'd been experiencing the past few months. She'd be scrolling through Instagram and see a friend on holiday with their family and be overcome with a sense of longing that she wished it was her.

Doing her best to clear all thoughts of Ben from her mind, Ari increased the speed of the treadmill, her legs pounding. Time flew, and what seemed like only minutes later, she was walking back through the front door of her apartment. She glanced at the retro wall clock at the entrance. She had forty minutes to shower, dress and grab a coffee before leaving for South Yarra. She slid her phone from her workout pants and hesitated momentarily. Was it too early to text Flo? Not if she was getting ready for work. And if Flo was sick, she would probably leave her phone off, or alternatively, she might need some help.

> Hey hon, you ok? If you're not working today and need anything dropped in, let me know.

She pressed send, wondering, even as she did, how she'd have time to take anything over if Flo needed it. She would be running late for work as it was after the airport trip.

> All good, short-lived illness. Feeling fine this a.m. Kayden's still not 100%, but I think he's ok for school. Trying to force some food into him. Thx for checking in. Enjoy your trip to the airport.

Ari smiled at the eye-rolling emoji Flo had added to her message.

* * *

An hour later, Ari turned into her parents' driveway for the second time in twelve hours. Her mother came straight out of the front door, pulling a small carry-on case.

'Is that all you're taking?' Ari asked, pushing open the car door and stepping out onto the driveway.

'Everything's already there. Don't forget, I have a house in Canberra and a second set of clothes and everything else. I usually only have my handbag. But I have some books I want to take back for a new friend this time.'

'A new friend?' Ari raised an eyebrow as she took her mother's bag from her. 'Does Dad know about this new friend?'

Ari grinned as her mother's laughter filled the air. 'I don't think he's got any reason to be worried. Bridie is an elderly neighbour. She's rather lonely, so I pop over to see her every now and again, and it turns out we have similar interests in literature. As you know, I always read the longlist of nominees for the Booker Prize and have well over a hundred books from the past ten years or so.'

'Are you giving her the winning books?'

'Yes and no. I've put together a selection of the titles I think should have won each year. So yes, she's getting the best of the books, but not necessarily the ones the judges agreed with me on.'

Ari put her mother's bag on the back seat and got back into the driver's seat. She accelerated out onto the road and travelled down to where it met busy Toorak Road. She hoped they'd left enough time to get her mother to the airport by eight.

'I know you said you can't talk about your research articles, but is everything okay at work? Dad seemed worried about you yesterday.'

Julia remained silent.

'Sorry, I know you hate us asking about work.'

Julia turned to face Ari. 'It's not that I hate you asking about work. In fact, I appreciate that you obviously care, but there are some things I just can't talk about. I only mentioned to your father that I was having an issue because I was afraid I was being a little distant with him. I didn't want him to think it was anything he'd done. It's a rather unusual situation, and I haven't quite worked out how to handle it. But I will. Now, you're probably wondering why I asked you to take me today...' Julia's change of subject signalled that this conversation was closed. 'I'm worried about Florence and think that you and I need to work together to make things happen for her.'

Ari wasn't sure what she'd expected from her mother, but it certainly wasn't anything to do with Flo. 'Why are you worried?'

'Arabella, she had a child six years ago and, to my knowledge, hasn't been on a date since.'

'Kayden's still young,' Ari said. 'Perhaps she doesn't want to get his hopes up by introducing a man who's gone again a few months later.'

'It's time she met someone,' Julia said. 'Which is why I wanted to talk to you. You're around intelligent and successful men all day. Who would be suitable for Florence? He needs to be happy to settle for someone less ambitious and obviously with a son.'

Ari fell silent. Was her mother really expecting her to set Flo up?

'Arabella?'

'I don't know, Mum. I'd need to talk to Flo first. And to be honest, I'm not sure who I'd recommend setting her up with. She'd probably be better with someone she meets herself through her work. She's around plenty of doctors and surgeons all day.'

'No, they wouldn't be suitable. We need to give her a man from your world. Opposites attract and all that. Now, can I leave it with you to arrange?'

Ari was about to object, knowing Flo would hate to think anyone was interfering in her love life, but stopped. Her mother, whilst annoying and far too controlling at times, was often right. Flo deserved to be with someone special, as did Kayden. Perhaps setting her up wasn't as crazy as it first sounded. 'Sure, I'll give it some thought. Now, which terminal am I dropping you at?'

'Qantas,' Julia said, folding her hands in her lap.

Ari glanced across at her. She wondered why her mother hadn't just picked up the phone if this had been all she'd wanted to discuss.

'You know,' Julia said, 'I'm proud of you.'

Ari's foot hit the brake, causing the car to lurch back before she released it and composed herself. 'What?'

'Well, not your driving, obviously,' Julia said, making a point of turning her neck from side to side.

Ari couldn't help but smile. She always knew where she stood with her mother.

'I'm referring to what you've achieved with your career,' Julia continued. 'You've worked hard and held off distractions. You made the right decision with Ben all those years ago. If you'd had a man distracting you, I doubt you'd have made partner so young.'

'Thanks, I guess.'

'But it's time to start thinking about your next steps,' Julia said. 'I can see you're getting restless. You're questioning what you're doing and thinking about the next stage. Aren't you?'

'Kind of,' Ari admitted. However, she was feeling dejected rather than restless. She was more surprised that her mother had noticed.

'You're a lot like me, Arabella. I see it in you, and like me, you need to be challenged. I know I haven't been able to talk much about my job due to the sensitive nature of it, but I can tell you now that what's kept my interest has been moving up to the next opportunity. Constantly being challenged and inspired.'

Was her mother right? Was this the problem? Her restlessness was because she was getting bored? The work had been routine for the past year or more. What used to seem like a challenge was more run-of-the-mill.

'I think you're ready for the next chapter,' Julia said. 'You've got the experience and now need to go through the formality. Apply to become a judge first, and then we'll look at how to reach the ultimate goal.'

'A judge? Ultimate goal?' What was her mother talking about?

'High Court justice,' Julia said. 'It's the obvious path for someone of your ability. I have contacts in Canberra who can help make it happen. We need to get you on the right path.' She patted Ari's knee, as if that cemented the decision.

Was her mother having an aneurysm or something else that would explain this? Ari opened her mouth about to say how ridiculous this all sounded but was cut off when Julia held up her hand.

'Give it some thought. There's no rush. You'll get your award tomorrow night, and when the interviews start, if you're asked what the next steps are for you, maybe drop entering the judiciary into conversation. Plant the seed now that you're picturing even bigger things.'

They travelled the rest of the way to the airport in silence. Ari wasn't sure what to make of this bizarre conversation. She'd be saying no to doing her mother favours in the future. One car ride to the airport, and she was now to not only become a matchmaker for Flo but she was also expected to become a High Court justice. She'd always thought her mother was strange, but surely now she was leaning towards crazy?

4

Flo signed off the documentation, double-checking she'd recorded the insertion site, the type of catheter used and noted the central line had been inserted without complications.

She'd been relieved to wake up that morning feeling fine and to find Kayden feeling better, too. He wasn't fully recovered but had begged to go to school. *Please, Mum. We've got soccer for sport this afternoon, and it's Tuesday, so Gigi's picking me up. I can't disappoint her.* As she couldn't afford to take time off to be home with him, he didn't have to beg. He didn't have a temperature, and saying he was strong enough to go to school was all she needed to hear. She'd dropped him at before-school care on her way to the hospital. His comment about Gigi reminded her that she'd better check on her grandmother and make sure she was feeling up to having an energetic six-year-old around. She checked her watch as the intensive care team moved into the room, ready to transfer the patient to the ICU.

'Great job, Nurse Hudson.' Doctor Marcus Benton smiled at Flo.

'Pretty routine,' Flo said.

'Yes, but when it comes to central lines, you're my pick to work with.' He indicated for Flo to follow him out of the operating area. 'Let's get cleaned up.'

'Well, if I'm honest, you're my pick to work with out of all of the doctors.'

Marcus raised an eyebrow. 'Should Stace be worried?'

Flo laughed. She'd known Stacey, Marcus's wife, for over ten years. She was a specialist surgeon and had clicked with Flo immediately. They shared a meal in the hospital's cafeteria on the odd occasion their breaks aligned. 'No offence, but definitely not. I love learning and appreciate that you explain what you're doing. Not all of the doctors do.'

'You know,' Marcus said as he tore off his gloves and turned on the taps to wash his hands and arms, 'it's never too late to go back into learning. Stace mentioned you once planned to be a doctor.'

'It was the plan at one stage. I did my nursing degree but then went back to study medicine. I got through three years part-time and then had to give it up.'

'Had to?'

Flo found herself blushing. 'Kayden got in the way.'

'Oh, of course.' Marcus lathered his arms with soap. 'But he's school age now. You could consider going back.'

'It'd be too much. It's hard enough working around him now. I couldn't add study to it or a bigger job down the track. It wouldn't be fair.' Marcus was, in fact, echoing words her father had used only a few months back when he'd encouraged Flo to consider her own future as well as Kayden's. *He'll be grown up one day and living his own life*, Mike had said. *You need to make sure you'll be happy with what you're doing when that day comes.*

Her mother had a different view. *Stop filling her head with unrealistic dreams, Mike. It's more than studying, you know. You need motivation and a drive Flo doesn't have.* It had been a slap in the face to hear the words, but on many levels, Flo believed her mum to be right.

'It wouldn't be fair to you not to,' Marcus said, 'if that was your goal.'

'Well, goals change,' Flo said.

'They can,' Marcus agreed. He turned to Flo and grinned. 'At least that leaves the ER nurse manager position in your hands. No one's going to complain if you're in that role. Have you submitted your application? I'm happy to write you a reference if you need it. So's Stace.'

Flo thought back to her mother's words from the night before. *It's too much, Flo. You've got Kayden to look after, and you're still struggling with your nursing duties from time to time. Until you're on top of them, you shouldn't be in a management position.* As much as she hated to admit it, her mother was right.

'I'm not sure I'm going to apply.'

Marcus's smile disappeared. 'What? It's a no-brainer. You'd be perfect for the job. All the staff respect you and love working with you. It's more pay, and the hours don't change. You just have more responsibility. I'm pretty sure you'd have a lot of say over the rosters, too, so you can make sure they suit you and Kayden.' His phone buzzed with a message. He dug it out of his pocket. 'Sorry, I have to go. But don't you dare not apply. Stace and I will both be on your case if you don't.'

Flo smiled as he made his way out of the scrub room, waggling his finger at her. It was nice that he was so supportive, but at the end of the day, he hardly worked with her. As her mother pointed out, if she was to take on a position such as the nursing manager, she needed to be across everything. While the patient hadn't had the wrong leg amputated, and it wouldn't have been her fault if he had, did she want the responsibility of having nurses working under her who could make those sorts of mistakes? Surely, it would come back to bite her then. No, she wasn't doctor material or management material. She was better off concentrating on doing her job and doing it well.

* * *

If dealing with her mother at the start of her day wasn't enough to contend with, getting to work had only increased Ari's frustration. The several deep breaths she'd taken before stepping into Jasmine's office hadn't calmed her down. She could only imagine the streams of steam that must be pouring from her ears.

'Relax, Ari.' Jasmine Leeds, co-council on the McGregor case, rolled her eyes. 'It's not that big a deal.'

Ari stared at her colleague. If anything was going to get her riled up it was being told to relax. 'Are you for real? This is a conflict of interest you should have declared at the start of the case. You'll need to recuse yourself, and we'll need to allocate new counsel.'

Jasmine rolled her eyes again. 'No one needs to know. I didn't even realise myself until now, which is why I'm telling you. I was at high school with him and haven't spoken to him since. I didn't register his name in the case files. It was only after meeting him this morning that he worked out he knew me and where from. I've literally had no communication with him in the past fourteen years.'

'You can't pretend you don't know him, and I can't risk my reputation of losing a case because you don't defend our client properly. I'm sorry, but that's how it is.'

'Fine, but the case was brought forward to tomorrow, so as long as you're ready, you can take it over.'

'Hold on,' Ari said, raising her hand. 'Tomorrow? Why is this the first I'm hearing about this?'

Jasmine shrugged.

Ari did her best to control her temper. 'I'm flying to Sydney tomorrow morning for the awards ceremony. I'm pretty sure you were aware of that.'

'I'm sure a finalist for the Australian Law Awards can handle something being thrown at them last minute. Get a later flight.'

Ari stared at Jasmine. So that's what this was. Jealousy. 'I'm sure I can,' she said. 'But, Jasmine, don't mess with me moving forward. I mean it. I don't care what your feelings are around my award nomination, but I will remind you that I'm a partner at this firm and do have some influence around here.'

Jasmine snorted. 'Not with Todd, you haven't. I'll recuse myself from the case and deliver you the notes in an hour.'

Ari nodded, keeping her mouth clamped firmly shut as she retreated from Jasmine's office. The moment she was in her own office, she slammed her hands down on her desk. 'Shit!'

'Everything okay?' Sophie, her friend and colleague, stuck her head around the office door. 'Jasmine's beaming like she just got a promotion, which I'm assuming from your reaction isn't the situation.'

'She's doing her best to undermine me. Turns out our client for the McGregor case is an ex-boyfriend of hers, and she's only just mentioning it. She also failed to let me know that the case was brought forward to tomorrow. So now it's me going alone on a case she, in theory, has done all the discovery for and was planning to defend.'

Sophie raised an eyebrow. 'That's not like her. She's usually good to work with.'

'It's the awards. I think she expected a nomination and is pissed that I got one and she didn't.'

'Sleeping your way to the top doesn't always do the trick,' Sophie said.

'Todd?'

Sophie nodded.

'That explains her comment that I don't have any influence with him. God, Soph, I can't turn up tomorrow unprepared. It's not fair to the client.'

'You'll be fine. I'll go and get the files from Jasmine now, and you can look over them. You can do this stuff standing on your head. You need to relax a bit, that's all.'

'Relax?'

Sophie nodded. 'You're a tad uptight, Hudson. You need to switch off from here occasionally and do something for yourself. Something that's not work.'

'I'm not uptight,' Ari objected, although she did recall Gigi using those exact words to describe her only a few weeks ago. *Ari, for goodness' sake, you need to relax for a night, not be working the whole time. The legal world won't collapse if you take some time out, you know, and sleeping doesn't count.* 'And I do switch off all the time.'

Sophie raised an eyebrow. 'That I highly doubt.' She put her hands on her hips. 'Okay, prove how relaxed you are. Be ready to go at six.'

'What? Where?'

'Yoga. No arguments. If the hot instructor, Sven, can't help you relax and focus on something other than work for ninety minutes, I don't know who can.' Sophie held up a hand as Ari opened her mouth to object. 'You're coming. No arguments. Trust me, Sven is worth showing up for.'

* * *

Gigi's response to Flo's text had been immediate earlier that morning.

Of course, I'm well enough to collect Kayden. It's Tuesday. Not even a rotten headache will stop me. It's much better than yesterday. See you tonight.

Now, as Flo knocked on her grandmother's door, she hoped it hadn't been too much for her having Kayden. She didn't suffer migraines herself but knew enough from her nursing how debilitating they could be. As the door opened, the dark circles under Gigi's eyes were impossible to miss, even with the layer of foundation Flo could see she'd done her best to conceal them with.

'Flo, my gorgeous girl,' Gigi said, her soft silvery curls brushing against Flo's cheek as she pulled her into a hug. 'How was work?'

'Good, busy as usual,' Flo squeezed her grandmother, appreciating the comfort of her gentle curves. 'How are you?' She pulled away, aware that the smile on Gigi's lips didn't reach her eyes.

Gigi averted her eyes from Flo's gaze. 'I'm fine, love – a bit tired, but good otherwise.'

'Are you sure? You look more than a bit tired.'

'I'm fine. No need for you to worry about me.'

'I do worry and we were all thinking of you last night, knowing that Mum's birthday is also a sad day.' A pang of concern fluttered through Flo as Gigi's eyes filled with tears. She touched her grandmother's arm. 'G?'

'Sorry, love, some years the anniversary of Ted's death hits me harder than others. This year's taken me a bit by surprise, if I'm honest. I said I had a migraine as it was easier than going into detail. I wasn't sure I'd be able to turn on a happy face for Julia's birthday and didn't want to spoil the night.'

'Oh, Gigi, I'm so sorry. You must miss him terribly.'

Gigi wiped her eyes. 'I do. Even fifty-eight years later. You'd think it was so long ago that I'd have forgotten about him by now. But he was the love of my life. I know how lucky I was to experience that kind of love, but it doesn't make it easier to accept it's gone, no matter how many years have passed.'

'If only Grandpa hadn't been travelling that route that day. Yours and Mum's lives would have been very different.'

Flo could have sworn she saw a flash of concern cross Gigi's eyes before her grandmother pulled her shoulders back and regained her composure.

'Come on in, and I'll put on a pot of tea,' Gigi said, signalling the discussion was over.

It was a trait she shared with Julia, and Flo knew better than to continue the line of discussion.

'Kayden's watching television. He was lacking a bit in energy today, love. He said he hadn't been well last night.'

'Did he eat anything?'

Gigi shook her head. 'And I even made banana bread.' She patted her protruding stomach. 'Which I really don't need to be eating. Kayden usually eats most of it, but saying no to that tells us that there's something not quite right. You might need to get him a check-up? Some blood tests, perhaps.'

Flo nodded. She'd give him another couple of days before booking him in for an appointment. It was quite likely it was a mild stomach virus, and he'd be back to his normal self in a day or two.

'Now, how was the dinner last night?' Gigi asked as Flo followed her along the passageway that led to the kitchen and open-plan family room.

Flo hesitated. She'd been delivered a kick in the guts the previous night. Her mother's low opinion of her capabilities always hurt, but last night had stung a little more than usual. But if she was honest, the kick in the guts wasn't entirely due to her mother's comments.

'Flo?' Gigi stopped and turned to face Flo, her concern-filled eyes jolting Flo from her thoughts.

'Sorry, thinking. Dinner was fine. Cut short with Kayden not feeling well and Mum preferring to go and pack rather than celebrate.'

'Oh yes, she's back to Canberra today, isn't she?'

Flo nodded. 'She asked Ari to drive her to the airport this morning.'

'That's strange,' Gigi said. 'Doesn't she normally park at the airport or get a taxi? Maybe she had something she wanted to discuss with her. Something confidential, perhaps.' She laughed. 'Julia's a pain in many ways, but she's good with secrets and good with advice.'

An uneasy feeling settled over Flo. Gigi was right about her mother being good with secrets. Flo herself knew this, for she had a secret of her own. A secret so awful that her mother was the only person she'd ever confided in. Surely, after all this time, she wouldn't say anything to Ari? She dismissed the thought as quickly as it arose. It was her mother who helped her decide how to deal with the most difficult situation she'd ever found herself in. To this day, she questioned whether it had been the right decision, but one thing she knew about her mother was that for all her flaws, she was level-headed and gave excellent advice.

What she hadn't given any thought to was her mother's seemingly excellent advice having the potential to unravel one day. But right now, Flo's gut was churning in the way it did when something bad – something very bad – was about to happen.

5

Ari changed into her gym clothes a few minutes before six, grateful she always left a bag of workout gear at the office, and now, as she followed Sophie into the yoga studio, she realised she was overdressed.

'Where are their clothes?' she hissed as they passed a group of scantily clothed women talking outside the studio. They were wearing shorts, so short they almost needn't have bothered, and crop tops that looked more decorative than supportive.

'It's hot yoga,' Sophie said. 'Everyone sweats, so the less, the better. There will be a couple of bikini wearers, and there's a guy who wears what looks like undies. He says they're swimwear, but I don't know.'

Ari looked down at her long leggings and tight T-shirt. 'I'm going to cook. You never said hot yoga.'

'Play it cool, okay. Sven will be in the studio, and you're a lot more appealing when you're not complaining.'

'Appealing? I'm not here to be appealing.' Sophie wasn't seriously trying to set her up, was she?

Her friend rolled her eyes. 'That's lucky 'cause you're not. Now be quiet as you can't talk in the room. We'll roll out the mats and get ourselves set up. Once we've done that, we lie down until the class starts. It'll help you acclimatise to the heat. And...' she winked '...it's a good chance to check out Sven.'

Ari followed Sophie into the heated room and rolled out a mat, grateful her friend had chosen an area at the back of the class. She'd done Bikram yoga once before, so she had an idea of what was in store.

But, she realised thirty minutes into the ninety-minute class, she'd forgotten the effect the heat had on her. She was fine one minute and then light-headed, feeling like she couldn't breathe the next. The undeniably hot instructor was by her side in an instant.

'Sit down in child's pose until you feel okay again.'

'I think I need to get out into the fresh air.'

'No, give it ten minutes first. It'll pass and be much better for you if you can stay until the end.' He gave her an apologetic smile. 'I try not to let anyone leave the class. You'll thank me later.'

Possibly, although she wouldn't be thanking Sophie for dragging her to the class, considering the gorgeous Sven had been the main attraction and the guy taking the class, whilst hot, was named Ryan and more likely from St Kilda than Stockholm. She'd been let down all around. Not that she'd come because of Sven, but it wasn't the point.

Ninety minutes later, Ari followed Sophie back out of the class, dripping with sweat and unable to decide whether she was angry at being forced to stay in the room or happy, as she did feel quite good.

'I'm impressed,' Sophie said. 'I thought you were going to leave about a third of the way into it. You did well to get through that and get back into the poses.'

'Very well,' a strong male voice agreed from behind them.

Ari turned to find the instructor smiling at them.

'Sorry to force you to stay, but if you leave once, you'll probably never come back. For most people, if they get to the end of a class, they'll return. The heat and the energy draw them in.'

'Mm, I think it might have been a one-off for me,' Ari said. 'Heat and energy aside, it's not my thing.'

'Relaxing's not her thing,' Sophie said, rolling her eyes at Ryan. 'I only got her here by challenging her to come. She's competitive, I'll give her that.'

'You also promised a Swedish instructor named Sven,' Ari said, regretting the words as soon as they left her mouth. 'Sorry,' she added for Ryan's benefit. 'I didn't come because of that. I was more making the point that Sophie's not exactly truthful with her promises and encouragement to get people to do things.'

'Ah, *Sven*,' Ryan said. 'Yes, he's incredibly hot, so I hear from the ladies. A real drawcard to the centre, isn't he, Soph?'

Sophie blushed. 'Fine,' she said, turning to Ari. 'Meet *Sven*.' She turned her hand over, indicating to Ryan. 'If he didn't open his mouth, he could definitely be from Sweden and quite possibly called Sven.'

Ari looked from Sophie to Ryan and back again. 'I don't get it.'

'She tells everyone about this hot Swedish instructor,' Ryan said, 'to get them through the door. They discover I'm the only instructor, and a large percentage stay, thankfully, even though they're obviously disappointed. I have no idea why you think it's so funny, Sophie.'

Sophie laughed. 'I have a fascination with studying what motivates people to do things. Telling them the health benefits of yoga rarely gets anyone to come with me, whereas promising them *Sven* does. And Ryan...' she winked '...I can promise you, no one is disappointed to discover you're my Sven. Now, I have to run. I've got a hot date with a client file and a microwave dinner. See you tomorrow, Ari.'

Ari watched as Sophie waved goodbye and headed out to the car park.

'So,' Ryan said, 'can I convince you to give Bikram a few more goes before you quit? I promise if you give me at least one session a week for a month, you'll want to be doing two sessions.'

Ari raised an eyebrow. 'You promise that?'

Ryan nodded. 'Cross my heart and all that. What do you say? It sounds like you need a distraction from everyday life, and it appears Sophie's challenging you to relax. Take up her challenge, and I'll give you that distraction.'

Ari thought about it for a moment. She was restless at work and in life. Her mother was convinced it was because she needed to step it up at work, but she wasn't so sure. If anything, relaxing and looking at life from a different perspective could do her the world of good. She smiled at Ryan and held out a hand. 'Okay, *Sven,* you've got yourself a deal.'

6

Flo groaned as she ended the call. Six months earlier, her real estate agent had warned her that the lease on the rental she and Kayden lived in was unlikely to be renewed as the owner had plans to renovate and sell. At the time, she knew she had two options. To be proactive and start looking for a new home or to bury her head in the sand, hoping he changed his mind, and do nothing. At the time, the second option had been the most appealing and the road Flo had taken. Of course, right now, she wished that she hadn't.

'What's wrong?' Kayden stared up at Flo, his eyes filled with concern. 'Are we being thrown out of our house?'

'No, nothing like that,' Flo said. 'But I think it would be fun to look for somewhere new to live, don't you? What I'd like to do is buy us our own house, and then we could do whatever we want to it. You always wanted to paint your room green, didn't you?'

Kayden nodded.

'Good. Now, don't worry about anything. I'll give some thought to where we might want to look for a house.' She looked closely at Kayden. He was still pale with dark rings under his eyes. 'You don't look that great. I think we need to make an appointment for you to see the doctor and work out what's wrong with you and why you're feeling so tired and run-down. You hardly ate any pizza tonight.'

Kayden shrugged. 'I'm not hungry.'

'Well, you're getting a little bit too skinny for my liking. I'll make an appointment. Now, how about you jump into the shower, and we'll watch a movie before bed if you like. While you do that, I'm going to give Aunty Ari a call and wish her luck for her big awards night.'

'Will she win a big trophy like they do in the World Cup?'

'I'm not sure about a trophy, but it will be an award of some kind.'

'And she's getting it for best player?'

Flo laughed. 'Kind of, but best lawyer. Now, go and get ready and then we'll choose a movie.'

As Kayden made his way to the bathroom, Flo went into the small kitchen to retrieve her phone from the charger. She looked at the room with fresh eyes, realising that while she'd made it homey and comfortable, it could use a coat of paint, and the cupboards needed some TLC. There was no point while they were renting doing anything to improve the property, but if they did have their own home, they could make it nice and keep it nice. She earned good money and had reasonable savings. The issue would be whether she could afford a house in the areas close to Kayden's school on one income. The pandemic had pushed the prices up for housing everywhere, but wages hadn't increased at the same rate. She picked up her phone, opened her contacts and found Ari. She hoped to catch her before the awards night started.

Ari picked up on the first ring. 'Hey, hon.'

'Just calling to wish you luck,' Flo said. 'Not that you need it if you talk to Mum. It's a formality, apparently, you collecting the award tonight.'

Ari laughed. 'Unfortunately, she's not the one deciding the award, and I think the other finalists might have something to say about that. It'd be nice to win, but I'm not expecting to. There are a lot of high-level people up for it.'

'Well, regardless of what happens tonight, have a great night and enjoy yourself. What's the hotel like?'

'Beautiful,' Ari said. 'Although it's been a bit of a rush, to be honest. I had to change to a later flight, so I only arrived at the hotel an hour ago. More time to get ready would have been welcomed.'

'I'm sure you look gorgeous. Are you wearing Mum's Chanel?'

'Of course! We have to give it to her, Mum certainly has taste.'

Flo could hear the smile in Ari's voice, and she pictured her looking stunning in the vintage black Chanel.

'I can't believe she has this gown,' Ari continued, 'let alone allowed me to have it adjusted so I could wear it. It'd fit you too, Flo, if you ever need to use it.'

Flo laughed. 'Where on earth would I wear Chanel, or anything other than scrubs? The last meal out I had was McDonald's with Kayden. I think it's safe to assume I won't need it. But make sure you send me some photos later tonight or tomorrow, won't you?'

'Will do. How's Kayden?'

'Not great. I'll take him for some blood tests and a check-up as soon as I can get an appointment. I'd hoped it was a bug that would pass, but I'm not so sure. He's pale and looking a little bit yellow around his eyes. I hope I'm imagining the yellow, but jaundice is a real condition. Anyway, I'll let you know once we see the doctor. So, are you going with anyone tonight?'

'Sophie and a few others from the firm. No man on the horizon at this stage, although if Sophie had anything to do with it, I would be bringing a hot Swedish yoga instructor.'

Flo smiled as Ari's laugh reverberated down the line. 'What's so funny?'

'Nothing. I'll tell you another time.'

'Okay. By the way, you don't happen to know of anyone renting out a property, do you? In my area or even further out from the city, I guess. There's not a lot available online and I already know I'd be lining up with a million others for each place.'

'For you?'

'Unfortunately. The landlord's agent called today, and my lease isn't being renewed.'

'You've got thirty days?'

'No, sixty. They're being reasonable, but I'm still going to have to move.'

'Sorry, hon, I don't know of anyone. But I'll keep my ears open. And you can, of course, stay with me if you can't find anything. I'd better go. Sophie's been texting me while we've been talking. They're waiting for me downstairs before we make our grand entrance.'

'Good luck and have fun.'

'Thanks, and don't worry about the housing situation, we'll work something out.'

Flo sat down on one of the stools at the kitchen counter when Ari ended the call and replaced her phone on the charger. Ari would do anything for her. Without a doubt, her twin would give up anything she asked her to, hand over the keys to the car and give them a place to live if they needed it. In reverse, Flo would do anything for Ari, too. However, the one thing that she knew her sister expected from her was honesty. And it was the one area where Flo had failed spectacularly.

* * *

Excitement and tension swirled in the air at Sydney's Star Event Centre. Ari was surprised at how nervous she was. She'd convinced herself that the award wasn't important, and she didn't care if she won, but right now, the way her stomach fluttered suggested she cared more than she'd like to admit. Her mother's words came back to her. *It isn't* just *an award, Arabella. It's recognition by your peers and leaders in the legal field. It's important.* Ari did her best to push all thoughts of her mother from her mind and instead ran her eyes around the event centre. The dimmed room was a sea of elegant black-tie attire with the murmur of hushed conversations. Ari's attention moved to the stage as the next presenter appeared from the curtained backstage area.

Sophie grabbed Ari's hand under the table and squeezed it. 'You're up,' she whispered.

Ari nodded, hoping Sophie couldn't feel the tremble in her hand, and plastered a smile on her lips, knowing the cameras would be on her the moment her name was announced as one of the six finalists for the award. You'd think it was the Academy Awards the way the awards were presented, but then, for their industry, it was the equivalent. She was only vaguely aware of her name being announced as one of the finalists before the presenter continued down the list. Polite applause continued as each finalist was named, and then it was time.

'And the award for Managing Partner of the Year goes to...'

Ari found herself holding her breath as the envelope was opened.

'Arabella Hudson, Partner at Premier Legal, Melbourne.'

Cheers erupted around the table as Ari's colleagues leapt to their feet. Ari's legs shook as she did her best to rise while Sophie drew her into a hug. 'You did it! You're amazing.'

Ari found she couldn't speak. She kept her smile firmly fixed to her lips as she made her way up onto the stage to accept the award. *Pretend you're presenting in court. Take a deep breath, and you'll be fine. You speak to audiences every day.* And she did; it just wasn't under these circumstances.

She accepted the award and congratulations from the presenter and turned to face her peers.

'Thank you,' she said, as the applause quietened, and everyone took their seats. She hesitated, considering the speech she had prepared. 'You know, I prepared a speech for tonight, but somehow now it doesn't feel quite right.' She paused. *What's wrong with me? I should be thanking people, not questioning why I'm here.* A murmur went around the room. Shit, had she said that out loud? She glanced at Sophie, who was no longer smiling but rather mouthing, 'WTF?'

'Not why I'm here, but why are any of us here?' Ari said, doing her best to recover. 'There's a simple answer to that question.' Relief washed over her as she saw lips turning back up in to smiles. 'Every person in this room embodies the spirit of justice and an underlying commitment to holding up the law. This honour isn't purely about me but rather a collective passion and dedication we all bring to our work. In saying that, I do, of course, need to thank some of the amazing team at Premier Legal...'

Ari's cheeks were hurting from the forced smile she managed to keep on her lips as she thanked the team at Premier Legal, their clients and the industry. The applause continued as she made her way to the back of the stage and was led to a private area where she was greeted by a photographer and journalist. She posed for the lens, answered the questions on autopilot, and once she was no longer required, debated as to whether she'd get away with making a quick exit or whether she should return to the table.

She asked herself the same question as earlier. *What's wrong with me?* This was the biggest night of her life and certainly her biggest career achievement, so why wasn't she lapping up the limelight and basking in the glory? She sighed. Because she'd had enough, that's why.

7

The next morning, Flo slipped her phone from the pocket of her scrubs and saw her father's name on the display. It was unusual for him to call her at work. He would normally text her in advance and ask her to call him when she was available. She stepped into the small break room used by most of the nursing staff and answered the call.

'Hey, Dad, what's up?'

'Have you heard from your mum?' The worry in her father's tone was unmistakable.

'No. Why? She'll be at work, won't she?'

'In theory, yes. But I didn't hear from her yesterday, which is unusual, so I left her a couple of messages this morning, which she didn't respond to. I called her office, but they're saying she didn't come in yesterday. In fact, they said she extended her leave beyond just having Monday off for her birthday, which doesn't sound right at all because if she was going to take leave, she would've come home.'

'That is weird, but you know Mum, she's an entity of her own.

She'll have a good explanation when she does get home. I'm sure you've gone a few days without speaking to her before?'

'Yes, of course, but yesterday was different. It was our wedding anniversary. Your mother doesn't forget things like that, and she was speaking about it on the weekend and apologising that she had to be at work this week. I'm a bit worried, if I'm honest, Flo.'

'Oh, of course it was! Happy anniversary. Have you got family sharing on your phone? You could track her and see where she is. I'm sure she said ages ago that she was going to set it up on both of your phones.'

Her father was silent for a moment. 'She mentioned it, but I don't think she ever did it. Anyway, I don't know how to use it, so it's not relevant.'

'I'm not sure what to suggest. I'll give Ari a call and see if she's heard from her. She had her awards night last night, so I was going to call her anyway. Mum's probably checked in with her to make sure she won.'

'Thanks. Let me know as soon as you've spoken with Ari, and of course, if you speak to your mum, tell her to call me. I'll give Gigi a call now, and I'll get off the line so you can call your sister.'

Flo stared at the phone as it clicked to silence, and she sighed. She had enough on her plate without having to track her mother's movements. It wasn't like her father to overreact, and her mother not communicating was hardly anything new.

* * *

Ari groaned, pushed her hand out and reached for her phone on the bedside table. She gingerly opened one eye, wondering how bad the hangover was going to be, before swiping at her phone's alarm and silencing it. She tossed it back on the bedside table and pulled the covers over her head as the events of the previous night came back to her.

The award. The drinking and celebrating. Then more drinking. It had gone on for hours, and it was unlike her to drink so much. Two or three glasses was usually her limit. She had vague memories of being on a dance floor at one stage with Sophie yelling in her ear, *You're the golden child. Everyone loves you.* Six months earlier, Sophie's words would have left her blushing and secretly bursting with pride, but last night they'd had quite the opposite effect. She pushed herself from the bed, hoping a shower would defuse the hangover.

She resurfaced ten minutes later feeling slightly better and knew a couple of paracetamol and a strong black coffee would help. It was a little after eight, and she had to be at the airport at ten for her eleven o'clock flight back to Melbourne.

She yanked on her jeans, grateful she had the day off, and did her best to ignore the shiny award that sat on the small table in the hotel room. She wasn't sure why she was so unenthusiastic about it. The award, in theory, encapsulated everything she'd worked towards. At this stage of her career, it was the highest acknowledgement she could receive from the industry and her peers. Was that the issue? It highlighted that this was her biggest achievement? Relationships, family, and children weren't even on her agenda, let alone on her list of accomplishments. How could she have reached her mid-thirties still obsessed with work? Surely there was a point somewhere along the line that maternal instinct or a need for a relationship would've kicked in. Or was that what was happening now? It was a bit early for a midlife crisis.

Her phone rang, distracting her from her looping thoughts. The way she was feeling right now, there was only one person in the universe she had the energy to speak to. Her favourite person.

She picked up the phone, smiling as the caller display announced it was, in fact, her favourite person.

'Hi, hon.' It was her automatic response when Flo was involved.

'How did you go?'

'I won.'

'That's amazing! You're amazing! Did you have a great night and celebrate?'

'My head is telling me I had a bit too good a night, but at least they've given me the day off.'

'How about Kayden and I take you out to celebrate on Sunday night? I'm working on Saturday, but we could go to that little Italian place you love in Lygon Street?'

'Hold on, before we talk about celebrating, how's Kayden this morning?'

'He's still not well. I've managed to get a doctor's appointment for him after work tonight.'

'Poor little man. Give him a big hug from me, and I'll give him one on Sunday night in person. Italian sounds great, and we can talk about your living situation at the same time.' Ari could hear announcements in the background of Flo's call. 'Are you at work? I thought you couldn't ring from there.'

'I am at work, and I usually can't, but Dad's called me. He's worried about Mum. He hasn't heard from her for the last couple of days and can't reach her. He wanted me to check with you whether she's been in touch. We hoped she might have called you to find out about the award.'

'No, she hasn't. Which, now that I say it out loud, is weird. I would've expected her to ring to say congratulations, or *I told you so,* if nothing else.' Ari laughed. 'Then again, she's so strange who knows whether she would congratulate me anyway. She's probably off doing something of her own. I'd tell him not to worry unless she doesn't turn up on the weekend or whenever she's due back. She's probably done it before, hasn't she?'

'She has, but yesterday was their wedding anniversary, remember? And that's why he's worried. He said she's never forgotten an anniversary, and he expected to speak to her yesterday. He said he tried contacting her at work, but they told him she'd taken leave. It is unusual. Anyway, I'd better get back to it. Let me know if you do hear from her, and of course, let Dad know, and in the meantime, congratulations. You're amazing!'

Ari smiled as Flo ended the call. Her sister was her biggest supporter. She always had been. She knew that Flo would do anything for her, which was how she felt about her twin, too. Her smile slipped as she turned her mind to her mother. It *was* unusual for her to disappear completely. But then again, her mother was unusual. She would give her dad a call later to see if he'd heard from her and, if not, to reassure him that she would no doubt appear at the weekend as if nothing had happened. He'd be better off enjoying the next few days before she returned and accused him of making a fuss.

* * *

Flo stood in the break room for a few moments after she ended the call with Ari. She knew there was probably no reason to be concerned about her mother, but it was still strange behaviour and hearing her father sound so distressed was a little disconcerting.

The door to the break room slammed open, and Phillipa, one of the ER nurses, beckoned to her urgently. 'All hands required on deck; we have a full ER already, and there's a car accident on its way in. It's going to be a busy afternoon.'

A familiar rush of adrenaline coursed through Flo as she hurried back to the main area of the emergency room. The doors swung open, ushering in a chaotic whirlwind of flashing lights and urgent voices. You'd think after thirteen years working in the ER, it would have become routine, but it hadn't. Every shift brought with it different ailments, different people and different outcomes. She let out a breath, hoping this would have a positive outcome, before hurrying forward to meet the paramedic team.

'Single vehicle accident, female driver, mid-sixties, unconscious with a head injury, suspected broken tibia and possible internal bleeding,' the paramedic said.

'Okay, thanks.' Flo's heart rate increased as she took in the oxygen mask and blood-soaked dressings covering the woman's face. That was normal, and to be fair, so was the blood that smeared her face and soaked her hair, but something about her wasn't quite right.

'In here,' one of the orderlies directed as they reached trauma room two.

Flo was jolted momentarily from her thoughts as the paramedic, with the help of two orderlies, lifted the woman from the stretcher onto the table. The priority was a primary assessment. She waited until the orderlies had cleared the area before prising open one of the woman's eyes, ready to shine a torch into it. She froze. A familiar grey eye stared back at her. *No. It couldn't be.*

'Flo, everything okay?' Nia, the assisting nurse, broke into her thoughts.

She shook her head and stepped back from the table.

'Flo?'

She was aware of the urgency in Nia's voice. The assessment needed to be done, and treatment needed to commence. But she couldn't do it. For a start, she could hardly move, but treating family members was against hospital policy. She met Nia's eyes with her own. 'Get another nurse and message Doctor Lee,' she instructed. 'The patient is a sixty-six-year-old female. Julia Elizabeth Hudson.'

Nia's eyes widened. 'Hudson?'

Flo nodded. 'My mother.'

8

Ari switched her phone off flight mode as the plane taxied toward the terminal at Melbourne Airport. She'd slept for the entire flight and, while a little groggy, was relieved that the headache that had been threatening earlier had gone. She glanced at her phone as it started pinging with messages.

She smiled as the screen lit up with texts mainly starting with:

Congratulations!

News of her award had no doubt travelled throughout the industry by now. A frown replaced her smile as she noted five missed calls from Flo's number and then a series of text messages, the last one being:

Call me, it's urgent.

Concern rippled through Ari as an image of Kayden appeared in her mind. She hoped nothing had happened since she spoke with Flo earlier. She'd call as soon as she was off the plane and in the terminal.

'Ladies and gentlemen, unfortunately, we are going to have a short delay as we are experiencing issues with the airbridge connecting us to the terminal. We ask that you retake your seats, and we hope to have you disembarking the aircraft as quickly as possible.'

A collective groan rippled through the passengers.

Ari remained seated in her window seat and stared at Flo's message. There was nothing she could do right now, but it didn't mean she couldn't call her from the plane. She pressed on Flo's number.

* * *

Flo gathered the blanket Holly had placed over her shoulders tighter, grateful for the support of her team. From the moment she'd identified the car accident victim as her mother, her colleagues had rallied around her. She'd been stood down from her shift, and both Doctor Lee, who was treating her mother, and the nurses on duty were doing their best to keep her informed.

'She's going into surgery now,' Holly told her, rubbing her back. 'You okay?'

Flo nodded, a tonne of thoughts swirling around her mind.

'Have you called your dad?'

'I tried, but no answer. I've called Ari, but she's probably on the plane back from Sydney, so she hasn't picked up.'

'You left your dad a message?'

Flo shook her head. 'I'll try again as soon as we've got more information. He'll be a mess. If possible, I'd prefer to wait until Mum comes out of surgery and we have more information.'

'Do you think that's a good idea?' Holly's tone was gentle. 'She has significant injuries. I think if it was my wife, I'd want to be here even if I was unable to do anything. If the worst happens, I don't think you'll want to tell him that you knew hours before you told him.'

Flo looked at her friend. 'You think she's going to die?'

'I'm being realistic. Your dad is already beside himself, from what you told me earlier, wondering where your mum is. He should be allowed to have the choice to be here, and I assume he is her next of kin and medical power of attorney, so he should be making her medical decisions.'

Holly was right, of course. Flo was only delaying calling her father again because she knew how distraught he would be and calling him made the whole thing real. Until she said out loud that her mother was in a critical condition, she could pretend that perhaps it wasn't true. It was some horrible dream she hoped she would wake up from.

'I'll call him again,' she said and made her way to the break room. She slid her phone from her pocket and took a deep breath before finding her father's number.

'Flo, hon, have you heard from your mum?'

The concern in her father's voice brought tears to Flo's eyes. She was a nurse, for God's sake – she made calls like this all the time. The difference, however, was this was her family, not a family of complete strangers. 'She's here,' Flo said.

'What? At the hospital? Did she stop in to visit you?'

I wish. 'There's been an accident. I don't know any of the details as Mum was brought in on her own. I'll find out more as soon as I can, but right now, she's been taken into surgery. She has a head injury, and I'm waiting for confirmation of other injuries.' She heard him suck in a breath at the end of the phone line.

'I'll be right there. Call Ari.' With that instruction, he ended the call.

Flo barely had a chance to take a breath when her phone lit up with Ari's name.

9

Ari stared at her phone after Flo ended the call. She wasn't sure where she thought her mother would be, but at no time had she expected her to have been in an accident. And why was she in Melbourne when she was supposed to be in the nation's capital? It was only an hour's flight from Canberra, so quite possibly a last-minute decision to come home, but wouldn't she have let their father know she was coming? Spontaneity was hardly a trait she associated with her mother.

It was not the time to start speculating about the circumstances. She needed to get off the plane and get to the hospital as quickly as possible.

It was nearly forty-five minutes later that Ari grabbed her bag from the baggage carousel and hurried to collect her car. She'd promised Flo she'd call Gigi, and as she drove out of the car park, she instructed the car's navigation system to call her grandmother. She quickly explained what she knew of the situation and told Gigi she would pick her up before backtracking to the hospital. She didn't want her grandmother driving under the circumstances.

After another forty minutes, with Gigi wringing her hands beside her, the two women entered the hospital emergency entrance and went in search of Flo. They were stopped by a nurse as they hurried through the hallways, her warm smile offering a sense of reassurance in the sterile hospital environment.

'You must be Ari,' she said, her gentle eyes conveying both compassion and competence 'I'm Holly. I work with Flo and we're good friends, so it isn't hard to recognise you. Come with me. Flo and your father are in the waiting room. Your mother's still in surgery.'

Ari and Gigi gratefully followed Holly to the waiting area. Ari's heart contracted the moment she saw her father's pale, worried face. His eyes filled with tears when he saw her, and she went to him and embraced him. After pulling out of his hug, she turned to Flo.

'Any news?'

'We're still waiting.'

'What do you know?' Gigi asked. 'Is she badly injured?'

'We're waiting for the doctors to confirm,' Flo said. 'She's got a broken leg and some cuts and bruises, but she also hit her head. Hopefully there'll be some news soon.'

Gigi nodded. 'Why was she in Melbourne?'

'All we know is that she was involved in a single-vehicle car accident, and her car ran off the road and hit a tree,' Flo said.

Gigi turned to Ari, her agitation obvious. 'You took her to the airport, didn't you?'

Ari nodded.

'Did she say anything unusual?'

Ari wondered what Gigi would define as unusual. The request to set Flo up and that she should become a High Court justice ticked that box, but from the concern in her grandmother's eyes, she had a feeling she was asking about something else. 'Like what, G?'

'It was her birthday the day before and also the anniversary of her father's passing. Did she talk about that?'

'About Grandpa's accident?'

Gigi nodded.

'A little bit at the birthday dinner, but not during the drive. She was upbeat and making all sorts of plans. The only thing out of the ordinary was her asking me to drive her.' Ari wasn't going to worry Gigi by telling her how unusually reflective her mother had been during the birthday dinner.

Gigi digested this information, the muscles in her face relaxing slightly. 'Okay, well that's good news. It doesn't sound like there was anything troubling her.'

Ari frowned. 'Are you worried that she did this deliberately?'

'No, of course not. I wanted to know if anything had upset her and she might have been distracted, that's all.'

'We have no other information,' Flo said. 'Once she's awake, I'm sure we'll find out more.'

The small group fell silent, each of them having the same thought. *If she wakes up.*

* * *

It was over two hours later when Doctor Lee appeared in the waiting area and beckoned Flo to join her in a small private room. 'Sorry it's taken so long. As I assume you already know, the CT scan revealed a subdural hematoma. There was evidence of significant brain swelling, indicating dangerous levels of intracranial pressure. We've placed your mother in an induced coma to minimise brain activity, thereby reducing the chances of further damage. The timeframe for swelling to reduce can be anything from days to weeks, but more likely weeks.'

Flo nodded.

'Would you like me to explain this to your family?'

'No, I can, but thank you. Were there other injuries?'

Doctor Lee nodded. 'Broken tibia, broken ribs and some lacerations to both the face and left arm. The arm needed stitching. The facial injuries were more superficial and should heal on their own.'

'Can we visit?'

'She's been taken to ICU, so usual visiting protocols apply, but yes. Give them an hour or so to get her settled. You'll, of course, be given staff privileges. And Flo...' Doctor Lee placed a hand on her shoulder '...if you have any questions or I can do anything at all for you or your family, please ask. You have my number, and I'm available to you twenty-four seven.'

Flo closed her eyes, doing her best to stop the tears that were threatening. The kindness, whilst lovely, was also a sign of how serious her mother's condition was. The doctor squeezed her shoulder, and she opened her eyes and nodded her thanks before exiting the room and returning to her family.

'We'll be able to visit as soon as they settle her in the ICU. She's got some minor injuries as far as cuts, broken ribs and a broken tibia, but the main concern is that she's hit her head, resulting in a traumatic brain injury. They've placed her in an induced coma to allow the swelling to reduce.'

Ari sucked in a breath. 'How long for?'

'It's unknown at this stage as everyone reacts differently, but I would expect it to be anywhere from one to four weeks based on my experience with other patients.'

'Will she be okay?' Mike asked.

'We can only hope so, Dad,' Flo said. 'Brain injuries must be monitored closely, and until the swelling has reduced, the doctors won't be able to tell how severe the injury is. It's quite possible she'll make a full recovery, but we're not going to know initially.' She stepped forward and hugged her father as tears filled his eyes.

'I don't understand why she was driving in Melbourne,' Mike said. 'And whose car was it? Hers was being serviced.'

'She probably came back for work,' Ari said.

'She would have told me if she was coming back early,' her father said.

'I guess we'll learn more over the coming days,' Flo said, 'or when she wakes up.'

'You okay?' Ari asked Gigi.

Their grandmother nodded; her round face paler than Flo had ever seen it. 'Can we visit her now?'

'Let's go up to the ICU floor,' Flo said. 'I'll let them know that we're there to visit, and as soon as they have her ready, we'll be able to go in and sit with her. It will probably be one of us at a time, but at least we can see her.'

10

Ari slipped away from the family to make some phone calls as they waited for the opportunity to visit Julia. She returned to the ICU area to find her father and grandmother had been allowed to visit and she and Flo could enter the room once they'd finished. Gigi looked like she'd aged ten years by the time she came out of her daughter's room.

'Try and prepare yourself,' their grandmother said. 'It's a shock seeing your mother so frail and beaten up. Hopefully the machines make it look worse than it is.'

Nerves rattled in the pit of Ari's stomach as she and Flo entered the room. Gigi was right. It was confronting seeing her mother hooked up to machines, her head bandaged, and her face bruised. Her leg was immobilised with a temporary splint.

'They'll wait for the swelling to reduce before setting it in a cast,' Flo explained.

Ari could only nod, her eyes fixed on their mother. She looked tiny in the bed and completely helpless, not at all like the formidable woman Julia Hudson was.

She'd been trying to think of a reason why she would be in

Melbourne instead of Canberra without telling any of them and also trying to figure out whose car she'd been driving; but Ari couldn't picture any scenarios where her mother would be on leave without letting one of them know. But then again, she'd lived in Canberra one week out of every two for the past thirty years and discouraged any of the family from visiting, saying it was a separate part of her life. Her job with the government made it impossible to combine it with family unless the family had been willing to move to Canberra. And Mike had not wanted to do that, and Julia had never pushed him, as she preferred living in Melbourne herself. She'd always said that this arrangement gave her the best of both worlds.

'We should probably let her rest,' Flo said, her voice quiet.

Ari glanced at her sister, the strain on her face undeniable.

Ari squeezed her mother's hand and followed Flo from the room. It was doing her head in not knowing what the circumstances were surrounding the accident. She made a beeline for her father when they entered the waiting room.

'Can we check your Internet banking and credit card statement? At least then, if she has charged a rental car to the account, we can go and speak to the rental people and find out from them why she was renting it.'

'I can't imagine she would have told the rental why she was renting the car and I also don't think you should pry into her movements,' Gigi said. 'Whatever reason Julia had for being in Melbourne is her own business. She's the only one who can tell us. Speculating could lead to all sorts of incorrect conclusions. I think you should leave it alone, Ari.'

Ari stared at her grandmother. 'Do you know something that we don't?'

'No, but I'd rather hear what happened directly from Julia and not go prying into her personal accounts without her authorisation. She is a very private person and she won't appreciate us interfering.'

'It's not interfering. It's caring about her,' Ari said. 'If she charged anything to her and Dad's credit card, then he's authorised to access it. At this stage, it's our only way of knowing what she's been doing the last couple of days.' She turned to her father. 'Can I take a look?'

He nodded, opened the app on his phone and handed her it to her. 'You'll only find a savings account and the credit card account. Our money is mainly invested. These accounts are used for bills and day-to-day expenses. Julia had work credit cards as well that I don't have access to, but if she was here for work, I can't imagine why she wouldn't have got in touch.'

Ari took the phone, hesitating for a split second when she saw Gigi's face. The worn wrinkles that usually made her face open and inviting, had deepened with worry. She was sure her grandmother knew something and didn't want her looking this up. Was she about to open a can of worms that was supposed to stay shut? No, her mother, whilst controlling and unreasonable at times, *was* an honest person. She'd drilled the importance of honesty and integrity into both of her daughters from day one, and anything but living to those standards was unacceptable.

She looked to Flo, who nodded. At least she had her sister on her side. She would be as desperate to know what was going on as Ari and her father were. She clicked on the banking app and when it opened, scrolled past the savings account to the credit card. She pressed on the credit card account and waited for it to open. There were a handful of transactions dated the previous day. She glanced up at her father, who was sitting with his head between his hands, possibly not wanting to know what was about to be revealed.

'There's a hotel charge,' Ari said, 'but there's no car rental. So, whose car was she driving?'

'And why would she stay at a hotel?' Flo asked. 'That doesn't make any sense.' She turned to her father. 'Did you have a fight or something?'

He looked up. 'Definitely not. I was expecting to hear from her yesterday for our anniversary. When she left for Canberra, everything was great. We'd celebrated her birthday the night before, and after you girls left...' he blushed '...continued the celebrations. I was gone early the next morning for golf. The last I know is that Ari dropped her at the airport, and I haven't heard from her since. It's all very strange.'

Ari stared at the phone and the credit card statement. 'Maybe she borrowed a friend's car. Do we know what type of car it was?'

'No,' said Flo, 'but the police will be here soon to talk to us. They'll have those details.'

Ari nodded. 'I guess we'll wait to hear from them then. The only other charge on the card here is a café, possibly near the hotel she's staying at. Not large amounts. Eighteen dollars last night and six this morning, which was probably a coffee. She certainly wasn't spending up big or entertaining based on this.' Ari didn't want to say more, but it was a relief to not find fancy restaurant bills or anything that would suggest her mother was with somebody else the previous night. Regardless, it still didn't make any sense.

Holly appeared in the ICU waiting area. She beckoned to Flo. 'The police are here to talk to your family. Are they up to it?'

'Yes,' Flo said. 'We need some answers. I'm hoping they might have them for us.'

'There's also a woman asking to see you. She says she's a friend of your mother's. We wouldn't normally let her into the ICU, but being staff, you can make that decision. Her name's Heather Reynolds.'

'She's Mum's best friend,' Flo said. 'I sent her a text to let her know the situation. You can let her in to see us. That's okay, isn't it?' she said, turning to the rest of the family.

'Of course,' Ari said before anyone else had a chance to answer. Their father had his head in his hands again, looking like he was doing his best to tune out everything.

Moments later, Heather, a tall woman in her mid-sixties, her long hair, once dark and now gently greying, appeared. 'I'm so sorry,' she said, going to Gigi and hugging her. Heather made the rounds, hugging each of the girls before sitting next to Mike and putting an arm around his shoulders. Ari knew that her mother would be grateful for Heather's kindness. They had been friends for at least twenty years, having met at a gardening course and instantly bonding over the beauty of the majestic tulip.

'We're hoping the police can tell us what happened,' Flo explained to Heather. 'All we know so far is that she was in Melbourne when she should've been in Canberra. She was staying in a hotel and was driving somebody else's car as hers was being fixed.'

'Possibly a loan car from the auto mechanic?' Heather suggested.

'Of course,' Ari said. 'That would make sense. Dad, if you give me their details, I'll call them and check.'

'Hold on a sec though,' Heather said, her forehead creased with frown lines. 'Do we know what type of car it was?'

'No, but hopefully the police can shed some light on that. They're here and ready to talk to us.'

'It's just,' Heather said, 'James's car went missing at some stage this week. I only noticed late yesterday when I opened the garage. I tend to park mine on the driveway, and since he passed away, I've garaged James's as I keep meaning to sell it. I'd assumed Henri borrowed it without telling me. My son might be thirty, but he's more irresponsible than any teenager I've ever met.'

'Did you call him?' Ari asked.

'Three times.' Heather's frown deepened. 'He only answers my calls if he wants something.'

'Has Mum ever taken one of your cars before?' Ari asked. 'I can't imagine her just taking it without asking.'

Heather considered the question. 'She's never taken one of our cars before. She does have a key to the house, but she's only ever used that to feed the cat when we've been away overnight. The car's probably with Henri.'

'I'm sure the police will have more information for us,' Ari said.

* * *

Twenty minutes later, they had as many answers as they were going to receive from the police. The car licence plate was confirmed as Heather's husband's car, and Ari couldn't help but notice the colour drain from Heather's face. 'I don't understand,' she said. 'Why would Julia take the car without checking with me first?'

It wasn't hard to guess why Heather was shaking her head as she ran through these questions. Ari was trying to make sense of her mother's actions, but it was impossible. She was in Melbourne unannounced, staying in a hotel and had stolen her friend's car.

'Do you think it's possible she hit her head before she got to Melbourne?' Ari asked. 'Mum's so ordered and controlled, and nothing she's done fits in with her usual M.O. If she'd had an accident in Canberra, it might explain everything.'

Flo nodded. 'That's probably the most logical explanation we've come up with so far, but I guess we'll have to wait for her to wake up before we know for sure. And realistically, with a head injury, she might not remember anyway.' She hugged Heather. 'I'm sorry about James's car.' The police had confirmed it was a write-off.

Flo's phone buzzed, and she moved away from Heather and slipped the phone from the pocket of her scrubs. 'Sorry, I'm going to need to take this. I'll be back in a minute.'

'The car is the least of my worries,' Heather said, turning to Ari. 'All I'm worried about is Julia.' She lowered her voice. 'And your dad. He doesn't look too good.'

Ari glanced across at her father, who'd lowered his head to his hands once more and was shaking it to and fro. Ari could only imagine what might be going through his mind. The thought of losing his wife was obviously far too much for him to bear. While she'd sometimes questioned what her father saw in her mother, she'd never had any reason to question how much he loved her. And that love, in the form of utter despair, was on full display right now.

11

Flo was tempted to throw her phone across the room as she ended the call with Kayden's school. Could the timing be any worse for him to need to be collected because he wasn't feeling well? She headed back into the ICU area where her family was gathered.

'Kayden's not well and the school have asked me to collect him.'

'Let me drive you,' Ari said.

'No, you take Gigi home, I'll be fine.'

Ari nodded, and Flo was glad to see she'd also noticed that their grandmother was struggling.

'I'll call you once I have Kayden,' Flo said, 'and check how everybody is. Do you think Dad will be okay if we get Heather to take him home? I don't think he should be driving.'

'Yes, I'll drop in and see him later and make sure he's okay. Then we'll need to work out some kind of roster for visiting Mum. I'm not sure how that's going to work, but we can organise it as we go.'

Flo took a deep breath. 'Let's worry about it all tomorrow. We've all got a lot to absorb and come to terms with. The reality is she could be in a coma for weeks, so sitting by her bedside every day isn't realistic. But let's not make any decisions today. I'll get Kayden sorted, and I'll give you a call later.'

Ari leaned forward and hugged Flo. For a fleeting moment, Flo wished she could enjoy the warm embrace and not have to endure the complexities and demands of being a grown-up. She squeezed Ari to convey her gratitude before pulling away. The situation was unexpected and overwhelming, but right now, Kayden needed her more than anyone here.

* * *

Flo took one look at Kayden when she entered the school's sick bay, and her maternal instincts quickly gave way to her professional ones. 'How long has he been like this?' she asked, taking in her son's pale face, clouded with pain as he doubled over, complaining of a sore stomach.

'A couple of hours,' the school's administrator said. 'Although he's only been complaining about his stomach in the last half an hour. It's swollen, and when I realised that I did suggest that we get a doctor in as I was concerned it might be appendicitis. You were already on your way, and since you're a nurse, we thought we'd wait for your opinion. We assumed you'd have your own doctor that you'd want Kayden to see.'

'Okay,' Flo said, 'but if you have another child presenting in this state, it's not even a doctor you need to contact. It's the ambulance. He's clearly very unwell. His entire abdomen is swollen, so unlikely to be appendicitis as it would be contained to the right side if it was.'

The colour drained from the woman's face. 'Shall I call an ambulance now?'

'No, I'll take him straight to the hospital.'

Twenty minutes later, Flo arrived at the emergency area of the hospital, and Holly was there to meet her with a wheelchair. She'd phoned ahead to let her know she was coming and what she needed.

'Oh my God, Flo, this day is beyond a nightmare.'

'As long as everyone's still breathing, it's not quite at nightmare status,' Flo replied. She passed her keys to Holly. 'And thanks, I appreciate this. Park it anywhere in the staff parking. If you can drop me the keys, I'm sure I'll be able to find it later.'

Holly nodded and climbed into the driver's seat while Flo hurried through the doors of the emergency department, pushing the wheelchair. She was given immediate priority, which under normal circumstances, she wouldn't allow for anyone, but this was her son, and he was pale, his eyes tinged with yellow, and when he wasn't bent double in pain, he could hardly keep his eyes open. There was something seriously wrong.

'Flo?'

Relief flooded through Flo as Stacey Benton entered the cubicle.

Stacey turned her attention to Kayden. 'What's been happening?'

Flo explained him feeling unwell, the fatigue, lack of appetite and now the yellow tinge to his eyes and face. 'I thought it was a bug going around,' Flo said, 'but it's more than that. His colour isn't normal, and his stomach's swollen.'

'No, it's not normal,' Stacey agreed. 'Let's get him a bed in the ward, and we'll run some tests. Has he been eating and drinking?'

'Not a lot,' Flo admitted.

Stacey nodded. 'Okay, after the tests we'll get him on an IV and pump some fluids into him. That'll help a little until we have some answers.'

She looked up at Flo. 'How are you holding up? I heard about your mum.'

Tears filled Flo's eyes. She'd been doing her best to keep them at bay, but Stacey's kindness and genuine concern were enough to push her over the edge. Her mother's situation was horrific, but to add something potentially serious with Kayden took her worry to a whole new level.

Stacey gave her a quick hug before turning her attention back to Kayden. 'Let's get this young man into a more comfortable bed,' she said to the attending nurse, 'and I'll order some tests. It might take twenty-four hours to get results,' she said to Flo. 'I'll do my best to get them pushed through quicker, of course, but I want to pre-warn you.'

Flo nodded. It was nothing new to her but hearing it as the mother of a potentially sick child was quite different to being the one delivering that news.

12

Ari was exhausted by the time she said goodnight to Gigi and drove the short distance to her parents' house. She wanted to check that her father was okay and plan for the following day before going home. She called Flo from the car but got her voicemail. She could only hope that there was nothing seriously wrong with Kayden.

She stopped in her parents' driveway and was surprised when she knocked on the front door that Heather opened it.

'Heather, I thought you would have gone home by now.'

'Your father's not in the best way,' Heather said, her voice low. 'I was hoping you or Flo would drop in and see him. You might need to stay with him tonight.'

Ari nodded. She wanted to be home in her own bed tonight, but of course, she'd do whatever her father needed.

'I think I'll go home now,' Heather said.

'I know I said it earlier, but I am sorry about the car,' Ari said. 'I can't imagine what Mum was thinking, taking it like that. The car, plus coming home from Melbourne early, and the hotel – it doesn't make any sense.'

'Don't give a second thought to the car,' Heather said. 'As I said, I had planned to sell it and the insurance will take care of it for me. It wasn't a car James particularly loved, so I wasn't holding on to it for sentimental reasons. As for it making sense, no, it doesn't. Hopefully, she'll wake up quickly, and we'll get all of our answers. You need to be careful not to assume anything negative. I've known your mother for many years, and have never known her to act on the spur of the moment. She'll have a good reason for why she was in Melbourne; we're just going to need to be patient. Now, I'll get going so you can spend some time with your dad. Call me if either of you need anything, won't you?'

Ari closed the door behind her mother's close friend and went in search of her father. She found him in the kitchen, a glass of whisky in his hand.

'Hey, love,' he said, barely glancing up from the glass. 'Want one?'

'No, honestly, I want to go to bed. It was a late night, last night, so I need some sleep. I wanted to see how you're doing and to ask whether you'd like me to stay tonight?'

Mike shook his head. 'No, you go home and get some rest. I'll go back to the hospital first thing in the morning. You don't need to come back then. I'll call you with an update.'

Ari considered her options. She needed to be in court tomorrow, but being with family right now was a priority.

Her phone pinged with a text. She glanced at the screen. It was Flo.

Back at the hospital. Kayden's unwell and needs some blood tests to see what's going on. I'm going to stay the night. Any chance you could bring some spare clothes with you tomorrow a.m., assuming you're coming back to see Mum?

> Of course. Do you want me to bring over a bag now? I'm with Dad, but can drop by your place for clothes, toiletries, etc.

> Tomorrow's fine. I can borrow what I need tonight from the supplies. One benefit of being on staff.

> Give Kayden a big hug for me, and I'll see you first thing.

Ari looked up at her father. 'No, I'll be at the hospital in the morning. We can make a plan then. I was going to pick up Gigi, but she's insisted on taking herself. How about I pick you up at eight?'

Mike shook his head. 'No, Heather's offered to pick me up and then I can collect my car when I'm ready to come home. How was Flo? Is Kayden okay?'

Ari nodded, deciding her father had enough to deal with tonight and didn't need to be worrying about Kayden, too. She would be up all night worrying for the two of them.

* * *

Flo stood and stretched; her eyes focused on the view from the hospital window. It was only just after six and still dark, but she'd hardly slept. The chair next to Kayden's bed was comfortable enough to sit in but not for a full night's sleep. Not that she was likely to have managed much sleep last night with worrying about Kayden and then, of course, her mother. She'd gone up to the ICU department during the night to check on her mother, but as she'd expected, there was no change.

Kayden was still sleeping, so she decided to go and get herself a coffee.

She left the room quietly and made her way past the nurses' station to the small staff kitchen.

She was deep in thought when a hand was gently placed on her shoulder. She jumped.

'Sorry,' Holly said. 'I saw you come in here and wanted to check how you're doing.'

'More to the point, what are you doing in the paediatric ward? Shouldn't you be down in Emergency?'

'My shift doesn't start for another half an hour. I thought I'd come and check on you first. What's happening with Kayden?'

'They ran some tests last night,' Flo said, as she added milk to her coffee. 'We're hoping to have the results back this afternoon, possibly earlier if Stacey has managed to get them pushed through as a priority.'

Holly nodded. 'Good. Now, you do what we tell all parents and look after yourself and try and get some rest while you wait for the results. He's in the best place possible.'

Flo nodded.

'And, looking at those dark circles forming under your eyes, you need to get some sleep. Have you managed to get your shifts changed for the next week or so?'

Flo sighed. 'I haven't got any sick days owing, and I think I'm out of annual leave too. I can't afford to miss work now, Holls.'

'How about we swap shifts for the next few days?' Holly suggested. 'I'll sort it out with Kim, who's doing the schedules. It'll be no problem.'

'But didn't you have plans to go away?'

'I did, but it turns out I need to keep looking in the romance department. Lisa ended things last night.'

'Oh no! I'm so sorry. I thought you two were good together.'

'Turns out we were both wrong about that.' Holly smiled. 'That's okay. I'd rather find out now than in a year or two. And as I have the next four days off after today, it means I can do your shifts instead of wallowing in self-pity.' She glanced at her watch. 'I'd better go. I want to put my head in and see a couple of patients before I start this morning. I'll pop back in later to check on you and Kayden. Let me know if you get the test results, won't you?' Holly drew Flo into a hug. 'And try not to worry too much.'

Flo returned her friend's hug, grateful for the comfort. The benefit of being a nurse was having access to the doctors and information she might not have as a regular parent. The downside, however, was knowing far too much and, of course, jumping to the worst conclusions. If Kayden was only fatigued and lacking in appetite, she wouldn't be too concerned, but the yellowing around his eyes and now of his skin was making her have all sorts of terrible thoughts.

As she walked, coffee in hand, back down the corridor to Kayden's room, Ari appeared carrying a sports bag. She held it out to Flo. 'A couple of changes of clothes for both you and Kayden, toiletries, and some snacks. I realised driving here that I forgot a towel, but I assume that, being on staff, you can get things like that?'

Flo reached out and took the bag from Ari. 'Thank you, and yes, I can get towels. Hopefully I'll be able to take Kayden home today though, so that won't be necessary.'

'Did you get any sleep?'

'Nope. How about you?'

'I surprised myself and did end up getting a few hours. I had such a late night the night before, and with all the worry of both Mum and Kayden, I think I collapsed. I'm going to have to go to work for a few hours now, but I'll come back mid-morning when Heather brings Dad in. I'll come and check on you and Kayden as well.'

Tears unexpectedly filled Flo's eyes.

Ari stepped forward and pulled her into a hug. 'Hey, it'll be okay.'

Flo snorted, a half-laugh and half-cry. She drew away from Ari. 'Mum's in a coma, and who knows what's wrong with Kayden, and you're telling me it will all be okay?'

'My gut tells me it will all be okay,' Ari said. 'My gut's usually pretty right about these things.'

Flo nodded. 'Sorry, I'm overtired and overwhelmed. It was a huge shock, realising it was Mum yesterday when she was brought in, and then, of course, Kayden on top of that.'

'Flo, you're one of the most resilient people I know. You can *tackle anything*.' She gave a small smile. 'You've got this. Now, let's get you back to Kayden, and I'll continue to work. Unless you'd like me to stay?'

'No, I'll be fine once I get this coffee and some food into me. Kayden will probably wake up soon, so I need to look less distressed for him. He doesn't even know about Mum yet.'

'I wouldn't tell him,' Ari said. 'Let's get him better first, and then we can let him know. It's not like she's a wonderful maternal grandmother who would be rushing in to see him anyway. I doubt he would even notice her not visiting. I'll have a word with Dad and make sure he puts on a happy face and doesn't mention Mum's accident if he visits. Now, call me if anything changes or you get the test results early, and I'll see you a bit later this morning.' She gave Flo's arm a quick squeeze before turning and hurrying back down the corridor.

13

Flo did her best to take in what Stacey was saying about Kayden's test results but was finding it difficult to concentrate. 'Hold on,' she said as Stacey started talking about a haematologist and the need for further testing. 'He has thalassemia intermedia?'

Stacey nodded. Flo had only dealt with thalassemia intermedia twice during her nursing career, but knew treatment could vary depending on the patient and the severity of their symptoms. 'We'll get the haematologist to check him over first,' Stacey said, 'and then I think we're best to consider a blood transfusion and see what impact that has. For some patients, it can be enough for management and may purely be a case of occasional blood transfusions.'

Flo nodded. 'That sounds manageable.'

Stacey cleared her throat and looked back at her chart, raising alarm bells for Flo.

'Is there something else?'

Stacey met her eyes. 'Flo, do you know what your blood type is?'

'A-positive.'

Stacey nodded. 'And Kayden's father?'

'I have no idea.' Heat rushed to Flo's cheeks. 'We're not in touch, and he has nothing to do with Kayden. Why?'

'Are you aware that Kayden has a rare blood type?'

She shook her head. Kayden hadn't had any illnesses since he was born that required his blood type to be checked.

'The reason we took extra blood during the night was that the test came back showing that he has Bombay blood type.'

'What?' Flo said. 'How's that even possible? The test results must be wrong. It's one of the rarest blood types in the world. I didn't think anyone in Australia even had it. Isn't it only found in India?'

'No, unfortunately it is found outside of India, but in such small numbers that finding donors is problematic. We reran his test to double-check, and unfortunately, it came back once again confirming Bombay. With you being A-positive, it must be from his father. Sourcing Bombay blood for a transfusion is going to be difficult. The best-case scenario for Kayden would be to get the blood from a relative with the same blood type. This, of course, would be his father and possibly other family members from his father's family. I know you've said that you're not in touch, but is it possible that you could reach out and explain the situation?'

Flo stared at Stacey. She had absolutely no idea of what she was asking. Her legs crumbled, and she reached out for a chair to steady herself.

Stacey was instantly by her side, holding her up by the arm. 'Let's get you sitting. I realise this is overwhelming.' She helped Flo to a nearby chair. 'Let me leave it with you for a little while to digest,' Stacey said, after Flo was seated. 'I'll go and do some research for alternative options for sourcing the blood, but unfortunately, as you know yourself, it's not going to be easy. If Kayden does have blood relatives on his father's side who you can get hold of, I strongly urge you to.'

Flo nodded as Stacey left the room. She dropped her head into her hands, doing her best to ignore the churning sensation in her stomach.

* * *

Flo had tried her best to remain upbeat in Kayden's presence, but the issue around his blood type was making the task almost impossible. She watched her son, his eyes glued to his iPad, a wisp of sandy hair covering his forehead, his cheeks alarmingly gaunt from his recent lack of appetite. An overwhelming sense of protectiveness enveloped her, not dissimilar to the way it had six years earlier, when he was a newborn. Tears welled in her eyes at the thought of anything happening to him.

'Why are you upset, Mummy?'

Flo quickly wiped her eyes and did her best to smile. 'They're tears of relief that you're going to be okay.'

Kayden frowned. 'Are you sure? You're not crying 'cause I'm sick, are you?'

Flo stood and moved across to sit on the edge of the hospital bed. She put her arms around her son. 'No, you're going to be fine. Doctor Stacey is going to run a few more tests, but she's already worked out what's wrong with you and how to fix you.'

'How will she fix me?'

'She's going to arrange for some blood with superpowers to be transferred to you. It will give you lots of energy back, and you'll feel normal again.'

'And I'll have superpowers?'

Flo laughed. 'That would be nice, wouldn't it? But the superpowers are more to clean your blood and make it all healthy again.

You might have to do it again every now and then in the future. We aren't sure how often, but it's something we can manage easily.'
Except for the fact you have one of the rarest blood types in the world.

Kayden smiled. 'That's good then.'

'Very good,' Flo agreed.

'Can I watch Messi now? There's a replay of an important Riyadh Cup match.'

'Of course.' Flo handed him the iPad and headphones and sank back into the chair beside his bed. If only his treatment could be managed so easily. What was she going to do? Stacey was checking as to whether blood supplies were available, but from a long-term perspective, she knew what the answer to that would be.

'Mummy?'

Flo jolted upright, realising she must have nodded off, to find Ari sitting on the bed next to Kayden, who was nursing a soft toy soccer ball.

'Look what Aunty A brought me.' His pale face lit up with a beaming smile.

'That's great, hon, and lovely of Ari.' She smiled at her sister. 'Thanks, your gifts are always perfect.'

'You're welcome. Any news?' Ari nodded her head towards Kayden.

'Kayden, I'm going to take Aunty Ari to get some coffee, and we'll be right back. You can keep watching your iPad if you like.'

Kayden didn't need to be told twice. He popped his head-phones on and started tapping at the screen.

'What's the news?' Ari asked as they stepped out into the hallway.

'He has what is generally a manageable illness. It's called thalassemia intermedia and is a type of anaemia. The initial treat-ment will be a blood transfusion, and then it will be a case of monitoring it and seeing whether that's enough for future treatments too, if and when they're needed.'

'Okay,' Ari said. 'That sounds like reasonably good news, I guess?'

Flo nodded. 'It is. But there's a complication. Kayden has a rare blood type, so getting blood is going to be difficult.'

'Can we all be tested?'

'I'm A-positive,' Flo said, 'which is common and as we're identical twins, you and I will be the same. Haven't you ever known your blood type?'

Ari frowned. 'No, I don't think so. I've never had any need. I did donate blood once. I guess they might have told me.'

'Anyway,' Flo said, 'as it's not from me, it has to be from his biological father.'

'Oh no,' Ari said. 'You don't even know who that is, let alone how to reach him, right?'

Flo swallowed, instantly transported back seven years to when she announced her pregnancy to the family.

* * *

'You're what?' Ari said, choking on a mouthful of cannelloni. She started coughing, eventually swallowing some water to compose herself.

If the situation hadn't been so awful, Flo would probably have laughed at the shocked reactions. Ari was choking, her father's wine glass was being held mid-air, and Gigi's mouth was wide open. The only one unaffected was her mother, who continued eating her meal.

'Pregnant,' Flo repeated.

'But how?'

Flo raised an eyebrow at her sister, choosing not to respond.

'I mean,' Ari corrected, her cheeks flushed red, 'who, not how? You aren't even seeing anyone, are you?'

'Can we not go into the details, please?' Julia said, placing her knife and fork on her plate. 'Flo's pregnant from a one-night stand with a man who she knows was returning to Paris the day after they were together. We have no surname or contact details and no known friends via whom we can contact him.' She held up a hand as Mike went to say something. 'I don't want judgement from any of you,' Julia said, 'because I think we all know that if we were honest, we've all been there and done that. I don't think there's one person in this room who hasn't had a sexual encounter that they are not proud of.'

Flo had dared to sneak a look at her grandmother and was shocked to see two red spots appear on her cheeks. If she wasn't the centre of attention and its awful announcement, she probably would have questioned her grandmother's past, but she knew better than to make the situation worse.

'So, we will all support Flo in her pregnancy and when she gives birth to the child,' Julia said. 'Now, who'd like dessert?'

* * *

'I assume you never heard from the guy?' Ari said, breaking into her thoughts.

'No.'

'Maybe there's some kind of blood donor registry in France,' Ari said. 'He was French, wasn't he?'

Flo stared at her sister. 'Registry?'

Ari nodded. 'Well, if he's got a rare blood type and he knows it, he might be a donor, and he might be registered. We might be able to track him down.' She thought for a moment. 'Imagine what a shock that would be for him, finding out all these years later that he has a son. Still, it would be a good shock. The only reason you didn't tell him was because you couldn't contact him. It wasn't like you held back the information on purpose.'

Flo thought she might be sick. Ari had believed every word she'd said all those years ago and still did.

'Look,' Ari continued, 'I'm going to visit Mum and check on Dad. I think he's already with her, and then when I get back to work, I'll start doing some research into blood registers. I'll see what I can find out.'

'No!' Flo forced a smile as surprise registered in Ari's eyes. 'I work here with some of the best doctors in the country. I'll check with them as to whether an international registry exists. I'm sure you've got enough work to do on your own. They'll have that information available to them.'

'Okay, well, if you're sure? I'd do anything for Kayden and for you, Flo. Tell me what you need.'

Ari's kindness brought tears to Flo's eyes.

'Hey, don't cry, hon. If we can't track down his biological father, we'll get the blood from somewhere – I promise. Money talks, and I've saved plenty over the years. It won't be an issue.'

Flo closed her eyes. Then she opened them again and took a deep breath. 'The thing is, I do know who Kayden's father is.'

'What? Who?'

'But,' Flo said, 'he doesn't know about Kayden, and it's going to cause huge problems if I tell him and if I make it public knowledge.'

'You lied to us?'

Flo nodded, having to turn away from the shocked expression on Ari's face. She wasn't surprised at Ari's reaction. She'd feel the same if she'd found out her sister had lied to her.

Ari struggled to compose herself. 'Okay, I wasn't expecting you'd ever lie to me if I'm honest, but that's not important right now. What's important is helping Kayden. I can only assume it was for a good reason. Is it one of the doctors here?'

'Why would you think that?'

'Because I can't imagine anyone else that you could have been with that would cause problems. A married doctor might be an issue. Although...' she frowned '...if he worked here, he'd have known you were pregnant and would know about Kayden. Was it someone famous?'

Nausea swirled in the pit of Flo's stomach. 'Can you stop speculating, please? I need to think about how I approach this.'

'Flo, you don't have a choice. You realise that don't you? Sure, we can possibly track down blood elsewhere, but if his father is contactable and you think he would give blood, you need to contact him. You'd do anything for Kayden, wouldn't you?'

'Of course,' Flo said.

'Good.' Ari squeezed her arm. 'Contact him today, and if you're going to do it in person, let me know, and I'll come with you for support. Hon, I know if you lied there'll be a good reason and I'll be there for you no matter what. Now, are you going to be okay if I go and check on Mum?'

Flo nodded, her head spinning with the realisation that her world was about to collapse.

14

Ari walked into the small waiting room area outside of the ICU. It was hard to believe that less than twenty-four hours had passed since she'd received Flo's phone call. So much seemed to have happened in such a short space of time. If somebody told her days had passed rather than hours, she would believe them.

She spied her father and grandmother huddled together on two of the chairs in a corner, deep in conversation.

'Ari, love,' Gigi said, her red-rimmed eyes meeting Ari's as she approached them. Her grandmother stood and hugged her. 'How are you holding up?'

'I'm okay. How are you? You look like you haven't had much sleep.' Her gaze travelled to her father, who was unshaven, and his rumpled clothes confirmed he hadn't changed since the previous day.

'You okay, Dad?'

Mike shook his head and sighed. 'Other than being worried sick she might not wake up, and that I can't work out why she was in Melbourne and hadn't told me.'

Ari nodded. Of the hours she had been awake overnight, she'd spent a good part of them trying to come up with plausible answers for that, too. 'Maybe we should concentrate on getting her better for now,' she suggested. 'Let Mum answer that question when she's awake.'

'I agree,' Gigi said, 'although I was telling your father that I had a strange phone call last night.'

'Oh?'

'It was close to eleven, and a man rang. He asked if I was Genevieve Greenway and whether I was any relation to Julia Hudson.'

'What did you say?'

'I asked him who he was and why he wanted to know.'

'And?'

'He sounded nervous and asked if there was any chance I knew where Julia was. He was a little vague but said something about her not turning up for an event in Canberra earlier in the week.'

'Was he someone she works with?'

'He said he was,' Gigi said. 'Although why would a work colleague ring that late at night? I asked how he got my details, and he said Julia had given him my phone number years ago, only to be used in an emergency. That she'd told him we were estranged, but I was still her next of kin, and if there was ever a reason to worry about her, he should contact me.'

Ari frowned. 'That doesn't make any sense. You're not estranged and Dad's her next of kin. What did you tell him?'

'Nothing. I asked what his name was, and he acted strange and didn't answer, so I ended the call.'

'Maybe I can get in touch with someone at her work and ask if she missed any events this week. That might help us narrow it down to who he was.'

'It was strange that she gave him my number.'

'If she really did,' Ari said. 'I guess it's another mystery that

Mum will be able to solve for us. How is she this morning? Have you spoken to any of the doctors?'

'She's the same,' her father said. 'It sounds like that's going to be the case for the next few weeks. I asked if she could hear me when I talked to her, and the nurses said it was possible. I think I'll stay here this morning and sit with her. Gigi's going to stay too.' He stood. 'In fact, I'll go in and sit with her now. Are you going back to work?'

Ari nodded. 'Unless I can be of any use here?'

'I don't think so. I'll call you if there's any change.'

'How's Kayden?' Gigi asked when Mike had left them.

'He's okay,' Ari said, 'but he needs a blood transfusion and is a rare blood type, which stems from his biological father. Flo's going to have to try and get in touch with him.'

'The Frenchman? How's she doing to do that?'

'I'm no longer sure he was a Frenchman,' Ari said and explained the rather cryptic conversation she'd had with Flo. 'It sounds like he's someone she shouldn't have been with and perhaps didn't want to admit to anyone who it was.'

'According to your mother,' Gigi said, 'it was a one-night stand with a stranger. I thought she handled that all rather well at the time. I remember being surprised that she didn't fly off the handle but instead was incredibly calm and matter-of-fact. It was very out of character. It would make a lot more sense that she was covering up something for Flo.'

* * *

Flo jumped every time her phone pinged with a text. What if it was him? She hadn't been able to get his number, but the staff member she'd spoken with had kindly offered to contact him and have him call her. She wasn't sure she'd ever dreaded something so much.

A little after one o'clock, she was dozing in the chair next to Kayden's bed when the vibration of her phone ringing jolted her out of sleep. She took the phone from her pocket, noted the unknown number and took a deep breath.

'Hello.'

'Flo?'

She'd recognise his voice anywhere.

'How are you?' Flo said, not sure what to say to him.

A deep chuckle could be heard at the other end of the line. 'Good, a little confused to hear from you. Is everything alright?'

'No, I'm afraid it's not. I'm at the hospital right now. Mum's been in a car accident, and my...' she hesitated '...my son is ill and requires treatment.'

'Oh, I'm so sorry. Will they be okay?'

'Honestly.' Flo sighed. 'I'm not sure. But it's the reason for my call. And as odd as this is going to sound, is there any chance you could meet me for a coffee? There's something I need to discuss with you.'

There was a brief silence before he spoke. 'How about you tell me what's going on? Whatever it is, you can tell me over the phone.'

Flo took a deep breath. 'It's about my son. It turns out he has a rare blood type and is going to need a transfusion.'

'Okay.'

'The thing is—'

'No!'

Flo stopped. Silence followed the outburst at the other end of the line. She waited.

'How old is your son?'

Flo closed her eyes. 'Six.'

'And?' The words were practically spat down the phone. 'Let me guess, he has Bombay blood?'

'Yes.' The word was barely a squeak.

'Jesus Christ. How could you have kept this from me?'

'I didn't want you to feel obligated to be involved.'

'Obligated to be involved with my own child?'

'You were going through a hard time already. I didn't want to add this on top.'

'Bullshit.' He spat the word out. 'That is absolute bullshit, and we both know it. There is only one reason you didn't tell me, and it has nothing to do with me, does it? You couldn't have cared less about what was going on in my life at the time. It was to protect yourself.' He let out a long breath. 'When does your, I mean *our*, son need the blood by?'

'They have enough supplied for an initial transfusion, but it's possible he'll need future treatment, and if you're willing, your blood will be a lot easier to obtain.'

'*If* I'm willing? Jesus, you're painting me as being some selfish arsehole who doesn't care about his kid. Of course, he can have my blood.'

'Thank you.'

'I'm sorry, but I have to get my head around all of this. I've got your number, and I'll call you back in the next couple of days. Obviously, call me if you need blood earlier than that, but if you don't, I'll be in touch soon.'

Flo didn't get a chance to respond. He'd already ended the call.

* * *

'We're in luck,' Stacey said, entering Kayden's room. 'The blood we've tracked down for the initial transfusion is being couriered from a processing centre in Sydney and should be on a flight in the next hour. We'll be able to do the transfusion later this afternoon or this evening.'

Relief flooded through Flo. 'That's amazing.'

'It is,' Stacey agreed. 'But it's a limited supply, and we've been unable to locate any other blood in Australia. Going overseas gets complicated. Have you been able to contact the person we talked about?' She glanced at Kayden, who had headphones on and appeared engrossed in his iPad.

'I've made contact with him, and yes, he's agreed to give blood. We'll need to provide him with the details of where to go.'

'That's great news,' Stacey said. 'As you know, blood from a family member will need irradiation to eliminate the risk of transfusion associated Graft-Versus Host Disease. We'll ensure that's in place as soon as we receive the blood. We should also find out which – if any – of his family members have the same blood type as a backup.'

Flo nodded. Stacey hadn't said it, but Flo knew she meant in case something happened to him, and they needed another source. She'd deal with this later. Now that she knew blood had been found for Kayden, she had more urgent problems to worry about.

15

The blood transfusion had taken place at eight o'clock the previous night, and it was amazing to see how quickly it had taken effect. The yellow tinge to Kayden's eyes and skin was almost gone, and he no longer looked pale and listless. They'd kept him overnight for observation, but on her early morning round, Stacey had confirmed that he could go home that morning after the haematologist did a final examination. They expected he would be available to do this mid-morning.

After ensuring he'd had some breakfast, Flo left Kayden engrossed in a book on soccer Gigi had given him the previous afternoon and went in search of her family to update them. Ari had messaged her to let her know they were in the hospital's cafeteria, so she made her way down to the ground floor and did her best to hide a smile as a crash of plates orientated visitors as to where they could get food.

Minutes later, she'd found the family and filled them in.

'That's wonderful news,' Gigi said, squeezing Flo's hand and handing her a coffee. 'You must be so relieved.'

'I am. His normal colour has almost fully returned after the transfusion. I've seen it before, of course, but it is a miracle what can be done.'

'That is good news, hon,' Ari said.

'He'll be okay to go back to school on Monday too, so hopefully, we'll all be back on track with Kayden and can concentrate on Mum.' Flo looked at her father. He was clean-shaven and wearing fresh clothes, but with pinched cheeks and dark bags under his eyes, he looked awful. Flo laid a hand on his. 'The doctors here are good. She's getting excellent treatment.'

Mike nodded. 'I know, I just want her better.'

He didn't say it, but Flo understood he was still struggling with not knowing why her mother was in Melbourne and why she'd taken Heather's husband's car without asking.

'I feel guilty,' he admitted.

'What? Why?' Ari asked.

'It was our anniversary. I suggested to your mother that I spend the week in Canberra with her, but she told me not to be silly. I didn't tell her, but I was relieved. There was a charity day at the golf club, and I didn't want to miss it. Maybe she was upset with me.'

'Dad,' Ari said, 'Mum needs you to focus on positive thoughts right now and be there for her while she recovers. If she'd been upset about you not going to Canberra, she would have said something. She wasn't backward in coming forward. When I drove her to the airport, she didn't mention you or the anniversary, so it certainly wasn't top of her mind.'

'Ari's right,' Gigi said, 'you need to move on right now and not worry about that. My Julia would have made it clear if she had an issue with you not going. And she had mentioned the anniversary to me and whether I thought you'd like to go away this weekend as a surprise. She was planning to book somewhere down at Sorrento. A holiday cottage she said you loved.'

'Seaspray Inn,' Mike said. 'Was she going to do that?'

Gigi nodded.

'Now I feel even worse.'

Flo looked to Ari, who shrugged. Her usually strong father was acting out of character, but then he was living on minimal sleep and a lot of coffee, so it was no surprise.

Flo put her coffee cup down and rose. 'I should get back to Kayden.'

'We'll pop in and see him before we leave,' Gigi promised. 'It'll be a nice surprise for him.'

'As this might be for you,' Mike said, looking at Ari.

'What surprise?'

'That one.' Mike's gaze shifted from Ari to the cafeteria's entrance.

Flo looked quizzically at her dad and turned away from the table. She took two steps towards the cafeteria's exit and froze.

* * *

Ari's eyes followed the direction of her father's. Her heart skipped a beat.

'Ben?'

Her voice conveyed the surprise that settled over her as she shot to her feet. She hadn't seen her ex-husband in over seven years. In fact, it was probably closer to eight by now. She hesitated as she reached the doorway and smiled. 'Wow, what a coincidence. It's been years. Dad mentioned he saw you at the golf club, but I wasn't expecting to bump into you.' She took a slight step backward and looked him up and down. 'You look great, super fit and tanned.'

Ben looked at her, a strange expression on his face. 'Your dad mentioned me?'

Ari nodded. 'Yes, that you'd moved back to Australia.' She hesitated, unsure of whether this was appropriate to say or not. She decided it would be rude not to mention it. 'I'm sorry to hear about your wife. We all are.'

'Um, thanks. I was sorry to hear about your mum. Is she doing okay?'

'Mum?' That made sense. It was quite likely someone at the golf course had mentioned the situation. 'No change. It'll be a few weeks, we think, before we know whether the swelling on her brain has subsided and whether there's permanent damage.' She smiled again, surprised at how good it was to see him. 'It's kind of you to come and check on her and us. After all this time, I wouldn't expect that.'

Ben blushed, and Ari was reminded of how attractive she'd found him when they first met. 'Why don't you come and say hi to everyone? They'd all love to see you.'

Ben pushed a hand through his hair, a nervous gesture he'd always had. 'Actually, that's not why I'm here. I—' He broke off his sentence, his eyes shifting from Ari and settling on something behind her. Ari turned and saw Flo, frozen in place, her face pale with a green tinge.

'Flo?' Ari walked over to her sister. 'Are you okay?'

'No, I'm not. I need to talk to you.'

'What? Now?'

Ben stepped towards Flo. 'Are you telling me you haven't told Ari?'

'Oh my God.'

Ari swivelled around to look at Gigi, whose hand was across her mouth, her eyes wide. 'What on earth is going on?' Ari asked, looking from her grandmother to Flo and then Ben.

'It's Ben,' Flo said, the words barely audible.

Ari frowned. 'I know who it is. But why are you all acting so weird? He's been in touch with Dad and has been kind enough after all this time to see how we all are.'

'Actually,' Ben spoke again, 'like I said, I'm sorry about your mum, but it's not why I'm at the hospital. I'm here...' he hesitated '...I'm here about my son.'

'Your son?' Now Ari was confused. 'Dad said you had a daughter.' She looked across to her father, who shrugged. He looked as confused as she felt.

'I do,' Ben said. 'But I found out earlier today that I also have a son. A son with a rare blood type who will require my blood.'

Ari's head began to spin. 'No.' The word sounded like a squeak as it came out of her mouth. She turned to Flo, her legs beginning to shake. 'Tell me no, Flo. Tell me no.' Even she could hear the almost hysterical slant to her words. Please do not let this be true. She honestly didn't think she could bear it.

Tears were flowing down Flo's cheeks. 'I'm sorry, Ari, I am. It was a mistake, a huge mistake, and I should have told you.'

Ari looked from Flo to Ben. Her sister and her husband. Sure, ex-husband now, but what—? Were they having an affair while she and Ben were married? She turned to Gigi and her father. 'Did you know?'

They didn't need to shake their heads. Ari could tell from their shocked expressions that this was news to them, too. 'So, Ben is Kayden's father.' It wasn't a question, more a statement of disbelief. 'You cheated,' she said to Ben. 'And you had a relationship with my husband,' she said to Flo. The hysteria in her voice was rising. It would never have crossed her mind that either of them would do something like this.

'It wasn't like that. It was one night, a huge mistake which a miracle came from,' Flo said, tears running down her cheeks.

'Miracle,' Ari spat, her wonder turning to anger. 'Are you for real? If it was such a miracle, how come neither of you ever told me? Hold on.' She turned her focus back to Ben. 'Did you say you found out today about Kayden?'

He nodded.

The air was sucked from Ari's lungs. 'I think I'm going to be sick.' She bent double, willing herself to stay in control. When she felt capable, she straightened and turned to her sister. 'Flo, how could you? This is unbelievable. You're seriously telling us that if Kayden wasn't sick, you would never have told Ben that he had a child?'

Flo nodded, unable to meet Ari's eyes and, in that moment, Ari felt heartbreak like she'd never known before. How could Flo have done something so awful?

She closed her eyes momentarily, willing the bile that was rising in her throat down.

'I can't do this.' She walked back to the table and picked up her bag. She hugged her father, then Gigi and walked out of the cafeteria without another word.

16

Flo's legs trembled, and she wished the floor would open up and swallow her. She'd known she was going to have to tell Ari, but it wasn't supposed to happen like this. She'd been rehearsing in her mind how she was going to deliver the news to her sister. How she'd planned to make sure Ari knew Ben hadn't cheated, to tell her the truth: that it had happened the night their divorce had been finalised. She wasn't sure it would make that much difference in the grand scheme of all her lies, but she'd hoped it might. If she'd tried to imagine the worst way Ari could find out, this was probably it.

'I suggest you take Ben somewhere for a private discussion,' Gigi said, crossing from the table to where Ben and Flo stood. 'You've given Ari a terrible shock, and if I'm honest, all of us. I have no idea how you're going to make this up to her, Flo, or if it's even possible, but right now, you need to put things right with Ben. Figure out how this is all going to work, assuming he wants Kayden in his life, that is.'

'Of course, I do,' Ben said. 'He would have been in my life from day one if I'd known. I never would have gone to London.' He shook his head. 'I can't believe you robbed me of his childhood.'

'No need to be so dramatic,' Gigi said. 'Yes, Flo has made some bad choices, but we all know it wasn't to rob you of anything. It was to protect her relationship with Ari.'

'And I thought you didn't want kids,' Flo said, her words laced with devastation. 'Ari said that was why your marriage ended.' And her mother had confirmed this detail when Flo had confided in her that she was pregnant.

'My marriage to Ari ended for several reasons. One being that *she* didn't want kids,' Ben said.

Flo's stomach churned as she digested this new piece of information.

'It appears Ari might have twisted that detail around,' Gigi said. 'Regardless, the first step is for you two to work out what happens now. And if I can give you one piece of advice, don't go barging into Kayden's room announcing you're his father. Work out a way to introduce yourself to him as a friend or something first once he's home and in his own environment. He's had a hard few days, and this needs to be handled with care.'

Both Flo and Ben nodded.

'Now,' Gigi added. 'I'll go and sit with Kayden while you two go somewhere quiet to talk. There's a nice courtyard garden near the front entrance. Why don't you go down there?'

Flo found herself following Ben down the corridor to the lifts and out of the hospital to the courtyard garden. Neither of them spoke, but she was glad of Gigi's suggestion.

When they reached the garden, Ben started pacing. Flo watched him for a moment and then stepped towards him and placed a hand on his arm. 'Can you stop?' She indicated to a bench on the edge of the garden area. 'Let's sit down over there.'

Ben followed her and sat down.

'I honestly don't know what to say,' Flo said, 'other than I'm sorry. When I found out I was pregnant, you'd already gone to London. But yes, Gigi is right. It was an incredibly selfish decision on my part not to tell you. I knew that it would end my relationship with Ari if I did.' A wave of sadness washed over her as she thought of her twin sister and the pain she'd inflicted on her.

'You had no right to play God,' Ben said. 'I should have been given the opportunity to make my own decision about this, and so should Ari. You've made it so much worse by letting her find out like this. She thinks I cheated on her and that we had some kind of affair. If you'd been honest when it happened, she would have known that she and I were already divorced, and it was a drunken, lonely moment for both of us. She would have been mad and upset, but she would have forgiven you.'

'You think?'

'She slept with Sean; did she ever tell you that?'

'What? Sean, your best friend?'

Ben nodded. 'And before our divorce was finalised. Way before you and I hooked up.'

'How did you find out?'

He looked her in the eye. 'Sean felt terrible, and he took me out for a beer and apologised. Said they'd bumped into each other at a networking event, and one thing led to another, and they ended up in bed together.'

'And you forgave him?'

'Not initially. I was pissed at him, and he ended up with a few bruises to show just how pissed. But once I'd calmed down and had a couple of weeks to give it some thought, yes, I did. He's only human. Ari's gorgeous, as are you. What guy is going to say no? He showed me a text that she sent him the next day. It said something along the lines of how sorry she was. That she'd crossed a line and hoped he could forgive her. She also said that seeing him had made her realise that she missed me, and while she didn't want to offend him, being with him was her way of being close to me, even if only for a short time.'

'She said all of that?'

Ben nodded. 'I forgave him. It was a night that wasn't supposed to have happened, and I knew she and I wouldn't be getting back together, so I decided not to dwell on it. I did ask him not to go there again, and that was it.'

'You stayed friends?'

Ben nodded. 'You underestimated Ari, and I think you're going to pay for it. Telling her back then would have been hard, and no doubt would've had some consequences, but lying all this time and only coming clean because you need something from me? You've shown all of us that you're not the honest, kind person we thought you were.'

As much as she knew his words were true, Flo still felt like she'd been punched. He was right. Her motives had been purely selfish, and she'd done her best to justify them to herself at the time. She'd told no one except her mother and now was regretting the advice she'd been so keen to follow.

* * *

'Are you pregnant?'

The frantic edge to her mother's voice was not something Flo had ever heard before. She nodded.

'By whom?'

Flo closed her eyes. She had to tell someone, but was her mother really the right choice? Maybe she should have told Gigi.

'Florence, I asked by whom are you pregnant?'

By whom? Even in this situation, her mother managed to make it sound like a grammar lesson.

'Ben.'

The silence that followed forced Flo to open one eye and check her mother hadn't had a heart attack.

'As in Ari's Ben?'

Flo nodded.

It was Julia's turn to close her eyes. She shook her head gently to and fro, appearing to be deep in concentration. Her eyes opened. 'Does he know about the baby?'

'No, it was just one night that shouldn't have happened and didn't mean anything. Ben was offered a job in London and will be there now. When I found out I was pregnant, I wasn't sure what to do. That's why I wanted to talk to you.'

A glimmer of a smile appeared on her mother's lips. 'Very good. Okay, we need to come up with a plan. I think we both know the outcome if you tell Ari. You will no longer have a relationship with your sister, and that is not an option. We're a family, and I'm not going to let your terrible choices ruin our lives.'

'What about Ben? Don't you think he has a right to know?'

'He has a right, but as he's never wanted children, which was one of the reasons Ari ended her marriage to him, I think he'd prefer not to know.'

Flo frowned. It was one of the reasons Ari had cited when she'd told Flo the marriage was over, but that didn't mean the news should be kept from him.

'It makes your decision a lot easier,' Julia said. 'You don't tell him, and you don't tell Ari. Your father and I will help you financially with the baby, and if you decide to keep it, we'll continue that support.'

'I'm keeping the baby,' Flo said, wrapping her arms protectively around her stomach.

'Oh, don't be so dramatic,' Julia said. 'It's not the 1920s. We're not going to send you off to some distant aunt to have the baby and then

*adopt it out. We'll organise the best prenatal care and aftercare for you
and be happy to welcome a grandchild.'*

* * *

'Flo?'

Flo looked at Ben, realising he was waiting for an answer to a
question she hadn't heard. 'Sorry, what did you say?'

'I asked you how you wanted to handle me being introduced to
Kayden?'

Flo sighed. 'I have no idea. Honestly, like Gigi said, he's been
through a lot the last few days.'

'Do you have a photo of him?'

Flo slipped her phone from her pocket and opened her photos.
A photo? Her camera roll was almost exclusively photos of Kayden.
She found one she'd taken the previous week of Kayden in the
back garden, grinning as he proudly held his soccer ball above his
head, and handed the phone to Ben.

He took the phone from Flo, closed his eyes momentarily and
then opened them, focusing on the screen. He swallowed, glancing
up at Flo briefly before turning back to the phone. 'He... he looks
just like I did at that age.'

Flo wasn't sure how to respond.

'He looks really happy,' Ben said.

'If you scroll through the photos, they're probably all of
Kayden,' Flo said.

Ben nodded and swiped the screen, stopping on the next
photo. He closed his eyes again and Flo's heart contracted as a tear
escaped the corner of one eye.

'I'm so sorry.' Her words were barely audible. How could she
have done this to him? Why had she ever listened to her mother
and decided that because Ben didn't want children it would be

kinder to him not to tell him. She knew why she'd listened. It allowed her to lie about the situation and protect her relationship with Ari. She shuddered, her own thoughts making her uncomfortable. That was not who Flo Hudson was.

Ben opened his eyes and handed the phone back to Flo. 'I don't think I can do this right now. All it's making me think of is how much I've missed out on. I think I need to focus on how we move forward.'

'How do we move forward?'

'Why don't Della and I drop in to your place tomorrow and say hello? We'll say I'm an old friend of the family, and I'd heard he'd been unwell. Della's four.' A hint of a smile appeared on his lips. 'And she's a handful, so she will probably cheer him up if he needs cheering up.'

Flo nodded slowly, a tear landing on her cheek. While the situation was her own doing, to say she was feeling overwhelmed was an understatement.

'Flo?'

'Sorry. It's been me and Kayden for so long. I don't know how I feel about all of this. Sharing him is going to be difficult.'

Ben's eyes hardened. 'Probably a lot easier than having missed out on his first six years.'

'Of course. Sorry.'

His eyes softened. 'No, I'm sorry. I get that this isn't easy for anyone. But I'm a good guy, Flo, and as mad as I am with you, I'm also excited.' He smiled. 'Like, really excited. I have a son.'

Flo wiped her cheeks, willing the tears to stop.

'I'll be there for him. We'll work something out. Don't worry. I'm not going to step in and make all kinds of demands to upset him or you. But I do want him in my life, and we'll take small steps over the coming weeks and months to work out the best way to do that.'

'What will you tell Della?'

'Nothing for now. Just that we're visiting friends – she'll be happy about that as other than a few kids she's met at kindergarten, she doesn't know many people in Melbourne. It's been a big upheaval for her, losing her mum and then being moved away from her friends in London.'

'I'm sorry about your wife,' Flo said.

Ben sighed. 'Me too.' He smiled. 'You would have liked her, Flo. She was a lot like you. Smart, caring, kind, hon—' He stopped. 'I guess the list can stop after kind.' He stood. 'Della's with my mum, but I should get back to her. I'd hoped to meet Kayden today, but another day won't matter if Della and I can drop by tomorrow?'

Flo nodded. 'I've got your number now, so I'll text you the address in the morning. We're in Box Hill.'

Ben's eyes lit up. 'Really? We're in Surrey Hills, so not far. We probably would have bumped into you at some stage.'

That comment silenced them both as Flo considered the shock that would have given her and wondered if he was thinking the same. Kayden looked like Ben did when Ben was little, so whether he would have noticed that or not, she wasn't sure.

* * *

Ari pushed her feet into her running shoes, drew her walnut-brown hair into a ponytail and was back out of her apartment door within minutes of returning home from the hospital. Her head was spinning from the revelations of the day, and she knew that the best thing she could do to get out of her own head was to go for a run. It was a beautiful winter's day in Melbourne, which was completely at odds with her mood. If there had been a thunderstorm with gale-force winds, it would've been more fitting.

However, she could hardly complain about a blue sky, even if the temperature was a little chilly.

She barely registered running through the city streets and along Southbank Esplanade, eventually crossing St Kilda Road near the Arts Centre and finding the track known to Melbournians as the Tan. While the track wasn't quite four kilometres in length, it wasn't unusual for Ari to do multiple circuits.

Her feet pounded the gravel track in a rhythmic beat. It was busy for a Saturday afternoon, which she welcomed. Being alone right now with her thoughts was not something that she wanted, and while the people around her were strangers and she wasn't conversing with them, she still felt like she had company. She had her AirPods in and turned up the music so that Pink's raspy tones were blaring in her ears. She loved Pink's no-bullshit attitude. She imagined integrity was important to Pink, not like her sister. She pushed the thought away, doing her best to rid her mind of Flo. It was practically impossible, though. How could her sister have done this to her? And Ben. Mind you, he was as much at fault in that he had an affair with her sister, but at least he hadn't kept the secret about Kayden's parentage.

She wondered if her mother knew the truth. Julia had been so understanding when Flo announced her pregnancy. She'd been matter-of-fact, even making the comment that everyone in the room was probably guilty of a one-night stand. It had seemed out of character that she hadn't lost her mind over it, as she was a woman who liked to control situations.

She dodged a couple of slow runners in front of her and increased her pace. She was back to the start of the run in what seemed like no time at all and continued. She would do at least two or three circuits and hopefully have stopped thinking about Flo by the end of it.

* * *

Fifty-five minutes later, Ari reduced her speed from a fast run to a walk. She was breathing hard and sweat ran down her back. She'd completed three laps in what was probably a personal record. She gave a wry smile. Next time she ran in a race, she'd have to get Flo to tell her something else she'd lied about. It certainly got her angry and got her going.

'Hey, Ari!'

She turned, still breathing hard, to find a good-looking guy smiling at her. He was dressed in running clothes but had barely broken a sweat. She smiled. He was familiar, but she couldn't place him.

'Sven,' he said and grinned.

She laughed. 'Ryan! Sorry, wrong context. I was trying to place you from work.'

He shuddered. 'Work. What a horrible thought. Gave *that* up years ago.'

She raised an eyebrow. 'What do you call teaching yoga then if it's not work?'

'A passion. Threw away the suit and tie about five years ago and never looked back. Now...' he folded his arms '...you probably didn't notice, but you ran past me twice in the last half hour. I was doing some yoga in the park.'

'No, sorry, I was pretty focused.'

'And fast. Are you training for the Olympics or something? That was impressive.'

She let out a sigh. 'Honestly, no. I've had a crappy day, and my release has always been running. The madder I am, the faster I go.'

'So, if I made you mad, you could probably win gold?'

She laughed. 'Right now, I'd say I'd have a pretty good chance.'

'Sounds like a rough day. How about I provide you with some distraction so you can get it out of your head for a while?'

Ari stared at him. Was he serious? She hardly knew him.

'Yes, I'm serious,' Ryan said, appearing to read her thoughts. 'Come on.' He held out his hand, and she had no idea what compelled her, but she found herself reaching for it.

'We'll go for a walk in the botanical gardens, and I'll show you my favourite place. It's guaranteed to relax you.'

Twenty minutes later, Ari laughed as she sat across from Ryan on the garden deck of Jardin Tan, one of the restaurants set amongst the beauty of the gardens. 'I assumed you'd be showing me some spiritual tree or space with healing energy, not getting me drunk.'

'Who said anything about getting you drunk?' Ryan raised his drink in a toast. 'I said I'd distract you, and I can guarantee this drink will.'

Ari took a sip of the exotic-looking cocktail. 'Mm, that's delicious. What's in it, and how do they make this foamy stuff on top?'

Ryan laughed. 'No idea. It's a Miss Saigon. A friend of mine loves them and had me try one a few weeks ago. I'd never had one before, but I liked it. Vodka and the rest is delicious.'

Ari smiled, placing her glass back on the table. 'I picked you as a yogi. No alcohol, vegan, cyclist and all that.'

'Cyclist?'

'Well, I can't imagine you driving a car and contributing to the pollution. Probably no coal-fuelled electricity either – you'd have solar panels and live next to a wind farm.'

Ryan burst out laughing. 'You concluded all of this after one yoga class?'

Ari shrugged. 'Guess I'm talking in clichés, aren't I?'

'You are. For the record, I am neither a vegan nor a cyclist, but I do enjoy yoga. I'm not particularly spiritual though. I also enjoy shooting guns and riding motorbikes.'

Ari raised an eyebrow. 'Guns?'

He nodded. 'I belong to a gun club. For sport. We shoot targets, not animals.'

'I guess I might have summed you up slightly incorrectly. Am I right in thinking you like meatballs, though?'

'Why, 'cause I'm Swedish?'

Ari laughed. 'You're quick, I'll give you that. I still have no idea why Sophie told me your name was Sven. I didn't think I was that superficial.'

'Well, it got you there and meant I met you, so who cares what her intentions were?'

Ari blushed as his eyes connected with hers. He was attractive, and while she wasn't on the lookout for a man, she had to admit, he was lovely. He was also doing a good job at keeping her mind off Flo, and the day she'd had.

'What did you just think about?' Ryan asked.

'What?'

'You looked happy for a moment, and then your face changed completely. It went dark, like you were remembering something bad.'

Ari sighed. 'Thinking about earlier, that's all.'

'I'm a good listener,' Ryan said. 'If you feel like talking about it. I'm also an impartial judge as I don't know anything about you or your friends, boyfriend or whoever has wronged you.'

'My sister,' Ari said. 'She has a six-year-old son who's been ill. He has a rare blood type and needs a blood transfusion.'

'I'm AB positive,' Ryan said automatically. 'If that's his type, I'm here to help.'

Ari stared at him. 'Without knowing more, you'd give him your blood?'

'Of course, it's not like you're asking for a kidney or bone marrow. Although, I wouldn't say no to exploring that either. Anything I don't need, he's welcome to.'

Ari smiled. 'That's kind, but he doesn't need any of your organs, and that's not his blood type, but thanks for offering.'

Ryan shrugged. 'So, he's unwell?'

'Yes, and his biological father can help him with the blood.'

'But the bastard won't. That's what you're about to say, isn't it?' Ryan's right hand clenched in a fist. 'What the hell is wrong with people these days?'

'Wow,' Ari said. 'We should get you running around the Tan and time it. I think you might beat me with that reaction. No, his father knew nothing about his illness until yesterday. In fact, he didn't even know he had a son. My sister lied to all of us about her son's biological father.'

Ryan relaxed his fist. 'Oh. Well, I'm sure she had good reason.'

'She did. It was my husband.'

Ryan froze. His expression one of utter surprise. 'You have a husband?'

Ari nodded and then couldn't help herself and started to laugh. 'I'm sorry,' she said, 'it's your face. You look more disappointed than shocked. I get the feeling my sister sleeping with my husband isn't necessarily an issue for you, but you're wishing I wasn't married, aren't you?'

Ryan composed himself, the muscles in his face relaxing. 'Well, it had crossed my mind that I'd quite like to get to know you. But if your sister's having babies with your husband, I'm assuming it's all a bit messy.'

Ari laughed even harder. 'I have no idea why I'm laughing. I'm so mad with my sister right now, but you're hilarious. Yes, it's messy, but Ben's actually my *ex*-husband if that's any consolation.'

Ryan lifted his glass. 'That's something to toast at least. Some good news for the day.'

Ari clinked her glass against his and sipped her drink while Ryan drained his.

'I think I'll order us another round in case you've got more shocks in store for me.' Ryan caught the attention of one of the waitstaff, placed the order and then turned back to Ari. 'Now, seriously, are you okay? That's huge news to have received. I don't know what I'd do if I found out my brother had got my wife – not that I have a wife – pregnant. Are you close with your sister?'

Ari nodded. 'We're twins.'

'Identical?'

She nodded again. 'We've had each other's backs all our lives, or so I thought. Flo's this kind, gentle person who would do anything for you. Until today, I would have said she has the most integrity of anyone I've ever met.' Tears filled Ari's eyes as she spoke. She did her best to blink them away.

'No wonder you're running at world record speed,' Ryan said, his voice gentle. 'It's probably skewed your view of everything. If your twin's someone you held up as having high standards, and she did this, what does it mean about everyone else?'

'Exactly.' Ari sipped her drink. 'Let's change the subject. It's all too raw, and while I'll need to deal with it at some stage, I prefer your original plan of distraction and relaxation. Tell me more about you. What was the high-flying job you gave up to become a yogi?'

* * *

When Ari arrived back at her apartment two hours later, a sense of calm had enveloped her. She'd stopped after the second drink as she didn't want to feel any worse the next day than she was already going to. But she had to admit, thanks to Ryan, one of the worst days of her life had ended surprisingly well. The anger she'd left the apartment with had dissipated.

She kicked her running shoes off and headed straight to the kitchen for a glass of water when her phone pinged with a text. She'd given Ryan her number as they'd said their goodbyes and she smiled, thinking he was already getting in touch. She extracted her phone from her pocket and dropped it on the kitchen bench. *Flo.* The fury she'd left the apartment with earlier returned in an instant. Running, a relaxing afternoon with Ryan and two cocktails weren't going to change the fact that her sister had betrayed her in a way that was completely unforgivable.

17

Flo was a bundle of nerves as she stared out of her lounge room window, waiting for Ben to arrive. She hadn't said much to Kayden, other than a friend of hers and Ari's was dropping in to see them. He'd hardly looked up from the television as a soccer match was being broadcast live from Spain.

The effects of the blood transfusion remained incredible. Other than a mild headache, Kayden had had no side effects and, within twenty-four hours of the transfusion, was looking and acting like himself, and was glad to be home. If Flo heard him say, 'I'm starving,' one more time, she'd scream. A happy scream, mind you. She was thrilled he was eating again. She'd done her best to put all other thoughts out of her mind for the morning and be grateful that he was healthy. But with worrying about Ari and the long-term implications of Ben in her life, it was hard to only focus on gratitude. The nail of her right index finger was taking the brunt of her anxiety and was already bitten to the quick.

On the dot of ten, a black Prado turned into the driveway, and Ben climbed out. He was wearing jeans and a hoodie, and Flo couldn't help but notice how good he looked. She checked herself.

This was Ari's ex-husband, not someone she was allowed to look at in any other way, even if she had failed on that account once already.

She watched as he opened the back door, speaking to his passenger. She drew in a breath as a gorgeous, blonde, curly-haired little girl appeared. She had perfect porcelain features, which were at odds with her rather dark and unimaginative clothing. She frowned. Della's outfit was completely black. Even her hair ties. It was an unusual choice for a little girl. Was she mourning her mother and showing it with her clothing? Immediately, Flo wanted to scoop her up into her arms and cuddle her. While her own mother wasn't maternal, she couldn't imagine losing her at the age of four. The reality that they might lose her at age thirty-six was hard enough.

Flo took a deep breath and called out to Kayden as she went to answer the door. 'Ben and Della are here. Can you turn off the TV and come and say hello?'

She sighed when there was no reply. He would be so focused on the game that she'd have to go and switch it off.

She opened the door, conscious of her heart racing a million miles an hour. She wasn't sure what was making her more nervous, that Kayden was unknowingly about to meet his dad or that she still felt awful for not telling Ben.

Flo forced a smile. 'Hey,' she said as Ben approached, his daughter's hand in one hand and a plastic bag in the other. She met Della's blue eyes.

'You must be Della. I've been looking forward to meeting you.'

'Really? Why?' Della offered Flo a defiant stare. 'Do you want to be my dad's girlfriend? Because I don't need a new mum.'

'Della,' Ben admonished. 'Where did that come from? I told you; I've known Flo for years. We lost touch when I moved to London, but I was close with her family. Say you're sorry, please.'

'Sorry,' Della mumbled. 'But Nanna said to Poppy that she hoped you didn't think you could replace my mum. My mum's dead, but I don't want a new one.'

Flo swallowed as the little girl looked down at her feet, her face filled with sadness.

'Dell,' Ben said, kneeling so he was eye level with his daughter. 'No one will ever replace Mum, okay? And Flo's a friend, nothing more.' He pulled her to him and gave her a hug, mouthing 'sorry' over her head to Flo.

'How about you come in and meet Kayden,' Flo said, doing her best to distract Della as she pulled out of Ben's hug. 'He's been looking forward to meeting you.'

'Okay,' Della said. 'Where is he?'

'Go down the hallway, and you'll hear the television. He was watching a soccer game, but I'll get him to turn it off.'

Della skipped off down the hallway.

'Sorry,' Ben said. 'Carrie's parents mustn't have known she was listening. I hadn't realised they were concerned. Once we've worked out our plans, I'll fill them in so they can understand there's nothing to worry about.'

'Would you like coffee or tea?'

Ben rubbed his hand through his hair. 'Can I meet Kayden first? I'm so ridiculously nervous, which is mad considering he doesn't even know who I am.'

'Yes, of course,' Flo said. 'Come through, and we'll get them to turn the TV off and go outside. There's some play equipment in the back garden and a sandpit, and if Della's into it, Kayden will love her forever if she's happy to kick a soccer ball with him.'

'I assumed from one of the photos you showed me at the hospital that he was a soccer fan.'

'Obsessed fan.'

Ben smiled. 'Good.'

Flo led him through to the family room, which housed the television, a comfy couch and two worn armchairs. 'Kayden, can you turn that off and come and meet my friend Ben?'

Kayden's eyes were fixed firmly on the screen, but he lifted the remote, flicked it off and then turned to Della and Ben. His reaction suggested he hadn't even noticed Della appear. 'Hi,' he said and smiled broadly at them.

'Hey, mate,' Ben said, holding out his hand that Flo couldn't help but notice was shaking. 'It's great to meet you.'

Kayden stood, held out a skinny arm and shook Ben's hand. 'Great to meet you too.' He turned to Della. 'Do you like soccer?'

'I like anything,' Della declared. 'Do you have a dog?'

'No,' Kayden said. 'My mum works too much and thinks it would be unfair to leave it home all day.'

'Cat?' Della asked hopefully.

'Nope. I do have a soccer ball, though,' Kayden said. 'Do you want to kick it with me?'

Della shrugged. 'Sure. But if you got a dog, you could play fetch. You should get a dog.'

'Okay,' Kayden said.

'Hey, buddy,' Ben said. 'Before you go out to play, Dell and I brought you a little present. We heard you'd been a bit sick and were hoping it'd cheer you up.' He held out the bag he'd been carrying.

'Thank you,' Kayden said and took the bag. He looked at Flo. 'Is it okay to look inside?'

She nodded. 'Of course.'

Kayden opened the bag and extracted a blue and white striped shirt. He held it up, his eyes bulging as he turned it over and saw number ten on the back. 'It's Messi's Argentina shirt,' he said. 'Mum, it's Messi's shirt!'

Flo smiled at Kayden and then at Ben. 'You picked the right present – that's for sure.'

'I'm a huge Messi fan,' Ben admitted. 'We debated between that one and the Miami shirt now that he's playing for them too. But Della said she didn't think you'd want a pink shirt.'

'I'd wear anything Messi wears,' Kayden said, 'but if I had to choose between this one and the Miami one, I'd choose this one.' He looked Ben in the eyes. 'Thank you. This is the best present ever.'

'Put it on,' Della said. 'Then we can go and play. I reckon it'll make you better at football.'

Kayden ripped his sweatshirt off and put the soccer jersey on. It was a perfect fit.

'Thank you, thank you,' he said again before turning to Della. 'Come on, let's go out the back. I've got lots of balls, so you can choose which one we use.'

Flo's smile evaporated as she watched the two of them disappear out into the back garden.

'Everything okay?'

'It's only just dawned on me that they're half-siblings. Della is Kayden's sister.'

'She is.' He let out a deep breath. 'I think that went okay for a first meeting, do you?'

'Okay? You bought him something he's wanted for ages. He'll love you forever.'

'As long as he doesn't think I'm trying to buy him.'

Flo raised an eyebrow. 'What do you call Messi's shirt?'

Ben pushed his hand through his hair and laughed. 'Buying him, I guess. It's hard to know what to do. You'd better fill me in on what you've told him so far about me so we can figure out how to make the fact I've suddenly appeared work.'

Flo nodded. 'Let me make some coffee, and we can chat.' She

hesitated. 'I know this probably doesn't mean much now, but I am sorry, Ben. I can see how much you want this to work with Kayden, and I'm kind of shocked in hindsight that I talked myself into thinking what I was doing was the right thing. Maybe it was the pregnancy hormones, I don't know. But I do know it was unforgivable.'

Ben nodded. 'I don't know what to say or think if I'm honest. But let's not dwell on all of that right now. I want to show you something my mum gave me this morning and asked me to bring with me.'

'You told her about Kayden?'

'Of course I did. She can't wait to meet him, and neither can Dad, but don't worry, they know it's going to be slow steps, and we need to work out the best way to introduce him to my family.'

Ben extracted his wallet from the back pocket of his jeans and took something from it. It was an old photo of a boy holding a fishing rod and grinning at the camera. Flo sucked in a breath. The only thing that gave away that it wasn't Kayden was the age of the photo. The colour fading suggested this was probably at least thirty years old.

'I was six in that photo,' Ben said.

'He looks so much like you!' Flo exclaimed.

Ben smiled. 'I know. Mum and Dad are going to be blown away. Do you have photo albums from when he was little? I'd love to see them.'

'I have about a million photos stored in the cloud,' Flo said. 'I've always meant to put them into albums but never have. I can show you some of them if you like?' *If you've got the next few hundred years free.* 'Let me get those coffees, and then we can start at the start, I guess, with the birth ones.'

* * *

More than an hour passed before it dawned on Flo that they hadn't heard a noise from the back garden in ages. 'We should check on the kids,' she said as Ben stared at another photo of Kayden when he was only a few days old.

He looked up and frowned. 'Della's not usually that quiet. I hope they haven't gone off somewhere.'

They stood and went over to the door that led to the back garden. The two children were sitting on the grass having a conversation.

'I wonder what they're talking about,' Ben said. 'It looks intense and unusual for Della. She usually can't sit still for more than a few minutes.'

'I'll offer them some food,' Flo said. 'Kayden and I made some muffins this morning. Hey, Kayden, Della,' she called, 'come and have some morning tea. We've got blueberry muffins.'

'In a minute,' Kayden called. 'Della's telling me something.'

They stood at the door watching the two children, who continued their conversation. Suddenly, Della stood up, hugged Kayden, and turned and ran towards Ben and Flo. She stopped when she reached them.

'Having fun, poppet?'

Della thought about Ben's question before answering. 'Kaydey's my new best friend.'

'Well, that's great to hear,' Ben said. 'You two looked like you were having quite a chat. What were you talking about?'

'How I sound different 'cause I'm from London, and how I call soccer "football",' Della said. 'Can I please have one of the muffins? Kaydey says they're delicious.'

'Does Kaydey?' Flo asked.

Della nodded. 'But you can't call him that. That's my name for him. He said no one had ever called him that before, so I'm the only one who can call him "Kaydey". Okay?'

Flo nodded, intrigued by this little girl. She couldn't imagine Kayden allowing a four-year-old to make the plans and call the shots, but she'd go along with it for now.

'I'll be in in a minute,' she said to Ben. 'I want a quick word with Kayden. The muffins and fruit are on the bench. Help yourself to drinks. There's plenty of cold water in the fridge.'

Flo waited until they were out of earshot before she approached Kayden. 'Just checking Della's not annoying you?'

'Annoying me? She's great. Did you know her mum died?'

'I did. It's sad.' Flo was surprised to hear that Della had told Kayden. From what Ben had told her, Della wouldn't speak about her mother, and he believed he was wasting a lot of money with the psychologist he was taking her to.

'Can I go in now?'

'Of course.'

Flo stood at the sliding door, watching as Kayden ran in to join Della and Ben. Ben said something, and Kayden laughed before sliding onto a stool next to Della at the kitchen bench. A lump rose in her throat. They looked like a perfect little family. A family that would spend time together and have a lot of fun. A family she wasn't part of.

18

It was hard to believe that two weeks had passed since Flo's shocking revelation about Ben being Kayden's father. Ari couldn't think of any time in their lives that they'd gone for such a long period without talking, and as much as she hated Flo right now, she also missed her unbelievably. While they would often go weeks at a time without seeing each other, they'd still text and speak on the phone every few days, if not every day. The number of times Ari had picked up the phone in the past two weeks to call her sister had surprised even her. She'd stopped herself each time, realising she just couldn't face her. She'd managed to avoid Flo at the hospital when she'd visited her mother and had refused Gigi's invitation to a family dinner when she'd learned Flo would be there.

She'd be lying if she said she wasn't curious as to how things had turned out for Flo with Ben. As angry and upset as he'd obviously been, there was still the question of Kayden, and Ben wanting to get to know him. Ari did feel a slight twinge of guilt when she thought back to her conversation with Flo when she had originally told her that she was ending her marriage with Ben because he had no desire to have children, whereas, of course, it had been her that felt that way. Regardless, that did not give Flo a reason to sleep with her husband or even her ex-husband, depending on when it had happened.

She manoeuvred her Lexus past a tram – muting her car radio as an ad came on promoting the Abba Voyage concert that was coming to Melbourne – and along Toorak Road towards Gigi's house. She'd planned to buy tickets for Flo, Gigi and herself for the concert, but there was no way that would be happening now. In fact, she doubted she'd ever be able to listen to Abba again. While she had declined the family dinner the previous weekend, she had promised her grandmother that she would come for dinner on her own. She knew both her father and Gigi were struggling with her mother still being in a coma, and she hoped spending some time with them each individually would help. She'd dropped in to see her father earlier that afternoon and was pleased that he'd been returning from the golf course.

'I feel guilty going out doing that,' he'd told her, 'but Heather stopped by last night and told me it's what Julia would want me to be doing and that I'm visiting her a lot and probably spending more time with her in the hospital than I normally do. With her being in Canberra, I didn't see her every day like I do now. It's quite strange.'

'Heather's right,' Ari had said. 'You need to look after yourself. Mum's getting lots of visitors, and we don't even know if she knows we're there. Being able to distract yourself for a few hours here and there might help keep you sane if nothing else.'

Now, as she arrived outside Gigi's house, she only hoped that the evening wasn't going to be full of her grandmother trying to convince her to talk to Flo and forgive her. For the past two weeks, she'd been grieving for her sister. But the sister she knew had died. She knew it sounded dramatic, but the betrayal was so extreme that she couldn't imagine ever feeling like she knew her sister in the way she thought she had.

It was quite bizarre, but the one person Ari wished she could talk to about this was her mother. Her mother had been vocal throughout their entire lives, always offering advice and guidance. And while at times it drove Ari insane, she also recognised that her mother tended to know what was in her best interest and guided her along those lines. She wondered what advice she would be handing out in this situation. She was still suspicious of what her mother might have known seven years ago when Flo announced her pregnancy. She pushed open the car door, determined to find out if Gigi knew more than she did.

* * *

Flo was amazed at how normal it was to have Ben and Della in the house. Only two weeks had passed, and they'd spent at least four afternoons together and most of the previous Sunday. It had seemed completely natural to be in each other's company.

'Have you spoken to Ari yet?' Ben asked as he sat down on one of the stools in Flo's kitchen. Della and Kayden were nearing the end of a movie, and Flo had offered to make herbal teas.

Flo shook her head, nausea swirling in her stomach as it did every time she thought of Ari and what she'd done to her. She added tea leaves to the pot. 'She won't take my calls or have anything to do with me. I tried showing up at her work earlier in the week, but they said she was unavailable and then had a security guard escort me off the premises. She's having dinner with Gigi tonight, so I'll probably hear from her as to how Ari's feeling about things.'

Ben sighed. 'Knowing Ari, she'll be masking her hurt with fury. I can hardly blame her. Maybe I should talk to her.'

'Not yet. It needs to be me first. I'm leaving her messages every day. Hopefully, she'll agree to speak to me at some stage. She needs some time. As much as I want to try and put things right, I know her well enough to know that giving her space is what I have to do right now.'

'I hope she'll come around, for all our sakes. I feel awful, Flo, really awful.'

Flo nodded. She understood how he was feeling. Regardless of the lies she'd gone on to tell, the actual act of her and Ben sleeping together would be hard for Ari to get past.

'On a completely separate note, thank you,' Ben said. 'These past couple of weeks getting to know Kayden have been amazing. Della's completely in love with him.' He smiled. 'I can't wait to tell her. She's going to be ecstatic.'

Flo nodded. She imagined Kayden would be, too. He and Della had connected in a way she'd never seen him do with any other child.

'How are you coping with everything?'

Flo was surprised at his question. 'Me?'

Ben nodded. 'I get that it can't be easy. Regardless of my feelings about what you chose to do seven years ago, sharing Kayden's a huge adjustment.'

Tears welled in Flo's eyes. She did her best to blink them away. She didn't want to appear any more selfish when it came to Kayden than she'd already shown herself to be. 'I'll get used to it,' she said. 'I know I'm lucky that it's you and not some deadbeat guy I'm suddenly having to allow him to spend time with. Your family are lovely too, so if anything, when he learns the truth, it's going to be a huge bonus for Kayden to suddenly have new people to love him.'

'And they will,' Ben said. 'Mum and Dad are beside themselves with excitement. Dad's already ordered a soccer net online and is hoping you'll let him take Kayden fishing. He's keen on that, as you might remember.'

Flo nodded. 'I'm sure Kayden would love to do all that when the timing's right. For now, can we continue to take things slowly? I still haven't worked out the best way to tell him who you are.' She pushed a cup of tea across to Ben.

'Any news on your mum?' Ben asked.

'The swelling's gone down a little, but not enough to bring her out of the coma,' Flo said. 'It's been so hard on Dad and Gigi too. I've never seen Dad like this before. To be honest, with Mum usually in Canberra, I've never realised how emotionally dependent he is on her. He's absolutely devastated. I hope Mum doesn't regress or that anything else happens. I honestly can't see him coping with anything more.'

'No, it's been a rough time for your family. Getting back to Ari, I know you said she needs time, but what if you force her to talk to you? You said she's having dinner with Gigi tonight. I'll watch Kayden and Della if you want to go and see her. It'll be harder for her to turn her back on you there, and Gigi's so wise, she'll probably act as a mediator.'

Flo's heart raced as she thought about his suggestion. 'You wouldn't mind?'

'Of course not. I know it might not turn out as you hope, but you won't know unless you try.'

Flo nodded. 'You're right.' She pushed her chair back and stood. 'I'll let Kayden know what's happening, and then I'll go. I'll try not to be too long.'

'Take as long as you want. It's still early. Kayden was hoping to play UNO after the movie, so I'll get them organised once it's finished.'

Flo flashed him a nervous smile. As much as she loved the idea of setting things right with Ari, the reality of making that happen was nerve-racking.

* * *

While she'd arrived at Gigi's wanting answers, once she'd crossed the threshold, Ari realised the last person she wanted to talk about was Flo, so she hadn't broached the subject. It wasn't until dessert that Flo's name was mentioned, and it was by Gigi, not Ari. Until that point, they'd been talking about Julia and the update they'd received that day that some of the swelling had subsided.

'You know,' Gigi said, readjusting her glasses before cutting a slice of her famous lemon cheesecake and sliding it across the table, 'the first I knew about Flo's relationship with Ben was when he turned up at the hospital the other day. What's strange is I always thought the story about Kayden's father seemed a bit off, but I was happy to believe it. I've been questioning myself over the past two weeks to try and work out why that was. I'm beginning to wonder if, subconsciously, I didn't want to know. I wouldn't have been able to keep it secret, but I would've shaken the two of them and demanded that they told you.'

'Except Ben didn't know about Kayden,' Ari said.

'I wasn't talking about Ben. I was talking about Flo and your mother. I can see that night clearly in my mind and hear her so casually telling us that we shouldn't be judging Flo because we've all had one-night stands, and we were lucky they didn't turn into pregnancies. At the time, I assumed Julia was drunk because it was so out of character for her not to go off the rails and berate Flo in front of all of us. I haven't asked Flo this yet because I'm not sure if I want to know the answer, but I have a strong suspicion that Julia knew. I'll be so angry with her if she advised Flo to lie, not only on your behalf but also for Ben and Kayden. He could've had a father in his life since the day he was born. We all know that while Ben might not have been suitable for you, and despite what's happened, he's a wonderful man. I'm sure he would've made a fantastic father and still will.'

'I've had the same thought,' Ari said. 'That Mum was behind this. But, even if she was, Flo wasn't a teenager needing guidance. She was an adult and should've made her own decision. My guess is that Flo was happy with what Mum suggested because it meant she didn't have to take responsibility or face up to what she'd done.'

'How do you think you would've reacted if Flo had told you at the time? Would you have been able to forgive her?' Gigi asked.

'I don't know,' Ari admitted. 'I still don't know whether they were having an affair or if it was a one-night stand after Ben and I divorced.'

'Would that make a difference?'

'I think so. I'm not sure how much of a difference or whether it means that I would forgive her, but to discover she'd been having an affair with Ben while we were still married would be something I couldn't handle. To find out they hooked up for one night after we were over isn't great, but certainly a different circumstance.' Ari thought back to her night with Sean, which, whilst it wasn't quite the same and certainly hadn't ended in a pregnancy, was something she wasn't proud of. She'd been relieved when Sean confirmed he'd told Ben, and Ben had forgiven him.

'I had another phone call from that man,' Gigi said, spooning a mouthful of cheesecake into her mouth. 'Wanting to know if I'd heard from Julia.'

'What did you tell him?'

'Nothing. I asked him a few questions, trying to work out who he was, but he gave me about as much information as I gave him. I found out his name is Scott Cohen, and that was about it. Another secret I imagine that we'll need to ask Julia about when she wakes up.'

'How are you coping with all of this, G? It can't be easy.'

Gigi sighed. 'I'm okay, love. Your mother has never been an easy person to be around, as we all know. I still wonder to this day what I did wrong with her. I hope we're not going to discover something awful has been going on when she wakes up.'

'Awful?'

Her grandmother nodded.

'You're thinking something between Mum and this guy?'

'I hope not. I really do. It would kill your father, but she's been going to Canberra every other week for thirty-odd years and living a separate life. Your father hardly ever accompanied her, and I only ever visited a few times, and the same with you girls. She always said it was easier to keep her two lives separate, but I'm beginning to worry that it's all a little too convenient.'

'Surely Dad would have questioned it?'

'Your father's a trusting man. Possibly too trusting for his own good. I can only hope that my daughter hasn't let him down.'

A knock on the door caused Gigi to freeze mid-spoonful. 'That's most likely to be Harriet from next door. She's been dropping in most nights when she gets home from work with meals for me. It's lovely of her, but she doesn't seem to realise that a jam sandwich or eggs on toast is more than enough right now.' She gave a wry smile. 'I made the dessert, but the chicken casserole was something she dropped in the other night. I didn't have the energy to make a main course, too.'

Ari stood. 'Why don't I let her in?'

'Better still, tell her I'm in bed, accept the food, and I'll thank her tomorrow. I don't feel like giving her an update tonight. She's lovely but nosy.'

A more insistent knock sounded at the door.

'She's not taking no for an answer,' Gigi said with a chuckle. 'I guess she saw the lights on.'

Ari hurried down the hallway to the front door. As much as her grandmother might find visitors annoying, Ari was pleased that her friends were rallying around her. She swung open the door, took one look at the visitor and slammed it shut.

19

The slam of the door reverberated in Flo's ears. She stood, shocked, staring at the carved wood. She'd expected an icy reception from Ari, but she hadn't anticipated her answering the door, and she certainly hadn't imagined it would be slammed in her face.

Tears threatened, but Flo blinked them back fiercely, refusing to let her vulnerability show. Inside, she was crumbling. She'd betrayed the one person who had always been there for her. She remained rooted to the spot. Minutes passed, and she lifted her hand, contemplating knocking again, but let it drop back beside her. Ari had made it clear that she didn't want to speak to her, and as much as she wanted to speak to Ari, she should be putting her sister first and respecting her wishes.

The door opened before she had a chance to turn and walk back to her car. It was Gigi.

Flo took one look at her grandmother's concerned expression and the tears that had threatened erupted. She hid her face in her hands.

'Oh, love,' Gigi said, pulling Flo to her. 'You need to let Ari come to you in her own time. She's not ready.'

Flo nodded, appreciating the comfort of Gigi's embrace. She pulled away, doing her best to compose herself. 'I know. Tell her I'm sorry.' She wiped her eyes on her sleeve. 'I need to explain what happened. That it wasn't an affair. I don't expect her to forgive me, but I need her to hear what I have to say. I miss her so much, G.' More tears spilt down her cheeks.

'Give her time,' Gigi said, her tone gentle 'You can't force it, and the more you try, the angrier she's going to get. You've had seven years to get used to this. She's had a couple of weeks. It's been a huge shock on top of everything going on with your mother, and she doesn't have the capacity for more. I don't think any of us do.'

Flo nodded. She knew Gigi was right, but it didn't stop her from wishing she could wave a magic wand and fix everything.

Gigi drew her into another hug before gently pushing her back towards her car. 'Go home, Flo. Ari will talk to you when she's ready. I'm sure of it.'

Flo followed her grandmother's instructions, walked back to her car, and moments later pulled away from the kerb. She was hardly aware of time passing as she made the journey back to Box Hill. Despite Gigi's assurances, she couldn't shake the feeling of helplessness that overwhelmed her. What if she couldn't mend her relationship with Ari? Losing her sister would be like something dying inside. Tears blurred Flo's vision as an overwhelming sense of grief enveloped her.

* * *

It was a little before ten when Ari arrived home from Gigi's. She was tempted to put her running shoes on and give the Tan a pounding, but it was late and not the safest time of night to be running around the streets of Melbourne. Gigi had done her best to calm her anger after sending Flo away, but she still felt it pulsing through her. Flo needed to leave her alone.

Her phone rang, and she grabbed it from her bag, ready to scream into it if it was Flo. But it wasn't. She stared at the screen, her anger evaporating instantly.

'Sven?'

Ryan's deep laugh reverberated through the phone line. 'The one and only. You were on my mind, so I thought I'd give you a call. How are you?'

Ari gave a strangled laugh.

'That good, hey?'

'I was contemplating another world-record run around the Tan, actually. But figured I was more likely to be running from rapists than my problems at this time of night.'

'Ah, problems. My speciality. Anything I can help you with?'

Ari moved into the open-plan living area of her apartment and sank onto her beloved cream snuggle chair. She gathered the soft pink blanket she'd draped over it, placed it across her lap and smiled. Ryan certainly had a knack for being available at the right time.

'My sister turned up while I was at my grandmother's tonight.'

'How did that go?'

'I slammed the door in her face, and that was the extent of our conversation.' Ari smiled as she heard Ryan stifle a laugh. 'It's not funny.'

'Sorry, it's definitely not funny. But I would have loved to have seen her face. She must have been shocked.'

Ari's smile turned into a frown. 'More than shocked. I heard her crying when my grandmother spoke to her.' Sadness settled over Ari as she replayed the scene in her mind. She missed Flo more than she was willing to admit. She sighed, doing her best to push the feeling of melancholy away. She hated Flo for doing this to them. 'Maybe I'm being unreasonable and should have let her speak to me.'

'Definitely not unreasonable, and give yourself a break. You have every right to be mad and every right to want some space. Of course, she wants to speak to you because she wants you to make her feel better by forgiving her or telling her everything's okay.'

'You don't think I should forgive her?'

'Absolutely not,' Ryan said. 'There's nothing she could say that would excuse what she did. She created a baby with your husband. I'm not sure it can get more messed up than that. I'd be planning to slam a lot more doors in her face if I were you.'

Ari was surprised at the venom in Ryan's tone. 'You sound like you hate her more than I do.'

'Do you hate her?'

Ari considered the question. 'I hate what she's done. It's hard to go from considering someone your favourite person on the planet to hating them overnight.' She sighed. 'I think I need more time before I make any decisions about anything.'

'Well, there is one thing you could give some thought to,' Ryan said. 'I believe you have a spot open for a favourite person on the planet. I'd be happy to help you fill that.'

Ari smiled. 'Auditions for the spot are, in fact, open – and I must say, you're doing a good job.'

Ryan laughed. 'Good. How about I buy you a drink one night next week? Or even better, come to a yoga class, and then we have a drink or even a bite to eat?'

Ari thought ahead to her schedule. She had long days sched-uled on both Monday and Tuesday. 'Do you have a class on Wednesday night?'

'We have a class every night,' Ryan said. 'On Wednesday it's from six until seven-thirty, and then we could go for dinner?

There's a Thai down the road from the studio. Very casual but delicious. How does that sound?'

'Perfect, and Ryan, I promise not to talk about my sister. You've heard enough about her.'

'No need to promise anything,' Ryan said. 'It's what's going on in your life right now, and if you want to talk about it, then I want to hear about it.'

'I'll see you Wednesday at the studio, and we'll go from there.'

'It's a date.'

Ari stared at her phone after Ryan ended the call. Had she agreed to go on a date? Yoga and a bite to eat wasn't a date, was it? She smiled. She had to admit, whether it was a date or not, she was looking forward to it. Once again, Ryan had helped take the edge off what, thanks to Flo, had been an awful day.

20

Flo sat by her mother's bedside, watching the rhythmic rise and fall of her chest, grateful that she was able to breathe on her own. Doctor Lee had confirmed that she was happy with the reduction in the swelling on the brain and hoped another week or two would be enough to bring Julia back to consciousness. Flo could only hope that whatever damage her mother had suffered wouldn't be irreversible.

'Hey, you.'

Flo looked up as Holly stepped into the ICU, her hair tied back in a neat bun, stethoscope draped around her neck and a clipboard in hand. Flo smiled. 'This is unexpected. What are you doing here?'

'Saying hi before I start my shift. How are you?'

'Honestly, you don't want to hear the answer to that.'

'That good?'

Flo nodded. 'I tried to apologise to Ari last night.'

'Tried? I assume it didn't go as you hoped?'

'It didn't go at all. She slammed the door in my face before I opened my mouth.'

'Ouch.' Holly grimaced. 'That's not much fun. Sound like she needs some more time.'

'That's what my grandmother said. I guess I should give her space until she's ready. Then there's the Mum situation, of course. We still don't have any clue as to why she was in Melbourne at the time of the accident or why she took her friend's husband's car. But I feel weirdly like that situation is on hold until she's brought out of the coma. It's like we've been given a slight break on that front until we have to deal with whatever the consequences are.'

'I get it,' Holly said. 'Hopefully, you'll be dealing with good news. Now, Pauline asked me to tell you that there's a guy out at reception insisting he see your mum. Said he knows her from Canberra and only recently found out she's here. He's been told family only, but he's insisting he *is* family.'

Flo stood. 'That's weird. We don't have any family in Canberra. What's his name?'

'Not sure. It's probably easiest if you came and met him, and you can let Pauline know whether he's authorised to visit.'

Flo followed Holly out of the ICU unit to the reception desk that was located outside the double doors. A man in his early sixties, dressed in a navy jumper and chinos, his salt and pepper hair combed neatly to the side, was sitting on one of the chairs in the waiting area directly across from the reception desk.

'That's him,' Holly murmured. She gave Flo a hug. 'I've got to get to work, but let me know if you need me, okay?'

Flo nodded and turned to Pauline, lowering her voice so it was barely audible. 'Holly said that guy's here to see Mum.'

Pauline's features were tinged with curiosity. 'Come with me for a second.'

Flo followed Pauline into the small break room that was positioned behind the reception area and closed the door behind them.

'I don't want to upset you,' Pauline said, 'but Mr Cohen is claiming to be Julia Hudson's partner.'

'What? That's ridiculous.'

'I've assumed he's got the wrong Julia Hudson, so we weren't going to let him in to see your mum without your authority or your dad's. But he turned up about an hour ago, quite upset, saying he'd only recently tracked her down. She's been missing for two weeks, apparently.'

'Missing from where? She lives here. Well, other than when she's at work.'

'I have no idea, but he was insistent,' Pauline said. 'Have a chat with him, and I'll alert security that we might need him to be removed. It's up to you whether you allow him to visit.'

Flo nodded and followed Pauline back to the ICU reception area. Flo made a beeline for the man, her arms folded across her chest. 'Can I help you?'

He looked up at her, his brown eyes suddenly alarmed. 'Sorry?'

'The duty nurse said you want to visit Julia Hudson. Can I ask why?'

'She's my partner,' he said. 'She's been missing for over two weeks, and I've only just found out through her workplace that she's here.'

'Your partner?'

He nodded.

'I think you've got the wrong Julia Hudson,' Flo said, forcing herself to take on a kinder tone. The man's tired expression suggested he was going through a rough time. 'The woman in the room here is my mother.'

His eyes widened. 'Your mother?'

'I'm sorry,' Flo said. 'Perhaps I can help you try and locate your partner?'

The man shook his head. 'This doesn't make any sense. I spoke with her mother, Genevieve, last night, and she wouldn't tell me much, but she did mention an accident and that Julia had been admitted to this hospital. What are the chances of two Julia Hudsons being here?'

Flo's heart rate quickened. 'Her mother's name is Genevieve?'

He nodded. 'Genevieve Greenway.'

Flo narrowed her eyes. 'That's my grandmother's name. Why were you talking to her?'

'Julia had a falling-out with her family years ago. She divorced, was estranged from her daughters, and her mother disowned her as a result. I've never met Genevieve, but Julia gave me her number and clear instructions that if anything was ever to happen to her, I was to contact her mother. That was it. And while I had no idea if anything had happened to Julia when she didn't come home, I decided it was time to reach out. Her mother gave me little information, to be honest, but did mention an accident, and this hospital.'

'My mother's happily married,' Flo said. 'She's not in a relationship with you or anyone else other than my father.' Or was she? Why would this man have Gigi's number as an emergency contact if Julia hadn't given it to him? Flo's legs began to tremble. She wasn't sure she could take much more right now.

'Look, I have no clue of what's going on either,' he said. 'All I can tell you is that I live in Canberra with Julia. She divorced over twenty years ago, has nothing to do with her family and spends every other week in Melbourne for work.'

Flo stared at him. 'You live in Canberra?'

He nodded.

Flo fell silent. What if this guy was in a relationship with her mum? What did it mean for her father and for all of them? But if it was true, then he also had a right to information about her mother.

'My mother lives one week in Melbourne and one week in Canberra,' she said. 'How long have you been together with your partner?'

'We've known each other for the past fifteen years and been in a relationship for the last five. You said your parents are still together?'

'Yes, and while she drives us nuts at times, we're not estranged from our mother.'

He shook his head. 'This is ridiculous. There's no way Julia would have lied to me about her marriage and children. Why would she? She can be a bit secretive at times, but she's not this extreme.'

Flo wasn't sure what to say. What had seemed unlikely only minutes ago now appeared to be a strong possibility. 'You'd better come and see her,' Flo said. 'That way, we'll know for sure if we're dealing with an even bigger disaster than we originally thought. I'm Florence. Most people call me Flo.'

'Florence?'

She nodded.

'And your sister is Arabella?'

Nausea churned in the pit of Flo's stomach. This man knew her mother. She nodded again.

'I'm Scott. Scott Cohen.' He pushed his hand through his hair. 'And as much as I don't want to believe any of this, I think Julia's going to have a lot of explaining to do.'

'Let me take you through to see her so you can confirm it's her. We'll need to get you a gown and some other protective clothing before you can enter the ICU.'

Scott nodded. 'Thank you.'

Flo organised the clothing in silence, her mind racing. What did this mean for her father, for their family? Had her mother who had such high moral standards really been having an affair?

Flo tried to push the thoughts from her mind, and few minutes later, dressed in the required clothing, they entered the ICU area. Scott followed Flo into the small room allocated to Julia. Flo looked at him, knowing how confronting it could be seeing someone hooked up to the machinery.

'Are you okay?'

He shook his head and sat down in the chair Flo had only recently been sitting in beside her mother. He took her hand, in a way that suggested it wasn't the first time he'd done this. 'Oh, Jules,' he said, lowering his head.

A chill swept through Flo at his words. She cleared her throat. 'This is your partner?'

He nodded.

'Look,' Flo said. 'I'm sorry to be so blunt, but can you prove it? I can see that you know my mother, but we've never heard of you and for you to suggest you're having a relationship with her is pretty hard to believe.'

'We live together. Is that enough for you? We're in Bellmore Gardens in Barton. It's Julia's place, but I moved in about a year ago.'

'But I've visited her there. So have my sister and my dad. You weren't there on any of those visits.'

Scott pushed a hand through his dark hair again. 'I don't know what to tell you. I travel internationally for work every few months, usually for two to three weeks at a time. Could she have timed your visits around my trips? My trips are always planned in advance, so she'd have plenty of time to organise that.'

He reached into his back pocket for his wallet, took out a photo and passed it to her. 'And here's a photo of us if you don't believe me.' She took a deep breath and brought the image to her eyes. Her mother, snug in ski clothes with Scott's arms around her and a stunning alpine backdrop, smiled back at her.

Flo looked up from the photo. 'You said you've known her for fifteen years?'

He nodded. 'We work together at the Bureau of Strategic Intelligence. We're in different departments, but both work from the same location, and of course, there's Project Enigma – which is what we've been working on together for the past six years. It's what turned our relationship from colleagues to a romance.'

'Project Enigma? She doesn't discuss the details of her work with us. Her work's always been confidential.'

'This isn't regular work. It's something we've been researching and working on together outside as a personal project. But regardless, we live and work together. I'm not sure what other proof you need? You can ring the HR department where we work. They'll confirm we work together.' He frowned. 'It's recorded on our files that we're in a relationship, but it's not public knowledge with the staff. I doubt anyone's allowed to disclose that information even if they did check our files.'

As much as she hated what she was hearing, Flo wasn't sure he needed to provide more proof. *Her mother had been having an affair. More than an affair. She'd been leading a double life.* Julia Hudson, the person Flo would have said had more integrity than anyone, was a liar and a cheat. However, when she thought back to the ill-advised path of lies and deception she'd followed herself many years ago with Julia's encouragement, was it such a surprise?

A lump rose in her throat as she wondered how she would face her father. He was already devastated at the prospect of losing her, and this would rip apart everything he'd ever believed in.

* * *

Ari couldn't shake the feeling of dissatisfaction as she closed the file and marked it ready for archiving. Another case closed. Another case won.

'Nice job, Hudson,' Sophie said, entering Ari's office and flopping down in the chair opposite her. 'No wonder they love you around here. I don't think anyone thought you'd get that guy off.'

Ari sighed. 'Wish I hadn't, to be honest.'

Sophie raised an eyebrow. 'What? Who *are* you? Where's my ball-breaking colleague gone? With the money his parents threw at the firm to defend him, you've kept us all fed for months.'

Ari laughed, grateful to Sophie for trying to lighten her rather dark mood. 'Winning at any cost doesn't feel all that good.'

'He was guilty?'

Ari nodded. 'He only got off because the police didn't follow proper protocol when storing his fingerprints. The judge agreed the evidence was mishandled, and it was ruled inadmissible. So, he walks away scot-free while the plaintiff has to deal with the loss of several hundred thousand dollars. They never did recover the artwork he stole.' She sighed again. 'Sometimes the legal system lets us down. The whole ethical duty clause we all abide by should be changed. Why should I give someone who admits to me he's guilty a great defence? I should be allowed to hand him over to the courts with a transcript of what he told me.'

'Your defence certainly sounded like you believed he was innocent. I sat in for some of it last week.'

'It sounded like it had to,' Ari said. 'Mind you, until this morning, I only *thought* he was guilty. He'd been lying to me all along, but my gut knew that. After the case was dropped, we had a candid conversation where he thanked me for "*going along with his lies*". I'm pretty sure he'll be out selling one of the paintings he stole to fund his next scam. I've got to say, Soph, there's part of me that's over this. I went into law wanting to make a difference. To do something good and contribute to society.' She held up the file she'd marked for archiving. 'I'm doing the exact opposite – defending scumbags like this.'

'Maybe you should consider swapping teams and joining the prosecution.'

Ari's phone pinged with a text. She picked it up, tutted as she read the message and threw it back down on the desk.

'Bad news?'

'No, it's Flo. Trying to use Mum as an inroad to get me to talk to her.'

'Really? You still haven't spoken? It's been weeks, hasn't it?'

'In addition to the million text messages, she attempted to talk to me on Friday night. I'm not interested. I don't know that I'm ready for the truth, assuming she's going to provide it. She crossed a line I never imagined she would. She told Gigi they weren't having an affair, but after all the lies, how do I know I can believe her? If it turns out they were having an affair behind my back, it's the end of our relationship. I'd never be able to trust her again.'

'You're not speaking to her in case that's what she tells you?'

Ari nodded. 'Partly that, and I'm still so mad I'm scared I might hit her if I look at her. The problem is, I can't imagine my life without Flo in it. As angry as I am with her, I've missed her the last few weeks. We were so close, Soph.' She sighed. 'It'll never be the same no matter what the story around her and Ben is, but not knowing might actually be better than finding out that they were sneaking around behind my back.'

Her phone pinged again.

'Flo again?' Sophie asked.

Ari glanced at the screen. 'Yep. Saying it's about Mum and it's urgent.'

'Hon, your mum's in a coma. You don't think there could be any truth to Flo's message?'

'Nope. The hospital has my details. I made it clear to them that

I want to be called directly and that I'm not having information relayed through Flo. Dad and Gigi know the same. If there was a complication or new development around Mum, I'd hear from one of them. Now, let's change the subject. Did you come in for anything in particular?'

Sophie grinned. 'A little bird told me you had drinks with *Sven*.'

'A little bird?'

'Yes, a little Sven bird. I did one of his classes yesterday, and he thanked me for dragging you to Bikram. How come this is the first I'm hearing about your date?'

Warmth crept into Ari's cheeks. 'Because it wasn't a date. *Ryan* saw me running at the Tan and invited me for a drink. It was after I'd found out about Flo and Ben. Not a date.'

'And you haven't heard from him since?'

'I've spoken to him. Now, what's happening with the Delaney case? Todd said you were hoping to delegate it?'

'What's with the change of subject, Hudson?' Sophie grinned. 'I knew you and Sven would hit it off.'

'He's a lovely guy. And yes, I'd say we're becoming friends, but nothing more.'

Sophie stood. 'I guess time will tell with that one. I'm not sure Sven will settle for only friends. A Nordic wedding, perhaps?'

Ari opened her mouth to object, but Sophie was already out the door, her laugh reverberating through the hallways of Premier Legal. Ari smiled. She had to admit, she was looking forward to Wednesday night.

She turned her attention back to her computer and opened her emails. At the same moment, her phone rang, and she instantly silenced the 'Thank You for the Music' ringtone. With her ban on all things Abba, she'd need to change that. Part of her was tempted to block Flo altogether, but she wasn't quite ready to do that. She just wished Flo would get the hint and leave her alone.

21

Flo stuffed her phone back in her pocket, anger and upset roiling inside her. She understood that Ari was mad with her, furious even, but she should still be picking up her phone. What if their mother was taking her final breaths? Wouldn't she want to be with her? And how was she supposed to deal with the Scott Cohen situation? She'd hoped Ari would agree to put everything else aside for the moment and come to the hospital and help her. Maybe she should have been more specific in her message. *Mum's boyfriend is at the hospital. Come and meet him.* Perhaps that would have got her attention.

She'd left Scott sitting beside her mother and made her way down to the courtyard area in front of the hospital, hoping to speak with Ari in private and work out a way to approach their father. She glanced at her watch. It was close to two, and he'd said he'd be coming in around three. She sent him a quick text.

> Can we meet at the hospital cafeteria when you get here? Don't come up to see Mum yet. The doctors want to run some tests, and we can't be in the room until they've finished. Meet you there at 3?

She was relieved when a thumbs-up emoji came straight back.

She took a deep breath as she made her way back inside the hospital and hurried to the lift that would take her back to the ICU. As angry as she knew Ari was with her, right now her own anger was channelled at her mother. How could she have put them in this situation? It would be bad enough if Julia herself had to tell them all about her second life and partner, but why should Flo be the one to have to break the news to her father?

As the lift opened to the ICU area, Flo was greeted with an empty waiting room.

'He's still with your mum,' Pauline said as she approached the reception desk. 'Are you going back in?'

'Would you mind asking him to come out?' Flo said. 'It'll save me having to dress up to enter the room again. Perhaps tell him visiting hours are over so we can get rid of him.'

Pauline pursed her lips and then nodded. 'I won't tell him that, but yes, he's had long enough with her.'

Moments later, Scott stepped back into the reception area, carefully removing his gown and mask.

Flo approached him, noticing the pained, weary look around his eyes. A wave of compassion washed over her. This wasn't only about her father and her family. This was about Scott, too. He hadn't done anything wrong other than love the woman who was currently in a coma. She reached out and touched his arm. 'How are you holding up?'

He managed a small smile. 'Not the best. I've spent the past two weeks trying to find her, imagining the worst – that she was lying dead in a ditch somewhere – to have a mild sense of relief discovering she was here. Learning she was in a coma, of course, was terrifying, but everything else takes it all to a new level.'

Flo nodded. 'I don't even know what to say. You hear of people, most often guys, having two separate lives, but it's not something you'd ever think your own mother would do. At least she didn't marry you, too.'

Scott sighed. 'I guess that would have been her downfall and explains why she rejected the one rather over-the-top marriage proposal I did make.' He gave a wry smile. 'She told me that her failed marriage taught her how wrong the concept was. That it went against her feminist beliefs; something about historical patriarchy and wanting to ensure she retained economic independence.'

'That sounds like Mum,' Flo said. 'But you stayed with her?'

'Of course,' Scott said. 'I was proposing because I loved her. That didn't change. I should have thought it through more or at least had a conversation with her about marriage before proposing, especially as she'd supposedly been divorced before. Anyway, that's hardly important. If she'd said, "*No, I'm actually still married*," that would have helped make things a lot clearer.'

'It's a shock, isn't it?'

He pushed a hand through his hair. 'I can't believe it. We have such a solid relationship.'

'And no one at work ever talked about her family?'

He started to shake his head, then stopped.

'What?'

'HR knows about our relationship, and they've kept it confidential, but no one else knows. It's a bit of a joke amongst our other colleagues that Julia's my "work wife" as we spend so much time together in the workplace. We've never spoken much about our relationship outside of work, as Julia's always insisted that we keep our personal relationship private. Now I know why. But, about six months ago, one of the staff, Kirsty, made a comment about Julia being my work wife, and she wondered how Julia's husband felt about that. Julia laughed and said, "Which one? I've got about six." Everyone laughed, and the conversation moved on. At the time I thought Kirsty was making a joke, but maybe she knew about your father, whereas she probably didn't know about me and Julia.'

'And no one else knows about you and Mum?'

'Outside of work, they do. Friends and neighbours.' He shook his head. 'Is it just you, and your sister, Flo, or do you have other siblings?'

'There's just me and my sister. Also, I have a six-year-old, so she's a grandmother.'

A wordless pause hung between them.

'You'll have to meet my dad,' Flo said. 'Have a conversation and work out how we move forward. We need Mum to wake up and explain herself, but there's no guarantee that's going to happen any day soon.'

Scott closed his eyes briefly, before nodding and reopening them. 'Have you told him yet?'

'No.' She glanced at her watch. 'He's meeting me in about half an hour in the cafeteria. I was going to ask if you'd be willing to join us. Let me explain the situation first, and then I could text you and ask you to come in.'

Scott nodded slowly. 'I'm not sure what I say to him. We're in a relationship with the same woman. A woman who lied to both of us. I doubt he'll believe me.'

'Your evidence is pretty compelling,' Flo said. 'Your address, for a start, and then that photo shows Mum was certainly out doing things she never mentioned to us.'

'I've got plenty of photos if you'd like to see them,' Scott said.

'Photography is one of my hobbies.' He frowned. 'I need my computer to show you them though. I don't have any on my phone. Work's strict about the personal data we're allowed to have on our phones.'

Flo nodded. She'd always thought the rules insisted on by her mother's work were extreme. Minimal personal details publicly available, no social media accounts, no publicly accessible photos. 'I don't need any more proof. I'm going downstairs to wait for Dad. Can you give me your number and I'll text you when we're ready for you to join us?' She held out her phone to Scott.

He took it and keyed in his number before handing it back to her. 'Good luck with your dad. I'm sorry you're the one having to do this. This was Julia's job, not yours. Assuming she does wake up from this coma. I'm beginning to think she might prefer not to.'

* * *

Flo hadn't expected her grandmother to walk through the hospital's front entrance with her father. Gigi had already visited earlier that morning, and she thought she wouldn't be back until the following day.

'Your father needed some company,' Gigi said before Flo asked.

Flo nodded, trying to decide how best to approach this.

'Any change with your mum?' her father asked.

'No, all still the same. Let's go and get some coffee. There's something I need to talk to you both about. It's not related to Mum's health,' she was quick to reassure them.

With coffee and a selection of muffins in front of them, Flo explained the situation as simply as she could. Gigi listened, her eyes growing wider with every word. Flo would like to think that Gigi's expression was one of total disbelief, but there was something in it that suggested she either knew something or had suspected something.

The last thing Flo had expected from her father was laughter. 'You're so naive, Flo. This man is clearly a gold digger. He's after her money. Probably read some news article about a woman in a coma after an accident and decided to try and cash in.'

'Have there been any news articles?' Gigi asked.

There hadn't, to Flo's knowledge. 'I don't think so. They've worked together for the last fifteen years, and they live together in Canberra. He said they've been together for five years, and he moved into Mum's place about a year ago.'

Her father's laughter subsided. 'That's not possible. I might not visit often, but I have been there a few times in the last twelve months. What does she do with him on those occasions? Hide him? You girls and Gigi have been to visit, too.'

'He said he travels internationally every few months for work. His theory is that she had us visit when she knew he'd be away. It's possible.'

'But where does he think she is the week she's in Melbourne?'

'It sounds like she's told him a similar story to what she's told us. That she has a job that's split between Canberra and Melbourne, so it's one week on and one week off.'

'Wouldn't he have come with her to Melbourne with her on some of her work trips?'

'I don't know, Dad. Like you said, we've been to Canberra and not known he existed.'

Mike shook his head slowly. 'No, she would never do something like this. Your mother's integrity is one of the things I love most about her. There's even that thing she says about it. How integrity isn't about what you do when everyone is watching; it's about what you do when no one is looking.'

'It's the measure of who you truly are,' Flo finished for him. 'I guess she had us all fooled.'

'No, I'm sorry,' Mike folded his arms across his chest. 'This guy's a con man. It's the only explanation.'

'He has photos of them together.'

Gigi drew in a breath.

'They're probably photoshopped,' Mike said. 'In this day and age, you can do anything. You should know that. All the Facebook scams. He probably got into her Facebook page and stole them from there.'

Flo thought of the photo he'd shown of them skiing. It had definitely been her mother with Scott's arms around her.

'Dad, I'm pretty sure Mum doesn't have a Facebook page. She's lectured us all a million times about not posting personal content online and that her work is very strict in what she is allowed to do. She works in national intelligence so she's hardly going to be doing anything risky. I think there's more to it than that.'

'Okay, so he's a guy she knows in Canberra who's decided to take advantage of the situation. I have no idea what his deal is, Flo, but your mother wouldn't have done this to us. There's no way she would have lied to any of us or led some ridiculous secret life. Is there?' He turned to Gigi for confirmation.

Flo couldn't help but notice her grandmother wringing her hands together. 'I hope not, Mike. I really do.'

'You hope not? Surely you know Julia wouldn't do anything like this?'

'I'd like to believe she wouldn't, but the last few weeks have given us revelations I never anticipated. So, while I might have agreed with you before the accident about her integrity, right now I think reserving judgement is a good idea. Seeing what's unfolded around the Kayden situation has had me questioning a lot of things.'

'This has got nothing to do with the Kayden situation,' Mike said.

'I disagree,' Gigi said. 'If you're going to insist that Julia's integrity is one of her strong points and a reason she couldn't be having a relationship with another man, then I think we need to examine that integrity. I have a strong suspicion that Julia was instrumental in *helping* Flo decide to lie to all of us about the Kayden situation.' Gigi turned to Flo. 'Would I be correct?'

Flo couldn't meet her grandmother's eyes.

'Well, whatever he says,' Mike interrupted, 'she can't be married to two people. Our marriage was legal. I know it was. She couldn't have been married again.'

'They weren't married. He refers to her as his partner. He told me she refused a marriage proposal, citing all sorts of feminist objections to it. Anyway, why don't you meet him? It's probably the easiest way to get to the bottom of all of this. Obviously, when Mum wakes up, she'll be able to explain.'

'This is ridiculous,' Mike said. 'There's no way she was in Canberra every week living with another man. I would have known.'

'Just meet him,' Flo said. 'He's convincing, and if you don't meet him down here, you'll see him in the ICU. He's shaken up and upset, but I don't think he has plans to disappear.'

'Okay, fine. Tell him to come and meet with us.'

Flo slipped her phone from her pocket and quickly sent Scott a message. His reply was almost instant.

'He's on his way.'

Her father nodded, and she couldn't help but notice how pale Gigi looked. 'G, are you okay?'

'Honestly, I'm not sure how much more of this I can take,' Gigi said. 'I've hardly slept the past two weeks, worrying about Julia not waking up. Now, I'm beginning to think I should be more worried if she does. What on earth is going to happen?'

'Nothing,' Mike said. 'She's done nothing wrong. We'll get rid of this guy, and then we'll go and visit as planned.'

Gigi nodded, but it was evident to Flo that she wasn't as confident as Mike that her daughter's integrity was as important to her as she'd led them all to believe.

* * *

Watching her father meet Scott resembled a high-stakes poker game, with each man studying the other's expressions and body language, trying to decipher the hand they held.

Mike refused Scott's outstretched hand and sat, indicating to the seat next to Gigi, across from him.

'I don't know what to tell you, mate,' Scott said. 'We're both in the same position. She's lied to both of us.'

'I'm not your mate,' Mike said, 'and how do I know you're not the one lying?'

'What's my motive?' Scott said. He pushed his hand through his thick hair. 'My partner's in a coma in ICU. Other than having her get better, I have nothing to gain here.'

'I imagine there's something to gain if she doesn't make it,' Mike said. 'Which is what I assume you're counting on. The house in Canberra for a start.'

Scott frowned. 'The house in Canberra is owned by the Bureau of Strategic Intelligence. It's only in Julia's name, not mine, so I would assume if Julia left the company for any reason, they'd take possession of it.'

'Why is it only in her name?'

'She was already living there when I moved in. We figured it was no one's business at work.'

'Does anyone at work know about your relationship? I would have thought there'd be rules around it working where you do.'

'There are,' Scott said. 'We had to inform HR that we were in a relationship and we did that before I moved in with Julia. It'll be on the file, but otherwise, no, I don't believe anyone at work is aware. I was telling Flo earlier that Julia had insisted we keep our relationship private. The reasons she gave me were obviously quite different from the truth.'

'What does she do for work?' Mike suddenly asked.

'She's a neuroscientist, but as for the details of her job, why don't you tell me,' Scott said. 'If you know her so well, you'd know that she isn't allowed to divulge much at all about her job. No one who works at the Bureau of Strategic Intelligence is allowed to. We're required to maintain strict operational security. Look, Mike, this situation is as bad for me as it is for you. How do you think I feel, discovering my partner has been lying to me for our entire relationship and that she's still happily married?' He shook his head. 'It's like something out of a movie. A bad movie. How she's got away with it blows me away.'

'Julia has been at home with us every Christmas and most of her birthdays for the past five years. How can you explain that?'

Scott frowned. 'She's never missed a birthday. But true, we've never celebrated Christmas. I'm Jewish, and I've always celebrated Hanukkah, which falls before Christmas. Julia's worked in the Melbourne office at Christmas to allow those who do celebrate to spend time with their families.'

Nausea began swirling in Flo's gut again. The complexity of what it appeared her mother had set up was horrific.

'She's never worked at Christmas,' Mike said. 'And it was her birthday the Monday before her accident, and she was with us.'

'No,' Scott said, 'her birthday's in February. The twenty-second.

She's at home for every birthday but always misses Valentine's Day.'

'Perhaps that's what she's told you,' Gigi said. 'But I can tell you with one hundred per cent certainty, Julia was born on August seventh.'

'And she's generally always home for Valentine's Day,' Mike said. 'It's the anniversary of our engagement, so she rarely misses that.'

It was starting to sound like a competition, and Flo wanted to change the direction of the conversation.

'What do we do now?' she said, looking from her father to Scott and back again.

'You'll need more proof than this, mate.' Mike emphasised the last word. 'You're having no more access to my wife until you can prove without a doubt that you were in a relationship with her. I'm her medical enduring power of attorney, and I get to say who can and can't visit.'

'What sort of proof do you want? I can show you photos of the two of us.'

'How about your phone?' Flo suggested. 'Do you have text messages from Mum? Emails or photos on it?'

Scott took the phone from his pocket. 'I've only had this phone a few weeks, so it'll be fairly limited, and definitely no photos. That's a work policy. As I mentioned before, Flo, I can share photos but will need to get my computer to do that.'

Mike rolled his eyes. 'How convenient.'

Scott ignored him and scrolled through the phone. He handed it to Mike. 'Like I said, it's new. I got it when Julia was last in Melbourne for work. There are a few messages from that week, and then she came back home and disappeared two days later.'

Flo watched her father's expression change as he scrolled

down the messages. The anger in his eyes quickly turned to surprise and then sadness. He handed the phone to her.

THURSDAY 3RD AUGUST

Hey, hon, missing you.

Me too. It's cold and lonely in Melbourne. Can't wait to be back with you. How did the meeting with the investor go?

Good, sounded promising.

Great news. Can't wait to hear more.

Love you. Chat tomorrow.

Will be in meetings all day. Will call you from the office. Love you too. X

FRIDAY 4TH AUGUST

Are you free to chat?

No, sorry. I am in meetings and will be working late. Love you. Can't wait to see you Tuesday.

Are you sure you can't get back earlier?

You know I can't. Chat tomorrow. Love you.

SUNDAY 6TH AUGUST

That phone call got me all hot and bothered.

Can't wait to see you Tuesday.

Ditto. X

Flo held the phone out to Gigi.

'No thanks. From the look on both of your faces, I take it the messages are real.'

Flo nodded as Mike pushed his chair back. He stood and

pointed a finger at Scott. 'More proof if you want anything to do with her. Otherwise, you'll need to wait until she wakes up, and we'll deal with it then.'

He didn't give Scott a chance to respond. He strode across the cafeteria and out through the double doors.

'Sorry,' Flo said.

'No need to apologise,' Scott said. 'He's had a shock. We both have.' He sighed. 'I'm going back to the hotel. If you're happy to give me your email address, I'll send through some photos later tonight if that's okay. Perhaps you could talk to your father and ask him to agree to let me see Julia when he's not going to be here. We can have some kind of schedule until she wakes up. As much as he feels like he's been done wrong, so do I. I don't want to see him or have any reminder of what she's done if I can avoid it. We'll deal with everything when she wakes up.' He turned to Gigi. 'Whilst not ideal circumstances, it is lovely to meet you. Julia led me to believe you'd had a falling-out many years ago and were no longer in contact.'

'The falling-out bit is likely to be true when she wakes up,' Gigi said. 'And yes, I think you're right that we'll deal with everything once Julia can provide an explanation. Trying to guess what she's done and why has the potential to complicate things even further.'

Scott stood. 'Honestly, I'm not sure that's even possible.'

22

Flo could never quite work out why the school needed to have a student-free day part way through the term when the school holidays weren't far away. Luckily, this one had coincided with her day off, so instead of running Kayden to school and doing chores, she'd agreed to a day out with Ben and Della. With all that was going on with her father and Scott Cohen, she should be at the hospital doing her best to ensure their visits didn't overlap, but the reality was she needed to switch off, even if only for a few hours, from her mother's situation. There was a lot to process, and she needed to distance herself from everyone to have any chance to do that.

She'd been grateful to Ben for looking after Kayden when she'd tried to speak to Ari on Friday night and even more appreciative of his wise words when she'd returned, upset from the unsuccessful visit.

He'd taken one look at her tear-stained face and drew her to him in a hug.

'I don't deserve this from you of all people,' she'd said, pulling away.

'It's not a case of deserving,' Ben said. 'It's a case of needing, and you certainly look like you needed that. I take it Ari was mad?'

'She slammed the door in my face. I didn't speak to her.'

Ben nodded. 'It's still early days. Give her some time. With your mum, too, as it's all overwhelming right now. My guess is Ari's going to miss Kayden, and she's going to miss you. She'll come around. It might not be this week or even this month, but she will. She likes to act all tough, but underneath, she's quite soft, and I know she loves you more than anyone or anything.'

He was right, and so was Gigi. As much as she wanted forgiveness from Ari, and it wasn't guaranteed, what she needed to do was to give Ari space and time.

Now, with Ben able to push his work until the evening, they were exploring Sherbrooke Forest in the picturesque Dandenong Ranges, with Kayden and Della running ahead to ensure they were the first to reach the waterfall.

'They get along so well,' Flo said as she and Ben walked side by side behind them. 'It's made me think that blood ties are strong, even if we're not aware of them.'

'Della loves him. At home, it's "Kaydey said this," and "no, I don't do it like that now because Kaydey doesn't."' He laughed. 'Turns out a big brother is what she needed, even if none of us knew it.'

They fell silent as the added meaning of his words settled over Flo – that Ben hadn't known he had a son. Flo glanced at him, and he grinned as a shriek of laughter echoed down the trail from ahead. Ben's relaxed manner suggested that she was the only one reading anything into what he was saying. She hadn't been able to shake her guilt and wasn't sure if she ever would.

After reaching the falls, and Della, in her excitement, slipping and almost falling in, they made their way back to the picnic area they'd started from, stopping at one stage to watch a lyrebird scratching for food in the leaf litter by the side of the track.

When they returned to the picnic ground, Kayden and Della, still full of energy, took Kayden's soccer ball from the car and kicked it to and fro while Flo and Ben organised a barbecue lunch.

'He's a great kid,' Ben said, watching Kayden run over to Della and demonstrate kicking the ball with the inside of his foot. 'You've done a fantastic job with him.'

Flo wasn't sure how to respond. As grateful as she was for his words, she continually experienced a need to apologise. She decided, on this occasion, it was best to say nothing.

'Mum and Dad want to meet him soon,' Ben said as he turned the sausages.

Flo nodded. She'd been expecting this.

'But,' Ben said, 'I want him to know who we all are before we go down that road. It'll be a shock that I'm his dad, but if he gets used to that, I think it'll be easier to introduce the rest of the family.'

Flo nodded again.

Ben raised an eyebrow. 'You're not contributing a lot to this conversation.'

Flo sighed. 'I'm not sure I have a lot to contribute. Everything you're saying makes a lot of sense. I can't imagine I'll ever agree that there's a good time to tell Kayden, so how about you decide when you're ready to? It's going to be a shock to him whether it's today or in a year.'

'I think the sooner, the better. He thinks we're all purely friends, which is fine, but I don't want to leave it too long, and then make it even harder. If we tell him soon, we can say that we wanted him to get used to Della and me before we dropped this on him. That we know it's a huge thing for him, and we'll give him some space if he needs it to get used to the idea.'

'You've given this a lot of thought, haven't you?'

'Flo, it's all I've been thinking about.' He smiled. 'I have a son. An amazing little boy, and I want him to know who I am. I want to spend a lot more time with him.' His smile faded. 'And I do get how hard that's going to be for you. Sharing him.'

Flo blinked back tears, doing her best to hide them with a forced smile. 'That's not something you should be worrying about. I can't make up the last six years to you, so we're going to have to make sure that moving forward everything's done in everyone's best interest. Not just mine. Boys need their mums in these early years, but having a man in their lives as they get older is incredibly important. He has Dad, of course, but a grandfather isn't quite the same.'

'I'd like to tell him tonight.'

Flo sucked in a breath. She knew it had to be done soon. She just hadn't expected it to be that soon.

'I was going to suggest that after I drop you both home, I take Della over to Mum and Dad's and then come back. Then the two of us could talk to Kayden.'

'I haven't worked out what I'm going to say.'

'He's only six. He doesn't need too many details. I'd suggest we tell him that we were good friends but lost contact when I moved to London. You had no way to get in touch when he was born, and it was when I came back to Australia that you were able to let me know. You can say you tried to find me if you like. I'm happy to go along with that.'

'Really?' The tears welled in Flo's eyes again. He could easily tell Kayden that she'd kept his parentage from him and caused a lot of damage to their relationship.

'Of course.' His eyes darkened. 'It's not in anyone's best interest, particularly Kayden's, to know the truth. Upsetting the relationship between the two of you isn't something I want.'

A lump caught in Flo's throat that made it difficult to speak.

'When he's older we'll need to address the issue that I'm Ari's ex-husband, but that's certainly not necessary now. I think he'll buy a simple explanation,' Ben continued. 'And if we try and focus on the future and what it means for him, then hopefully his questions will be around that.'

Flo cleared her throat. 'What does it mean for him? We haven't worked that out yet. There's no formal arrangement in place or anything.'

'Do you want a formal arrangement? I'd prefer that we take it slowly. Yes, I'd love him to spend a few days a week with me, but that doesn't have to happen straight away. Perhaps he could come for a sleepover to start with every now and then. I'm sure we could make it work. You're at the hospital some weekends, so it would make sense that if you're rostered on, he spends that time with me and Della. I'd be happy to keep it flexible to start with, and if it's not working for either of us, we reassess the situation then.'

Flo could hardly argue with this. Another man might have come in and demanded his parental rights with 50 per cent custody, or worse, based on her deception. She looked over to Kayden, who was bent over laughing at something Della had said. Kayden's world would be dramatically improved with the addition of Ben and Della in his life, so why did she feel like *her* world was crumbling?

* * *

Ari couldn't believe it was only Tuesday when she opened the door to her apartment a little after seven. She'd done her best to push the dissatisfaction of winning the case for her *scumbag* client the previous day from her mind and had spent a good part of the day writing up a recommendation for the firm around the types of cases and clients they moved forward with in the future. She wasn't sure how it would be received, but she was a firm believer that if you wanted to see something change, it was up to you to make it happen.

Her phone rang as she made her way through to the kitchen, the caller display showing Gigi's name. 'G, everything okay?'

'I take it you haven't returned Flo's calls or your father's?'

'Dad rang?'

'He said he was going to, but he might have forgotten after the events of yesterday.'

'I got Flo's messages that something had happened with Mum, but as I didn't hear from you or Dad, I assumed it was her way of trying to get me to talk. I ignored her.'

'Not on this occasion, I'm afraid. It's not to do with her health, so there's nothing new to worry about on that front. It's something from out of left field. Flo said she sent you an email. Can you do something for me?'

'Of course.'

'Read the email and then come over. We need to discuss the content.'

'I take it it's bad news.'

'It's certainly not good,' Gigi said. 'I'll see you soon.'

Ari replaced the phone on its cradle and flipped open the screen of her MacBook.

She opened her email program and scrolled down to the email titled:

Please Read. It's not about you and me.

* * *

Thirty minutes later, Ari stood outside her grandmother's front door, her heart racing and her thoughts swirling.

'Tell me it isn't true,' she said as Gigi's door opened. Although one glimpse of Gigi's ashen face told her it was. 'A double life? There's no way Mum would do that. Integrity's her thing.'

'It appears that she's slipped on the integrity front. Wine?'

'Got anything stronger? Like a shotgun perhaps?'

Gigi opened her arms. 'I've got a hug. Will that help?'

Ari nodded and moved into her grandmother's arms, allowing some of her anger to fade. 'I can't believe she'd do this to us. You hear of guys having two families, but women... How's it even possible?'

'I guess she has a job that enabled her to do it, as a man would. Plus having grown-up kids isn't the same as having two families with small children.'

'But people must know,' Ari said, pulling out of Gigi's embrace and following her down the passageway to the open-plan area at the back of the house. 'She works with people in Canberra who must have known what she was up to. While we didn't visit much, we still did visit occasionally. Surely, she couldn't have got away with that when this guy was supposed to be there? How did she make that work?'

'I have no idea,' Gigi said, 'other than I assume she arranged for us to visit on a week Scott was working away. He told Flo his job includes a fair amount of international travel. She probably hid all traces of him in the house and acted as if she lived there alone. Hopefully, she'll wake up soon and can explain everything to us.'

'If she's lied for the last five years, do you think she'll come clean now?' Ari asked.

'I honestly don't know. I would hope so, but it's a bit like the Flo situation, isn't it?'

'How do you mean?'

'Well, she was backed into a corner and had to tell us the truth. It wasn't at her own volition. Your mother's situation is the same. It's all come out because of the accident, and I can't imagine she's going to be rushing to fill us in. In fact, she'll probably slip straight back into a coma the moment she realises we're on to her.' Gigi's bottom lip quivered, and Ari could see she was doing her best to contain her emotions.

'G, are you okay?'

'I'm sorry, love, I've been trying to stay strong but I'm feeling particularly low right now.'

'Come and sit down,' Ari said, taking her grandmother's arm and guiding her through to the comfortable lounge area. 'Let's get you settled, and I'll make a cup of tea. Or would you prefer wine?'

'A cup of tea would be perfect, thank you.'

A few minutes later, Ari sat across from Gigi, both nursing their drinks.

'You know,' Gigi said, 'I've always prided myself that Julia showed such integrity throughout her life and took a strong moral stand on most issues. I think that's what's hitting me the hardest. That my daughter is not the person I thought she was. That she's had us all fooled.'

'And Flo's followed in her footsteps,' Ari said. 'They're both liars and not little white lies – we're talking devastating, life-changing lies.'

'It might be in their blood,' Gigi said. She met Ari's eyes briefly before glancing away.

'In their blood? What does that mean? Please tell me you're not hiding things from us too.'

Gigi shook her head slowly. 'No, nothing like that.' She sat up a little straighter. 'Now, enough of my wallowing in self-pity. I did have another reason for asking you here tonight.'

A laugh, sounding more like a small shriek, escaped Ari's lips. 'There's more?'

'Possibly. But hopefully, it might give us some answers. I found something the other day that I've been debating whether to mention or not.'

'Found what?'

'You may not know this but your mother's kept diaries for years,' Gigi said. 'Actually, they're more like scientific journals with all sorts of information about psychological studies and goodness knows what.'

'How far do they date back?'

'The ones I have here are her early ones,' Gigi said. 'She brought around some boxes one day and asked if I could store them for her. I thought of them a few days back and got them out. Of course, she made me swear I'd never look at them, but considering everything that's happened, I thought they might provide some interesting information. The problem is, the boxes I have are from her teenage years through to 1980, so before you and Flo were born and before she started her job in Canberra. If we want more recent information, then I'm assuming that if she continued journaling, the relevant ones will be at the house.'

'You think they'll talk about Scott?'

'Well, if she's known him for fifteen years and they've been romantically linked for the past five, it would be interesting to see what she's documented about that.'

'I'll stop in and see Dad tomorrow after work,' Ari said. 'See if he knows where they are and if I can have a look at them.'

'Good,' Gigi said. 'I'm thinking you might need to talk to Flo too.'

'I'm not interested in anything she has to say.'

'I know what Flo and Ben did was unforgivable, but I'm hoping you can put the other situation to the side for a moment while we work out what's going on with your mother.'

Ari sighed. 'Even seeing her is going to make me irate. Look at what happened on Friday night. I've never slammed a door in someone's face before, but later, I thought she was lucky it wasn't my fist. I don't think I've ever experienced this much anger towards someone.'

'It's not just anger. You're hurting. Of course you are. What Flo did was terrible, and it's going to take time, if ever, to get beyond that hurt and anger. But right now, your mother's giving you plenty of additional reasons to be angry. Is there any chance you could put the situation with Flo to one side while we try and get through this?' She reached over and squeezed Ari's hand. 'For me? For your father?'

Ari rolled her eyes. 'It's not hard to see where Mum gets her manipulation skills from.'

Gigi gave a wry smile. 'Sorry, love, but you're the strong one among us. We need you to help us get to the bottom of all of this. I think showing a united front that we're a family is important right now.'

'Fine. I won't object to being in the same room with her, but that's as much as I'm going to offer. She needs to be told that I won't tolerate any discussion about Ben or Kayden, and everything that comes out of her mouth needs to be about Mum, or I'll walk out of the room.'

'Fair enough. I don't blame you.'

'But...?' Ari's grip on her teacup tightened as she waited for her grandmother to lecture her on why she should forgive her sister.

'No buts,' Gigi said. 'If I was in your shoes, I don't know how I'd react. I think the best thing you can do is give yourself time and see how you feel. There's no rush. Hopefully, you'll be able to forgive her at some stage, but that's your call. People can't betray you and think time is going to make everything better. It's not always realistic or fair.'

Ari was surprised at her grandmother's words. It was refreshing to hear that she wasn't going to pressure Ari into anything. 'I have to be honest,' she said to Gigi, 'as much as I don't want to hear anything out of Flo's mouth about Ben or Kayden, I've been worried about him. Have you heard how Kayden's doing? I realised I didn't even ask the other day when I saw you.'

'He's fine so far,' Gigi said. 'The transfusion seems to have worked, so hopefully, if they can bank some blood for the future and continue to bank it, it will be enough if he does regress.'

Ari nodded. 'Good. As much as I don't want to see Flo, I do miss seeing him. None of this is his fault.' She sighed. 'And if I'm being completely honest, I miss Flo like crazy too. Not talking to her has made me appreciate how close we were. How lucky I was to have a sister who I thought had my back no matter what.'

'Oh, love,' Gigi said, opening her arms and drawing Ari into a hug. 'I'm so sorry this has happened.'

'Me too, G. A few weeks back, we were a normal, happy family. Now we're a complete mess. How did it happen that quickly?'

'Honestly, I have no idea. The only thing we can do now is hope your mum wakes up soon and we get some answers. Hopefully, ones we're looking for.'

23

Flo found herself pacing, unable to stand still after Ben dropped her and Kayden home. He would be returning in an hour, and she was dreading telling Kayden the truth. Her phone pinged with a text, and she quickly grabbed it from the bench. It was Gigi.

> Did Scott send you those photos last night? Your dad wants more proof before he'll allow him to visit ICU.

Flo had forgotten all about the photos.

> No. Did he say he sent them?

> Yes. I'll ask him to resend them to both of us.

> Thanks. I'll be at work tomorrow and will visit Mum and see you then if you're going to be at the hospital.

> Is everything okay?

Flo stared at the text. How could her grandmother decipher from the brief exchange that anything was wrong?

Another text arrived.

> I was surprised not to hear from you today.

> Out with Ben and Della. About to tell Kayden who Ben is.

> If you need to chat later, I'll be up. Good luck.

Flo put the phone back on the bench as Kayden appeared at the entrance to the kitchen.

'Is dinner nearly ready? I'm starving.'

Flo stared at him. Was she that nervous she'd forgotten to cook dinner?

'It'll be ready in ten minutes. Now,' she said, improvising, 'what would you like in your omelette? I've got ham, cheese, mushrooms and spinach.'

'Nothing green,' Kayden said. 'Can we do something nice for Della, not this Sunday but the one after? Maybe have a party and a cake?'

Flo looked over to him as she took the eggs from the fridge. 'Is it her birthday?'

'No, but she told me she misses her mum a lot, and I thought it would make her happy. She's worried she'll miss her mum's birthday because she doesn't know when it is and doesn't want to ask Ben in case it makes him sad.'

Flo's heart contracted. A four-year-old was worried about her father. 'Of course, we can do something. It's really nice of you to think of it.'

Kayden nodded. 'It must be hard for Della to not have a mum. At least I never knew my dad, so it's not like I lost him. He wasn't ever here. Maybe he's dead too. Della said that maybe he's with her mum and they're friends now. That would be good, wouldn't it?'

Flo busied herself, collecting more ingredients from the fridge. Did this conversation have to happen an hour before they told him? 'Ben's coming back tonight for a little while,' she said, hoping to change the subject.

'With Della?' Kayden's face was hopeful.

'No, by himself. He wants to talk to you. We both do.'

'About what?'

Flo forced a laugh. 'We'll tell you when he gets here. Now, how about you go and wash up? The omelette will only take a few minutes.'

Kayden nodded and bounded out of the room, thankfully not asking any further questions.

They'd finished packing the dirty plates into the dishwasher when headlights turned into the driveway.

'Ben's here,' Kayden called in delight. 'I'll let him in.'

Flo switched the dishwasher on and followed Kayden down the hallway.

'Hey, buddy,' Ben said, grinning at Kayden. The grin didn't hide Ben's nervous demeanour. He met Flo's eyes over Kayden's head. 'Ready for a chat?'

'Sure,' Flo said. 'How about some hot chocolate for everyone first?'

Kayden turned and stared at her. 'But that's our comfort drink. That's what you say whenever something goes wrong.' He looked between the two of them. 'Am I in trouble? Did I do something wrong?'

'No, of course not,' Flo said. 'Forget the hot chocolate – I wasn't thinking. How about a glass of wine?' she suggested to Ben.

He nodded. 'Sounds perfect. Do you want a hand, or can

Kayden show me his soccer cards? You had a few new ones, didn't you, bud?'

Kayden grabbed his hand and led him in the direction of his bedroom, leaving Flo to get the drinks.

She took two glasses of her favourite Cab Sav and a juice box into the small lounge area and waited while Kayden showed Ben the cards. She stared at the wine. Part of her would like to gulp it down for some Dutch courage, but she didn't.

It was only a few minutes before Ben and Kayden reappeared, Kayden talking a million miles an hour about the two special cards he was hoping to get for his collection.

'Come and sit down,' Flo said, holding out the juice box to him. His eyes lit up as she knew they would. It was usually strictly water between dinner and bedtime.

Kayden sat down next to her, and Ben sat propped on the edge of the chair across from them.

Flo cleared her throat. It was up to her to tell him. 'So, we have some news for you.'

Kayden nodded, sucking on the skinny straw poking out of the top of his drink.

'Some good news, we hope,' Ben added, a nervous smile twitching on his lips.

'It's about your dad,' Flo added.

Kayden stopped sipping, his gaze growing big with surprise. 'My dad?'

Flo nodded. 'You see, when I was pregnant with you, your dad had moved to London, and I didn't know how to contact him, so he never even knew about you. But now he's back in Australia, and I've been able to tell him all about you.'

Kayden stared at her. 'Does he want to meet me?'

'He wants you to be part of his life,' Ben said.

Kayden shook his head. 'I don't know him. I've never even met him. I don't have to be, do I?' His eyes pleaded with Flo's. 'I like it better without him.'

Flo put an arm around his shoulders and pulled him to her. 'There's more to it that we need to tell you before we make any decisions.' She looked at Ben and nodded.

He cleared his throat. 'The thing is, Kayden, it turns out that I'm your dad.'

Flo held her breath as she waited for a response from Kayden. He'd frozen beside her, his body completely stiff. He looked at Flo, who nodded in confirmation.

'You're my dad?'

Ben nodded. 'And this is the best news I've ever had. To find out that I have a son. A son as brilliant and as clever and funny as you.'

'You're my dad?' Kayden repeated, pulling out of Flo's embrace. His tone was full of wonder.

Ben nodded again. 'And I'd like to be part of your life. I would have been there every day if I'd known when your mum was pregnant. I feel like I've missed out on a lot not being around while you were little, but we can make up for that right now if you'll let me.'

'What about Della?' Kayden asked. 'If you're my dad and you're her dad, what does that mean?'

'Della's your half-sister,' Flo said.

A smile played on Kayden's lips. 'Della's my sister? This is the best news ever.'

Flo couldn't help but feel a tug of sympathy seeing the hurt flash across Ben's face. Kayden was a lot happier about his sister than his father, by the looks of things.

'Does Della know?'

'Not yet,' Ben said. 'I'd like to tell her tonight when I get back home.'

Kayden nodded. 'You're really my dad?'

'I am.'

Kayden stood and walked over to where Ben sat. He didn't say anything. He just leaned down and put his arms around Ben's neck. Flo closed her eyes. She wasn't sure her heart could take much more.

24

After leaving Gigi's and tossing and turning for a good part of the night, Ari found herself staring out of her office window the next morning, relieved she wasn't scheduled to appear in court. The view, looking over the tops of most of the city's buildings to Port Phillip Bay, usually gave her pleasure, but today she wasn't even seeing it. The revelation about her mother's double life was all-consuming. She had so many questions and, unfortunately, the only person who could fully answer them was her mother. What if she died or was severely brain-damaged? Would she get away with what she'd done? Ari's emotions swung from disbelief to anger to sadness. What had happened to their family in a matter of weeks? Anger returned at this thought. It wasn't a matter of weeks. Both her mother's and Flo's actions had been set in motion years ago. It was just the fallout that had occurred in the last few weeks.

She thought back to her conversation with Gigi the previous night, suddenly overcome by another surge of anger towards her mother. All these years later Gigi was still mourning the loss of her husband, and now she was left questioning where she went wrong with her daughter. Ari had to admit she couldn't wrap her mind around her mother's actions. Had she really believed she could get away with living two lives?

It was quite possible the journals Gigi mentioned would give some insight into her mother's mind.

She turned her attention back to her computer and clicked on her schedule. She never took personal days or sick days, but today, with only a few meetings to rearrange, she decided her time and energy would be more effective focusing on her mother and not on work. She quickly sent off a few emails requesting changes to the meetings, packed up her briefcase and made her way to the lifts and underground car park.

She sent her father a text to let him know she'd be dropping in and twenty minutes later was standing outside her parents' South Yarra home.

Her father opened the door at the same time she reached for the doorbell.

'I saw you pull into the drive,' he said. 'Is everything okay? I had a phone call from Gigi this morning saying you'd visited her last night.'

'I did,' Ari said. 'Flo emailed me about the situation with Mum and this Cohen character, and Gigi wanted to fill me in.'

Her father's face fell at the mention of her mother's supposed partner.

Ari placed a hand on his arm. 'I'm sorry, Dad. I hate that she's done this to you.'

'To us,' Mike said. 'Assuming it's true. But until I hear it from her own lips, I – for one – don't believe it is.' He held the door open wider. 'Come in and I'll make some coffee. I was planning on going back to the hospital after lunch, so it's good timing to visit now. Although shouldn't you be at work?'

'Couldn't concentrate,' Ari said, stepping into the house and following her father to the kitchen. 'I'm thinking I might even put in for a few days' leave. My caseload isn't too hectic this next week or two, so I think it could work. I need to get my head around a few things. Now...' she directed her father towards one of the stools at the island bench '...you sit, and I'll make the coffee.'

Mike sat as instructed, and Ari set about making strong black coffee, the way they both liked it. She brought the two cups around to his side of the island bench and sat down next to him.

'I still don't believe she'd do what this Cohen bloke's saying,' Mike said. 'I know she can be forthright and opinionated, but a whole other life doesn't sound like her.'

'It doesn't sound like anything a decent wife or mother would do,' Ari said. 'But I'd say that about many of the things Mum's done. I hope it's not true, but it sounds like it might be. Gigi said that Cohen was going to send through more photos as proof. There'll be other things that can prove their relationship. Joint bills, bank accounts, that sort of thing. Friends they socialise with would be another.'

'The house in Canberra is owned by your mum's work, and all utilities are covered. I don't think there'd be any joint bills. As for friends, I'm not sure how we find that out. Cohen can tell us anything he wants.'

'We need to wait for Mum to wake up,' Ari said. 'In the meantime, there's something that Gigi mentioned that I'm interested in exploring that might give us some insights into what she was up to. Do you know if Mum has any journals here? Gigi said she's always written journals, but the ones she has at her house finish around 1988. I vaguely remember her writing in books as we were growing up. If she's continued then it's likely that they're stored here somewhere.'

'She was always writing in notebooks,' Mike said. 'Said it was work-related and would bore me. I think you'll find some of them locked in the fireproof cabinet in her office.'

'She locked them away?'

'Purely for fire protection and, of course, theft. They were handwritten, and she didn't want to lose them if there was a fire, and with the nature of her job, everything is confidential. The key is in the small vase on the bookshelf next to the photo of you being admitted to the bar.'

'Have you ever accessed them?'

Mike shook his head. 'No. The confidential bit applies to me, too.'

'Can I have a look at them?'

'I'm supposed to say no to that,' Mike said. 'She'll be furious if she finds out we've been looking at highly confidential information. But under the circumstances, go for it. I'm not sure there'll be anything personal in them, though.'

'Her work's highly confidential. I doubt she's allowed to be writing any detail in a personal journal.'

Her father shrugged. 'Well, she writes something in them.'

Ari took a sip of her coffee before sliding off the stool. 'I'll go and have a look. See if there's anything interesting.'

'She also has some storage boxes in the large, locked cupboard in the back of the garage. Did you want me to have a look there?'

'That'd be great. Thanks. I'll check the ones in her office and then come and find you.'

* * *

Ari trod softly on the polished wooden staircase, the rich grains and warm tones a testament to her father's style. She stopped at the top of the stairs and turned into her mother's office, which sat directly across the hallway. It was strange entering her mother's domain without her there. When they were kids, it had been a no-go zone, and even as an adult, Ari couldn't remember

entering the room without her mother's permission and
presence.

She pushed away her thoughts, stepped inside the office and
made her way directly to the bookcase housing the vase her father
had mentioned. It sat between two photos. The one of her being
admitted to the bar and, on the other side, a photo of Flo with
newborn Kayden in her arms. Ari averted her eyes, picked up the
vase and turned it upside down. A small key dropped into her
hands.

She looked around the room. A floor-to-ceiling bookshelf lined
one wall. A locked cabinet the other. She walked over to the locked
cabinet, inserted the key and opened it. It wasn't hard to see who
she'd inherited her organisational skills from. The shelves were
filled with journals. All neatly lined up with information on the
spines as to the date the journal related to. She took a random
book from the shelf and flicked through it. Her mother's distinct
handwriting filled every page. It took a moment for Ari to understand what she was reading. It didn't appear to be confidential
information but rather an analysis of some of her mother's work
colleagues.

Date: *27 April 2018*

Study: *Evaluating Managerial Influence Strategies within Intelligence Agency Departments*

Objective: *To investigate the effectiveness of managerial influence strategies on decision alignment within the departments of
the Bureau of Strategic Intelligence and determine whether
influence can be used in matters of national security.*

Ari scanned the rest of the journal but found it to be written in unnecessarily complicated language for a study that appeared to compare how influencing two groups of employees with different management methods impacted the project they were working on. She replaced the journal and picked up another. It was of a similar nature. Entry after entry followed the progress of experiments seemingly conducted on human behaviour within the Bureau of Strategic Intelligence.

She couldn't find any references to herself or the family. She looked along the spines of the journals. It appeared they were all related to her workplace and not family life.

'Ari.' Her father's voice drifted through the house. 'I think I've found something.'

Ari replaced the journal she'd been reviewing and hurried back down the stairs to the lower level and through the internal access to the garage. Her father had unlocked the large storage cupboard, which revealed numerous boxes. He had one open and was leafing through a journal similar to the one Ari had found. He held it up as she entered the garage. 'Personal journals from the past thirty-two years. Based on the dates, this is the most recent one. There are pages and pages about you and Flo and advice and suggestions she gave you.' He flicked through more pages and frowned. 'Did your mother talk to you about becoming a High Court justice by any chance?'

'She did on the way to the airport. Why, what does it say?'

Her father held out the journal to her. 'Skip down to the "Study" heading.'

Ari noted the entry was written on the day of her mother's birthday, before jumping forward to the section her father had highlighted.

Study: *Arabella's Career Progression*
As Arabella continues to excel in her legal career, it becomes

ever clearer to me that her capabilities are boundless. Becoming a partner at such a prestigious law firm has been achieved, and now it is time to look to greater things. My vision for her to serve on the High Court is a recognition of her unparalleled potential.

Method: *The need for subtlety; Arabella is fiercely independent, and any direct push could backfire. I will ask her to take me to the airport tomorrow so that we have time alone together. I will drop the suggestion casually into conversation to plant the seed. This task requires patience. It will take time to gently guide Arabella to see the broader horizon.*

Ari's eyes moved from the page to meet her father's. 'She did mention it, not as subtly as she's suggesting here. I didn't take her seriously.'

She looked back at the journal and began flicking through the pages. 'It's like we're puppets in her little theatre or something. She's controlling and influencing everything we do.' Ari put the journal down, took another from the box, and flicked through it. Entry after entry stared back at her with her mother talking about one project she was working on and then another.

'Hey.'

Ari's head snapped up as Flo walked into the garage. The two sisters stared at each other for a moment until Flo looked away, her eyes flitting nervously from Ari to the journals.

Flo cleared her throat, her words tumbling out nervously. 'Can we put everything else on hold for a moment? This Mum situation is extreme, and I think we need to deal with it together.'

Ari studied her sister. She had dark rings under her eyes, her skin was pale, and her usual calm demeanour was noticeably absent. In reality, she was probably looking at a reflection similar to her own. Had something else happened? 'Is Kayden okay?'

Flo looked at her father. 'Did Gigi tell you?'

'Tell him what?' Ari said. 'Is he okay? The transfusion was successful?'

Flo nodded. 'Health-wise, he's good. We'll have to keep monitoring him.' She cleared her throat. 'We told him about Ben last night.'

Ari stared at her. 'We?'

Flo's cheeks coloured. 'Ben came over so we could tell him together. He's spent some time with Kayden over the last few weeks, getting to know him. We weren't sure how he was going to react to the news.'

'And?' Ari wasn't sure why she was asking. It was unlikely she'd be happy with any answer Flo returned.

'He was happy about it. He loves Della, and he and Ben get along already. He seemed a bit shocked still this morning, but it was a good shock. He was asking a lot of questions about how the future's going to work as far as spending time with Ben and Della and getting to know Ben's parents and family.'

Ari's jaw tightened as she tried to process this information. Other than her anger at Flo, this was why she didn't want to talk about the situation. She'd divorced Ben and, at the time, had been sad that it meant the end of spending time with his family. But a clean break was also important for everyone. She didn't want to know what a family she was no longer part of was doing. Now, through Kayden, the two families would be connected again. 'How could you? I can't even begin to understand what you were thinking.' Ari practically spat the words at her sister, noting, with some satisfaction, Flo flinch.

'Ari,' Flo's voice wobbled as she tried to speak. 'I never meant—'

'No,' Ari said, holding up her hands to stop Flo. 'There's nothing you can say that will make this okay. Honestly, I'm only not walking out of here right now because I promised Gigi I'd try and be civil. But that extends purely to the situation about Mum. I don't want anything to do with you otherwise.' She threw the journal she was holding across to Flo, annoyed that the tears welling in Flo's eyes were getting to her despite her best efforts to remain unaffected. 'Take a look at this. Mum appears to have journaled every event in our lives, and from what I've read so far, also appears to have steered and manipulated us into how we've navigated through life.'

'I don't think she would have done that,' Mike said. 'It's her recordings of things that have already happened.'

Ari rolled her eyes at Flo, as she'd done a million times before at the rose-coloured glasses through which their father viewed their mother, and quickly averted her gaze, catching herself. Flo was the enemy. She'd be civil, but she wasn't going to be friendly.

They spent the next half hour pulling journal after journal from the boxes and flipping through them. It was impossible not to stop at some sections and read through what their mother had planned and how, in her eyes, it had come off.

'You know,' Flo said. 'I'd like to read these from the first journal and see in order how many life decisions she's influenced, but what's sticking out at this point is there is no reference at all to her life in Canberra.'

'See,' Mike said, 'I told you that guy was a scammer. She hasn't mentioned him once.'

'I meant she hasn't referred to her life in Canberra in anything I've read. Have you found anything, Ari?'

'Not in these ones. The dates and entries are for her Melbourne life only. You can see when the dates jump a week, which would be when she was in Canberra. Are there any other boxes, Dad?'

Mike shook his head. 'Only the ones in her office. They're work-related, aren't they?'

'From what I saw, they are,' Ari said. 'But about people at work, rather than the work itself. I only flicked through them, so I'm not sure if she mentions Scott Cohen in them.'

'Do you think this means she has a whole other set in Canberra?' Flo asked.

Ari put down the journal she'd been reading and looked from Flo to her father. 'It would make sense. She's kept her two lives separate for so long. It's likely she'd have documented her Canberra life in the same way.'

'That Cohen guy didn't mention them,' Mike said. 'We asked for proof, and so far, all we've had is a chain of text messages and a photo.'

'Photos,' Flo corrected. 'He sent me through quite a few last night. I wanted to show you today. I think he's telling the truth, Dad.'

Mike turned to Ari. 'What do you think?'

'I haven't even met him. I can't see any purpose to this so-called scam, other than perhaps assuming if Mum died, he'd inherit her estate.'

'But that would go to Dad,' Flo said.

'Yes, but Scott Cohen claims to have had no idea that Mum was married. It's quite possible he thought he was her next of kin and the main beneficiary of her estate.'

'You're talking like Mum's going to die.'

'Sorry,' Ari said. 'Lawyer in me talking. I'm trying to figure out his angle if he has one. It's a huge gamble to assume she's going to die and try and cash in on it. I know she has a Will, as she used

Jordan Sloger at my firm. It's possible she's listed Cohen as a benefactor.'

Mike shook his head. 'No, I've got a copy of it. She's left some personal items to you girls, but otherwise, our Wills are basically the same. Everything would go to me if she were to die and vice versa. That seemed fair, and it would allow the surviving spouse to decide how to distribute the money. If we both die, our estates will split equally between the two of you.'

'He could possibly contest and prove they're in a de-facto relationship,' Ari said, 'but again, it doesn't seem likely. Assuming he's earning a decent wage he's most likely contributing to their living expenses, even if the house is leased to Mum. But back to the journals. I'd like to go and see what she has in Canberra. If she has something like these ones, we might find all of our questions answered.' She glanced at her watch. 'I could probably get there this afternoon. Do we have a key to her house?'

'I do,' Mike said. 'Which also doesn't make sense. If she's living with this guy, why has she given me a key? Imagine if I'd surprised her one day and turned up. How was she going to explain that to either of us?'

'Let's stop speculating,' Ari said. 'I'll go and see if I can get some answers. I suggest no one mentions it to Cohen. Give me a chance to go through the house and see if there are signs of him living there and whether I can find more journals.'

'Okay,' Flo said. 'But what do we do about Scott in the interim? My gut is that he's telling the truth. Do we allow him to visit Mum?'

'It might be a good idea,' Ari said. 'We don't want him returning to Canberra and finding me rifling through his house.'

'Your mother's house,' Mike corrected her, then sighed. 'But yes, fine. Tell him he can visit as long as it's when none of us are there. I'll make my visits in the afternoons from now on so he can go in the morning. I don't want anything to do with him until we have confirmation that he's legit. And to be honest, I don't want anything to do with him then, either.'

25

As the plane made its final descent into Canberra International Airport, Ari closed her eyes and leaned back in her seat, an image of Flo's strained face dominating her thoughts. She'd done her best that morning to keep the conversation civil, but her suppressed anger had manifested into a dull headache. She was trying very hard to change her thought pattern. She wasn't here to waste more energy on Flo. She was here to get some answers. She ran through a mental checklist of what she needed to do once she'd picked up the rental car and driven to her mother's. The search of the house was the priority and likely to provide the most information. She'd already rung her mother's workplace and organised a meeting for the next morning. She also wanted to speak to the neighbours and find out from them what they believed her mother's situation to be.

It was a strange feeling turning the key in her mother's front door an hour later. Not that she'd been here many times, but it felt like trespassing, particularly with the knowledge that this was a house her mother supposedly shared with Scott Cohen.

She let herself in and was faced with a console table housing an array of photos. Seeing her mother with a man she assumed was Scott was jarring. There was part of her that still hoped to find out this was all a big mistake or a con like her father was clinging to.

Ari left her bag by the front door and walked from room to room, surprised at how homely the house was. When she'd last visited, it'd seemed rather bare. Her mother preferred a minimalist existence, so she hadn't done too much in the way of making it comfortable. It had the necessary basics, which, to be fair, were still lovely but lacked the cosiness that the photos, artwork and even cushions seemed to create. Perhaps Scott's influence was more prevalent when her mother wasn't hiding his existence.

She entered the master bedroom, spying reading glasses and books piled high on one of the bedside tables. The other side only had one book. That would be her mother's side. She was strict about finishing one book or project before moving on to another. Julia had insisted Mike do the same and only have one book on the go. Perhaps Scott had more backbone than her father when it came to saying no. She stepped into the walk-in wardrobe and stopped. If her father wanted evidence that her mother was living with a man, it was staring her right in the face. One side of the wardrobe was lined with her mother's clothes, neatly arranged in a similar fashion to her clothes at home. The other was similarly orderly. Men's shirts, jackets, pants and shoes.

She moved into the en suite. It was almost identical to the en suite in her parents' house. Her mother's creams and lotions were prominently displayed on a shelf above the sink. Her favourite shampoo, conditioner, and body wash positioned with labels facing out on the shelf in the shower. A man's electric shaver sat neatly at one end of the shelf next to a second electric toothbrush.

Ari moved back into the bedroom and sank down onto the bed. How could her mother have done this to them? And to Cohen too? Her eyes brimmed with tears. Her mother had let her and Flo down many times throughout their childhoods, particularly in their teenage years. Missing school awards, sporting events and even some of their birthdays. Always citing work as the reason. It was bad enough when Ari thought her mother's work was more important than she was, but now, it wasn't work. It was another life.

The doorbell rang, jolting her from her misery. She stood. What should she do? Should she answer it? She was basically trespassing. She should probably let Scott know she was in his house. She made her way slowly down the stairs, hoping the person would assume there was no one home and go away. Although the rental car in the driveway was a giveaway that she was there.

The doorbell rang again and glancing through the small window that looked out to the front path, she could see a rather short elderly woman.

Ari opened the door. 'Can I help you?'

'I was hoping Julia might be home. I'm a friend of hers. I live next door,' the woman said, pointing to the next-door property. 'Bridie Andrews,' she added.

Bridie? The name was familiar. 'The books,' Ari said.

'Sorry?'

'My – I mean Julia – mentioned to me that she was bringing you some books from her Booker Prize collection.'

The woman wore a puzzled expression. 'Yes, that's right. I've been a tad worried. Julia dropped the books in a few weeks ago. She stayed for a cuppa and, when she was leaving, said she'd drop back in later in the week to see which book I'd started on. But she never did. She's usually here every other week, so I'm hoping she's okay.'

'Would you like to come in?' Ari opened the door wider. 'I can fill you in a little on her whereabouts. I'm afraid there's a bit of a situation.'

* * *

A few minutes later, the older woman sat across from Ari in one of her mother's upright armchairs. She looked around the room. 'This is nice. I don't think I've been in this room before, or if I have, Julia's spent some time making it cosier.'

'You've been here before?'

'Once or twice. I only moved in three months ago, and Julia tends to visit me, so I haven't been here often.'

'Have you met Scott, Julia's partner?'

'Partner?' Bridie frowned. 'I thought he was her husband. But, no, I haven't met him other than to wave to when he's gardening. My back verandah overlooks part of Julia's back garden. I don't mean to pry, but sometimes I do see movement in the garden that takes my attention. He seems friendly and keen on the garden.' She smiled. 'And then he does like to do the special bow with that large gardening hat of his. I feel like I do know him without having met him. I'm sure I'll meet him at some stage. As I said, Julia usually visits me, and I don't like to interrupt their evenings. I know she works hard and is in Melbourne a lot.'

Ari's heart rate slowed with disappointment. For a split second, she'd hoped Bridie knew nothing of Scott. Although how the photos and men's clothing would be explained, she had no idea. She did, however, wonder for a moment if this woman had mistaken her mother for someone else as she doubted her mother had ever been described as *so lovely*. She realised she needed to be careful about what she said. If Bridie thought Julia was with Scott, she would know nothing about the Melbourne family.

'I'm afraid I've got some rather bad news,' Ari said. 'Julia was involved in an accident in Melbourne a couple of weeks ago.'

Bridie's hand flew to her mouth. 'Will she be okay?'

'She's currently in intensive care. We're hoping for a full recovery, but right now, things are a little unknown. She's experienced some head trauma, so they've put her in an induced coma to allow the swelling to subside. Hopefully, she'll wake up soon, and there won't be permanent damage.'

'That's awful,' Bridie said. 'Oh, gosh, I'm so worried.'

'Bridie,' Ari said, 'did Julia ever mention any other family members to you? Family in Melbourne perhaps?'

The older woman looked puzzled again. 'We didn't talk much about family. I know she worked one week in Canberra and one week in Melbourne. She has grown-up children she adores and sees when she's in Melbourne. And possibly a grandchild. Don't quote me on that, though. My memory for detail isn't the best.' Bridie sighed. 'Sorry, as I said, I do get a little confused.'

'Have you met her children?' Ari asked.

'No, I haven't met anyone. As I said, I've only lived here a few months.' Bridie stopped. 'Can I ask who you are and why you want to know this information?'

Ari stared at the older woman. Should she tell her who she was? At this point, she wasn't sure why she was playing along with her mother's lies. 'I'm one of her daughters,' Ari said. 'I live in Melbourne but wanted to come and look for some journals to see if we can work out why she was in Melbourne when she had the accident. She was supposed to be here.'

Bridie's face relaxed. 'That's a relief. I was beginning to get a little worried with all the questions. It's nice to meet you, although not under these circumstances. Did you find the journals?'

'I haven't had a chance to look yet. I'll look tonight and then go into her work tomorrow and see what else I can find out. Her life here is a little different to what we'd been led to believe back home.'

Bridie drew herself up to her feet. 'I should let you get on with things. Could you keep me informed as to Julia's progress, and when she does wake up, tell her I was asking about her?'

'Sure. Why don't you give me your number, and I'll stay in touch.'

* * *

'You're kidding me.' Flo muttered the three words for what must be at least the tenth time as she scanned the pages of her mother's journal, her mouth hanging open, her eyes wide.

'Mum!'

Flo jumped at the sound of Kayden's voice.

'I've called you lots of times. Can't you hear me?'

Flo looked up to find Kayden standing across the kitchen table from her.

'Sorry, I was caught up with this.' She held the journal up before laying it shut on the table in front of her. 'Now what's happening?'

'Della wants me to spend a day with her and Ben on the weekend. Can I go?'

'Sure, I guess. But how did she contact you? She's four. She doesn't have a phone.'

Kayden held up Flo's mobile phone. 'She sent you a message from Ben's phone. But she also asked me when we were out walking the other day. We're going to make a fort in the kitchen and have lunch in it.'

Flo took the phone from him and listened to the voice message Della had recorded. She couldn't help but smile. 'She sounds very excited at the idea. But why are you checking my phone?'

'It beeped, and you didn't answer when I called you.'

'Okay, but next time, hand it to me.' She didn't want Kayden reading messages about Julia or her falling-out with Ari.

'Can I go?'

Flo nodded. 'We might need to check with Ben that he's agreed to Della's invitation, but if it's okay with him, then yes, you can go if you want to.'

'Is it weird that Ben's my dad?' Kayden asked. 'Only I think it is, and I'm not sure what to call him. Della said I could call him Dad, but that would be extra-weird.'

'He's happy for you to call him Ben. It's a big adjustment for all of us to have him in our lives. You might feel comfortable calling him Dad at some stage, or you might prefer Ben. Spend more time getting to know him. There's no pressure.'

Kayden nodded. 'Can I go out the back and kick my ball?'

'If you give me a hug first, you can,' Flo said, laughing.

He squealed and hugged her quickly before pulling away and rushing to the back door.

Flo's smile slipped as her attention was drawn back to her mother's journal. She flipped it open on the page she'd been reading before Kayden had interrupted her.

Date: 16 November 2004

It's rewarding to watch the seeds I've so carefully sown with Florence beginning to bloom. It's almost poetic the way her life is mirroring her namesake, Florence Nightingale. Even in the womb, I knew I wanted her to embody the spirit of such a strong and caring woman, and now, as she considers her university pathways, my gentle guidance and reminders that 'you have a healer's touch' are coming to fruition.

Her curiosity has at times wandered, most recently towards

the arts, but I've been able to guide her gently back to her true calling.

Tomorrow, I will be sharing the news that I know will help cement in her own mind her future path. I've secured her a volunteer placement at St Xavier's for the Christmas break. Once she steps into that world, I'm sure there will be no turning back. Maintaining the right level of encouragement for Florence is crucial. It's important to acknowledge her achievements and provide positive feedback to keep her motivated. However, I must also ensure that her confidence stays aligned with the path of becoming a nurse – a respectable and stable role, yet not one that overshadows Arabella's trajectory. Arabella is being groomed for success and leadership, and it's important that Florence's development does not interfere with this.

Flo stared at the page. She remembered quite clearly the day her mother told her about the volunteer holiday work. She was seventeen, and it was the long summer break before starting her final year of schooling in January. She'd enrolled in an intensive art class, exploring numerous painting mediums and had been excited about it for months. While her mother had been talking about nursing for years, she secretly harboured ideas of applying for art school. She had natural talent and wanted to explore it. When her mother had told her about the volunteer position, she'd said no, that she had other commitments. She couldn't remember the exact details of the conversation, but she did recall eventually feeling like she had no choice and that it would be selfish of her to do something for pleasure rather than something of service.

She turned the page.

Date: *4 December 2004*

Florence's art class announcement was a surprise today. I hadn't realised she was serious about pursuing the arts as a career. It, of course, is not an option, which I made clear. She came around and will be starting the volunteer position on 15 December. It is crucial she completes this vacation work as it will assist with her university application, which will be submitted early in the year. I would have preferred Florence to elect the nursing pathway of her own volition, but if this is not to be, then I will continue to sow the seed of guilt that will remind her of her dedication to service.

For her own sake, she must believe that her pleasures are secondary to her duty to others. As cruel as it may seem, eradicating the small potting shed in the yard that Florence turned into an art studio would be a kindness to remove the temptation from her path.

Flo threw the journal onto the table and closed her eyes, doing her best to push down the bile that was rising in her throat. *Remove the temptation.* It's interesting that she didn't clarify in the journal what this entailed. She should have written: *I will burn Florence's art studio to the ground and ensure she thinks it was her fault,* because that's what had happened. Flo had asked Gigi to pick her up from school that afternoon, excited to show her finished artwork to her grandmother. While the converted potting shed was small, she'd still made it hers. It housed all her paints, canvases, and equipment, and she'd proudly hung her latest painting ready to show Gigi. When they arrived home, the shed was ablaze.

She'd been told later that a candle was the culprit. A candle her mother assured her she must have left burning the previous night. Her mother had gone on to convince her that events like these were often signs that we were following the wrong path.

Wiping tears from the corners of her eyes, Flo slid her phone across the table and picked it up. She put it down again, her tears falling faster. Her instinct was to ring Ari, but of course, she couldn't. She wondered if Ari had read through the journals she'd taken home with her and found similar entries showing how her life had been shaped. She stood and stretched. She'd taken an entire box of journals from her parents' house, and as much as it was making her feel physically ill, she was going to read through them all tonight once Kayden was in bed. Her mother's second life was one level of betrayal, but this was another altogether.

26

A few hours after her conversation with Bridie, Ari sat in her mother's lounge room with a glass of wine in hand. If she could determine the outcome of her mother's situation, what would she want it to be? She sighed. She could almost picture her mother explaining the details in a matter-of-fact way, making them all feel like they were in the wrong or stupid for even suggesting the situation wasn't okay. She'd seen her do it so many times before. The difference was Ari couldn't see her getting away with it this time.

Her phone pinged with a text, breaking into her thoughts. She picked it up, and her heart sank.

> I assume you're a no-show for dinner?

Her date with Ryan. With everything going on, she'd completely forgotten.

She rang his number.

'I'm so sorry,' she said before he had a chance to speak. 'I flew to Canberra this afternoon and have been so caught up in what I'm doing that I completely forgot what day it is.'

'So, I'm not technically being stood up?'

Ari smiled, hearing the playful tone in his voice. 'Technically, you are being stood up. But you're not *deliberately* being stood up. Can I make it up to you? Saturday night, perhaps?'

'Sounds great. Now, more importantly, is everything okay? Why are you in Canberra?'

Ari sank back against the couch and relayed her day to Ryan.

'I'm sorry,' he said when she'd finished telling him the story about Scott. 'That's terrible. First your sister and now your mother. You're not having the best run.'

'You could say that. I was trying to work out before your text what the best outcome could be in the situation with my mother, and honestly, I don't have a clue. Her betrayal runs deeper than the situation with Scott Cohen. I haven't read all the entries in the journals we found, but even the sections I did read suggest she's also been controlling and manipulating Flo and me since we were little kids. Flo and I each took a pile of them away to read so I hate to imagine what she's discovered. I didn't bring my stack with me on this trip, but I've read enough to know I don't want anything more to do with her.'

It was half an hour before Ari ended the call, feeling a little lighter, having been able to decompress with Ryan. She realised as she sat staring at a large, framed photo of her mother and Scott, that what she'd said to Ryan was true: no matter how the situation played out with her mother, she didn't want anything more to do with her. A tear ran down her cheek as her mind filled with images of Flo and her mother. How was it possible to lose two important people in her life so quickly? Betrayal wasn't something she'd ever associated with her sister or mother, and now here she was, discovering it to be a trait they both shared.

She wiped her eyes, doing her best to shake off the sense of loneliness that settled over her, and reminded herself she wasn't

alone. She had Gigi and her father, and for that she was truly
thankful.

27

Flo's head pounded as she gratefully accepted a steaming cup of coffee from Holly before her shift the next morning. She'd been up until two, reading the journals she'd taken from her parents' home. Her nurse's training told her that, without a doubt, she was suffering from shock. The more she'd read, the more she'd found herself wanting to curl up in the foetal position. Her entire life had been orchestrated by her mother. She was no better than a puppet.

'You okay?' Holly asked, sipping her own drink. 'You look tired or hungover. Hopefully hungover from an amazing date?'

'I wish. No, just tired.'

'Your mum?'

'Definitely my mum,' Flo said, unable to mask the bitterness in her voice. 'I'm embarrassed to even call her that.'

'Oh, hon, it must be rough with this second family stuff.'

Flo stared at her. Her anger this morning towards her mother had nothing to do with Scott Cohen. This went way back. But she wasn't ready to share this with Holly. The person she needed to speak to was Ari.

'I'm assuming that's the issue,' Holly said. 'Although you look like you've seen a ghost. Are you okay?'

'I wish I had seen a ghost,' Flo said. 'The reality is, I've seen what my mother is capable of, and I'd say she fits more into the mould of a devil than a ghost.'

'How is she capable of anything right now?'

'It's past behaviour. Realistically, I need to speak to Ari.'

'And she still won't take your calls?'

Flo swallowed the lump that rose in her throat as soon as she thought of her sister. She'd never seen such hurt and anger in Ari's eyes before. To think she'd caused that was heart-wrenching. 'I saw her yesterday but what we discussed wasn't relevant to the Ben situation. It's more complicated than that. Nothing's changed about how she feels right now, so I'm probably better off leaving her alone. If she decides she wants to reach out, then we can talk.'

Holly gave her a strange look.

'What?'

'I don't know, Flo. If someone who's so level-headed, kind and caring ends up with this amount of drama and grief, where does it leave the rest of us?'

'In a position to not make one bad decision like I did. Although, I'm beginning to realise I was helped with that decision.'

'Oh?' Holly raised an eyebrow.

'Nothing.' She indicated to her coffee cup. 'Let's finish these and get to work.'

* * *

After the phone call with Ryan, Ari had slept fitfully in one of her mother's spare rooms. She seemed only capable of catnapping, then waking with a million thoughts churning through her mind. She'd ended up giving up on sleep and spent the early hours of the morning once again searching her mother's house, looking for journals. She'd even got up into the attic, but other than dust and cobwebs, there'd been nothing of interest.

Now, as she stood outside the Bureau of Strategic Intelligence, she wished the reason for her trip could be for something different. To take her mother out for lunch, perhaps. She'd never visited her mother's workplace before, but even from the outside, she could tell she was going to be impressed. She'd called the previous day and arranged a meeting with the one colleague her mother had mentioned in passing: Kirsty Lenehan. She wasn't sure what she was hoping to learn from Kirsty. She already had concrete proof her mother was leading a double life, but she'd be interested to hear what the woman could tell her. From what Ari understood, Kirsty and Julia had worked together for a few years.

Over a cup of coffee, Kirsty confirmed it was four years. 'I can't tell you anything about our work,' Kirsty said, 'but yes, we've worked together for four years. I'm so upset to hear about Julia's accident. Is there any news?'

'Not a lot,' Ari said. 'The doctors have confirmed that the swelling on her brain has reduced slightly, but not as much as they'd hoped in this timeframe. It might be weeks until she reaches the point that she can be brought out of the coma.'

Kirsty nodded. 'Can I ask why you're here?'

It was a direct but fair question. Most people would be by their mother's side at a time like this.

'Did Mum talk about her family in Melbourne much?'

Kirsty raised an eyebrow. 'Family?'

'As in her husband and daughters?'

'I didn't even know she was married.' Kirsty blushed. 'Actually,

I assumed she was one of those women with six cats. Don't get me wrong, she's probably lovely, but she does come across as rather standoffish at work. It was only after getting your call asking to meet that I realised she had a daughter.'

'Two, actually,' Ari said. 'Do you know a man by the name of Scott Cohen? I believe he works here.'

Kirsty nodded. 'Yes, Scott's been here for years.' Her eyes lit up. 'He'd be someone to talk to about your mum. He mentioned to me recently how much time they've been spending working on some personal project. Something they do outside of work, I think. Human Resources might be able to tell you more about that as the organisation is very strict about full disclosure on any projects of a personal nature.'

'I'm not sure they'll tell me anything, but I'll certainly ask. Are you aware that they were also in a relationship?'

Kirsty's eyes widened. 'As in a romantic relationship?'

Ari nodded.

'Wow, no, I had no idea.' She hesitated. 'I did joke about Julia being his work wife, questioning if her husband knew. That was purely to stir him up though. I didn't realise they were in a relationship or that she actually had a husband.'

'If he's to be believed, they've known each other for fifteen years and been in a relationship for five.'

'I would never have picked it. I wonder if they disclosed it to Human Resources? I'm pretty sure it's in our contract. Wow, she was having an affair with Scott?'

Ari nodded again.

'I don't know what to say.'

'You're obviously surprised.'

'Surprised? Shocked is probably more apt. While I don't know much about Julia outside of work, never in a million years would I have predicted this. The one thing I'd say about her was she was a straight shooter. She told it like it was but also had your back. She seemed principled. It might be part of the job here that we're all held to high standards, but I can't see that differing in her personal life. I guess it's fair to say that I didn't know her based on what you've told me.'

Ari thought back to the journals she'd started reading. She wondered if Kirsty would think her mother was such a straight shooter if she'd seen the content of those. A sudden thought occurred to her.

'This might seem like a strange question, but did you ever see my mother writing in journals? We've found boxes of them in Melbourne detailing her life with us and are expecting she might have boxes here in Canberra too that talk about her life here.'

'And you figure they'll fill in the details for you of what she has or hasn't been up to?'

Ari nodded. 'We have enough proof that she's been living two lives, but an explanation as to why might help us understand a little more.'

Kirsty took a long sip of her coffee before placing the cup back on the table. 'You know that everything that takes place here is completely confidential.'

'I do.'

'So, without giving you specific details, I can confirm that Julia spent a lot of time writing in journals. I can't tell you how many there are, but I do know that they're stored in a vault.'

Ari's mouth dropped open. 'A vault? They might be her personal scribblings as we found work-related ones locked away at home.'

'Possibly, but she's added them to her own personal area. When an employee leaves the Bureau they have the option to go through those items with Human Resources, and if they are confirmed as personal and make no reference to the organisation or projects, they may remove them from the premises. Otherwise, they're shredded.'

'All of the answers we need might be in a vault?'

Kirsty gave her a look brimming with sympathy. 'I'm sorry I can't be of more help. But yes, the answers are possibly in the journals in the vault or in the vault Julia keeps firmly shut in her head.'

Ari sighed. 'I guess I'll investigate whether there are any legal avenues to access those files. If Human Resources are willing to go through them, then they might release them to us.'

'Possibly, although I'm not sure that you'd get authority from anyone to do that while Julia's still alive. Her power of attorney might be able to request access, but I don't think any detail will be released to anyone but Julia. Especially, as other than possibly having an affair, something that's not actually illegal, she hasn't done anything wrong.'

* * *

Ari's mind churned as she loaded her bags into her car at Melbourne Airport. The flight had passed in what felt like minutes, with her unable to think of anything but her mother and this situation. Kirsty's words – *hasn't done anything wrong* – were a joke. Her mother had betrayed both her father and Scott Cohen in the worst possible way and, at the same time, betrayed her, Flo, and Gigi. Her thoughts began to manifest as anger as conversations with her mother from the past resurfaced. Excuses as to why her mother refused invitations to weddings, family birthdays and celebrations. It had never made sense to Ari that Julia said she worked on the weekend during her Canberra week and couldn't come home on a Friday. Seven days on, seven days off. That was hardly normal for a government job. But now it made sense. It wasn't work. It was her other life.

Ari's thoughts intensified as her Lexus followed the Tullamarine Freeway towards Melbourne city. As she steered off at Flemington Road, the car seemed to have a mind of its own, and a short time later she found herself taking a ticket for the car park at the Dominion Hospital. She hadn't planned to visit her mother, and with her in a coma, she wasn't sure why she'd come. But she needed answers. Perhaps she could will her mother awake and demand an explanation.

Ten minutes later, she stood at the entrance to the ICU unit, accepting a bundle of protective clothing from the duty nurse.

'You missed your sister,' the nurse said. 'Her shift ended about forty minutes ago.'

'That's okay. I came to visit my mother, not Flo.'

'Your mother already has a visitor in with her. It would be best if you waited for that visit to end before you go in.' She nodded in the direction of the waiting area. 'If you'd like to take a seat, I can let you know when she's free.'

'Do you know who the visitor is?'

'A man. Looks to be in his sixties. I can check the visitor log for you if you like. Sorry, he was signed in before my shift started.'

'No, that's okay. I can wait.' It was probably her father. An uneasy stirring started in her gut. Or it might be Scott Cohen. She was about to ask the nurse to check when a man stepped out from the ICU unit. 'Is that him?' she asked in a low whisper.

The nurse nodded.

Ari took a deep breath and stepped toward the man. 'You must be Scott.'

He met her eyes, lines of confusion creasing his forehead. 'Flo?'

'I'm Ari. Flo's my twin sister.'

A look of understanding spread across his face. 'I was wondering how Flo had suddenly grown her hair so long. It's good to meet you.'

Ari forced a smile. 'Could we speak for a moment?'

'Sure.' Scott indicated to the double doors that led back out to reception and the waiting area. They found two empty chairs and sat down.

'I owe you an apology,' Ari began. 'I've spent the past twenty-four hours in Canberra and a good part of that at your house. I have a key, but I will admit, as soon as I saw evidence that you lived there, I felt like an intruder.'

Scott sighed. 'Look, it's your mother's home too and in your shoes, I'd probably have done the same thing. Honestly, it's the least of my worries right now. Hopefully, you'll all believe me now. Your father included.'

'Until Mum wakes up, I don't think he'll believe she's done anything wrong. Can I ask you what you're hoping will happen when she wakes up?'

Scott pushed a hand through his hair. 'Honestly, I don't know. I'm not going to stay in a relationship with someone who has another family. I guess I'm hoping for an explanation that gets us all through this and makes sense. The problem is, I can't imagine any scenario where this can possibly have a happy ending for everyone.'

'You'll leave Mum?'

'I'm not sure. Like I said, I need an explanation. She's the love of my life, and I assumed I was hers. It's unfathomable to think we've known each other for so long, and I believed she was divorced and estranged from you and Flo. I can't get my head around that, nor that I'd never heard of you through some of our work colleagues. Surely, she'd have spoken about her family to some of them?'

'I had coffee with Kirsty Lenehan yesterday. She had no idea you were in a relationship with Mum.'

'I could have told you she'd say that. Julia insisted we keep our relationship private,' Scott said. 'She told me she was worried that people would be uncomfortable working with us on projects together if they knew. Of course, now I know why she was really keeping our entire relationship a secret.'

'Wasn't it against your employment contracts to be in a relationship?'

Scott glanced at his watch. 'I'm really sorry, but I have to get going. If you're happy to walk me down to my car we can keep chatting, or I can phone you later tonight. I've got a meeting in about forty minutes and need to be back at the hotel for the Zoom call.'

'I'll walk down with you,' Ari said.

'HR were notified as per company policy,' Scott said.

Ari sighed. She wasn't sure why she'd even asked the question as Kirsty had said something similar. It was blatantly obvious that her mother was a liar and a cheat. 'I guess it's a nightmare I'm hoping to wake up from. I met one of your neighbours while I was there, too. An older woman. Bridie Andrews. Have you met her?'

Scott shook his head. 'No. This will sound rude, but I tend to keep to myself. I'm not interested in befriending the neighbours. Don't get me wrong, I'd be happy to help her if there's an issue, but I'm not one for small talk or getting involved in the business of strangers.'

'It sounds like she and Mum were friends. She said Mum helped her out from time to time and had lent her some books. Mum never mentioned that?'

'The books ring a bell,' Scott said, 'but no, I didn't know Julia was helping her out. But keep in mind I work long hours, and I travel sometimes for work. Julia and I have been so focused on the project we've been working on that, as unhealthy as it's going to sound, the majority of our discussions revolve around Project Enigma. There's little time for other discussion and certainly not about the neighbours.'

'Project Enigma?'

Scott nodded. 'There are some interesting commercial conversations taking place.'

'She hasn't told us about it other than to say she was close to being able to announce something, but I think that was around articles in scientific journals, not something bigger. We're used to her work being confidential so it's not unusual that she didn't talk about it.'

Scott ran a hand across his chin stubble. 'It was a personal project so she could have told you, but I guess as it was *our* project, she needed to be careful with what she disclosed. She's obviously been forced to lie to your family and to me, depending on who she's been talking to.'

'It does seem strange,' Ari said, 'that you've never met your neighbour and your work colleagues didn't know you were in a relationship with Mum.'

They reached the lift, and Scott waited for Ari to step in before joining her. 'I take it that our work colleagues now know about our relationship. The one Julia insisted be kept confidential?'

An uneasy feeling settled on Ari's shoulders. If her mother woke up, she might not be too impressed that Ari had told Kirsty, who may have shared the news around the office. She gave herself a shake. 'At this point, I'm not too concerned if people discover the truth about my mother. She's dug her own hole. I'm more interested in getting to the truth about everything. To be with someone for five years and not know your neighbours and to hide it from your workplace all seems a little unusual.'

They travelled in silence for a few moments before the lift

came to a stop. As they stepped out into the underground car park, Scott turned to face Ari. 'Look, I'm sure you're searching for anything that suggests your mother wasn't leading a double life, but you're not going to find it. I, for one, wish it wasn't true, but even if she wakes up, there's going to be no getting around what she's done.'

Ari had the good grace to blush. 'Sorry, wishful thinking, I guess.'

Scott nodded. 'Don't worry, I've been trying to come up with scenarios where you're all lying to me, too, but there's not a lot of hope for me there. I think for now, we wait and pray that Julia wakes up and we get an explanation that can at least let us know where we all stand and hopefully answer the multitude of questions we have.'

It was Ari's turn to nod. 'You're right.' She gestured in the direction of her car. 'I'm parked over there. I think I'll get going too.'

'You're not going back in to visit your mother?'

'No. I need to drop in and see Dad on the way home, and right now, I don't think I can look at her.' She wasn't going to tell him that anger had initially driven her here, and that she'd planned to will Julia awake. Even as she had the thought, she realised how stupid it sounded.

After saying farewell to Scott, Ari climbed into the driver's seat, exhaustion settling over her. She wondered momentarily whether Project Enigma had anything to do with her and Flo. Had her mother used her journals and the twins as case studies for something she was now going to commercialise? She dismissed the thought as quickly as she had it. It wouldn't make sense for Scott Cohen to be working on a project that made any reference to her and Flo when he'd been led to believe that their mother was estranged from them. She also had to remind herself that she'd dealt with cases before where the evidence stacked against her client was impossible to ignore and painted them as guilty, yet they'd been innocent.

Even with the evidence stacked so high against her mother, a persistent itch of doubt was lingering at the back of her mind. Was it wishful thinking, or did she need to follow her instinct and explore why something wasn't sitting quite right?

28

Flo stepped inside her grandmother's front door, desperate for coffee. She'd been up most of the night reading her mother's journals and had woken, after only a couple of hours' sleep, with feelings of anger, betrayal and resentment flooding her. She wondered how much influence, if any, her grandmother had in her mother's decisions.

Gigi welcomed her with a hug and took her through to the open-plan kitchen area. 'Tea, coffee?'

'Coffee would be great.' Flo slid onto one of the stools by the island bench, concern filling her as she took in her grandmother's worn expression. She looked ten years older than she had just a few weeks ago. 'How are you coping? This can't be easy.'

Gigi sighed. 'If Julia would wake up, then we could get some answers. Instead, I'm lying awake all night, going through a million different scenarios, trying to work out what they all mean. I don't know what we'll do if she doesn't wake up. I think the not knowing will be worse than whatever horrible truths we might learn from her.'

'Has Ari spoken to you since we found the journals?'

'She called this morning from Canberra.' Gigi glanced at her watch. 'She's probably back in Melbourne by now. She was flying home this morning. She said that she didn't find any more journals, but one of Julia's colleagues confirmed that Julia has a personal storage area at work, and she believes there are more notebooks or journals stored there.'

'Can we access them?'

'No. The only scenario where we can get them will be if Julia doesn't make it and her possessions are left to someone in the family. Then Julia's work would go right through them to make sure they didn't reveal any confidential information, and if they didn't, would return them to us.'

'Did Ari tell you about the journals we do have? About what Mum says in them?'

'Only briefly. She didn't give me any details. She said she was surprised by some of the content.'

'That's an understatement.' Even as the words came out of her mouth, Flo regretted them. If Ari hadn't told Gigi what the journals said, it would be for a reason. Possibly to not put more stress on Gigi when she was already so distraught.

Gigi's arm froze mid-air as she went to pour the coffee. She looked up at Flo. 'What do you mean by that?'

'Oh, nothing. Forget I said anything. It's just Mum and her ramblings.'

'Florence? Don't lie to me. What do they say?'

Flo sighed. 'I shouldn't have said anything. No doubt Ari didn't because she wouldn't want to distress you any further.'

'Well, I'm more worried now that I know you're both hiding something from me.' Gigi finished pouring the coffee and passed Flo her cup.

'From what I've read,' Flo said, 'it appears Mum has been conducting some kind of experiment on Ari and me.'

'What?'

'The journals document so many parts of our lives and how Mum *helped* us make decisions to steer us on paths she wanted us to go down.'

'She always had a clear vision for what she thought you'd be best suited to. But that was from watching and observing your interests and then helping you cultivate them.'

Flo shook her head. 'Our lives were being planned for us while we were in the womb. Did you know that our names were picked to represent the women she expected us to become? That we'd follow in their career paths and Ari, in particular, would achieve great things?'

Gigi snorted. 'Don't be silly. She named you both after strong, high-achieving women. She didn't expect you to become them.'

'Really? She named me after Florence Nightingale and then pushed me towards nursing when I was a little girl. I was never given a doctor's kit, only the nurse's uniform. She had me visiting the children's ward to read books to other kids when I was only about ten, and in high school, she had me volunteering at the hospitals during school holidays.'

'But that was because you were interested in all of that.' Gigi frowned. 'Wasn't it?'

'The more I think back, no, it wasn't my interest initially. It was Mum telling me why it should be and praising me whenever I showed interest in something related to medicine. But, as soon as I showed interest in anything else, she shut me down quickly. Remember my art studio?'

Gigi nodded.

'She burnt it down to get rid of all of my supplies and make me realise that art school or anything in that line was silly.'

Gigi's face paled. 'No, she wouldn't have done that. I remember that day clearly. You left a candle burning.'

'Until now, that's what I believed. But she burnt it down. And there's more than that. Her journals are clear: she wanted me to be a nurse and nothing more. She wanted Ari's career to be what we celebrated and me to have an altruistic career that gave to people but didn't allow me to get too full of myself. One of her last entries was the night of her birthday. That night she'd told me I'd be no good as the nurse unit manager. She documents it in the journal, saying she wants me to stay at the level I am.'

'But why would she want that? It makes no sense.'

'I've no idea, but all I can assume is that it's about her being in control. That we're her puppets.'

Gigi was staring at her. 'I find this hard to believe.'

'She's done the same to Ari. Named her after Arabella Mansfield, who was the first female lawyer in the US, and mapped out while she was still in the womb her progression from high school to law school, to the bar, to becoming a partner and then eventually a High Court justice.'

'High Court justice? Is that something Ari's even interested in?'

'Assuming Mum's already been in her ear, then yes, probably.'

'This is madness. Does your father know anything about this?'

Flo hesitated. She hadn't for one minute considered her father might have been part of this. But she guessed anything was possible. 'I don't know.'

'Is he mentioned in the journals? Was your mother manipulating him too?'

'You know, that's a good point. He wasn't mentioned at all. Maybe they were in on it together.'

29

The darkened sky outside Ari's office window confirmed, once again, that she'd be one of the last to leave the office. She'd originally planned to take the rest of the week off, but at the last minute, decided to go in to take her mind off the situation with her mother. She unplugged her laptop from the external monitor she liked to use when in the office and slipped it into her bag.

She'd left her car at home so exited the lifts at ground level rather than going all the way to the basement car park. She walked through the revolving door, shivering as she was hit with the full force of a gusting city wind. It was one of the things she disliked about working in the CBD – the wind tunnels the narrow streets tended to create.

Pulling her coat tight around her, Ari turned to walk towards Elizabeth Street and stopped. 'Ben?'

Ben smiled and stepped towards her. 'I was hoping to talk to you.'

Ari frowned. 'Really? Why didn't you call? How long have you been waiting?'

'About an hour. I called your office earlier, and your assistant said you generally left anywhere between six and eleven. I figured I could wait that long.'

'You'd wait until eleven o'clock?' Ari smiled. 'You always were a bit mad. Next time call me. If I'd parked in the underground parking, you wouldn't have even seen me leave.'

He raised an eyebrow. 'I didn't think of that, and I wasn't sure you'd take my call. Look, can I buy you a drink or even dinner if you haven't eaten? That little Italian place is still tucked down that laneway near Queen Street. I rediscovered it with Della the other week.'

Ari hesitated. Did she want to have dinner with Ben? If it was Flo standing in front of her, she'd walk right past her, and yet Ben was as responsible for what had happened as her sister was. It was unfair to Flo that she didn't feel the same resentment towards her ex as she did her sister.

'How about the Italian place for a glass of wine then?' Ben suggested.

Ari couldn't help but laugh. 'I see right through you, Ben Mitchell. You know that all you have to do is get me through that door and one smell of the garlic, and I'll be ordering three courses.'

Ben shrugged. 'That sounds good to me. What do you say?'

'Sure, why not?'

They walked the short distance to Queen Street, and Ari followed Ben down the small laneway that led to the Italian restaurant. It had been a favourite of theirs, and they'd been regularly enough that the owner, Lorenzo, had always come out to greet them. *My favourite couple*, he'd exclaim.

Ben held the door open for Ari, and she was pleased to get inside to the warm and the oh-so-delicious garlic smell.

'My favourite couple!' Lorenzo's booming voice greeted them. The abundance of greys in his formerly dark hair showed that years had passed since they'd last visited. Ari wasn't sure whether to correct him or not. She looked to Ben, who shrugged as if to say, *your call.*

Instead, Ari accepted Lorenzo's bear hug before following him to what used to be her and Ben's favourite table.

'You have an amazing memory,' Ari said to the Italian.

'Always for my favourite customers. Although,' he tutted, 'if I was relying on you to stay open, I would have closed years ago. Where have you been?'

'London,' Ben answered. 'Work took me there seven years ago. Only back in Australia in the last few months.'

Lorenzo's eyes widened. 'And you came straight back here. Now I do feel honoured.' He winked at Ari. 'Two glasses of my special Barolo and Barbaresco coming up.'

Ari waited until he left them to organise their drinks. 'He'd be upset if we told him the real story.'

'No more upset than I am. That's why I came to talk to you. I wanted to apologise to you in person. What I did was awful, and there are no excuses, and I don't intend to make any. I wanted you to know how sorry I am.'

Ari nodded. 'Thank you. I appreciate that. You're right. There are no excuses. And while it isn't quite the same, I know that Sean told you that we hooked up after you and I broke up. That was crossing a line, and I shouldn't have done that. I should have reached out to you at the time when he did, but to be honest, I was too embarrassed. I'm glad you forgave him.'

'Flo mentioned you've barely spoken to her since you found out.'

'I'm not ready to. You both crossed a line, but she took it to a completely new level,' Ari said. 'I feel like I don't know who she is at all. I think that I'm shattered on many levels. First, that she'd sleep with my husband – that's low enough – but to then lie to such an extreme and not even tell you about Kayden. I don't know how she's been able to live with herself.'

'That's something we definitely have in common,' Ben said. 'It was such an out-of-character thing to do.'

'Or we never knew the real Flo,' Ari said. She stopped talking and smiled as Lorenzo returned to the table with two glasses of wine. He placed one down in front of each of them. 'It is still the best red in Italy. Enjoy!'

Ben picked up his glass and raised it in a toast. 'A bit unconventional being here together, I know, but here's to the good times we had in this restaurant.'

Ari raised her glass. 'And to all the other good times.'

They sipped their wine.

'As much as I don't want to keep bringing it up, I did want to tell you what happened that night I was with Flo.'

'I honestly don't want to know.'

'Not details,' Ben said, his face turning red. 'But the circumstances around it. I got the impression from Flo that you thought we were having an affair.'

Ari hesitated. This was why she hadn't allowed Flo to explain. She wasn't sure she wanted to know. There was no turning back once she knew the details. She remained silent, part of her wishing she'd said no to coming here with Ben.

Ben appeared to take her silence as a cue to continue. 'I would never have done that to you, and neither would Flo. I bumped into her the night our divorce came through. I'd been set up on a blind date, my first date since you and I split. I was stood up, and Flo and some of her friends from work happened to be in the bar. When I first saw Flo, I thought it was you, and I realised how much I wanted to see you. To hold you and say I was sorry that it hadn't worked out. To make sure you knew I still cared about you. But then I realised it wasn't you and I must have seemed really depressed to Flo. She felt sorry for me and offered for me to join them. We ended up drinking too much, and one thing led to another. It wasn't planned and would never have happened if we hadn't coincidentally ended up in that bar that night. I hadn't seen Flo since you and I separated.

'I felt terrible the next day. I would never have said it to Flo, but I would have given anything that day to not be divorced. I never wanted that, Ari, you know that. Too many drinks and it wasn't hard to fantasise that your identical twin, who wanted to be with me that night, was you. In addition to being violently hungover, Flo was beside herself when she realised what she'd done. She couldn't believe it. Neither of us could. I've since learned that your mother talked Flo into lying about the pregnancy and about who Kayden's father was.'

'She could have gone against my mother,' Ari said. 'She was an adult, and she had a mind of her own. Not telling me was one thing, but not telling you that you had a kid! How can you forgive her for that?'

'I have to,' Ben said. 'For Kayden's sake. I want him to have stability and know he has two parents who'd do anything for him. If I stay angry with Flo, he'll pick up on my resentment. It's not going to help the situation. And...' he raised an eyebrow '...while we can blame Flo for everything, it sounds like both you and Julia led her to believe I didn't want children.'

Ari looked away. He was right. 'I'm not sure that excuses her behaviour.'

'No, of course not,' Ben said. He sighed. 'Unfortunately for Flo, I'd say she's made one major mistake in her life, and this happens to be it. And as much as you won't want to hear this, the one good thing that came out of this big mess was Kayden. Imagine if we didn't have him.'

Ari sipped her drink, the wine caressing her throat with its velvety warmth. She placed her glass down and smiled at Ben. 'I assume you're still in high demand in the advertising world. You can certainly still sell a concept.'

'I'm not trying to sell anything,' Ben said. 'I'm serious about Kayden. I've known him for a few weeks, and already I can't imagine my life without him. You've known him for six years, and I'm guessing you're missing him a lot right now. He's missing you. He was asking Flo if you were sick too, like Julia.'

Ari sighed. 'You're right, of course. It's not his fault, and yes, I'd probably rather be in this situation and have him than turn back the clock and not have him at all. But why did it have to be with my husband?'

'*Ex*-husband.'

'By less than twelve hours by the sounds of it.'

'Ari, we'd been separated for months.'

'And that makes it okay?'

'No, of course not. At the end of the day Flo and I should never have been together, no matter what the circumstances were. Mum's been asking how you are,' Ben said, veering the subject in a different direction. 'She was furious when she found out what had happened. So was Dad.' His cheeks coloured. 'I don't think I've ever faced a lecture that severe. Mum also said to tell you that they miss you.'

'I miss them too,' Ari said. 'I miss all of you.'

'Really?'

She nodded. 'The timing wasn't right for us. I was so focused on my career that I was acting like a crazy person.'

'*Was* so focused?'

'Yes, was. Something's changed in the last few months. That drive's faded, and I'm beginning to feel a lot of what I do is unethical and ridiculous. I'm thirty-six, and considering I'm not even in a relationship, I'm leaving it late if I decide I do want kids or a family. I kind of can't believe I've done that.'

Ben leaned back in his chair, studying her. 'I'm surprised to hear you say that.'

Ari shrugged. 'I've been doing a lot of reflection lately and since Mum's accident even more.' She thought of the journals and that the way her life had unfolded was due in part to her mother's manipulation. 'I've probably left it too late, but it feels like time for a change.'

Ben cleared his throat. 'Do you think…?'

Ari placed a hand on his. 'Stop. If you're going to ask what I think you are, then no. We had our chance and went in different directions.' She stopped as the edge of his lips flickered into a smile. 'What?'

'I wasn't going to go down that path. I was going to say, do you think you want to have kids after all?'

Ari withdrew her hand and gave an embarrassed laugh. Of course he wouldn't want to go down that path again. She'd broken his heart. Why would he come back for more? Not that she was interested in exploring that with him anyway. 'Maybe. Honestly, I don't know what I want right now. There's so much upheaval at the moment. Has Flo told you what Mum's done?'

He nodded. 'A bit. She didn't go into too much detail but did mention Julia's partner and the life she's been leading in Canberra.'

'Did she mention the journals we found?'

Ben frowned. 'No. What was in them?'

Ari picked up her wine glass and took a large gulp. 'Enough evidence to show that our mother was a psycho… is a psycho. I guess I shouldn't speak in the past tense.'

'Psycho?'

Ari nodded. 'She literally orchestrated almost everything we ever did. All our decisions and life directions. They were pre-planned. Even our names are supposed to be symbolic of who we needed to become. It's quite disturbing.'

'Ah, that makes sense then. I spoke with Flo the other night, and she was distracted. Sounded quite upset. I asked her if she was okay, and she said she wasn't. That she'd found out a bunch of information about Julia and was completely freaked out.'

Ari's heart sank in a shared sense of sorrow. She gave herself a shake. Flo had destroyed their relationship, not her.

'She said she'd picked up her phone about ten times to ring you,' Ben said, 'but then put it down again. She didn't want to put this on you with everything else.'

Ari's heart contracted. 'I've wanted to ring her about a million times. I miss her,' she admitted.

'Why don't you?'

Ari stared at him, ready to jump down his throat and stopped. Why hadn't she? She considered her words before she spoke. 'For my entire life, Flo has been the most important person to me.' She felt her face flush. 'Sorry, but you know that's true. I put her before you even in our marriage.'

Ben nodded but didn't comment.

'I always thought that no matter what, we had an unbreakable bond. That we'd do anything for each other. And then she lied. I'm beginning to believe that the lies she told after she slept with you were bigger than the act. I would have been angry, don't get me wrong, if she'd admitted what had happened, but to drag it out for seven years until there was no choice but to be honest. You've got no idea how much that hurts.'

'I do actually.'

'Sorry. Of course, you do.' She considered Ben for a moment. 'How do you forgive her for that?'

'Part of me wants to yell and scream and try to get full custody of Kayden if I'm honest.'

Ari sucked in a breath. 'Please don't do that. She's an amazing mum and it would destroy Kayden. God, Flo would be devastated. We all would.'

'But,' Ben continued, 'I then remind myself of the Flo we knew before she and I hooked up. She was an amazing person. Gentle, kind and would do anything for either of us. Do you remember that time we both had gastro and she insisted on coming around and nursing us? Cold compresses on our foreheads, cleaning up our messes.'

'Holding my hair back as I hung over the toilet for the fiftieth time,' Ari added.

'Exactly. And then remember our sixth anniversary? She booked the hot air balloon and champagne breakfast. Had organised with both our employers for the day off.'

'You know,' Ari said. 'She told me later that she was worried about us and wanted to do something special to make sure we stayed together.'

'I guess she knew that we were nearing the end. Anyway, it was those things and about another hundred examples I could give you that helped me forgive her. In all the time I've known you and known Flo, the Kayden situation was the only time I saw Flo make a bad decision. I know I've made a lot of bad decisions over the years, but I haven't been punished for them in the way I could punish Flo if I chose to.'

Ari nodded. 'In my entire life it's the only bad decision I've seen Flo make too.' She lapsed into thought.

'You okay?'

'Would you mind if we cut this short? There's something I need to do.'

'Do you have time to finish your drink at least?'

Ari picked up her wine glass. 'Definitely.'

* * *

After hugging Ben, Ari hurried home and retrieved the journals she'd taken from her parents' house. She'd been reading through them in chronological order previously, and still had a lot to get through to reach the current day. She quickly eyeballed the spines of the journals she'd yet to read and extracted 2017 and started flicking through.

Date: *14 May 2017*

To say I'm in shock is an understatement. Florence came to me today with what should have been exciting and wonderful news. And would have been if we could fast-forward three years and she was settled and married as per the plan. But, no. She's 'knocked up' in the most unfortunate of circumstances. I've been questioning all day as to where I went wrong, but can't pinpoint it. I don't think anyone who knows Florence would believe she'd done something as despicable as this. The only thing I do know is that no matter what happens, Arabella can never find out. It would destroy everything that underpins our family's values and relationships. I honestly think it would be the end. I know that I need to allow the dust to settle before making any further recommendations. I can't even speak to Michael about it – he'll be devastated.

I'm back in Canberra tomorrow. Perhaps I'll seek advice from colleagues. Scott's likely to have some insightful wisdom. It's an unusual situation.

Ari looked up from the journal momentarily. So, it was

confirmed. Her mother knew but didn't want to be embarrassed. She stared at the entry, the reference to Scott even more jarring.

She turned the page.

Date: *21 May 2017*

A week away helped clear my mind and seek advice on the Florence baby situation. I'm not sure I agree with any of the advice given. Scott, as I should have known, advised total transparency. That honesty was the only way forward or we'd be dealing with repercussions down the track. Of course he, like everyone else, believes I was asking for a 'friend'. I couldn't disclose that it was my daughter.

Ben has already gone to London and has no clue about the pregnancy. According to Florence it was a one-night stand so there is no reason for further communication. I'll be talking to Florence this afternoon about my expectations for her keeping quiet about the real circumstances surrounding her pregnancy. I can only hope that she, as she has done in previous situations, agrees.

Ari read on to the next journal entry that documented Julia's discussion with Flo.

In many ways I'm proud to have raised a daughter with such a strong moral compass, but the determination on this occasion is not serving her. I can see it will take more than one conversation to have her agree to my plan. I have at least had her promise not to speak to Arabella until I'm present. That will buy me a little more time and opportunity to convince her that telling the truth will destroy her relationship with her sister forever.

Ari shook her head. Flo had wanted to tell her the truth, but her mother had apparently worn her down. She flicked through the next few entries, pausing when she found the entry that confirmed Flo had been manipulated.

Florence has agreed that my plan is the only way forward to not destroy her relationship with Arabella and to keep Ben out of the picture. Reminding her that Ben didn't want children, which was part of the reason he and Arabella parted, made this easier. Perhaps subconsciously, she's been looking for a way out, and I've provided it for her. I would do anything for my girls to ensure their future happiness.

Ari laid the journal down. If this had been an isolated event that her mother had documented, she probably still would have thought that Flo should have told her the truth. But having read through years of entries of the incredible lengths her mother had gone to in order to manipulate their lives, she was beginning to realise that Flo had little option but to go along with her mother's plan. She'd been brainwashed by her.

She thought of Flo. Having learned from Ben that it was a one-night stand that Flo had regretted after, and now to have learned that she had wanted to tell Ari the truth, her anger softened a little towards her sister. But Julia hadn't held a gun to her head. Flo was still her own person, and Ari was supposed to be the person she loved most in the world. If she forgave Flo and let her back in, she might betray her again. And right now Ari didn't have the capacity to handle that.

30

Anxiety bubbled within Flo throughout her early morning shift. She'd been riddled with bad dreams during the night, all focused around the situation with Ari. At one stage she'd woken gasping for air, her pyjamas soaked with sweat, and her heart thumping.

'You look distracted,' Holly said, taking a patient's chart out of Flo's hands. 'You've been standing next to this bed for at least five minutes. Luckily, the patient's asleep, or he'd be worried something was seriously wrong with the intent way you're reviewing his chart. What's his name, by the way?'

'Who?'

Holly nodded towards the bed. 'The way you've been analysing that chart I assume you've memorised everything.'

'Very funny. I'm a little distracted thinking of Ari.'

'I'm sorry you haven't been able to work things out with her. You must be missing her. You two were always so close. Now, Pauline's been looking for you. The doctors are with your mum, and I think there's some discussion about weaning her off the medications and bringing her out of the coma.'

'Really?'

Holly nodded. 'They're with her now, and that Scott guy is there. You might want to get in and hear what's going on.'

'Thanks.' Flo gave her a quick smile and hurried from the room. She reached the ICU as doctors, one of them Doctor Lee, appeared from her mother's bedside with Scott Cohen beside them.

'Flo,' Doctor Lee said, smiling warmly at her. 'We have the results from yesterday's tests and have seen a significant reduction in the swelling around your mother's brain. We feel the timing is right to reduce the medications and to try to bring her out of the coma. As you know, it can take a few days, sometimes longer, for the patient to wake up. But we will start the process today if you'd like to let the rest of your family know.'

'Did the tests show anything else?' Flo asked. 'Any damage?'

'We won't know the full extent of the damage for some time,' Doctor Lee said. 'As you know, upon waking, your mother may experience confusion, disorientation, weakness and possibly temporary, or even permanent, neurological deficits. We'll need to observe her and see how she's been affected.'

'If she wakes.'

Doctor Lee nodded. 'Yes, it's always a possibility that she might not. I feel it's unlikely on this occasion, but we can't completely discount it.' Doctor Lee glanced at her watch. 'I'd better get on. If you have any questions, message me, okay?'

'Thanks,' Flo said, appreciating that being on staff was affording her some extra care. She watched as the doctors made their way to the lifts to exit the ICU.

'How long do you think it will be until she wakes up?' Scott asked.

Flo turned her attention to her mother's partner. 'It's unknown. It could be hours, more likely days, hopefully not weeks. Everyone's different.'

'Okay, thanks.'

Flo kept her fists firmly in her pockets. 'Can I ask you something?'

Scott nodded.

'Did my mother ever ask your advice on things that you perhaps thought were rather odd?'

'Like what?'

'Well, like situations that a friend's daughter was in.'

Scott nodded. 'Yes. I've been reflecting on this realising that the *friend* she was always asking advice for was, in fact, herself and you two girls. I feel rather stupid, to be honest, that I never picked up on this. I've been dishing out advice for years, having no idea that this was for Julia's daughters. Mind you, it was rare that she agreed with anything I said. I think she liked to use me as a sounding board.'

'We found some journals that document a lot of the major milestones in both our lives,' Flo said. 'It appears she's had quite an influence over us.'

Scott's eyes lit up with interest. 'Does she mention me too?'

'No, the journals we've found appear to only be relevant to Ari and me. There are, however, more journals filed away at her work in Canberra that we don't have access to. I imagine they'd go into detail about your relationship with her. I've seen a few references to you in the journals we have, purely where she says she's going to ask your advice. She obviously valued your input.'

'But there's been no other references to me?'

'Not that I've seen, but I haven't read every journal. Ari has some of them, and there are a lot to get through.'

'I guess she wanted to try and keep the two lives separate,' Scott said. 'It'd be interesting to read the journals from her work to see if she was asking you or your father for advice on things that were happening in Canberra.' He shuddered. 'It feels wrong if she was.'

'Everything feels wrong,' Flo agreed.

They sat in silence for a moment. 'I guess we might get some answers when she comes out of the coma,' Flo said. 'We'll need to give some thought to her visitors,' she added. 'As much as we all want answers, we can't overwhelm her initially. We'll need to be guided by how she is and what we think she can handle.'

Scott nodded and smiled. 'I can see why she was committed to keeping you in nursing. You're good, Flo.'

Flo wasn't sure whether to be pleased with the compliment or angry at the accurate description of *keeping you in nursing*. She found it easier not to respond.

* * *

Ari had been surprised by the flutter of nervous energy that had overcome her moments before Ryan picked her up for their date. She'd been looking forward to seeing him but hadn't realised how much until her apartment intercom had rung announcing he was downstairs.

Now, as she sat across from him at the Sapphire Room, an upscale restaurant recently opened at Southbank, she was grateful for the calming effects of the red wine they'd ordered.

'I should probably follow in your footsteps and throw in my job,' Ari said. Ryan had shared more details of the financial analyst role he'd walked away from five years earlier.

Ryan laughed. 'I'm not sure I'm the best example of a career change. But I'm happy with my choice. I was hating what I was doing. Everything was about money and making more and more of it for clients and, to some degree, myself. My life revolved around work, and that was about it. I had no social life and did little outside of the office.'

'That sounds familiar.'

'And then the wife of a friend of mine died,' he said. 'She was only forty-six and was killed instantly in a head-on collision.'

'That's terrible,' Ari said.

'It was. Matt, my mate, was devastated, as you can imagine. I went out with him one night a few months after she passed, and he was telling me how much he regretted their lifestyle. They'd chosen not to have kids but were working ridiculous hours to save for an early retirement. They'd hoped to travel the world in their fifties. She never made it, but instead left this world having done a lot of hard work to leave behind a small fortune she never got to enjoy.'

'And that triggered something in you?'

'We have no idea how long we have left. It could be years. It could be months or even days. Everyone says to live in the moment, but how many people do? Not many. I decided, as a legacy to Matt's wife, that I would live in the moment. That I'd try my best to only do things I enjoy. I'm lucky that I'd set myself up financially with investments, so I can afford to earn a minimal amount through yoga and live off a combination of that and the interest I earn on my investments. I'm hardly living a poor yogi's lifestyle. Quite the opposite, in fact. But it's not about money or material possessions. It's about trying to experience happiness and joy as much as possible. To surround myself with people I love and share the happiness.'

'I could do that,' Ari said. 'I've worked my butt off for years and hardly spent any of my earnings. It's mostly invested, but I could consider doing something else. Even if it's only to take a year off to find out what I want to do.' A vision of her mother entered her mind.

'What or who are you thinking about?' Ryan asked. 'Your face is like an open book, you know? Whatever you're thinking about looks like it's hurting you.'

'My mother. There's part of me that would find walking away from work incredibly satisfying, even if only to see her horrified reaction.'

'Not a reason I'd recommend for walking away.'

Ari smiled. 'No, but it would be a silver lining.'

Ryan reached across the table and entwined his fingers through hers. Ari smiled, enjoying the sensation of butterflies that flittered inside her. She hadn't felt date nerves in years. Mainly because she'd barely dated since she and Ben broke up, but also because she hadn't been attracted to anyone she'd been out with until now.

'I know I've been giving you all sorts of advice about trying new things and travelling and changing your life, but there is a stipulation in all of that.'

'What's that?'

He leaned across the table until their faces were almost touching. 'That I'm one of those new things you try.' Their lips met, and Ari found herself thinking of nothing other than how right this moment felt.

31

Flo was grateful to be able to drop Kayden off with Ben and Della the next morning. She turned into Ben's parents' driveway and was greeted by a harmonious blend of Victorian and contemporary architecture.

'Are you sure you're ready to meet Ben's parents?'

'My new granny and gramps, you mean?'

Flo glanced in the rear-vision mirror at Kayden, who was gazing out of the window at the large home.

'That's what Della calls them,' he added. 'They might want me to call them something else. By their names, maybe?'

'What would you like to call them?'

'I don't know,' Kayden said. 'I'll see if they're nice first. If they're like Grandma, then I might need to call them what they tell me to call them.'

Flo's heart contracted at the quiver in his voice.

'Kaydey!' Della, wearing a bright blue T-shirt, came racing out of the front door towards the car, Ben a few steps behind her.

Kayden grinned, unclipped his seat belt and pushed open the car door.

Della threw her arms around him the moment his feet touched the driveway.

Ben grinned at Flo, and she couldn't help but grin back. It was hard not to fall in love with Della and her enthusiasm for Kayden. She climbed out of the car as Kayden and Della ran off towards the house.

'He's a bit worried about meeting your parents,' Flo said. 'He's not sure what to call them.'

Ben nodded. 'Thanks for the heads-up. They're out until lunchtime, so I'll have a chat with Kayden and reassure him that he can call them whatever he chooses. He's calling me Ben, so he might want to call them by their first names. They won't mind. They can't wait to meet him.'

'It's a weird situation,' Flo said. 'Like we need to navigate a divorce and sharing of custody, but we missed out on the relationship and the marriage.'

Ben laughed. 'I guess. It's unusual, but we'll make it work. And Flo, don't worry, I'll make sure Kayden's comfortable with my parents and everything that we do.'

A scream of laughter wafted out of one of the upstairs windows.

Flo smiled. 'With Della around, I think he's in good hands. They've become so close, so quickly.'

'I know,' Ben said. 'You've got no idea what Kayden's done for her. She was so sad about Carrie. I know she's only young, but I honestly was worried that it was going to ruin her forever. Did you notice the blue shirt today? It's the first day since Carrie's funeral she hasn't insisted on wearing black. What you're seeing—' another shriek came from the house, '—and hearing is what she was like before Carrie got sick. I think having someone else to love has brought that Della back. It's amazing.'

'For him too,' Flo said. 'The only difference is, he hasn't lost anything. He's gained a whole new family.' A lump rose in her throat as the words left her lips. A family she wasn't part of. She glanced at her watch. 'Speaking of family, I'd better go. We're meeting at Gigi's about Mum and everything that's going on.'

Ben reached out and laid a hand on her arm. 'Flo, have you spoken to Ari since Friday?'

'No. She'll tolerate me at Gigi's today, but she's not likely to be in touch otherwise. Why?'

He pushed a hand through his hair. 'The thing is, I went and saw her after work on Friday night. I needed to apologise, and I had hoped what I'd said might have helped your situation with her.'

Flo's heart rate quickened. 'She accepted your apology?'

He nodded. 'I explained that it was a one-night stand and that she and I were officially divorced at the time. I apologised, of course, and we chatted for quite a long time. She misses you, and I had hoped you might hear from her.'

'I haven't. But Ari's not one to rush and do things. She might be waiting until we see each other today. Did you get the impression she might forgive me?'

'I did,' Ben said. 'I can't guarantee anything, but she might be ready to talk.'

Flo smiled. 'Thank you. Whatever you said would have helped with that. I appreciate it.'

'You're welcome.' He frowned. 'I hope you're all going to be okay, Flo. Ari mentioned how much of a mess your dad is over all of this. I'm not surprised. He was so devoted to your mum. If there's anything I can do, even if it's to get him out on the golf course for a break, let me know.'

* * *

Ben's words about her father being a mess played over in Flo's mind as she pushed open Gigi's front door and made her way along the passage to the open-plan living area. From the cars out the front, she knew her father and Ari were already there.

'Hey, love,' her father said, standing as she entered the living area. She walked over to him and hugged him, his usually solid build feeling noticeably thinner.

'Coffee?' Gigi asked, holding up a cup.

Flo extracted herself from her father's embrace, nodded and sat down next to Ari. She turned to her sister. 'How are you?'

Ari glared at her, and Flo turned away, doing her best to hide the utter disappointment she felt. She had to admit Ben's words about his conversation with Ari had left her hopeful for some kind of reconciliation with her sister. But Ari had shot down any idea of that already.

'Any news from the hospital?' Gigi asked.

'Nothing more than we just have to continue to wait.'

'I'm beginning to wonder what we're even waiting for,' Ari said. 'We know she's a liar and a cheat and has been ruining our lives since we were children. Controlling our movements, forcing us into decisions that suited her. Do we think she's going to wake up and tell us some other version of events that we're going to believe?'

Silence fell in Gigi's kitchen.

'Because I can tell you, that's not going to happen,' Ari said.

'Hold on a minute,' Mike said. 'Controlling your movements and forcing your decisions? That's a little unfair, isn't it? Your mother would have offered you help and guidance, of course, but she hardly *forced* you to do things.'

'Dad,' Ari said, appearing to ignore her father's words, 'how involved were you with Mum's decision-making when it came to Flo and me?'

'What do you mean?'

'I mean,' Ari said, 'the journals we've found that go into detail about plans for Flo and me date back to when we were about four, but they also clearly outline that from the day we were conceived, she'd mapped out a pathway for our lives and moulded and manipulated us into being the people she wanted us to be. Practically every major milestone or decision we've made has been orchestrated by her.'

Mike shook his head. 'I think that's a huge exaggeration. Your mother always supported your dreams. She didn't make you do anything.'

'Did she ever talk to you about how, for instance, Flo would make a wonderful nurse and shouldn't, therefore, be studying to become a doctor? That she was going to make sure Flo gave up on the idea of study and did what she was destined to do?'

Mike's cheeks flamed red. 'Of course not. She wanted Flo to succeed, but she was worried, too. Protective, I guess.'

'What do you mean,' Flo said.

'She was worried, that's all,' Mike said. 'That with Kayden and everything else that you were setting yourself up for failure. That you wouldn't have the time to study and wouldn't succeed. She was worried that it would affect you negatively, possibly even send you into some kind of depression, and she didn't want to see that happen.'

'So she stopped me from even trying?'

'She didn't stop you. She gently reminded you of your obligations. I supported her with that. I don't want to see you get hurt either.'

'Oh my God,' Ari said. 'She manipulated you too. Didn't she?'

Mike raised an eyebrow. 'Of course not. We discussed issues, and often, I agreed with her. I know you both think your mother was controlling at times, but perhaps you didn't hear the full story behind her concerns like I did. She spent too much time, if you ask me, worrying about the two of you and wanting you to have wonderful lives. If it had been left to me, I would have let you get on with things. Let you learn from your mistakes and experiences, but Julia said she didn't want you to be traumatised by bad experiences. She wanted to help you lead the best and happiest lives you could.'

'She had you brainwashed too, didn't she?'

'She said that?' Gigi asked. 'About not being traumatised?'

Mike nodded. 'She never elaborated on it, but it was a huge thing for her. I always assumed that she'd seen things at work that made her think this way. It was hard to tell with everything being so confidential.'

Gigi nodded, her features adopting a faraway look.

'Gigi?' Flo said. 'What are you thinking?'

Gigi opened her mouth, appearing to be about to share her thoughts then closed it again. 'Nothing. Trying to digest everything.'

Flo stared at her grandmother. She was thinking about something specific. You could easily tell from the lines of concern etched deep into her forehead. She was tempted to pry further when her phone rang.

'Sorry,' Flo said, taking it from her bag. 'Kayden's with...' She stopped herself and glanced sideways at Ari. She wasn't sure whether mentioning Ben was off-limits. 'I'd better check in case it's him.'

She glanced at the screen. It wasn't Ben, it was Holly. She hesitated a split second before answering.

'Holls?'

'It's your mum, Flo, she's coming around. I know the hospital will contact you all soon, but I thought I'd give you a heads-up.'

Flo's heart raced as she listened to Holly's words. It was quite likely they were about to get some answers. 'Thanks for letting me know.'

'The thing is,' Holly said, 'that Scott guy's here, and I wasn't sure you'd want him to be the first face she sees when she comes to.'

'No, definitely not. I'll be straight there. In fact, we probably all will. Thanks again.'

Flo ended the call and looked from Ari to her father and then to Gigi.

'What's happened?' Gigi asked. 'Is it news about Julia?'

Flo nodded. 'She's waking up.'

Mike jumped to his feet. 'Let's go.'

'Hold on a minute,' Gigi said, lifting her hands to indicate they needed to stop. 'Julia's been in a coma for the last few weeks and left us with a huge mess to deal with. As much as I know we all want answers on a range of things, let's not rush her, okay?'

'We deserve some answers,' Ari said.

'We do, but let's see how she is before we become too demanding. The Scott situation is the first that needs some answers. The journals and the information they contain can wait.'

'But—' Ari didn't get to finish her sentence before Gigi cut her off.

'No buts,' Gigi said. 'I'm simply asking you to wait until we know what impact the head injury has had. She's like to be disorientated and confused. Even regarding Scott. We'd be better to wait until she's fully functioning to ensure we get the truth.'

32

They arrived at the ICU within thirty minutes of receiving the call. Flo instructed the family to sit in the waiting area while she went to speak with the nursing staff and doctors. 'We won't all be able to go in and see her at once,' she reminded them. 'It'll probably be a maximum of two. So, Dad and Gigi to start, I think.'

'Not that prick,' her father said, startling them all with the venom in his voice.

Scott stood up from the chair he'd been waiting in when they arrived, took a step towards them, but stopped, no doubt sensing the anger emanating from Mike.

Flo glanced at Ari. 'I need to go and find out what's happening. Can you look after this?' She nodded from their father to Scott.

Ari nodded and took her father's arm as he stepped towards Scott, fists clenched. 'Dad,' she murmured. 'He has every right to be here.'

Mike stopped and turned to Ari. 'Until I hear the words from your mother's lips that this man is her *partner*, he has no right to be here. I'm her husband, her medical power of attorney, and I've been overly accommodating of this— this prick up until now. Either you ask him to leave, or I'll make him.'

Ari wasn't sure she'd ever seen her father so angry. She knew he was worried about her mother and doing his best to push everything other than her recovery from his mind, and this was spewing out as anger towards Scott. As far as they knew, Scott was as much a victim of their mother's deceptions as everyone else.

'Okay, let me deal with it.' She dropped his arm and beckoned to Scott. 'Can we have a word?'

Scott looked from Mike to Ari, nodded and followed her to the corner of the room.

'Dad's pretty upset that you're here. He's not going to let you see her. Can I ask if you'd mind giving us some space for the next hour or two? As soon as we know what's happening, I'll call you. I'll also make sure you can visit Mum once Dad's no longer in the building.'

Scott hesitated.

'Look, I know you want to be here, and you feel you have every right to be, but ultimately, Dad's got the say in this. Legally, you don't have a lot on your side right now. Yes, you might be having an affair with Mum, but the law will side with her husband for any medical decisions. You could probably fight for visitation rights and possibly win, but that's unnecessary, as you have that anyway. You just can't be here when he is.'

Scott managed a small smile. 'I guess I should listen as you obviously know the law.' He pushed a hand through his hair. 'I just don't want to leave her. I need to talk to her. Find out what on earth is going on.' He looked away, brushing his eyes with the back of his sleeve. 'Sorry, this is hard.'

'It's hard for all of us. Now, can I ask you to leave? I'll call you in an hour with an update, and then we'll go from there.'

Scott nodded. 'I'll go for a walk. There's no point going back to the hotel if I'm likely to see her this afternoon.'

It was on the tip of her tongue to tell him that seeing Julia today would be unlikely, but she didn't. She'd give him an update in an hour when she had a better picture of what was happening.

She watched as he walked out of the ICU waiting area towards the lift before rejoining her father and Gigi.

* * *

Flo returned about five minutes later with ICU outfits for all of them. 'We can visit two at a time,' she said. 'She's conscious but disorientated, so don't expect much at this stage. I know we've all got a lot of questions for her, but like Gigi said earlier, today's probably not the day to ask them. Let's see how she is, and we'll go from there.'

'You go in with your father,' Gigi said to Flo. 'Ari and I can go in second.'

'Are you sure?' Flo asked.

Gigi nodded. 'There's no hurry. The main thing is she's waking up.'

'You, okay?' Ari asked Gigi after Flo helped her father put on the ICU scrubs and disappeared into Julia's room.

'Worried,' Gigi said. 'Very worried as to how this is all going to turn out. It feels like this family is imploding.'

Ari couldn't disagree with that. While she would respect her grandmother's request and not rush in demanding explanations from her mother about the contents of her journals, she couldn't imagine any scenario moving forward where she or Flo would forgive her. But right now, that wasn't what Gigi needed to hear. She took her grandmother's hand and squeezed it. 'I keep trying to think of some way this all turns out okay, but no matter which angle I look at it, I can't see a positive outcome.'

'The Scott Cohen situation is the most worrying,' Gigi said. 'I'm devastated for your father, to be honest. For all of us.'

'I'm praying Mum's going to deny it all, that there's some logical explanation,' Ari said. 'Again, not that I can even begin to imagine what that would be, but I'm holding on to a sliver of hope.'

'We all are,' Gigi said. 'You know, her friend Heather came around to see me the other night. Such a lovely woman. Brought a small lasagne and a quiche, worried that I might not be eating.'

'I should message her,' Ari said. 'Let her know that we're here and Mum's waking up.' She reached into her bag for her phone, glancing at Gigi as she did. 'Is there anyone else we should let know?'

Gigi frowned. 'Not that I can think of. If she has friends or colleagues in Canberra, Scott can let them know once he's spoken with her.'

The reference to the Canberra friends made Ari think of the elderly neighbour, Bridie. She should probably let her know, although she might be better to wait until they knew the extent of Julia's injuries before getting the older lady's hopes up.

33

A knot tightened in Flo's stomach as she watched her father take her mother's hand. The breathing tubes and equipment had been removed, and Julia's eyes were closed. She looked pale and vulnerable in the hospital bed. As much as Flo wanted to shake her and demand answers, there was part of her that felt sorry for her mother, too. She'd been involved in an awful accident, an induced coma, and was about to face the firing squad.

She held her breath as her mother's eyes flickered open.

'Mum? It's me, Flo. You're in the hospital. You were in an accident.'

Julia stared at her before shifting her gaze to her husband. Her eyes flared wide, and Flo couldn't determine whether it was anger or shock. Her mother pushed his hand away.

'Julia, it's Mike. Oh, thank goodness you're awake. I've been so worried about you.'

Her mother opened her mouth, but no words emerged.

'Mum, you might find it difficult to talk,' Flo said. 'You had a car accident and have been in an induced coma for the past few weeks. The doctors had an endotracheal tube down your throat, which will leave your throat dry and sore, and your muscles will be weak too. There's no hurry to try and talk. It will all come back over the coming days.'

Julia gave a small shake of her head, her eyes wide as she stared at Mike.

He looked to Flo. 'Do you think she knows who I am? She looks freaked out to see me.'

He was right. She did look freaked out.

'Perhaps we should give her some space.' Flo turned her attention back to her mother. 'Mum, do you want us to go?'

Julia looked at Flo and gave a small shake of her head.

'Okay, she wants us to stay,' Flo said, but then Julia turned her focus to Mike and gave a small nod.

'You want Dad to go?'

Julia nodded again.

Flo looked at her father, the shock on his face evident.

'I guess I should leave the room?'

Flo nodded. 'For now. Keep in mind she's disorientated, and it will take some time for her to be thinking straight again. It could be some days before she's back to normal.'

Mike nodded. 'Should I tell Ari or Gigi to come in?'

Flo looked to Julia, who gave a small nod of her head. 'I guess so.'

Mike hesitated, then left the room.

Flo took her mother's hand. 'You've had a rough few weeks,' she told her. 'We're not sure of the details, but you were involved in a car accident in Melbourne. You were driving James's car.'

Julia's eyes widened.

'Don't worry,' Flo assured her, 'Heather's not worried about the car. She's worried about you. You had a nasty head injury, which is why you were placed in a coma to allow the swelling to go down. You also broke your tibia and a rib and have quite a few cuts and bruises. That's all mending nicely, though.' She smiled, realising that regardless of everything that was going on behind the scenes, her immediate reaction was relief that her mother was awake.

'Mum?' Ari said, entering the space. She looked to Flo. 'Is she okay? Dad said she didn't want him in here. He's pretty upset.'

'It's likely she's confused,' Flo said. 'Best to do what she says for now. She's not talking. She's communicating with nods and shakes of her head. Yes and no questions are, therefore, the best, but we need to be careful not to tire her. The medical team will be back to run tests soon.'

'You've had us worried,' Ari said. 'Are you in pain?'

Julia gave a small shrug.

Flo could see Ari struggling not to ask the many questions she was obviously dying to ask.

'Gigi's here too,' Ari said. 'She's been worried, as we all have. Is she okay to visit?'

Julia opened her mouth and flinched. She closed it and gave another small nod of her head.

'There's a man here too,' Ari said.

'Ari!' Flo couldn't believe Ari was going to mention him now. This revelation was likely to give her mother a heart attack. They should at least wait a few days.

Ari ignored her. 'A man by the name of Scott Cohen.'

Confusion registered in Julia's eyes.

'Do you know him?'

Julia nodded.

'He'd like to visit you. Is that okay?'

Julia looked from Ari to Flo, then nodded.

Flo sucked in a breath. Her mother had asked her father to leave but was okay with Scott Cohen visiting. This was not looking good.

Despite the 'two visitors at a time' rule, Gigi crept quietly into the room. Tears filled her eyes the moment she saw Julia staring at her. 'Oh, thank goodness.' She placed her hand on top of Julia's. 'You've had me so worried.'

Julia managed a small, apologetic smile.

'All of us have been worried,' she added. 'Hon, Mike's upset in the waiting room. Said you didn't want to see him. Are you sure? He's been here every day by your side, willing you to wake up. I can call him back in if you've made a mistake?'

Julia shook her head. There appeared to be no mistake. She closed her eyes.

'We'll stay a few more minutes, Mum. We can see how exhausted you are,' Flo said.

Julia gave another slight nod but didn't open her eyes.

* * *

A few minutes later, they regrouped in the waiting area.

'Did she say anything else?' Mike asked.

'Nothing. Just a few nods and headshakes,' Flo said. 'It's likely she'll have no recollection of us visiting and certainly no recollection of telling Dad not to visit. It'll take time. Dad, why don't you drive Gigi home? I'll stay a bit longer and see what the doctors say after they've run some tests this afternoon. We can come back again tomorrow and try again then.'

Mike stood, the strained expression in his eyes and cheeks no longer as prominent. His relief that Julia was awake appeared to outweigh the potential complications that lay ahead. 'I'm happy to follow your lead. If she's confused like you say she is, then it's probably more overwhelming than anything. We've been patient for the last few weeks. A few more days won't hurt.'

'Did you want me to stay with you?' Ari asked Flo.

Flo was surprised at the offer from Ari, but knowing what Ben had said to her, she hoped that it was a sign that her sister was getting closer to the point of being able to talk. 'No, I'm good, but can we have a quick word?'

They moved out of Mike and Gigi's hearing.

'What are you going to do about Scott?' Flo asked.

'I'll let him know that she's awake, can't speak, but said he could visit. I'll tell him to make sure it's this afternoon while we're not here and that we'll let him know when it's best to visit next. We can't have him and Dad here at the same time.'

'Why do you think Mum said no to seeing Dad, but Scott could visit? That doesn't make any sense.'

'It probably makes sense to her,' Ari said. 'Who knows what bombshells she's going to drop when she's ready to talk? Now, I'll go with Gigi and Dad, and I'll call Scott from the car when I'm on my own. Let's not tell Dad she wants to see him.' She hesitated as if she had something else to say but thought better of it and turned away from Flo and rejoined her father and Gigi.

Flo said quick goodbyes to her father and Gigi and then went in search of more information from the medical team.

* * *

It was over an hour later that Flo was sitting back beside her mother's bedside, waiting for Julia to wake again. The medical team had run a few tests and confirmed what Flo already knew; that Julia was likely to be exhausted and disorientated and they would need to give her a few days, possibly longer until they could tell what long-term damage, if any, had been done.

Flo hadn't realised her own eyes had flittered shut until she felt a hand rest on her shoulder. She opened her eyes to find Heather smiling at her.

'Sorry to wake you. I came as quickly as I could when Ari texted. How's Julia?'

'Exhausted,' Flo said. 'She's not talking yet but was able to communicate through a few nods and shakes of the head. She looked horrified when I told her she'd had an accident in James's car, so I expect you'll get an apology and an explanation when she does wake up properly.'

'That's the least of my worries,' Heather said. 'All that matters right now is getting her better and back to Mike. He's been so distraught through all of this.'

'I have to go and pick up Kayden. Did you want to stay with Mum for a while?'

'No.' The word came out as a faint croak but was a clear no.

Both women turned their heads to look at Julia. Her eyes were closed, her face strained, confirming she'd put a lot of effort into enunciating the word.

'Mum,' Flo said, 'did you want Heather to leave?'

There was no response.

Flo picked up her mother's hand. 'If you have the energy and would like Heather to leave, give my hand a squeeze.'

Flo registered the faintest of squeezes.

'If you'd like me to leave, give my hand a squeeze.'

Again, the faintest of squeezes.

'Okay, we'll leave you to rest and be back tomorrow.' Flo leaned down and kissed her mother's cheek. 'Love you.' Flo wished she could retract the words the moment they left her lips. She wasn't sure her mother was deserving of any of their love right now.

She indicated for Heather to follow her out of the ICU.

'She asked for both of us to leave?' Heather asked.

Flo nodded. 'She's exhausted and needs time to rest. She asked Dad to leave earlier, too. It's unlikely she has any idea of what she's asking for.'

'Do you think it would be okay to come back tomorrow?'

'I was going to say yes, but seeing how tired she got today with visitors, I'd suggest we don't overdo it during the next few days. She'll be moved to the ward later today or tomorrow, and while they're more lenient on visitors, we need to let her rest. If you're happy to wait a day or two, I can let you know when she's ready to see you.'

Heather drew Flo into a hug. 'You've been through a lot the past few weeks. How are you?'

Flo closed her eyes, grateful for Heather's warmth. She withdrew and opened her eyes. 'I'm doing okay. If we can get to the bottom of this situation with Mum, then hopefully things can return to some kind of normal.'

Heather hesitated, and in that moment, Flo could have kicked herself. How could they not have thought to ask Heather? 'You know something, don't you?'

Heather averted her eyes from Flo's.

The realisation was as if she'd been slapped. 'Mum's had you covering for her for years, hasn't she?'

Heather looked startled. 'What, no, of course not. I love all of you as much as I love your mum. I'd never do anything to hurt any of you.'

'But you knew about Scott?'

'I didn't know she was in a relationship with Scott,' Heather said. 'But she has mentioned him from time to time. I thought he was a friend of hers. Someone from work. She never elaborated, and you know what Julia's like. She's only going to tell you what she's happy for you to hear.'

'How long do you think they've been *friends* for?'

'I honestly don't know,' Heather said.

'He says fifteen years. Can you believe she'd do something like that?'

'I'd like to say no,' Heather said, 'but Julia is the one friend I can honestly say I don't know all that well. She puts her walls up and is a closed book most of the time. Some of that is, of course, because she can't discuss her work, but I think that's the way she likes to do things. She's the only person who can tell us what's been going on, and that, of course, is only *if* she chooses to.'

* * *

Ari called Scott from the car on the way home and confirmed that, yes, Julia had said she would be happy to see him. The relief he conveyed sent shivers down Ari's spine. It was one thing for the two of them to be having some kind of relationship, but the fact their mother had kicked their father out of the room and wanted to see Scott was more alarming than she cared to admit. Things weren't looking bright for their family unit.

Scott said he would call the hospital and check if he could visit that afternoon, and if not, he would clear it with Ari the following day before going in so as not to run into Mike.

Ari sighed as she ended the call. Their mother's actions moving forward were going to determine what happened to their family. She guessed that that was no different than it had been all along. Her phone pinged with a text. She smiled as she saw the caller ID light up as *Sven*. She probably should change that at some point to Ryan, but she had to admit, it made her smile every time she saw it.

> Had a great time last night. Can we do it again soon? x

She stared at the message. She'd had a great time, too, so why was she hesitating? Thoughts of her mother and Flo crossed her mind, and she quickly dismissed them. But then, an image of Ben entered her mind. He was a great guy, and she'd not appreciated what she'd had back then. She'd put work ahead of her marriage and made a mess of it. Was that why she was hesitating, or was it because she felt so lost right now? Her family was imploding, and she had no idea what she wanted when it came to work. It was a terrible time to consider adding a new relationship into the mix. Her phone pinged again.

> I bet you're way overthinking this. 'Yes, a drink would be nice,' is fine. x

Ari smiled again. In the short time she'd spent with Ryan, he seemed to get her. She quickly typed into her phone.

> Yes, a drink would be nice. Later in the week if that suits you. Have a few busy days.

> Sounds good. Let's aim for Thurs. I'll message Wed night to see if it still suits you.

Ari's smile widened. Ryan was a pleasant distraction amongst everything else that was going on.

34

Flo dropped Kayden at school, waved, and rejoined the line of traffic. Her shifts this week enabled her to do the morning school run. Ben had offered to pick Kayden up each day, which felt strange, but with everything going on, Flo knew she couldn't ask Gigi or her father.

She'd had mixed feelings when she'd arrived at Ben's parents' house to collect Kayden the previous night. He'd had a wonderful day with Della and Ben and, from what she observed when she picked him up, had been thoroughly spoilt by his new grandparents.

They'd greeted her warmly, although she could tell Ben had asked them to. She'd made a point of speaking with Susan, Ben's mother.

* * *

'I don't expect you to forgive me,' she said. 'It was a terrible thing to do to Ben and to all of you. I do want you to know that I'm sorry, and I hope we can move forward from this. I know Kayden is excited to get to know you.'

Susan didn't mince her words. 'Flo, we're heartbroken for Ben that he missed out on those early years, but we also recognise that if you had told him, he wouldn't have gone to London. He wouldn't have experienced the love he had with Carrie, and we wouldn't have Della. So, while you did the wrong thing, it's not our place to judge you. All we can say now is that we hope you won't stand in the way of Ben sharing access to Kayden with you.'

'I won't.'

'Because,' Susan said, 'I do understand how hard this must be for you. Know that we'll love him like we do Della, and ensure he feels that love from us. How's Ari taken all of this?'

'Badly,' Flo admitted. 'She's refusing to talk to me about it. I'm hoping she'll come around, but I'm not convinced she will.' She sighed. 'And I don't blame her. It's made me even more apprecia-tive of Ben's reaction. I certainly don't deserve how wonderful he's been.'

Susan squeezed her arm. 'Ben losing Carrie helped put things in perspective for him. It's not something you'd wish on anyone, but it certainly makes him appreciate what he does have. As much as Kayden coming into her life has helped Della, it's helped Ben, too. When he first came home from London, he was a mess. He's done his best to hold it together for Della's sake, but it hasn't been easy. So, as much as you've been beating yourself up about the whole situation, know that it's also done some good. I also want to let you know that the Bombay bloodline comes from Pete's side of the family. The three who have it are all willing to start banking blood.'

Flo had to swallow down the large lump that had formed in her throat. It wasn't hard to see where Ben's generosity of spirit came from. She hoped it was a trait that Kayden had inherited.

At that moment, Kayden came racing out of the house with Della and a small Pomeranian at his heels. He flew into Flo's arms for a hug. 'I've had the best day ever,' he declared. 'Granny Sue made a delicious cake.'

Flo met Susan's eyes. 'Granny Sue?'

Susan shrugged. 'Della came up with it. So now I'm Granny Sue and Pete's Pappa Pete.' She laughed. 'We sound like cartoon characters, but that's fine. It'll probably change again next week. We don't mind what they call us as long as they're here with us.'

'Can Kaydey come again tomorrow?' Della asked. 'Maybe he could live with us now that he's ours.'

'Della!' Ben said. 'Kayden's not *ours*. He's his own person who we're lucky enough to also have as part of our family.'

'I have two families,' Kayden said proudly. 'Two families with yummy cakes. However, my other grandma isn't a good cook. She prefers to feed me carrots.'

Della giggled. 'That's why you should live here. We don't eat yucky food.'

Ben laughed. 'I'm not sure that's the best selling point, Del. Now, why don't you two go and get Kayden's bag while I speak to Flo for a minute.'

Della and Kayden ran off, and Susan followed them into the house.

'How's your mum?'

'Awake,' Flo said. 'But not up to talking yet. She's disorientated.'

'But that must be a good sign? That she's awake, I mean.'

'Let's hope so. I take it all went well today?'

Ben smiled. 'It did. He fits in perfectly. He's so polite. Mum's in heaven telling Della to practise her manners to be like Kayden. You've done such a good job with him.'

Flo wasn't sure why every time Ben praised her, she felt like bursting into tears.

'Now, what does your week look like? I'm working from home, so if I can be of any help taking Kayden to school or picking him up, let me know.'

Flo stared at him. 'Really?'

'Of course. If we can be a team with this, it will work. You work shifts, and I have heaps of flexibility because I work from home. My workday often starts after Della's in bed with the time difference between London and here, so my days can be quite free. I'd much rather have Kayden here than learn he was in after-school care.'

Flo nodded. So would she. 'Well, I'm working day shifts this week. That means I can drop him off at school. He'd normally go to Gigi a few afternoons and after-school care on the other days, but I think Gigi's got too much to handle right now. If you'd like to have him on her days, that would be great.'

'Let me have him every day,' Ben said. 'Honestly, Della will love it too. She's at kindergarten for a few hours tomorrow and Wednesday, and we can walk down and meet Kayden after school. It's only a ten-minute walk from here. I can drop him over to you once you get home. Let me feed him when Della eats, and then all you'll need to do is the bedtime stuff.'

'I don't know what to say.'

'Say yes. I'm not doing you a favour, Flo. He's my kid, remember? I'm being his dad.'

Flo nodded, the lump that had appeared in her throat earlier growing even bigger.

'Hey, bud,' Ben said as Kayden and Della came racing back out of the house, the fluffy dog on their heels once more. 'How would you feel if Del and I picked you up after school each day this week and brought you back home with us? You and Del can play, and after dinner, I'll take you back home once your mum gets home from work.'

Kayden's eyes lit up, and he turned to Flo. 'Am I allowed to?'

She nodded.

He turned back to Ben. 'Do you think Granny Sue would make another cake?'

Ben laughed. 'I'm sure she will. What do you think about coming to us after school?'

Kayden's smile widened. 'Yes, please.'

Della threw her arms around Kayden in delight, and he hugged her back. 'You're the best brother I've ever had,' she said. She'd then lowered her voice, but not low enough to avoid Flo's sharp hearing. 'Imagine when you get to live here all the time. You'll have your own room and everything.'

* * *

Now, as Flo accelerated onto the main road and headed towards the hospital, she wondered how it would all pan out. Of course, Kayden wasn't going to live with Ben all the time, but Della's words had hit home. There was a real possibility that in the not-too-distant future, he would spend more time with Ben and Della. He *would* have his own room, and he'd consider himself as much a part of their family as he did hers. She let out a loud sigh. She should feel happy for her son. At least one of his families was a loving, united group – a total contrast to her family, which was falling apart in a spectacular fashion.

* * *

Julia stared at the man holding her hand. Scott Cohen. She recognised him. She'd known him for years. She knew that. But how well did she know him?

He was caressing her hand as if they were intimate friends, but she was married, wasn't she? To Mike. No, that wasn't right either. Mike was her ex-husband. Although everyone was saying that wasn't the case. They were happily married. At this stage, she had no idea.

'I was so worried, Jules. It took me two weeks to even track down where you were. Then I find you're here, and you're not divorced or estranged from your daughters like you'd led me to believe. It's all been quite a shock, to say the least.'

Jules. He was calling her Jules. That wasn't right. No one called her Jules, did they? Maybe they did. She closed her eyes. And estranged from her daughters... what was that about? Everything was so confusing. It was as if her memory had shut down and was a fuzzy mess. She recognised everyone, but what she was being told didn't sound right: that she was married *and* in another relationship.

And then there was Heather, asking her about her double life. What double life? She worked in Melbourne one week, and Canberra the other, and the detail of the work she did as a neuroscientist was confidential. She knew that. The only thing that was still out of reach was any information about what she'd been working on. And no one could tell her because it was top secret. If she hadn't felt so frustrated, she probably would have laughed at the irony of that.

'Do you remember the ski trip we took last winter?' Scott was saying. He fished out his phone and held up a photo for her to see. It was her, with Scott's arm around her and the snowy Alps in the background. She looked happy in the photo, so why couldn't she remember being there? And why would she choose to go skiing? She'd hurt herself at Thredbo that time and vowed she'd never risk breaking a bone again. Hadn't she? Maybe he'd talked her around. It was possible because even though she'd scared herself, she did love the freedom and exhilaration of flying down the slopes.

'Scott?'

Relief flooded Julia as Flo entered the room.

'Hi, Flo. Don't worry. I know your family will be here soon. I'll head off in about five minutes. I have to go back to Canberra for two nights,' he added. 'I was about to tell Julia. I don't want either of you to worry, but there were storms last night and the large gum tree in the back garden has come down. It's done some damage to the back verandah and to the roof of Julia's home office. I need to organise some repairs and check for other damage.'

Why was Scott going to her house? That didn't make any sense. And if there was damage, he didn't need to arrange repairs, the house wasn't hers. It belonged to her work.

She looked at Flo. 'Do I work for the Bureau of Strategic Intelligence?'

Flo smiled encouragingly. 'You remembered. Yes, you do. So does Scott.'

Scott works for Strategic Intelligence. Julia closed her eyes. He was a work colleague, and she had vague memories of sharing information with him about Project Enigma. She couldn't remember the details, but at least now she could place him. She opened her eyes. 'Then it's their house. We need to let them know.'

'She's right,' Flo said. 'You shouldn't be fixing it. They own the house.'

'I already contacted them,' Scott said. 'They're happy to arrange for someone to clear the tree away and fix the damage, but we need to inspect the internal damage and whether any of our valuables were affected so that they can be claimed on insurance.'

Our valuables. Julia tried to reach into the depths of her memory. She looked at this man, and he was familiar and friendly, but she wasn't attracted to him, and yet she was, apparently, in a relationship with him. She'd asked Heather, who at first had seemed cagey and not wanting to answer but had eventually said that yes, she was aware that Julia had worked with Scott for many years. She didn't know the details of the relationship, but Julia referred to him quite often. But Scott was saying they lived together. She wished her memory would return.

Scott leaned over and kissed her forehead. She shuddered. Surely that wouldn't be her reaction if she loved this man? Mind you, she'd felt the same when Mike had tried to hold her hand.

'I'll call you once I'm home with an update, and I'll be back here in two days. Okay?'

Julia nodded. There wasn't much else she could do. There was part of her that felt mildly sorry for him. He obviously loved her, and if the situation was reversed, she was sure she'd be devastated.

She waited until he left the room and let out a groan.

'Are you okay?' Flo was immediately by her side.

'I don't remember him being anything more than a work colleague,' Julia said. 'I can't believe I would have a whole other life in Canberra, other than the job that is. But why would he make this up? He's got nothing to gain from it.'

Flo looked away.

'What?' Julia asked. 'What aren't you telling me?'

'Ari went to your house. You do live with him. There are photos as you walk in; his clothes are in the closet, and his belongings are strewn throughout the house. Ari said the house was cosy and lived in.'

Julia gave a snort. '*Cosy and lived in*. Well, that hardly sounds like me, does it? You've been to visit, Flo. Would you say the house was cosy and lived in when you visited?'

'No, but we're assuming you removed all traces of him when we came.'

That silenced Julia. Eventually, she nodded. 'That would make sense. I do remember that I'm methodical, so if I was doing something so underhand, I'd do it to my best ability.'

'You don't remember him?'

'That's the thing. I do remember him from work. We worked on various projects together, and he's saying he was involved in Project Enigma. That's a bit hazy, but it will no doubt come back to me. But I don't think he's my *partner*, as he keeps saying. Only I don't understand why he'd say that if I wasn't. Maybe if I died and he wanted to claim my worldly goods, but that's a big gamble.'

'And they'd go to Dad, anyway, wouldn't they?'

'Mostly,' Julia said. 'I do have some items in a vault in Canberra that are worth something. But even if I was his partner, they wouldn't be going to him. My Will is clear as to where they go.'

'And where's that Will?'

'I have two Wills. That one's with a solicitor in Canberra. If something happens to me, there are clear instructions left with the Human Resources department. When an employee dies, there are certain things that need to be processed internally. We have a vault for our belongings, and HR goes through it. I have a file with all the numbers they need, including the solicitor's.' She frowned. 'How come I can remember that and can't remember that I'm having an affair and can't remember what I actually *do* for my job?'

'You've had a head injury. Partial memory loss isn't uncommon and is often temporary. Now, should I be contacting the solicitor to let him know you've had an accident?'

'I'm still alive, so probably not.' She frowned. 'You know, I can't remember the solicitor's name. That's strange.'

'You can't remember your relationship with Scott,' Flo said, 'so why would you expect to remember the solicitor?'

Julia remained deep in concentration. 'I don't know. It's like my brain isn't quite working. It's foggy or something.'

'You've been in a coma,' Flo said. 'You may find it takes a bit longer for everything to get back to normal.'

'If anything happens to me, contact Human Resources, and they'll give you the solicitor's information.'

'Okay, will do.'

'Are you okay, Florence?'

'What do you mean?'

'You don't seem quite yourself. You're saying all the right things, but there's an edge to your voice, and your body language tells me you're here out of obligation.'

'We all want some answers, Mum, that's all. Until you get your memory back, we might all seem a little upset.'

Julia nodded. 'That's understandable. This situation with Scott is highly unusual. But is there something else going on?'

'What, this isn't enough for you?'

'I get the feeling that there's something no one is telling me. Arabella had an edge to her the other day, and you do, too.'

'All evidence suggests you've been having an affair for years. You don't think that gives us the right to have an *edge*?'

Julia's eyes narrowed. 'It does, of course. But I feel like there's more. I know you two girls, Florence, and I'm sure there's something else.'

Flo remained silent, causing Julia to sigh.

'If there's an issue, I can only do something about it if I know what it is.'

Flo didn't respond. Instead, she looked at her watch. 'I'd better go. I think Gigi said she'd be coming to visit a little later. Why don't you try and get some rest? It's the best thing for you right now.'

* * *

Julia wasn't sure if rest was the best thing for her. What she needed was her memory back. Reading people's behavioural patterns and emotions was something she was good at. She was a neuroscientist, so it made sense that this was an area of expertise. Flo was giving off a vibe that was full of emotion. Full of questions and anger.

'Hello, love.'

Julia glanced up as her mother shuffled through the door. So much for her coming in later. She must have passed Florence on her way out. Gigi looked terrible. She was thinner than Julia remembered, her face tight and drawn, and she had large bags under her eyes.

'How are you holding up?'

'Mum, I should be asking you that. Are you okay? You don't look the best.'

'It's been a worrying time,' Gigi said. 'First the accident and then the Scott Cohen situation. But this isn't about me. We need to get to the bottom of what's been happening with you.'

'I wish I knew, myself,' Julia said. 'I wish I could remember. Did you see Florence? She just left. She's angry and emotional towards me.'

Gigi sat down in the seat next to the bed, her eyebrows raised. 'No, I missed her. What did she say?'

'Nothing, it was all in her manner. I asked her if there was more than the Scott situation, but she wouldn't elaborate.'

'I think the Scott situation is enough for everyone right now. She also had a bit of a scare with Kayden when you were first brought into the hospital. He needed a blood transfusion, and that created issues of its own when they found out he has a rare blood type.'

'Rare blood type?'

Gigi nodded. 'One of the rarest.'

'But they were able to get him blood?'

'This time, but the plan is that his father will donate, and it will be stored.'

Julia's heart rate increased. 'Father? But we don't know who that is.'

Gigi fell silent, her face giving away that she was debating whether to say more.

'What aren't you telling me?'

Gigi sighed. 'I wasn't going to burden you with any of this until you were fully recovered. But we know who Kayden's father is. Flo had to ask him for blood.'

Julia closed her eyes, wishing the bed could swallow her. She'd tried her best to protect Flo and Ari's relationship, and she could only imagine what damage this had done. She opened her eyes and met her mother's. 'How's Ari taking it?'

'Not the best. She's not speaking to Flo.'

'That's fair enough and explains the icy vibes.'

'I asked everyone to let you recover before bombarding you with questions, but how could you?'

Julia had to avert her eyes from the pain she saw in Gigi's. She hated that she was the one causing all this upset.

'How could you advise Flo to do something so deceptive? For Ben to miss out on the opportunity of being a father and for Flo to live with the burden of deception.'

'It was simple,' Julia said. 'I couldn't bear the thought of Ari going through the trauma that learning what Flo had done would cause her. I knew it would break her heart, and I wasn't going to stand by and watch that happen.'

'But encouraging her to lie had such awful consequences.'

'Only because the truth came out. I know how awful it sounds, but if Kayden didn't have a rare blood type, no one would be any the wiser. I'd do the same thing if it happened again.'

Gigi dropped her gaze from Julia's. 'I'm shocked you'd tell such lies. As Aunt Mary always said, the truth hurts for a little while, but lies can hurt forever. I'm worried that there will be no forgiveness from Ari on this. That the hurt will last forever.'

Julia froze, her breath catching in her throat. That saying – *the truth hurts for a little while, but lies can hurt forever* – had been one of Gigi's older sister's favourites. She was transported back to the night of her eighth birthday. The night her mother and Aunty Mary had thought she was asleep. But how could she sleep? Her father had taken his last breaths that afternoon on the side of the road in what she'd imagined was a tangled mess of metal. But she'd overhead Aunty Mary and Gigi talking, and Aunt Mary had said those exact words to her mother.

She gasped for air, her heart suddenly racing.

Gigi's face filled with alarm. 'What's wrong? Shall I get the nurse?'

Julia shook her head, doing her best to settle her breathing as she gulped in the air.

Gigi got to her feet. 'Julia, you're scaring me. You're white as a sheet. I'm going to get someone.'

Julia reached out and grabbed her mother's arm as she turned. 'No. Sit.'

Gigi hesitated, then did as she was told.

Julia closed her eyes, her heart still racing, but she managed to get her breathing under control. She took a deep breath, opened her eyes, and focused on her mother's now-ashen face.

'*You* lied.'

35

The two women sat staring at each other. Julia repeated her words. 'You lied. The most horrific thing that's ever happened to me in my life, and you lied.'

'I have no idea what you're talking about.'

'Dad. The night of the accident. You and Aunt Mary were talking. I heard everything.'

The colour drained from Gigi's face.

'You lied to me about Dad. There was no car accident.'

Gigi's lower lip began to tremble. 'You've known all this time?'

'No. I mean, I guess, yes, I must have, but I must have blocked it out. It's as if those words Aunty Mary used to say about lying triggered my memory.' She sank back against the pillows and closed her eyes, conscious of a tear rolling down her cheek. 'How could you?'

Gigi took Julia's hand, but she snatched it away.

'Julia, I couldn't tell an eight-year-old that her father committed suicide on any day, but especially not on her birthday. It's been bad enough that every birthday we've had the memory of his death. What would you have thought if you'd known that it wasn't an accident? That it was a deliberate act?'

Julia opened her eyes. 'I would have thought that he didn't love me.'

Gigi nodded. 'But he did. When he returned from Vietnam, he was battling demons.' She sighed. 'When I think back, I realise how low he was and that it's unlikely he'd even remembered your birthday. He wouldn't have done that to you if he had.'

'But he still killed himself.'

'He did. And I've never forgiven myself. I should have seen how much he was hurting.'

Julia stared at her mother, who'd clearly blamed herself for the past fifty-eight years for her husband's death. 'Have you ever spoken to anyone about what happened?'

'Mary.'

'I meant a professional, not your sister,' Julia said. 'It wasn't your fault, and they could probably have helped you see that.'

Gigi shrugged. 'I doubt it. I was busy socialising with my friends, working, and raising you, and I didn't give Ted the attention he needed. I should have been a better wife. I would have noticed if I was.'

'Is that why you never explored another relationship?'

Gigi nodded. 'I couldn't risk missing the signs again.' She wiped a tear from her cheeks. 'I'm not going to apologise for not telling you. I thought it was the right thing then, and I still do now. It was an awful time, Julia, that's all I can say.'

'Just as awful as Ari learning what Flo did would have been,' Julia said. 'Perhaps now you can understand why I thought it was the right thing then and *I* still do now.'

Gigi wiped her eyes again. 'I think I'm beginning to understand, but I am sorry that you overheard us and didn't feel that you could tell me. No eight-year-old should have had to live with that.'

They fell silent as they both thought back to that night fifty-eight years ago.

After some time had passed, Gigi reached for Julia's hand. This time, she didn't pull hers away.

'I think a lot of your actions stem from that night,' Gigi said.

'How do you mean?'

'I mean, that you've spent the last thirty-six years directing your girls along pathways that set them up for success and minimised any chance of them getting hurt.'

'Because of Dad?'

Gigi nodded. 'I'm sure any psychologist worth their weight would tell you that while you had no control over what happened to your dad, you've made sure you've had full control over what has happened with your daughters and their lives. The only thing is, while you might have been doing it out of love, I'm not sure they'll see it that way, and I'm not sure they'll ever forgive you.'

* * *

Flo waited until she was home to call Ari. Ben wasn't dropping Kayden home until seven, so she decided to make use of the spare half hour. She sent Ari a text in advance of calling her, hoping her sister would pick up and have a conversation.

> Need to speak to you about Mum and her Will.
> Would you be open to discussing?

Ari called her moments later. She offered no greeting or pleasantries and just dove straight into questioning Flo. 'What do you mean she has another Will in Canberra?'

'It's what she told me. In a vault in Canberra there's information that's important if she dies and one of the items on that list is the name of her solicitor. It seemed a bit strange, that's all. I asked her if she wanted me to contact her solicitor to advise him or her of her situation, but she said no, as she wasn't planning to die, but also couldn't remember their name.'

Ari was silent.

'Ar?'

'Sorry, I'm thinking. It's strange that she doesn't have everything in one place. It is possible to have multiple Wills, but you must be clear that they refer to different assets. Sometimes, people do it if they want different executors to deal with different assets. Knowing how anal Mum is about everything, I'm sure she would have covered her bases. Does Dad know about this other Will and whatever the assets are?'

'I don't know,' Flo said. 'I'll check with him and get back to you. Look, I'd better go. Kayden will be home any minute. With your legal background, I thought you might want to know.'

'Okay, thanks.'

Silence hung over the phone line. Flo took a deep breath.

'Ben mentioned that he spoke to you last week about what happened.'

'And?'

'And, I wondered if there was any chance we could talk. Try and move past it.' Flo closed her eyes as a snort clearly reverberated down the phone line. 'Okay, sorry. I shouldn't have asked.'

The click of the phone call ending confirmed that, no, she shouldn't have.

* * *

Ari threw her phone onto the desk in front of her. It had been on the tip of her tongue to ask Flo how things were going for Kayden with Ben, but she couldn't. Part of her wished she could move past it, but every time Flo mentioned either of them, she felt like a dagger was being driven into her heart.

Her phone rang, and she was tempted to ignore it but saw *Sven* light up on the caller display. 'Hey, you! I wasn't expecting to hear from you until Wednesday night.'

'Hey, yourself. That was the plan, but I was thinking of you and wondering how you're going. So, as my life motto of trying to live in the moment directs me, I decided there was one way to find out how you're doing. Hence the call.'

'How am I going? I'd say an accurate description is that I'm being quite unreasonable. You?'

Ryan laughed. 'That's an interesting self-assessment. What unreasonable things are you currently doing?'

Ari sighed. 'Usual stuff. Refusing to talk to my sister. Making her life more miserable than it probably already is.' She glanced at her watch. She was home early, and it was only a few minutes after six-thirty. 'Hey, are you teaching tonight? There's a class at seven-thirty, isn't there?'

'Sure is. Don't tell me you're going to come!'

'Don't have a heart attack, but I am. I need to start listening to your advice about switching off and relaxing. I thought running did that for me, but it doesn't. I ruminate the entire time about whatever problem I'm fixated on. But I didn't find that when I did your yoga class.' She laughed. 'I was so fixated on the heat and trying not to pass out that I didn't have time to reflect on anything else.'

'Come on over,' Ryan said. 'I'll warm up a mat for you.'

Ari smiled as she ended the call.

* * *

'It's no wonder you're feeling so stressed,' Ryan said a few hours later after the yoga class had finished. Ari had stayed behind when the rest of the class left and was enjoying chai tea with Ryan.

'We promised my grandmother we'd hold off on the questions for Mum until she's got her memory back, assuming she gets it back. It's probably better for her if she doesn't. She's going to be facing the equivalent of a firing squad.'

Ryan ran his finger around the top of his teacup, deep in thought.

'What are you thinking about?'

'I'm trying to work out a motivation for your mother's lies. There's the other guy, and then there's covering up your sister's pregnancy and the journals. It's all extreme. Are you sure she works for the Strategic Intelligence place, or is that made up too? A cover for whatever it is she really does.'

Ari laughed. 'Your thought process is as bad as mine's been the past few weeks. I've had so many bizarre thoughts pop into my head about who she is. But no, she does work there. I spoke with Human Resources yesterday to see if there was a chance of accessing some of her belongings that are stored in a vault.'

'And?'

'They said no. Not while she's alive. If she was dead, I could possibly, depending on how her Will is left.'

'I think it will be easier to ask her,' Ryan said. 'If she can't remember then she'd be able to speak to HR about accessing her own files. And is avoiding your sister the long-term plan?'

'Possibly. I don't know if I can ever trust her again.'

'I get that. My brother let me down a few years ago,' Ryan said. 'Stole some money from me and denied it. We found out it was him. He was caught up with drugs and gambling and not in a good place. I walked away from him, but he got himself cleaned up and asked forgiveness. When I hear myself talk about it, it sounds like a no-brainer. The guy cleaned himself up. Of course, he should be forgiven. But the reality is, he's been in and out of trouble and lied and stolen from me and my parents since he was a teenager. This wasn't a one-off event, and most likely won't be the last time he lets us down.'

'What did you do?'

'A lot of soul searching. My dad has written him off. He's no longer welcome at the family home or at any family gatherings. Mum's devastated, but she understands. He's doing it to protect them from being hurt again. He doesn't think Mum can handle another round.'

'And you?'

'I thought about how I'd feel if something happened to him. I realised that even though he'd let me down, I know there's part of him that loves me, and there's part of him that hates himself for what he does. So, while I don't like him at times, I would miss him if he was gone. Understanding that told me that I shouldn't wait until it was too late, and I forgave him. I'm still wary of him, I'll admit, but I make a point of catching up with him for a meal a few times a month.'

Ari thought about what he'd said. 'I'd miss Flo if she wasn't around. We all would.' That was an understatement – she'd be devastated.

Ryan smiled. 'Then that might ultimately be as much as you need to know. You're hurting, and it will take some time, but if your heart's telling you that one day you'll have a relationship again, then don't wait too long in case it's too late.' He wiped his brow in mock exhaustion. 'This is all a bit heavy for what, our third date?'

Ari raised an eyebrow. 'This is a date, is it?'

'Definitely, and I intend to kiss you in a minute, so you have no doubt that it is.'

A tingle of anticipation ran up Ari's spine.

'Okay,' Ryan said. 'We've talked about your mum and your sister, and the last agenda item...' he grinned '...before I can kiss you, is work. Tell me more about why you're feeling so underwhelmed by your job.'

'We can pass on the work stuff, if you like?' Ari raised her eyebrows suggestively.

Ryan groaned. 'No, I know it's something that's affecting you, so let's see what we can do to help in that area before we move on. When I do kiss you, I want your total focus on that and not on work or anything else.'

Ari laughed, enjoying the build-up he was creating. 'It's funny,' she said, 'but I'd already been feeling restless at work, and then to read Mum's journals and see how many of my decisions were influenced by her took the level of dissatisfaction up a notch. On paper, I'm quite successful, but reading the journals makes me think it's Mum's success, not mine. I'm beginning to wonder if I've ever made a decision in my life without her influence.'

Ryan reached across and took her hand. 'Does she know about me?'

'Not yet.'

'Then there's one decision you've made without her. One of your best decisions.'

Ari smiled. 'I'd have to say I'm beginning to agree with you on that one.'

'And,' Ryan continued, 'you're no doubt selling yourself way too short. Even if your mum helped you find your pathway into law, it's not like she's sitting next to you during every case telling you what to do. You're good at your job because you have talent and ambition. Without those two things, it wouldn't matter what your mother suggested. You wouldn't get far, especially in law. You may find that the restlessness is a signal that you need a change, nothing more.'

'You think?'

'I do. Five years ago, I was feeling like you. Working long hours, beginning to question the point of it all.'

'So, you walked away from the financial markets.'

'Not initially. To start with, I took six months' leave without pay and travelled. I went to some remote parts of Thailand and Cambodia and volunteered on some housing projects. When I say housing projects, I mean helping to repair basic huts. It was hard work but rewarding and gave me a sense of purpose I hadn't previously had. I travelled around and experienced different places and people. It gave me a much better appreciation for what I have but also made me realise I couldn't go back to an industry that was looking to make the rich richer. So here I am, still trying to work out what my path should be but enjoying the journey as I do that.'

'Maybe I should do that,' Ari said. 'Take some time off and travel. Experience something new and see if it helps me work out what the next stage in my career should look like.'

Ryan intertwined his fingers with hers, lifted her hand to his lips and kissed it. 'I highly recommend it, and if you want a travelling companion, I'd love to experience something new with you.'

Ari leaned across the table, her head inches from his. 'There's nothing to stop those new experiences starting right now.' She leaned closer and their lips met.

36

Thoughts of Ari plagued Flo the next day as she willed her shift to end. She'd started at six, which meant she was able to finish before the end of the school day and collect Kayden. With him spending so much time with Ben recently, she'd been looking forward to an afternoon of the two of them.

Now, shortly after arriving home, she pushed all thoughts of Ari away as she waited for Kayden to change out of his school uniform. She knew she should have waited for her sister to extend the olive branch, but she'd been unable to help herself. Now, she wished she hadn't tried. Ari's reaction had left her feeling worse than if she'd said nothing at all.

'Mum.' Kayden came into the kitchen, his hand clutching his stomach. 'My belly's sore.'

Flo shot to her feet and hurried over to him. After the last time his belly was sore, she wasn't going to take any risks.

'Let's lie you down and give you a quick examination,' Flo said, putting an arm around him and helping him to the couch.

'I think I'm going to be sick.'

Flo grabbed the rubbish bin, thankful she'd emptied it earlier that morning, and held it in front of Kayden. He vomited and started to cry.

'Hey, it's okay,' she said, rubbing his back and helping him lie down once he'd finished. 'Now show me where your tummy hurts.' She was doing her best to stay calm and infuse her voice with as much of her confident nurse tone as she could, but her heart was racing. After the last episode that had landed Kayden in hospital, she was worried.

He clutched the lower right side of his abdomen and cried harder. This wasn't the same belly bloating as when she'd been called to the nurse's office at school.

'Let's take your temperature, and then we'll do a little test on your tummy before taking you to see a doctor. Okay?'

Kayden didn't answer but continued to cry.

Flo hurried to the kitchen cupboard and fetched the thermometer. She held it against his forehead and waited for the beep. 'Low-grade fever.' That wasn't a surprise. 'It isn't too bad, but you have got one. Now, I'm going to touch your belly for one moment, okay?'

Kayden continued crying but allowed her to pull up his shirt. She pressed the lower right side of his abdomen gently and then released it. Kayden's crying intensified, and he swatted at her hand.

'Sorry, hon, I had to check something. Now, I'm going to help you to our car, okay? We need to get you to the hospital. The pain in your tummy is common but does need some treatment.'

And quickly, she added in her own head. He was exhibiting textbook signs of appendicitis. Her heart rate continued to race as she helped him to the car. He couldn't sit properly, so she helped him lie across the back seat in a way that she was able to put a seat belt on him. They were less than ten minutes from Box Hill Hospital.

'Try to stop crying if you can,' Flo said as she backed out of the driveway. 'I know it hurts, but crying might make it hurt more.'

The volume reduced slightly, but the tears continued to flow.

Flo switched the car radio off the second Abba's 'Fernando' started to play. She wasn't sure she could *tackle anything* right at this moment and hadn't been able to stomach Abba since Ari had learned the truth about her and Ben. It was too much of a reminder of what she'd lost. Instinctively, she instructed her car navigation system to call Ari, and cancelled the call as quickly as she started. She didn't want to worry Gigi or her father and realised that on this occasion, she would have to do this herself. She didn't have the luxury of calling on family to be there for her.

The cries from the back seat caused a panicky feeling to rise within her. Assuming she was correct, and it was appendicitis, what did this mean for Kayden's thalassemia intermedia? It affected the immune system, so an operation would lead to the risk of infection. It also could result in blood loss, and another transfusion might be needed. There were other complications that Flo did her best to push from her mind. The thought of a blood transfusion reminded her that while she might not have a family to call on, Kayden did.

She instructed the navigation system to call Ben.

* * *

Ari had found herself unable to contain her smile as she stepped out of the lift at Premier Legal and into the company's foyer. What should have been a yoga class and a cup of tea the night before had turned into much more with Ryan, and it was after midnight when he'd insisted on driving home with her to ensure she got there safely. She'd spent the morning working from home in a much more leisurely fashion than she normally would.

'What's that smile for, Hudson?' Sophie asked, appearing from the staff kitchen that led off the main passageway that also connected Ari's office.

Ari grinned at her friend. 'Sven.'

Sophie raised an eyebrow. 'Really? You two hooked up?'

Heat flushed Ari's cheeks. 'Well, I wasn't expecting you to ask outright, but yes, it's possible. After yoga last night, we were talking, and one thing led to another.'

'That's fantastic news. Are you seeing him again?'

'Definitely.' Ari wasn't going to tell Sophie that she was seriously considering his suggestion of going travelling together. It was far too early to be having thoughts like that. But in comparison to the previous conversations she'd had with Sophie about Ryan, this time she was ready to admit she liked him. 'Thanks for the introduction. It's early days, but I feel like this could become something.'

Sophie squealed with delight and gave Ari a quick hug. 'You've made my day.' She glanced at her watch. 'But I need to go and meet my client. I'll drop by your office a bit later.' She winked. 'I want all the details about last night. I already have a picture cemented in my mind of a naked Sven, and you might need to fill in some blanks for me.'

'Sophie!' Ari said, laughing as she swatted her away. 'I would never kiss and tell... well... *tell* that much.'

She continued laughing as she made her way along the corridor to her office. It felt good to forget everything else and enjoy the moment.

Her moment was ruined as she pushed the door to her office open, and her phone rang. Flo's ringtone. She ignored it, equally annoyed by the call but also surprised that Flo rang off almost as quickly as she'd started the call. Perhaps she'd finally worked out that Ari wasn't ready to speak to her.

* * *

By late afternoon, Ari once again found herself distracted. She was thinking about her mother's situation with Scott Cohen, and an uneasy feeling crept into her gut. It was becoming a familiar feeling when she thought about her mother. One that, if it was work-related, would tell her she'd missed something. If this was one of her legal cases, she'd be going back through the files, combing through evidence and leaving no stone unturned. But this wasn't a case, and she wasn't sure what she was even looking for. She decided it wouldn't hurt to talk with her mother again.

She finished early and went to the hospital.

She was relieved that her mother was on her own, and there was no need to make small talk with Scott or any of her family.

'Mum,' Ari said as she sat next to her mother's hospital bed, 'when you had your accident, I flew to Canberra to check on your house and to see if I could find out any details as to why you were in Melbourne that day, and not back in Canberra. Do you remember why you were in Melbourne?'

Julia's eyes filled with pain, then she closed them.

'Mum?'

Ari waited, but Julia didn't reopen her eyes, so she continued. 'Do you remember when I drove you to the airport the day after your birthday?'

'Vaguely.'

'I asked you about a problem you were having at work, and you said it was something unusual, but you couldn't talk about it. You'd told Dad you were having trouble with someone but also didn't elaborate as to who or what the issue was.'

Julia pressed her lips together.

'I wondered if whatever it was had something to do with why you came back to Melbourne before you had your accident. I rang your work and they said you'd taken leave, so you weren't here for work.'

Julia stared blankly at Ari.

'Mum?'

'I'm trying to remember what it was. I get this sick feeling in my stomach every time I think about work. I can't figure out if I did something wrong or what was going on.'

'Have you asked Scott?'

Julia nodded. 'He says he has no idea. From what he knew, everything was better than alright before I had my accident. He and I were working on something rather big. I have vague recollections of the project, but that's all. Did I mention it to you?'

'You never talk about anything to do with work.'

'This wasn't technically a work project. It's something that I've been working on with Scott for years. We've had interest from an investor with talk of a buyout if the commercial viability is proven. I don't remember any of that, to be clear, but Scott's filled me in as much as possible.'

'At your birthday dinner, Dad mentioned you were having problems with a colleague at work,' Ari said. 'Was that Scott?'

Julia closed her eyes. 'I don't think so. I can't remember. When you say that I get a sick feeling in the pit of my stomach, but I have no idea why. I probably wouldn't have referred to Scott as a work colleague though.' She opened her eyes, her cheeks instantly reddening as she saw Ari's expression. 'Oh, yes, I guess I might have. See that pile of papers on that shelf?' Julia pointed to a shelf near the hospital's window. 'There's a newspaper amongst all of that. Can you bring it here?'

Ari moved from her chair and picked up the newspaper.

'Open it to page five,' Julia said. 'There's an article there that speaks about the project and how it could answer numerous questions about human behaviour and brain functionality.'

Ari opened the paper and scanned the headlines. 'Your project is really worth millions?' she asked after reading the information.

Julia nodded. 'Possibly. Not just my project though – it's mine and Scott's. There are no guarantees of course, but it appears that an official valuation will place it at quite a high value.'

'You don't seem excited.'

Julia shrugged. 'It's hard to be excited when my memory's so hazy. There's something about it that I can't put my finger on.'

'You probably need to give yourself a break,' Ari said. 'Your memory is likely to return soon, and then you'll be able to recall everything. Though surely Scott can tell you more about the project if you were working on it together?'

'He's shown me some of the research papers we've produced,' Julia said. 'I remember bits and pieces of the papers and snippets of conversation I've had with him about the project, but that's all. It all looks incredibly complicated, and I'm not sure my brain's going to allow me to get back to a place where it all makes sense. He says the commercial discussions have been postponed, but I'm not sure how I'll ever be able to have them if I don't remember.'

'Can Scott do the meetings?'

'He says he can, but he'd rather have me there. I guess we'll see how much time we can buy.'

'Have you given any thought to the Scott situation and what you're going to do?'

'Honestly, I want to bury my head in the sand,' Julia said. 'I still can't believe I've put myself in this situation. I know I'm struggling to remember things, but I feel like affairs and cheating aren't on my radar at all. Although—'

'Although, what?'

'I came back to Melbourne early for something, and every time I think of the affair, I get this awful churning in my stomach. I'm nauseous now, even thinking about it. So that's not normal, and

I'm concerned that my physiological reaction reflects my guilt. I've done enough study in this area to know that it's not unheard of for your brain to block out the memories of something you consider traumatic. However, the guilt might still manifest physiologically. If it wasn't so awful, I'd probably be writing up a report on all of this. If I was able to separate myself from it, I'd probably find it quite fascinating.'

'Do you think Project Enigma was going to be your undoing?'

'What do you mean?'

'Well, you said you'd been working on it for years with Scott, and he said your relationship turned into something more than colleagues because of that project. Now it's at a position where investors might get involved or you could be bought out. It's obviously massive, and once all that moves forward, it will probably garner a lot of publicity.'

Julia was silent as she thought about Ari's theory. 'It's possible, I guess. Regardless of the relationship, I can't get my head around the investor scenario. From what I remember, Enigma was a passion project. Not something built for commercial gain, just observations and data over many years. I can't remember exactly what Scott and I had planned. He's filled me in, but I'm surprised I wanted to go down the investor route as it would make the project and findings public and me accountable. I'm not sure I was ready for any of that. Maybe, if he and I were as close as he says, I'd changed my mind.'

'I think you need to assume that was the case. It's unlikely you could have kept your relationship with Scott secret with journalists poking around.'

'Although, let's assume I wasn't having an affair with him, and we were work colleagues who'd developed this study. There's no reason anyone would assume we were having an affair, would they? As I said, affairs are not even on my radar.'

'Mum, you live with Scott in Canberra, and whether affairs are on your radar or not, you've definitely been having one.'

The colour drained from Julia's face. 'And that's why I almost don't want my memory to return. I can't begin to imagine what I was thinking, but I'm pretty sure I'm going to despise myself once I know.'

* * *

Ari was surprised to feel a flicker of sympathy for her mother when she left her room. It was one thing to have to own up to your deceitful ways, but when they were a shock to you, too, that had to be hard. The fear on her mother's face as she contemplated her memory returning and learning what she'd been up to was uncharacteristic. Julia was known for being in total control of everything as her journals showed.

She wondered whether her mother would be as shocked if, and when, her memory returned, and she had the full knowledge of her motivations. Ari doubted she or the rest of the family would ever hear what those true motivations were.

She made her way to the lifts, debating whether to go back to the office or do some work from home. Her caseload was beginning to pile up, and she wasn't giving it the attention it currently needed. The lift opened, and Scott Cohen stood on the other side.

'Ari.' He smiled and stepped out. 'How's she going today? Any improvement on the memory?'

'Bits and pieces, but she's still grappling with the lies and deception side. How did you go in Canberra? Did you get the tree damage fixed?'

'Yes, it's all repaired. The damage to the furniture was minimal and it appears nothing of value was destroyed.' He rubbed a hand over his chin. 'Would you have a few minutes? It might be a bit unorthodox under the circumstances, but I'd love your advice on something.'

'Sure,' Ari said uneasily. 'There's a quiet area over by that window.' She pointed to the free space. 'Why don't we sit over there?'

'What's the issue?' she asked once they were seated.

'It's Project Enigma – the thing that we were working on as a side project,' Scott said. 'I'm not sure what to do. Julia only has vague recollections of the project, and there are meetings scheduled with investors in the coming weeks. I've done my best to delay them as I don't feel comfortable going ahead with them without Julia, but I'm also aware that it's an opportunity that, if she was her normal self, she wouldn't want to miss.'

'Who owns the intellectual property of Project Enigma?' Ari asked. 'Is there a contract in place?'

'No, it's only been Julia and me working on it to this point, and I don't think either of us thought it necessary to draw up a contract. I guess we figured if we were to sell it or have investors, we'd do it all then. Up until now, it's been more of a hobby than anything else.'

Ari frowned. 'My mother's not one for hobbies. I'm surprised she wouldn't have done everything properly.'

Scott cleared his throat. 'I know you don't want to hear this, but Julia and I were in love. We weren't thinking of commercial arrangements or contracts. We were excited by something we were creating together. We could see the applications the study has and the amazing contribution it could make. Neither of us were doing it for money. It's more about the notoriety and the status of our discoveries. I believe we would have made history. I still do.'

'Regardless, I'd recommend you have a contract drawn up before you speak with investors. To make sure it's all covered.

However, with Mum's current memory issues, she's not of sound mind to sign that. You'll have to wait and hope she does get her memory back.'

'Are you suggesting I postpone the investor meetings indefinitely?'

Ari nodded. 'Under the circumstances, I would recommend that yes, you do that. I'm sure they'd understand, with Mum having been in a coma and everything. But if they can't be postponed, is there any reason you can't attend them on your own?'

'I could, but now realising Julia is married, and not divorced like I thought, I feel her interests need to be represented. I don't want anyone to think I'm trying to take advantage of the situation. What if you stood in for her? I have the knowledge about the study, and you have the legal knowledge to make sure we go about things the right way.'

He flushed with embarrassment. 'Look, I'm not imagining there's going to be a happily-ever-after for Julia and me on a personal level, but we can't walk away from the work we've done. There's too much at stake. It's quite a breakthrough for neuroscience. When Julia's back to her full capacity, she can step back in, but until then, it would be good if someone she trusts was involved. If our personal relationship is over, I don't want anyone to think I'm taking advantage of Julia's current situation. While I can't get my head around what she's done, professionally, I've always had the utmost respect for her and would like to see the project through, if nothing else.'

'I'm not sure I'm the right person to talk to, Scott. I can see you're passionate about this project, but I'm still trying to digest the fact that my mother is a liar and a cheat and numerous other things that have come to light. In my professional capacity, I'd suggest you engage a lawyer and have your interests represented.

Feel free to give them my details and if they make contact, I'll be able to advise who's representing Mum. The one thing I do know for sure is, it won't be me.'

37

'Your diagnosis was correct,' the emergency doctor told Flo after Kayden had undergone tests including an ultrasound. 'We'd like to prep him for theatre to avoid any chance of rupture. There is a concern about his blood type. Have you had blood banked yet?'

Flo nodded. 'Yes, we have blood from his father. He's on his way now too, so he will be available to donate. However, he only donated a few weeks ago, so it wouldn't be within the safe guidelines.'

'For Bombay, we might have to revise those guidelines,' the doctor said.

'There are three members of Kayden's extended family, in addition to his father, who are willing to donate.' Flo thought back to her conversation with Ben's mother.

He smiled. 'That's good news. I'd suggest you get in touch with them in case we need to call on them urgently.' He smiled at Kayden. 'Okay, matey, let's get your tummy fixed, shall we?'

Kayden nodded. He was pale, and Flo could tell he was scared. She stroked his forehead. 'You'll feel a lot better once this is done. Your tummy will still hurt a bit, but nothing like it is now.'

'Is Ben coming?'

Flo nodded. 'He should be here any minute.'

'And Della?'

'I'm not sure, but she'll definitely be in to visit after your operation.'

Flo moved out of the way while the nurses checked Kayden's vitals and started to prep him for surgery.

'I'll be able to be with you right up until the operation,' she told Kayden. 'Once you're asleep, I'll let the doctor do his job, and then I'll be there waiting when you wake up.'

'Ben, too?'

Flo nodded, hoping that Ben would arrive before Kayden went into surgery so he could reassure him.

'Hey.'

Flo turned to find Ben, slightly out of breath, behind her.

'What's going on, bud?' he said, placing a hand on Kayden's hair. 'I hear you've got a sore belly.'

Kayden nodded. 'Can you be there when I go to sleep and when I wake up?'

'Of course, I can,' Ben said. 'There's nowhere else I'd rather be.'

Kayden shut his eyes, his face relaxing with relief.

Flo met Ben's eyes and saw that, like hers, they were raw with emotion.

* * *

Fifteen minutes later, with Kayden in surgery, they waited together in a small area. The nurse had promised to bring them through to recovery before Kayden was brought around.

'Thanks for coming,' Flo said. 'He was asking for you.'

'Really?'

Flo nodded. 'It means a lot to me too. I went to ring Ari when I realised what was wrong with Kayden and, of course, couldn't. And I couldn't worry Dad or Gigi about what's going on. It meant a lot to know you would be there for him.'

'I should always be the first call, Flo. From now on, make sure I'm your go-to person when it comes to Kayden. Okay?'

She nodded.

'But I do think you should let Ari know what's going on.'

'I can't deal with her today. I'll tell the family once he's in recovery. They can't do anything anyway.'

Ben nodded. 'Okay, but I might pop out and make a quick call. I promised Della I'd let her know what was happening. I was in the car when you called, and so she overheard that Kayden was sick. She freaked out. She associates hospitals with Carrie, so she's terrified Kayden won't come home.'

Flo's hand flew to her mouth. 'Oh no, the poor little thing. Go and ring her. A laparoscopic appendectomy takes between thirty and sixty minutes usually. You've got plenty of time.'

Ben nodded. 'Okay, I'll be quick.' He turned to leave but then hesitated and turned back to Flo. He drew her to him in a hug. 'He's in good hands, Flo; he'll be fine.'

* * *

Ari still couldn't put her finger on what didn't sit right with her about Scott Cohen. She was attempting to leave the hospital for the second time after speaking with him and had only made it to the front entrance when she bumped into Gigi.

'Come and have a coffee with me before I visit your mother,' Gigi insisted. 'I feel like I haven't seen you in ages.'

Ari laughed. 'You've seen more of me these past few weeks than you ever normally do.'

'I know,' Gigi said, 'but it's always about your mother or Flo or whatever other drama's going on.' She sighed. 'To be honest, I'm exhausted by the entire thing. Part of me thinks it's time to curl up and not wake up in the morning.'

'Don't say that, G. We'd miss you terribly.'

Gigi sighed. 'I know, and I'd never do anything like that. This whole situation has been a bit much. I can't go into any detail yet, but I had a conversation with your mother yesterday, which has left me rather shaken up.'

'Oh?'

'Leave it with me for now, love. I need to process a few things before I share what we discussed. It's not about the current situation. It's about the past. But I'm beginning to realise that the impact of what happened all those years ago shaped Julia into the person she became. So, in that respect, it has everything to do with the current situation.'

'You're sounding cryptic.'

'I know. I need to work out what to do with the information I've learned and whether you should hear it from me or her. Now, tell me something nice that's got nothing to do with any of the disasters that seem to have been unfolding around us.'

'I'm thinking of taking some time off work,' Ari said. It was only by putting the thought into words that she realised it was something she was really thinking of doing. 'A few months or maybe even longer. However long it takes to get some perspective on what I'm doing.'

A look of astonishment flashed across Gigi's face. 'Really? What are you going to do?'

'I'm not sure. I think I might travel. Possibly give thought to other types of work I might want to try. I'm not enjoying my current work. I think I'd like to do something that gives back rather than aims to make as much money as possible.'

'What's brought all this on? Your mother's journals?'

Ari considered this. 'They've contributed, I guess. But I was feeling restless before Mum's accident and before we were aware of the journals.'

'Well, I'm excited for you,' Gigi said. 'I think you're wise to think about doing something like that.' She smiled. 'You've always had great ideas, Ari.'

'I'm questioning whether I've *ever* had an original idea,' Ari said. 'Mum's journals suggest I haven't, or if I have, it was probably quashed. And I can't take all the credit for this one. I have a new... friend.' Her cheeks burned as she admitted this to Gigi.

Her grandmother grinned. 'Now, this is more like the type of nice information I want to hear. Tell me about this person.'

'His name's Ryan,' Ari said. 'He's about my age, and he walked away from a high-paying job five years ago and hasn't looked back. He takes time to appreciate life, and he's rubbing off on me a little.' She laughed. 'He even has me going to yoga.' Her phone pinged with a text. 'That might be him now.' She slipped her phone from her bag and glanced at the screen. It was an unknown number. She was about to dismiss the message when her gut told her to check it. She swiped it open and gasped.

'What is it?' Gigi asked.

'Kayden's in the hospital,' Ari said. 'In surgery for an appendicitis.'

'This hospital?'

'No, Box Hill.' She stood. 'I'm going straight there. Do you want to come with me or stay here with Mum?'

'I'll come with you,' Gigi said. 'Thank goodness Flo messaged you and that you checked the message.'

'It wasn't Flo,' Ari said. 'It's from Ben.'

Gigi's brow furrowed. 'Flo didn't let any of us know. Surely, she'd rise above everything for something this important? What if

Kayden has a reaction during surgery or the unthinkable happens? How could she?'

Guilt stabbed at Ari. She knew why Flo hadn't contacted her. It was unlikely she would have responded. There were many text messages on her phone from Flo in the past few weeks she had refused to read, let alone acknowledge, and too many calls to count that she'd let go unanswered. She was gutted that things had gone this far. She hadn't even seen Kayden since finding out about Ben, and for a six-year-old who was used to seeing his aunt regularly, that was unforgivable. After all, he hadn't done anything wrong.

'Let's not get on Flo's case when we get there,' Ari said. 'She'll be worried enough as it is, and it's quite likely she asked Ben to message us.' Even as the words came out of her mouth, Ari knew that scenario was unlikely. She'd said no to Flo enough times now that her sister would have felt like she couldn't call her.

* * *

Having Ben beside her while they waited in the private room Kayden had been lucky enough to be allocated while the surgery took place was a godsend. He'd managed to distract her with random questions about Kayden, which, of course, gave her an opportunity to share stories about him.

'It's hard to believe you've been back in our lives for less than a month,' she said after describing in detail his most recent birthday party at Ben's request. 'It might be because you were a part of the family when you were with Ari, I'm not sure, but it feels completely natural that you're here.'

'For me too,' Ben said. 'There are times when I feel so bad that I've missed the first years of his life, but you know, then I remind myself that I wouldn't have Della if you'd told me you were pregnant. And I wouldn't have had the love I had with Carrie. So, if you're still beating yourself up about not telling me, know that there's a small part of me that's glad you didn't. You know that I loved Ari, but my relationship with Carrie was so different. She loved me with a fierce passion that Ari never had for me. She made me realise what can exist as far as love. It was short because of her cancer, but it was brilliant.'

'Are you going to thank me too then?'

'Jesus!' Ben said, his face turning bright red. 'You weren't supposed to hear that.'

Flo turned around to find Ari standing in the doorway with Gigi next to her.

'It's fine,' Ari said. 'You found the love you deserved, and it's not what's important right now.' She stopped talking, walked up to Flo and enveloped her in a hug. 'He'll be okay, Flo – he's a tough little guy.'

Flo melted into Ari's arms, tears rolling down her cheeks at the unexpected gesture. 'How did you know we were here?'

'Ben,' Ari said. 'And I'm so sorry you knew I wouldn't pick up if you called. Now, how long is the surgery going to be?'

'We're not sure, but it shouldn't be too much longer. It's a standard procedure, assuming they got to it before it burst.'

'It didn't burst,' a nurse said, appearing in the doorway. 'You can come to recovery now. They'll be waking Kayden up in a few minutes.'

'We'll be waiting for you,' Ari called as Flo and Ben hurried after the nurse.

* * *

'You know,' Gigi said, 'I've done my best to stay out of this situation between you and Flo, but if today tells you one thing, it's that it must stop. I don't have your mother's powers of persuasion, or whatever it was she used to make you do what she wanted you to, but today, I'm going to plead with you to see what you can do to put the situation behind you. For Kayden's sake as much as all of ours.'

Ari nodded. She didn't need Gigi telling her what she had to do. She'd already made her mind up about that on the ride to the hospital. Ryan's words had come back to her. *You're hurting, and it might take some time, but if your heart's telling you that one day you'll have a relationship again, then don't wait too long in case it's too late.*

They'd moved on to talk about her work, but as much as she was hurt and angry with Flo, she couldn't imagine her not being in her life ever again. She hadn't put a timeline on forgiving her sister, but she knew at some point she would, so Ryan was right. Why wait?

Those final words, *in case it's too late,* had sent a shiver down Ari's spine. She'd never forgive herself if something happened to Flo and they hadn't made up.

It seemed like hours but was less than one when Kayden was wheeled back into the room by the orderlies, Flo and Ben flanking his bed. His eyes were open but drooping. They lit up as soon as they saw Ari.

If he hadn't come out of surgery moments before, she would have scooped him into a big hug, but instead, she had to settle for squeezing his hand. 'Hey, big guy, you trying out a new hospital this week?'

Kayden managed a weak smile. 'My dad's here, Aunty A. Did you know I have a dad? His name's Ben.'

Ari had to blink back tears at the love Kayden conveyed in those few words before his eyes closed again, and he drifted back into sleep. She looked up at Ben, who was wiping his eyes. 'I can't believe he said that.'

'With such pride,' Gigi added. 'It was a lovely moment. It looks like you've made quite an impact on him, Ben.'

'And him on me,' Ben said. He looked from Flo to Ari. 'Would you like Gigi and me to go and find some coffee or cold drinks for everyone?'

Flo opened her mouth, but Ari spoke before she had a chance. 'That would be great, thank you. We'll text if Kayden wakes up while you're gone.'

Ari waited until Gigi and Ben exited the room before turning to Flo. 'I'm sorry. We should have had this conversation weeks ago. I don't know why I didn't let it happen, to be honest. A friend of mine thinks I want to punish you by dragging it out longer than necessary and he's probably right.'

'I deserve to be punished.'

'We agree on one thing at least.' Ari held her hands up when she saw Flo's shattered face. 'I'm kidding. Sorry, you'd normally laugh at a joke like that.'

'Laughter hasn't been on the top of my list the last few weeks.'

'I know, and I should have spoken to you after I read Mum's journal entries from when you got pregnant and when she advised you of how to handle it.'

'I can only imagine what they said. I truly believe the woman's a psycho from what I've read. Her manipulation skills are top-level.'

'That's an understatement,' Ari said. 'I saw from Mum's journals that you wanted to tell me as soon as it happened with Ben, but she talked you out of it.'

'And I shouldn't have let her. I've thought back to that day again and again and tried to work out what it was that stopped me from doing what I knew was right.'

'It was *who*, not what,' Ari said. 'Probably the only good thing to come from these journals is realising that she's had us brainwashed our entire lives. I've only got half of the journals, and I can see major decision after major decision influenced by her. It's our early years that are particularly interesting or, more aptly, completely messed up. Have you read the parts where she talks about the strategies she put in place from when we were little to ensure we came to her with any problems? That she reinforced time and time again that we needed her guidance and all of that?'

'No, I've mainly got teenage years. She talks about doing that?'

Ari nodded. 'And when I think back to some of the things she's convinced me of and even my choices of friends, boyfriends and my career path, it's quite frightening. I'm beginning to wonder if I've ever decided anything for myself. But, back to you and Ben. I hate that it happened, and I'm guessing it will take me some time to come to terms with it, but I can see from the journals that you did want to do the right thing both when you slept with him and then later when you found out you were pregnant. Julia – honestly, I don't want to call her Mum any more – she made sure you did what she thought was best for the situation.'

'I still should have had the backbone,' Flo said.

'Based on the manipulation she's managed throughout our entire lives, you didn't have a chance. Our backbones were extracted at birth. She made sure of that.'

Flo placed a hand on Ari's arm. 'I'd never deliberately hurt you – you know that, don't you? The night with Ben should never have happened, but I can guarantee you that there's never been anything else I've done that I've hidden from you. You've always been the most important person in my life, Ar. You share that spot with Kayden now, but you're still everything to me.'

A tear rolled down Flo's cheek, causing a lump to rise in Ari's throat. She closed her eyes momentarily before stepping towards her sister and embracing her. 'Let's get things back to normal, okay? These past few weeks have been so awful, not only because of everything we've found out about Mum but not being there for each other.'

'You'll forgive me?'

Ari nodded. 'Life's too short. I need to, for all our sakes. I'll probably find it a bit weird having Ben back in our lives, but having seen Kayden's pride moments ago, I can get over that. And anyway, from what I've been reading in those journals, we've been through a lot weirder our entire lives, even if we weren't aware.'

'Thank you,' Flo said, her cheeks wet with tears. 'I mean it, Ar. I promise I'll never let you down again.'

Ari pulled her into another hug as Gigi and Ben reappeared.

'Sorry to interrupt,' Ben said, handing Ari a coffee cup. 'I wanted to make sure I was here when Kayden woke up again.'

'Have you called Della to let her know the operation was a success?' Flo asked.

Ben nodded. 'Mum's going to bring her in to visit. I hope that's okay. She was pretty upset.'

'Of course, it's okay,' Flo said. 'He'll want to see her too.'

'How weird,' Ari said, 'to think Kayden has a sister.'

'And a dad.' They all turned as the words, practically a whisper, came from Kayden's lips. 'I have a mum and a dad and a sister. I'm so lucky.' His eyes closed again, leaving the adults in silence.

'You know,' Gigi said, 'I think Kayden's summed it up when it comes to his family. Now, if we could get to the bottom of this situation about your own mother, then perhaps, by some miracle, we'll consider ourselves lucky too.'

Flo gave Ari a look that she had seen many times before. It was going to take more than a miracle.

38

Julia had been shocked to hear of Kayden's appendicitis the previous evening when Gigi had phoned from Box Hill Hospital but equally relieved to hear that the operation had been a success. The news that Ari had forgiven Flo had also been a huge relief.

'Perhaps the family won't be destroyed after all,' she'd said to Gigi.

'I'm not sure if that forgiveness will extend to you,' had been Gigi's response. 'Sorry, love,' she'd added. 'It's been a long and worrying afternoon. Ignore me. You've got bigger things to worry about with Mike and Scott.'

Gigi had been right. The situation with Mike and Scott was awful, and now, as he sat across from her, Julia was finding it hard to meet Mike's eyes as he did his best to keep her entertained. She spent most of the time he was with her trying to work out why he kept coming back. Today was no exception. Her mind was still foggy, and while some things had come back to her, there was still a lot of missing information. But the one thing that wasn't missing was her sense of morality. If the situation had been reversed, the likelihood of her being within ten feet of the room, let alone the hospital, was zero. She would have found the entire situation humiliating. She realised he'd stopped talking and turned her attention back to him.

'Are you okay? You seem distracted.'

'I was wondering why you're here,' she said. 'I've been cheating on you for years apparently, and you're visiting every day making chit-chat. Why would you do that?'

'Because I don't believe you cheated. Until you have your memory back and can categorically confirm you're in a romantic relationship with this Cohen character, I'm giving you the benefit of the doubt.'

Julia stared at him. Was he delusional? 'What if you find out it's all true? That I remember why I've done what I've done?'

'Then I'll be interested to hear the reasoning behind your actions. I've never known you to do something you aren't proud of, Julia, so that's why I don't believe this.'

'What about my lies around Kayden and Flo?'

'Are you sorry you did that?'

'Honestly?'

'Yes, honestly.'

'No, I'm not. I can see why Ari's upset, and Ben and his family are too, but ultimately, I think I did the right thing. It would have destroyed our family back then, and I wasn't ready for that. Ari probably wouldn't have made partner. She'd have been so distraught, and who knows where Flo might have ended up. We all assume Ben wouldn't have gone to London if he'd known, but it's also possible that Flo would have gone with him, meaning we missed out on Kayden's childhood.'

'Instead, Ben missed out.'

'I didn't say what I did wasn't flawed. I'm saying I'd probably do the same again if put in that position.'

'This is why I want to hear your reasoning for your secret life,'

Mike said. 'I just know that there'll be a reason that you can justify your actions with, like you just did about Kayden and Flo. I'm not saying I'm going to agree with it, and I'm positive I won't like it, but I know you'll have a thought-out and considered motive for anything you've done.'

Julia sighed. 'You're an amazing man, Mike Hudson. To have that kind of belief in me when I'm seriously worried I've let you down.' Mike placed a hand over hers, and she enjoyed the warmth momentarily before pulling it away. 'Sorry,' she said, seeing the hurt in his eyes. 'I love that you're so confident that I'll be able to explain my actions, but my guilt has manifested in a physiological way that concerns me. My gut churns every time you touch me, and I can only imagine that the reason for that is my guilt. You don't deserve to have had someone treat you like I have.'

'Let's not jump to any conclusions,' Mike said. 'You seem to be remembering more and more each day. I think you'll find it won't be long until you remember your work, your living arrangements in Canberra and the reason you were in Melbourne when you had your accident. Once you're able to put all the pieces together, then we'll have some answers.'

* * *

Julia was relieved that there'd been an hour separating her visits with Mike and Scott, so they hadn't bumped into each other. Now, as Scott filled the chair across from her, Julia stared at him. Of course she knew him: they'd worked together for years. But a sudden sense of familiarity washed over her. She really knew this man. Everyone had been telling her this, but it wasn't until this exact moment that she believed them.

'Were we happy?'

Scott smiled. 'Of course, we were. So, happy. We have many

things in common, Jules. Our work is what got us together to start with, and we've had years working on Project Enigma together, which has strengthened our bond.'

'What about friends?'

He shook his head slowly. 'You liked it just being us and regardless, you never really had time for them with being in Melbourne for work every other week. That's what you told me. But I've now realised there was obviously more to it than that.'

'And you were happy with that? Not socialising?'

'I caught up with Bill on the weeks you were in Melbourne to play squash. My parents are dead, as you know – or possibly don't – so family hasn't been a strong thing for me in recent years. We were happy in each other's company. We didn't need anyone else.'

'Why are you still here?'

'What?'

'Well, you've found out that I'm married with grown-up children and a grandchild. If our situations were reversed, I'm not sure I'd be staying. You've been lied to and betrayed, and yet you're still sitting here every day. Why?'

Scott flushed red. 'Having learned the truth about your situation I'm not sure why I'm still here. I guess it's because I love you and I'm still finding it hard to believe you would have lied to me.'

'And you're hoping I'll end my marriage and move to Canberra to be with you permanently?'

Scott's cheeks went from red to crimson.

Julia sighed. 'I'm sorry to sound so callous, but I'm finding this difficult.'

'How do you think I feel? You don't remember the man you were living with. Jules, babe, I'm heartbroken.'

Julia stared at him. *Jules, babe?* What was with that? No one had ever called her that. Surely she didn't— She closed her eyes, cutting off her own thought.

'Julia?'

Nausea overcame her, and her head started pounding as an onset of memories flooded back to her. Wave after wave of memories from her life in Canberra pummelled her. Her eyes flew open.

'No!'

'What?' Scott reached for her hand; concern etched in every wrinkle on his face. 'Julia, what's happening? Should I call a nurse?'

Julia shook his hand away. 'Don't touch me,' she practically spat through gritted teeth.

Scott recoiled. Shock clouding his features.

'I remember.'

"I love you."

39

A WEEK BEFORE JULIA'S ACCIDENT

Julia checked her watch and groaned. It was after eleven, and she was still at work. She'd promised Mike she'd ring him after dinner, and of course, now it was too late. She slipped her phone from her handbag to find a text message from him that had arrived three hours earlier.

> Assume you're working hard. Love you. See you tomorrow. Let's go out for lunch. I'll book Enrico's.

She smiled. She often wondered if the situation was reversed how she'd feel. If he was the one away every other week working ridiculous hours or at least saying he was. How would she know what he was doing? But they'd been married for forty-two years, and she trusted him with her life, as she knew he did her. It would be good to be home. Even though she didn't enjoy the focus being on her, she knew he'd be planning something for her birthday, and it would be nice to see the girls and Kayden, too. She'd been so caught up with Project Enigma the past few months that she'd neglected the girls' progression, Ari in particular. It was time to harness the restless feeling she knew Ari was experiencing and direct her to great achievements.

'You still here?'

Julia's head jerked around to face her office door as a voice broke through the quiet of the office.

'Scott, what are you doing here?'

'I wanted to talk to you about Enigma.'

Julia shuffled some papers on her desk and switched off her computer. *Project Enigma.* It was a completely confidential project he should know nothing about and wouldn't if she'd been sensible and only used her personal computer for it. But no, she'd been silly enough to think saving a copy to Strategic Intelligence's cloud would keep it safe. She'd never anticipated Scott Cohen accessing her studies. 'It's not something I'm interested in discussing. I'm heading home. It's late.'

Scott closed Julia's office door and came and sat down in the chair across from her. 'No, let's talk about it now.'

Julia leaned back in her chair and eyed him carefully. She'd worked with Scott for fifteen years, and while they'd had to work quite closely in recent years on work-related projects, there was something about him that she couldn't quite pinpoint, but that she didn't like. She'd shuddered recently when she'd over-heard someone refer to her as Scott's work wife. Yes, they'd spent a few months working quite intensely on a project together, but she worked closely with other staff members as well. Whoever had started that nickname should have been fired.

'As I mentioned earlier in the week, you need to add me as a contributor to the project.'

Julia snorted. 'And, as I told you earlier in the week, absolutely no way. This is a personal project I've been working on. The fact you've been privy to information around it is quite unusual and upsetting if I'm honest, and the fact you've shared my findings with external parties is something I should probably prosecute you for.'

'As if,' Scott said. 'Me sharing it is the only reason you're in the position you're in now. I have existing relationships with the investors who've reached out to you. It's only because of me that they're aware of the project and its capabilities and it's because of me that they're likely to invest.'

'I don't recall ever telling you or anyone, for that matter, that I had a project and was looking for investment. You have no idea what I'd planned to do with my findings,' Julia said. 'But it was for me to determine. You have nothing to do with it.'

'Incorrect. It's *our* personal project,' Scott said, 'as many people in the office can attest to.'

Julia raised an eyebrow. 'Really? How did you figure that when no one even knew about this project until recently.'

He smirked. 'Ask around. You'll find a lot of staff know how close we are and that we spend a lot of time outside the office together.'

Julia's stomach started to churn. She'd hoped he wasn't serious earlier in the week, but now she could see he was deadly serious. 'Scott, I'm not adding you to a project you had nothing to do with. It wouldn't be fair to anyone.'

'Let me tell you what wouldn't be fair,' Scott said. 'That would be your husband and family hearing about the secret affair you've been having.'

Julia's mouth dropped open. 'What affair?'

'Jules, babe, you've been in love with me for years. Surely, you're not going to deny that?'

'Don't be ridiculous. You'd never be able to prove that. Not when we've never had an affair. Mike wouldn't believe you anyway. He knows me better than that.'

'I think Mike's in for a big shock if you don't do what I'm asking you for. First, he's going to hear about the data breach you're responsible for, as will everyone at Strategic Intelligence, and then he's going to hear about your affair.'

'You're delusional. The cyber-attack we experienced last week was nothing to do with me.'

Scott laughed. 'You and I know that, but your system shows unauthorised activity last Monday night, eight hours before the cyber-attack happened. It appears you had data files open that were able to be accessed externally.'

'My system shows nothing of the sort.'

'It does,' Scott said, folding his arms across his chest. 'At the moment, you and I are the only ones aware of this. If we can't reach an agreement right now, I'll escalate it. Surely, you realise you're messing with the wrong person?'

'You could get fired if you've tampered with my system,' Julia said, her pulse racing as she realised that Scott's technical skills and system access could, in fact, leave her exposed.

Scott laughed again. 'That I doubt. I'm an expert in what I do, Jules, which is why they hired me. If I choose to use it to my own benefit, well good for me. Now, are you going to add me to the project? I'd be quite happy to share the notoriety it will bring, and the reality is I'm much better at commercial negotiations than you are. Between us, I think we have a bright future. We'd make a good team.'

Julia stood. 'Let's get this straight. You're threatening my job and my marriage unless I give you credit for a project you had nothing to do with?'

'You can look at it like that,' Scott said. 'Or you can look at it as a business proposition. Your career, marriage and life will run a lot smoother if you agree to my proposal.'

Julia unplugged her computer and slid it into her briefcase. 'I won't tolerate threats being made against me or my family. I suggest you rethink your *proposal* and, ideally, don't approach me again. I'm flying back to Melbourne first thing and will be back in a week. When I return, I'm happy to move forward as if this conversation never happened. For the sake of your career, I suggest you consider this a generous offer.' She turned her back on him and walked out of her office, doing her best to ignore the *this isn't over* smirk that played on his lips.

40

Julia stared at the man sitting across from her hospital bed. 'You said you were going to ruin my marriage, so this is how you were planning to do it? Set me up to look like a criminal, which would ultimately have had me fired and possibly put into jail, and on top of that lead my family to believe I was living a second life with you? How would Project Enigma have progressed anywhere with me accused of criminal activity?'

Scott stood, pushing a hand through his hair. 'It was a threat, Julia. One I was hoping you'd return from Melbourne after your trip and give in to. When you didn't return, and I heard about the accident, it gave me a window of opportunity, which I took.' He smiled. 'I could hardly believe my luck if I'm honest. I was given the impression that you were unlikely to survive, and I had access to the Project Enigma files. I couldn't have asked for a better scenario. But I realised I was going to need a convincing story to prove that this was *our* project and not yours.'

Julia shook her head. 'How you ever got a job at Strategic Intelligence baffles me. This is the most ridiculous plan I've ever heard of.'

'Not if you'd died. Your family believes I'm your partner. In fact, I think they're all still wondering how you're going to choose between Mike and me.'

Julia continued to stare at him. Would her family really believe this lunatic over her? And how had he been able to access her house to set this up in the first place? 'You literally moved yourself into my house and pretended we were in a relationship! What did you do, break a window?'

'No, Shelley in Human Resources is young enough and dumb enough to hand over your keys. *I'm one of her closest friends, Shelley. Someone needs to feed her cat and pack up clothes and other items to send to her.* It wasn't exactly hard.'

So much for confidentiality, Julia thought. 'Did you honestly think I'd go along with the relationship story when I woke up?'

'I didn't think it would be an issue,' Scott said. 'I assumed with the extent of the head injury you'd received that you wouldn't make it, or you'd be a vegetable. The prognosis was hardly good. If I'd thought you were going to wake up and be okay I would have stuck with my original plan. You can't imagine how relieved I was initially when you woke up and believed me. All I had to do was get your family to believe me and to convince them that you couldn't be trusted, so if you did turn around and say you were the sole contributor on the project, I'd convince them all it was another of your lies.'

Julia started to see where he was going with this. 'Let me get this straight. You thought you'd tell people that we'd been in a relationship for years, worked on this together for years, and I wasn't giving you credit?'

'Exactly.'

'I'd die or be in a vegetative state, and you'd claim the commercial benefits from the project?'

'Now you're getting it.'

Julia shook her head. 'You're completely crazy – do you know that? I have years of research documents and journals to back up my work. You have nothing. If someone asked you detailed questions, you wouldn't be able to answer them. I have experiments and reports with quite intricate detail, which only I understand. You never would have got away with it.'

Scott folded his arms across his chest. 'I disagree. I've accessed all of the Project Enigma files and understand it well enough. Your research and detail are brilliant, I'll add, and so comprehensive that Enigma could be developed without further input from you.'

'Well, that's never going to happen,' Julia said. 'I want you out of this room now and out of my life. I'll be speaking with the police, my lawyer, and Strategic Intelligence.'

Scott turned and took a step toward the entrance to the room.

'And don't come near me again,' Julia added.

He hesitated, took another step forward and instead of exiting the room, pushed the door shut and turned and glared at Julia.

Julia's heart thumped. 'What are you doing?'

'Exactly what I should have done the first day I visited you in the ICU.' Scott walked towards her; his eyes darkened with hatred.

Julia's fingers desperately searched the bed for the emergency call button, but before she could grasp it, Scott wrenched the cord from her grip. Her mouth opened wide in a silent scream as he yanked the pillow from beneath her head. With a swift, brutal motion, she was pinned to the bed as he pressed it against her face.

41

'Aunty A,' Kayden said, his eyes lighting up as Ari entered his hospital room with a large soft toy dog. She leaned down and kissed Kayden on the head and handed him the dog.

'I know he's not real, but who knows, if you play your cards right, you might convince Mum one day to get you a real one.'

'I've already got one,' Kayden said, his eyes shining. 'At Dad's house. It's Granny Sue's, but Della said we could say he's ours too.'

Ari pushed the hair from his eyes. 'Where is everyone? I wasn't expecting to find you here alone.'

'Mum had to work. Dad's here, though. He went to get some coffee.'

Ari sat down in the chair beside Kayden's bed. 'Is it weird having a dad all of a sudden?'

'Yep. I was calling him Ben, but I don't know. Dad kind of seems better. I never had one before. Did you know that?'

Ari smiled. 'I think you did always have one. Ben's always been your dad. It's just that neither of you knew that. I think it's wonderful, and I can't wait to meet Della. She sounds like a lot of fun.'

'She is.' Kayden's smile dropped, and he winced. 'My tummy hurts.'

'I bet it does. It'll take a few days, I think, before you're feeling better.'

'Am I interrupting?'

Ben stepped into the room.

'Hey,' Ari said. 'No, Kayden's telling me that his tummy hurts. But he was also telling me how much he loves having a dad.'

Ari smiled as both Kayden and Ben blushed. 'It's pretty awesome,' Ben agreed. 'Best surprise I've ever had. Now, how are things with you?'

Kayden groaned. 'Can I watch my iPad? You probably want to talk about boring stuff, don't you?'

Ben laughed. 'You've certainly got adults worked out.' He passed Kayden his iPad and headphones and helped him get set up. He stood back from the bed as Kayden was instantly engrossed in YouTube. 'Can you hear me, buddy?'

When he got no response, he turned to Ari. 'Thanks for what you did yesterday with Flo. I know how hard this has all been but forgiving her will make a huge difference for everyone moving forward.'

'For me too,' Ari said. 'I missed her. Not having Flo by my side made it even harder to deal with everything else that was going on.'

'How are things with your mum?'

Ari frowned. 'Nothing's changed on the memory front, but it's this guy who claims to be her partner. He's quite charming and saying all the right things about wanting to protect her interests with a project that has potential buyout or investor options. But all along, something hasn't sat quite right. And it's more than the fact she's been having an affair. I can't quite put my finger on it, but alarm bells have been ringing since I made a trip to Canberra.'

'Okay, walk me through it. Let's see if we can put our collective finger on what it is.'

Ari smiled, remembering how patient Ben had been when they'd been together. There had been many times when something hadn't sat right with her about a client or a case, and he'd patiently listened to the details she was allowed to share and, often, helped her pinpoint the issue. 'Like old times.'

'Good old times,' Ben added. 'Now, begin. You landed in Canberra, and then what?'

Ari retraced her steps from the Canberra trip for Ben.

'The house looked legit like he lived there?'

Ari nodded. 'His clothes were in the walk-in robe, photos everywhere. The place was quite homey, which was strange. I guess that would be his touch and not Mum's.'

'Okay, what else do we have? Who else did you meet?'

'The neighbour. Elderly woman, failing eyesight. She's only lived there a few months but has become friends with Mum. She was worried that she hadn't seen her for a few weeks.'

Ben gave this some thought. 'Anything else about her?'

'She didn't know Scott. Said she'd waved to him when he was gardening, and he was always friendly, but she hadn't met him. He's a keen gardener, apparently, so he would often acknowledge her but never went over to talk. That was a bit strange but not completely crazy if she'd only been there a few months. I asked him about Bridie, and he said he knew of her but he'd never met her, that he liked to keep to himself.'

'Okay, did you meet anyone else?'

'Her work colleague, Kirsty. She didn't know much about Mum's personal life. Said she'd assumed she was a cat lady, so any relationship was a surprise to her. Said she knew Mum and Scott worked together on Project Enigma but had no idea they were in a relationship. Human Resources, however, confirmed that Scott had been added recently to her file as an emergency contact. They wouldn't tell me more than that.'

Ben ran a hand through his hair. 'No wonder you're finding this confusing. I'm not sure—' He stopped mid-sentence.

'What?'

'The old lady, Bridie. The bit about her only ever seeing Scott when he was gardening.'

'Yes, she said she saw him quite regularly, that he was obviously a keen gardener.'

Ben's lips curled into a smile. 'I think we might have worked out that knot in your gut.'

Ari stared at him. 'I'm not following.'

'Do you remember years ago when your mum moved into that house? It was around Christmas time. You and I had been married maybe three years. She'd insisted they move her into a house with a large garden after that apartment she'd been in with the noisy neighbours.'

Ari nodded. She remembered her mother's fury at the neighbours who worked shift work and insisted on playing loud music when they returned home from work, which was often in the early hours of the morning.

'Remember your dad telling her she was mad to take on the garden of a large property when she was only there during the week? That maintaining it would be a nightmare?'

Ari stared at him, realisation hitting her. 'And she rolled her eyes and told him that he was the mad one. That, of course, she wouldn't be expected to touch the garden. Strategic Intelligence owned the property, and all property maintenance, including gardening, would be their responsibility. That they'd made it clear that tenants were not to touch the garden and if they wanted to plant anything they had to get permission.'

Ben folded his arms, a satisfied smile on his face. 'That might be the key to undoing all of this. What if Bridie was waving to a gardener?'

'But all of his belongings were there. He lives there.'

'Or made sure it looked like he did.'

'You think it's a set-up?'

'I'm putting it out there. It's been a few years, but I've spent enough time around your family to feel like I know your mum and the double-life thing is hard to comprehend. Give Bridie a call and ask her if she's waved to Scott in the last couple of weeks. He's been here most of the time.'

Ari's heart began to pound as she slipped her phone from her bag. She found Bridie's number and crossed her fingers, hoping the elderly lady would have her phone close by. It appeared she did when, within the first two rings, she picked up.

'Ari? Is that you?' Bridie's voice was a little shaky and unsure.

'It is, Bridie.'

'Oh good. I did key in your details properly. I'd been hoping to hear from you. How's Julia—?'

'Bridie, can you tell me something?' Ari said, cutting her off. 'Have you seen Scott in the garden during the last week or two?'

'He waved to me this morning,' Bridie said. 'He was busy cutting back some bushes and mowing. I'd hoped it was a sign that he was getting the house ready for Julia's return. I was going to head over and ask him, but I didn't want to interrupt him.'

'And it was Scott? The same man you've waved to in the past?'

Bridie gave a little chuckle. 'Definitely. My eyesight isn't the best, but there's no mistaking that large hat he wears. It's almost like a sombrero. He makes me laugh each time. He doffs it – you know, takes it off and does a showy little bow. It's nice of him. I can see why Julia loves him so much.'

'Bridie, thank you. I have to go. I'll ring you later with an update on Mum.' Ari ended the call before Bridie could respond. She turned to Ben. 'You're right – she's waving to a gardener.'

Ben nodded. 'And from the sounds of it, Scott Cohen is about to have a contract drawn up that gives him partial ownership in your mother's project. A project he quite possibly isn't entitled to any ownership of. The entire thing might be an elaborate set-up.'

'For Dad's sake, I hope so, I really do.' Ari leaned forward and hugged Ben. 'You're amazing, and I'd better go. Get that bastard away from Mum as quickly as possible. Last week, I thought your coming back into our lives was breaking up our family, but instead, you're the thing that's going to bring us back together. Well, save Mum and Dad's marriage at least.'

'Go,' Ben urged her. 'Flo's working, so find her and tell her.' He grinned. 'See, we're still a good team, Hudson.'

Ari grinned, dropped a kiss on Kayden's forehead and hurried from the room.

* * *

Ari arrived at the hospital within forty minutes of leaving Ben and Kayden and rushed to her mother's ward. She'd rung Flo from the car.

'Meet me at the reception desk at Mum's ward. It's urgent. I think I can prove Cohen's lying.'

'What? How?'

'I'll tell you when I get there. We need to tell Mum and get him away from her. He wants her to sign some contracts, and while I don't think they'd stand up in court with her memory the way it currently is, I don't want to risk it.'

Anxious energy surged through Ari as she exited the lift on Julia's floor of the hospital.

'Ari.' Flo hurried from the reception desk where she was

talking to one of the other nurses. 'He's with her now. Pauline at the nurses' station told me he only arrived a few minutes before I did and he didn't appear to have any papers or anything else with him.'

'Good,' Ari said. 'Now, let's go and tell Mum that her gut feeling was right all along. She didn't cheat on Dad.'

'Are you sure?'

'Yes. I'll fill you in later, but for now, I want him away from her.'

The two sisters hurried through the double doors, past the central nurses' station to Julia's private room and pushed open the door.

'Get off her!' Flo's scream pushed Ari into immediate action.

She didn't hesitate. She rushed towards Scott Cohen, who was straddling their mother on the bed, a pillow pushed firmly against her lifeless body. She yanked on his shirt, pulling him backwards off the bed. She registered a sickening thud as he crashed to the floor, his head hitting hard.

Flo raced to the bed, pushed the emergency button and went to work checking her mother's vital signs.

'She's not breathing,' she told Ari. She started CPR compressions as the door burst open, and Holly, with another nurse directly behind her, rushed in.

'What's happening?' Holly asked, surveying the scene.

'She's been smothered with a pillow,' Flo said, stopping to give her mother two rescue breaths. 'I started CPR less than a minute ago. Call security, and one of you help me. Ari – continue sitting on that prick until security arrive and they've called the police.'

Ari nodded, thankful that Flo was able to quickly assess their mother and advise the other nurses on what to do. Restraining Scott wasn't difficult. He was face down on the floor holding his head and groaning.

LOUISE GUY

'Thank God,' Flo said when Julia coughed as she started to regain consciousness.

'We'll get her started on oxygen,' Holly said. She turned to the other nurse. 'Get Doctor Lee or one of the trauma team.'

'It's okay, Mum,' Flo said as Holly placed an oxygen mask over Julia's mouth.

'Is she okay?' Ari asked.

Flo nodded. 'She's breathing on her own. She's probably in shock, though. The doctors will give her a thorough examination.'

'But she stopped breathing...' Ari said.

'Hopefully not for too long. Tests will help us see if there's been further damage.'

Two large security officers stepped into the room at that moment.

'Get this bitch off me,' Scott hissed, still clutching his head.

'You can let him go,' one instructed Ari, and she stood while the security officers roughly tugged Scott to his feet. 'We'll get him out of here. The police have been called, and we'll hand him over to them. They'll want to speak with both of you, so don't go anywhere if you were planning to.'

Ari nodded and turned to Holly. 'Is she going to be okay?'

'We've got her stabilised,' Holly said. 'The doctor will be here in a minute and will run tests.'

Ari noticed Flo's hands begin to shake and drew her into a hug. 'She'll be fine. She's a tough old thing. We should know that by now.'

Flo nodded. 'Let's call Dad. He needs to know.'

42

A week after the chaotic scenes in Julia's hospital room, the family were gathered around Julia's bed, waiting on an update from Ari, who'd been working with Julia's legal counsel.

'He's been charged with attempted murder,' Ari said, 'but there will be more charges to face regarding the fraudulent behaviour around Project Enigma and also for misrepresenting himself as Mum's partner. He'll be facing a long jail term.'

'What about the photos of your mum and Scott?' Gigi asked. She turned to Julia. 'Did you ever go skiing with him? Quite a few were from a ski trip.'

'I don't imagine I did,' Julia said. 'I still can't be completely sure.'

'You didn't,' Ari said. 'He photoshopped you onto the body of his sister. He was silly enough to leave some of the originals on Instagram. The ones in the house were obviously the same.'

'I told you,' Mike said, his cheeks puffed out. 'And you all told me I was being silly.'

'Sorry, Dad,' Ari said. 'He forged the mobile phone messages easily enough, and from what I've learned, he also managed to tamper with documents at Strategic Intelligence. It's still early days, so I imagine we'll find out more in the weeks and months to come as to what he did and what he thought he was going to achieve.'

'What about all his belongings in the house in Canberra? How did he do that?' Gigi asked.

'I can answer that,' Julia said. 'He told me before he tried to kill me. He convinced one of the staff at work to give him a key so he could feed my non-existent cat. It's quite unbelievable the lengths he was willing to go to.'

'I'm intrigued to know what he would have done if Mum hadn't had the accident,' Ari said.

'He had access to all sorts of information at Strategic Intelligence. It appears he's been planning to take credit for my work for some time and had set it up to look like we were more than friends.'

'The letter to the human resources department about your relationship was months before the accident,' Ari said.

'That makes sense,' Julia said. 'He threatened me that day in Canberra that he'd be saying we were having an affair. I guess the accident gave him the perfect opportunity to take it that step further.' She sucked in a breath. 'Imagine if I'd died. You would have had no reason not to believe him.'

'Thank goodness you didn't,' Flo said. 'I can't believe this happened. I'm so sorry, Mum. And I'm sorry we ever doubted you.'

'Your father didn't,' Julia said, smiling at her husband. 'Which means a lot. But to be fair to everyone, I think I would have doubted any of you if you'd been in the same situation with that amount of evidence against you. I'm just thankful that Ari worked it out.'

'Ben was the one who asked the right questions so I could

work it out,' Ari said, 'and your friend Bridie was the key to all of it, not that she will have known it.'

Julia chuckled. 'She'll love it when I tell her. She spends half her life reading thrillers or listening to audiobooks. This would fit nicely into her whodunnit obsession, I'm sure.'

'When do we get to take you home?' Mike asked Julia, but his eyes were focused on Flo.

'Possibly as soon as Friday,' Flo said. 'Mum's memory hasn't fully returned, but the doctors believe she will make a full recovery over time. She doesn't need to be here for that. Once her leg heals, she'll be as good as new.'

'Almost,' Julia said. 'Apparently, breaking a tibia at my age might have a few long-term effects, but that's okay. I'm alive, and I'm not having an affair, so that's one relief.' Her smile faded as the words left her mouth.

'You, okay?' Mike asked.

She gave herself a little shake. 'I'm being silly. I felt so guilty thinking I'd been having an affair that I haven't been able to shake an uneasy feeling that seems to have followed me around.'

'Maybe you're feeling guilty about the advice you gave Flo when it came to Ben and the pregnancy,' Ari said. She folded her arms and stared at her mother. While she was glad that they'd sorted out the Scott situation, they hadn't broached the matter of the journals with their mother yet. Her relief that her mother hadn't cheated had quickly been replaced with resentment as she gave thought to her entire life and how much it had been manipulated.

Julia locked eyes with Ari. 'I'd give her the same advice if it happened again.'

'Please tell me you're kidding?'

'Like I said to Gigi, it isn't necessarily the right advice, but if I was put in that situation, I'd still believe it would keep our family intact and save you both from a tremendous amount of pain.'

'As long as the truth didn't come out,' Ari added.

Julia nodded.

'What about everything else you've done?'

'Ari.' Gigi held up a hand as she spoke the word in a warning tone. 'Not now. Let's get your mother better and home, and then we can talk about other matters. We agreed we'd let her memory return before we did. Otherwise, it's unfair. She can't defend her actions if she can't remember them.'

'Why don't we leave Mum and Dad to talk?' Flo said. 'There's a bar across the road from the hospital. I don't know about any of you, but I could use a glass of wine.'

'Good idea,' Gigi said, getting to her feet. She put an arm around Ari's shoulders, not giving her a chance to object, and guided her out of the hospital room.

* * *

Five minutes later, the three women sat in a quiet corner of the Wellness Bar and Grill, nursing glasses of pinot gris.

'Here's to a happy ending for Mum and Dad,' Flo said, holding up her glass.

Gigi raised hers, but Ari refused. 'I can't toast her. Don't get me wrong, I'm glad she's alive, and I'm glad she hasn't betrayed Dad, but she's betrayed us since we were little kids. Even if she gets her memory back and tries to explain, what could she say that would make it all okay?'

'She probably won't have the right words,' Gigi said. 'But I might. I've come to realise over the last few days that I'm responsible for Julia's controlling and manipulative ways.'

'You can't take the blame for her,' Ari said. 'How can any of this be your fault?'

'Because she's my daughter, and I'm beginning to see that what I did to her years ago has impacted every action in her life ever since.'

'What *you* did to her?'

Gigi nodded. 'It wasn't what I did, but what I let her believe.' She looked from Ari to Flo. 'I'm afraid I've also kept a secret that appears to have done a lot of damage. You know that your grandfather died when Julia was eight.'

They nodded.

'What you don't know is the exact circumstances of his death.'

'The car wreck,' Ari said.

Gigi shook her head. 'There was no car wreck, and Ted's death wasn't an accident.'

Ari and Flo exchanged a confused look.

'He suffered from severe depression,' Gigi said. 'The black dog, as they call it. He couldn't shake it. It was Vietnam that did it to him. He was thirty-seven when he returned, having been a captain for his tour of duty. The number of men and boys he saw die on his watch was horrific and he brought his nightmares home with him. Like many others, I now realise that he suffered from PTSD. He couldn't handle it and, within a year of returning, took his life. He hanged himself at a local park.' She paused, tears filling her eyes. 'If that wasn't bad enough, it was on your mother's birthday.'

Flo squeezed Gigi's hand. 'I'm so sorry, G.'

Gigi wiped her eyes. 'Me too, love. I'd do anything to be able to go back in time and help him. When it happened, your Aunty Mary convinced me it would be best for Julia if we led her to believe it was a car accident. It was so unusual for Mary to suggest lying as she'd always been so against it, that I knew how damaging she thought the truth would be. I agreed with her that we didn't want Julia blaming herself or thinking he didn't love her. His choice of date was, of course, particularly heartbreaking.'

'It's terrible,' Ari said, 'but I don't understand why you think Mum's behaviour was your fault.'

'A few days before we found out that Scott was a con artist, something I said triggered a memory for Julia. It turns out that she overheard Mary and me talking the night Ted died. She heard all the details of his death and knew from that day that her father killed himself on her birthday.'

'Oh no,' Flo said.

'She didn't tell anyone she knew, and I think it traumatised her. She never spoke about it and, from what I can gather, convinced herself that the story about the accident was true to the point that she believed it. It was only in regaining parts of her memory recently that this came back to her. She remembered everything. It makes sense to me now because after Ted died, she changed. She went from being a happy, carefree little girl to an anxious and controlling one. She had to know where I was going; when I'd be home, who might be visiting; whether we needed to use the car and a million other small details that she'd obviously felt she needed to control. She had no control that day Ted died, but suddenly she realised that there were things in life that you can control.'

'Like her family,' Ari said.

Gigi nodded. 'I didn't go into detail with her about her journals, but I did ask her what she was thinking advising Flo to lie to you and to Ben. Do you know what she said?'

Ari and Flo shook their heads.

'She said she couldn't bear the thought of Ari going through the trauma that learning what Flo had done would cause her. So, she chose the path that she thought would have the best outcome, and she made it happen. She was protecting both of you. I think you'll find the journals you've found documenting every occasion that your mother deemed necessary to help plan your lives. Her actions, while unorthodox and way off mark, were a sign of her underlying love for the two of you. She wanted you on a pathway that would bring success and happiness while avoiding any trauma or sense of failure.'

Flo snorted. 'If this was true, she'd be encouraging me to go for promotions, not discouraging me.'

'She's protecting you from the disappointment if you don't get them,' Gigi said.

'What about burning down my art shed when I was a teenager?'

'Again, I think you'll find if you talk to her that she knew life as an artist would be difficult. Life in a secure job in health, however, would give you financial stability. Look,' Gigi said, 'I'm not saying that what she did was in any way healthy or good. I'm saying that I'm beginning to realise why she's behaved as she has. She studied to be a neuroscientist so she could understand human behaviour and I imagine therefore learn how best to control it. I'd say she's taken everything to an extreme and ended up hurting people, which was the exact opposite of what she intended. I'm not asking you to forgive her, but I am asking you to spend some time thinking about it before you start attacking her.' She turned to Flo. 'Think about what you'd do for Kayden to protect him and then put yourself in your mother's shoes.'

Ari sighed. 'You know, as much as I hate her journals and what she's done, I'm so happy that she didn't betray Dad that I'll probably forgive her at some stage. Everything that's happened in the last month or so has shown how important family is. And if I'm going to forgive her down the track, why wait?'

Flo nodded. 'She can't continue controlling us, though. We

need to make that clear. At least she didn't set out to be malicious or deceitful,' Flo said. 'Not like Scott Cohen.'

Ari raised her glass. 'Let's toast the fact that we're still a family. A slightly different-looking family than a few weeks back, what with Ben on the scene and Kayden now having a dad, but we *are* a family.'

'Now, if we can get Julia home, we can start getting back into some kind of normality,' Gigi said. 'I'd be happy to never see the inside of another hospital – that much I do know.'

43

Julia's eyes filled with tears as Mike put a protective arm around her as, with the aid of a walker, she stepped through the front door of the family home for the first time in over six weeks. A big sign in childish scrawl said:

Welcum Home!

It had been fixed to the wall in the front entrance with a gorgeous arrangement of soft pink majestic tulips sitting below it.

Gigi, Ari and Flo stood waiting for her.

'Welcome home, love,' Gigi said, a broad smile on her face.

'Thank you,' Julia said. 'And please thank Kayden for the wonderful sign. He's done an amazing job.'

Ari raised an eyebrow at Flo. They'd been speculating as to how quickly Julia would point out Kayden's spelling mistake, but it appeared she was deliberately not mentioning it.

'Is he here?'

'No,' Flo said. 'He's with Ben and Della. We weren't sure how you'd be feeling, so we thought we wouldn't overwhelm you today.

He's dying to introduce Della to you, so when you're up for it, I'll bring them both round.'

'Sounds lovely.'

Flo glanced at Ari again, who shrugged with a helpless *I have no idea* action. There was no doubt that she, too, was wondering where their critical mother had gone.

'Come into the lounge room,' Mike said. 'We've prepared some nibbles, and we'll open the champagne if you're up to it?'

'Sounds lovely,' Julia said again, allowing him to steer her towards the lounge.

'And there's a surprise for you,' Gigi said.

Julia hesitated. 'I'm not great with surprises.'

'This is a nice one, love. It's one of your favourite people who I will add, has been good to me since you've been in hospital.'

Julia looked from Gigi to the rest of the family. 'With the exception of Kayden, my favourite people are already here.'

'Not all of them, I hope!' Heather appeared in the doorway, a huge smile on her face. 'It's so good to have you home again.' She moved towards Julia as if she was going to hug her and stopped, her face twisting in confusion. 'Julia, are you alright?'

Julia's eyes were wide as if she'd been caught in the headlights.

'Mum,' Flo's voice was filled with concern. 'Everything okay?'

Julia closed her eyes and shook her head.

* * *

'Come and sit down,' Flo said, gently guiding her to her favourite couch. The rest of the family stood in silent concern.

Julia sank into the couch and dropped her head into her hands. The entire time she'd been in the hospital, the story Scott had spun about their affair had seemed implausible, but until her memory returned, even she'd believed the evidence was too damning not to be true. But it wasn't words that had scared her. It was an overwhelming internal sensation that seemed to haunt her. Anytime she allowed her mind to wander to the prospect of an affair, it was like being punched in the gut. She was gripped with a mixture of nausea and heartache. Nausea, she assumed, was guilt and heartache for what she was putting Mike through. After forty-two years, cheating was unthinkable, and her reactions were no doubt physiological.

'Mum,' Ari said. Her voice was gentle. 'You're scaring us.'

Julia did her best to lift her head from her hands, her emotions spiralling from disbelief to grief.

She looked at Mike. 'All along, I knew something had happened, but I couldn't remember what. At one point, I honestly believed what Scott was saying was true. My heart told me there'd been an affair, but my head was trying to convince me otherwise. I truly couldn't believe I would do something like that. It goes against every value I possess. But I was wrong, wasn't I?'

'Mum,' Flo said. 'What do you mean you were wrong?'

'Julia.' Gigi's tone was shocked. 'You're saying there was an affair?'

A tear rolled down Julia's cheek. She nodded. Her gaze fixed firmly on her husband. 'It just wasn't me.'

* * *

Mike's face paled. 'What are you talking about?'

Flo looked to Ari, whose eyes were wide in horror.

'It's all coming back,' Julia said. 'I remember coming to Melbourne, and I remember crashing James's car.' She dropped her head into her hands. 'I'm wishing I couldn't remember.'

Gigi placed a hand on her shoulder. 'I think you need to tell us what happened that day to try and help us all understand the situation.'

Julia nodded, wiping her eyes on the back of her sleeve. She kept her eyes firmly focused on the window, looking out to the leafy back garden, and began to speak.

'It was our wedding anniversary coming up. I'd planned a special surprise weekend away, but it was one of the first years in our entire marriage that I wasn't going to be home on the day. I felt bad about that all the way back to Canberra. I usually go straight from the airport to work, but I had a bag full of books to give to my neighbour, Bridie. I went home first and took the books over to her. She's lovely, and I ended up staying for a cuppa. Ironically, it turned out that it was her wedding anniversary too, and she was feeling rather down as she'd lost her husband three years earlier. She was telling me about how wonderful their marriage was and how she'd do anything to be able to turn back time and spend every minute she had with him. It sounded like in the last year of his life, he was off playing golf a lot and wanted her to go with him, but it didn't interest her. If she'd known she was going to lose him, she would have been his golf partner week-in, week-out to create more memories and share more time together.'

'Poor Bridie,' Flo said.

Julia nodded. 'I thought the same, and I suddenly felt awful that I'd prioritised work over my marriage. There'd been years of me having to say no to events for you girls and celebrations with your father, and here I was, having turned sixty-six the previous day, once again putting work first. I remember sitting there think-ing, what the hell are you doing? You could be dead next week, and what will you have to show for it? Decades serving a company that anyone could have done.'

'I think you're underselling yourself there,' Mike said.

Julia didn't meet his eye. 'Perhaps, but you know what I mean.

We all like to think we're indispensable, but the reality is if we're not there, someone else will do it. Perhaps not as well or with as much experience, but they'll muddle through, and the job will be done. The only place I realised that I was truly indispensable was in my marriage.'

Mike reached for her hand, but she refused to look at him and pushed her hands firmly underneath her legs.

'So,' Julia continued, 'I made a decision to come straight home and spend our wedding anniversary together.'

'But you didn't come home,' Mike said.

Julia turned and looked at him. 'Yes, I did. I arrived back around four and caught an Uber to the house.'

Confusion crossed Mike's face. 'But you were driving when you had your accident, weren't you?'

'And your accident was the day after your wedding anniversary,' Flo added.

'I got to the house,' Julia continued, 'to find you...' She stopped, closing her eyes, her face contorted with pain.

'Mum?' Ari said.

Julia opened her eyes. 'To find you and Heather together in the family room. You passed Heather a beautiful bunch of red roses and then took her in your arms.'

'What!' Ari, Flo and Gigi all spoke at once. They turned and faced their father.

Mike's pale face took on a green hue.

'So,' Julia continued. 'For the first time in my life, I didn't know what to do. I was so shocked I could hardly stand up. The Uber driver hadn't left and saw me almost collapsing on the front lawn. The guy was lovely. He could see the two of them through the window as easily as I could and must have put two and two together. He bundled me back into the car and drove off. When I could finally speak, for some reason, I gave him Heather's address and got him to drop me off there. I have no idea what I thought I was going to do. Confront her once she'd got home, maybe. Who knows? At the end of the day, it was Mike I had to confront. But I wasn't ready to do it.'

'Oh, Mum,' Ari said. 'I'm so sorry.'

'Julia,' Mike said. 'I— let me explain—'

But Julia cut him off and continued. 'I waited about an hour, and Heather didn't come home. It was about then that it dawned on me that she was probably staying at our house. They weren't expecting me home, and who knew how long this had been going on. I used the spare key Heather gave me years ago and let myself in. Helped myself to James's car keys and carried on my way. I wasn't sure what to do. I couldn't tell anyone what had happened. I couldn't bear the humiliation of it right at that moment. I found a hotel in the CBD and curled up in a ball for the next fourteen hours, trying to work out my next move. When I crashed the car, I was on my way to Gigi's.'

'My house?'

Julia nodded. 'I wanted your advice. I was at a complete loss. My marriage, my friendship, everything was about to end, and I didn't know how to handle it. I'd tried to protect the girls all their lives. How was I going to do that now? It was awful. I'm not sure I've ever felt so low in my life.'

'You didn't...?' Gigi's hand flew to her mouth. 'Please tell me you didn't.'

'Do what Daddy did? No, I think I was tired and exhausted and didn't see the T-intersection and went straight through and hit the tree. Nothing more than that.'

'Julia, you've got it all wrong.' They all swung their heads to the doorway where Heather stood rooted to the spot.

'There was no affair.' Mike's voice increased in intensity. 'Julia, I didn't give Heather flowers.'

Julia rolled her eyes. 'Then tell me – what did I see?'

'You saw me,' Heather said, 'doing my best to convince Mike that *he* should book a late-night flight to Canberra to surprise you for your anniversary. I was quite mad with him that he'd allowed you to go back instead of staying in Melbourne that week.'

'It's true,' Mike said. 'And Heather brought the flowers for me to take to Canberra with me. For *you*,' he clarified.

'That's not what I saw,' Julia said. 'You two were all over each other.'

'No,' Heather said, 'he was hugging me to thank me. And he gave me the flowers back because as much as he loved the idea of surprising you, he didn't think you'd like it. He reminded me of the surprise party he threw for your fortieth birthday and how you'd made us swear we'd never do anything like that to you again. I didn't think Mike surprising you by himself, without a room full of people screaming *surprise*, was at all the same, but he did.'

Julia's cheeks flamed red as she turned to her husband. 'Is this true?'

Mike nodded. 'After that surprise party for your birthday I promised I'd always check with you before organising anything. I keep my promises – you know that.'

Julia nodded slowly. 'Yes, you do. Of course, you do. I don't know why I didn't open the front door and confront you both that afternoon.'

'I wish you had,' Mike said. 'We could have spent our anniversary together and none of this would have happened.'

'I'm sorry I ever doubted you.' She turned to Heather. 'And you, too, Heather. I don't know what to say really, other than I'm so sorry about the car, but I also need to thank you, I suppose. For caring so much that you'd ask Mike to do that. God, what a mess. Can you both forgive me?' Julia asked, looking from Mike to Heather and back again.

Heather stepped forward and sat beside Julia on the couch, resting a hand on her knee. 'There's nothing to forgive. All that matters is that we've got you back with us and you know Mike and I would never do anything like that.'

'Never,' Mike agreed. 'I love you. I always have and always will. In the forty-two years we've been married I've never wanted anyone else and I know I never will. You're all I've ever needed and all I've ever wanted.' He wiped his cheeks as tears streamed down them. 'Sorry, but I don't think you have any idea of what the last few weeks have been like.'

Julia looked from Mike to Heather, then to Ari, Flo and Gigi, taking in their weary eyes and strained faces. She didn't need a degree in neuroscience to be able to identify the signs of stress they all exhibited. 'Actually, I think I do.'

44

Ryan's mouth hung open as he sat across from Ari, absorbing the details of how her mother's situation had played out.

'Crazy, hey?' she said, taking a sip of her wine.

'*Concerning* is a better description,' Ryan said. 'That a guy like Cohen exists is awful to start with, but to go to those extremes for money. It makes you wonder what lengths he would have gone to if your mum hadn't had the accident.'

'A very avoidable accident as it turned out. Considering my mum hates surprises, for her to think it was a good idea to surprise my dad for their anniversary was a very strange thing to do.'

'How are your parents now?'

'They seem to be okay,' Ari said. 'Mum was even talking about retiring. I think she's finally beginning to realise what's important to her and working like a woman possessed, isn't it. I doubt she'll stop working completely, but at least the situation has her thinking.'

'I think it shows what an amazing family you are.'

Ari leaned back in her chair. 'Amazing? Are you sure you didn't mean nuts or something?'

Ryan laughed. 'Not at all. Life's hard. We get put into all sorts of bizarre situations as we navigate through it, and it's not about what we've done, it's about how we handle it. Look at your dad, for starters, unwilling at any point to believe anything that was said about your mum until it came from her lips. Incredible! If he'd believed what was being said he could have been a basket case. Instead, he stood strong and believed in their marriage and their love.' He reached across and took her hand. 'That's what I want in a relationship. To know that whatever's thrown our way, you'll believe in me and know that I love you.'

Tingles ran up Ari's arm. It was what she wanted too, and she loved that Ryan was able to reflect on the bigger picture. He was right. Her parents had a very special relationship and stopping to acknowledge that was important. She leaned across and kissed him. 'You're amazing, did you know that?'

Ryan shrugged. 'Not amazing. Just being me with someone I think's amazing.'

She kissed him again. 'You're the best thing that ever happened to me. I've never felt like this.'

He raised an eyebrow. 'Really, what about Ben?'

Ari shook her head. 'No, it was different. Funnily enough, I overheard Ben describing his love for his late wife as being short but brilliant. That they loved each other with a fierce passion that he'd never experienced before, and I get that he never felt that with me, because I didn't either. And the reason I know I didn't feel like that with Ben is because it's a totally new feeling.' She blushed. 'One I'm experiencing for the first time.'

A wide smile spread across Ryan's face. 'Really?'

Ari nodded.

'That feeling, which I agree is a totally new feeling for me too, hit me the first night you came to the studio to meet Sven.'

Ari laughed. 'Well, Sven, all I can say is thank God Sophie

convinced me to come along. I think my family will be happy too when they meet you.'

Ryan raised an eyebrow. 'So, I'll get to meet them? You haven't just made up all these wild stories to keep me interested?'

'I wish I had made them up. But no, I'd love you to meet them. In fact, I spoke to Dad last night, and he said Mum has some news she wants to share with us about the investors and her job. They've invited us all round on the weekend for lunch and to fill us in.'

Ryan raised an eyebrow. 'All?'

Ari nodded. 'Gigi, Flo and Kayden, and I think she might even be bringing Ben and Della. I think Mum wants to thank him.'

'Your husband?'

Ari laughed. '*Ex*-husband. Do I detect a hint of jealousy?'

'Definitely. Although I should thank him. He could be your current husband, and then it's unlikely you'd be sitting here with me.'

'Very unlikely,' Ari agreed. 'I'd love you to meet him. The *all* included you. If you'd like to come, you can hear whatever the final part of this saga is first-hand.'

'You've told them about me?'

'Gigi, my grandmother, yes. It appears she's ensured everyone else is aware of you, and Mum, of course, wants to meet you.'

'So she can determine if I'm suitable and put me in one of her journals?'

Ari laughed. 'Exactly. Now, are you journal-worthy?'

He reached across and took her hand. 'I'd love to be journal-worthy. Are things likely to calm down, or are you about to tell me that there's something even more peculiar going on?'

Ari didn't respond. She was enjoying the sensation of his touch and wondering if the timing was right for what she did want to say.

'Should I be worried?' Ryan said. 'I was expecting you to assure me that all the extreme stuff was behind you, and the family I'll meet at the weekend are actually half normal.'

Ari smiled. 'Definitely not half normal, and I'm not sure whether what you'll think I'm about to suggest is extreme, but I do have a proposition for you.'

* * *

The rest of the week passed quickly, and Ari was surprised at how nervous she felt at the thought of spending the day with her family. 'You sure you're ready for this?' Ari said as she parked behind Flo's car in the driveway of her parents' South Yarra home. 'We can keep driving and go out for lunch somewhere without irrational people being involved.'

Ryan laughed. 'Should I be concerned that you're worried about introducing me to your family?'

'It's not their opinion I'm worried about,' Ari assured him. 'It's your opinion of them.'

'My opinion couldn't be any lower,' Ryan said, his eyes twinkling. 'Your sister's a liar, your mother's a control freak, your ex-husband, who I'm sure I'm going to hate on sight, is going to be here, and who knows what criminal behaviour your grandmother's been up to. The bar's been set so low you don't need to worry about what I think.'

Ari gave him a playful slap on the arm. 'Fine, but don't say I didn't warn you.'

Ari's nerves continued to make their presence known. It was the first time she'd brought a man home since she'd started dating Ben. The irony wasn't lost on her that he'd be there today. They climbed out of the car, and Ari calmed a little when Ryan took her hand and gave it a squeeze.

'Don't worry. I'm sure I'll love them,' he said as they walked up the driveway.

The front door opened before she had a chance to respond, and a little girl peeked out at them. Her eyes grew wide, and she slammed the door.

Ryan laughed. 'Well, that's a nice welcome.'

'Kaydey,' they heard the little girl call. 'There's a ghost at the door. Quickly, your mum's ghost is here.'

The door reopened, and this time, Mike smiled at them. 'Hey, love,' he said to Ari, stepping forward to embrace her. 'Sorry about that. I think Flo might have forgotten to mention to Della that you're twins.'

Ari hugged her father before pulling back. 'This is Ryan, Dad.'

The two men shook hands.

'Nice to meet you, son,' Mike said as Della reappeared with Kayden beside her.

'See,' Della said, pointing at Ari. 'It's a real live ghost.'

Kayden laughed. 'It's Ari, Dell. My Aunty A. She and Mum are twins.'

Della continued to stare at Ari as Kayden moved in for a hug.

'My tummy's still sore, so you need to be careful,' he said.

Ari introduced Ryan to them, and Mike ushered them inside. 'Everyone's out the back,' he said. 'We thought a barbecue would be the way to go today.' He clapped Ryan on the back. 'How about I show you around and, most importantly, show you the kitchen? There's a fridge with a few beers we should probably investigate.'

'Sounds good to me,' Ryan said. He smiled at Ari and followed Mike's lead.

Ari looked down as a small hand slipped into hers. Della looked up at her. 'Kaydey's lucky. He's got two families and an aunt. I don't have any aunts or uncles.'

Ari crouched down. 'Well, if Kayden's your half-brother and

I'm his aunt, that must make me your half-aunt, too. Don't you think?'

Della nodded. 'That makes sense. And if by the end of the day you like me, maybe you could be my whole aunt?'

Ari smiled. 'I can tell already that I like you, Della. So how about we call it now? I officially declare myself as your *whole* aunt.' She held up her hand and wiggled her small finger at Della. 'Pinkie promise?'

Della looped her own small finger with Ari's and shook it. Then she let go and raced away from Ari down the hallway towards the back garden. 'Aunty A's here,' she yelled at the top of her voice.

Ari looked at Kayden, and they both laughed. 'Guess I have a new niece,' she said. 'Are you okay with sharing me?'

Kayden nodded. 'Yep. Della's mum died, so she needs a new mum, and while she waits, having an aunt would be nice.'

Ari's heart squeezed at the thought of Kayden and Della discussing her needing a new mum. She wondered if Flo would spend time with the little girl and help fill that space until perhaps there was another woman in Ben's life. She couldn't imagine he'd be rushing into a new relationship while he was still grieving.

'Grandma's being nice,' Kayden said as he and Ari made their way through the house to join the others. 'Like really nice.'

'Oh. What did she do?'

'She asked me about soccer and even got me to show her who Messi is on the iPad. She didn't ask me about school at all. She also said that when my tummy's better, and her leg's better, she wants to take me and Della to Werribee Zoo.'

'Really?'

Kayden nodded. 'Della's never been there, and she's never seen a real lion, so Grandma said she'd take us. We might even stay in tents overnight and go on a safari. How awesome would that be?'

'Very awesome,' Ari said as they reached the bi-fold doors that opened out onto the back lawn. Her father was already out there with Ryan, introducing him to Flo, Ben and her mother. Gigi was sitting off to one side, watching the introductions taking place.

'I'm going to go and play with my *sister*,' Kayden said. 'Is that okay?'

Ari couldn't help but smile at his deliberate use of the word. She hoped Kayden and Della would form the kind of sibling bond she and Flo had. 'Of course.'

As he made his way over to Della, who was sitting on the grass at Ben's feet, she couldn't help but notice Ben laughing at something Flo was saying. They looked comfortable together. As Ari watched them, a subtle twinge clenched at her heart. She did her best to push it away, but it remained. She knew it would take time to get used to seeing them together.

Ari glanced at Gigi and smiled as her grandmother patted the seat beside her.

She made her way across the freshly mown grass to the spot Gigi had picked in the shade of her father's meticulously cared-for Chinese elm. 'How are you, G?' she asked, sitting down on the chair next to her.

'Wonderful,' her grandmother replied. 'And that Ryan... he might be the reason.' She winked. 'He's certainly a bit of alright.'

'Did Dad introduce you?'

Gigi nodded. 'Yes, he said a quick hello before he was dragged off to meet the others. He's promised to come and chat with me once he's met everyone. From our short conversation, I thought he was lovely.'

'He is,' Ari said. 'I'm lucky to have met him.'

Gigi reached over and squeezed Ari's hand. 'I'm happy for you, love, really happy. Hopefully, the craziness of the past few weeks won't send him running.'

'Let's hope not,' Flo said, joining them. 'Where on earth did you meet him? He's gorgeous and so nice.'

'Introduced by a friend,' Ari said. 'And you're right, he's both gorgeous and nice. Now, tell me about you.' She cleared her throat, unable to make eye contact with Flo. 'You and Ben look comfortable together.'

Flo looked from Ari to Gigi, colour marking her cheeks. 'There's nothing going on.'

'I didn't say there was.'

'Your tone implied it.'

Ari shrugged. 'I was making a comment, nothing more.' She was not going to admit to Flo that the thought of her and Ben getting together made her stomach churn.

'Ari, I would never go there with Ben again. We'll co-parent Kayden and be as friendly as possible around each other, but no more.'

'Like I said—' Ari began, but Flo cut her off.

'I need you to believe me. Not having you in my life has been one of the hardest things I've ever had to experience. I never want to go there again.'

Ari nodded. 'It'll take time, but I'll certainly try.'

A lump rose in Ari's throat as Flo blinked away tears. She wanted to believe her sister, she just didn't want to get hurt again.

'Good,' Flo said. 'Now, Dad said to get everyone some drinks, and we'll be eating in a few minutes. You might want to rescue Ryan too,' Flo said, looking over to where Ryan was engaged in an animated conversation with their mother. 'That can't be good.'

Ari stood. 'No, I'd say it probably isn't. I'll go and rescue him and then come and help with the drinks.'

Ari hurried over to where her mother and Ryan were talking.

'Arabella dear, I was enjoying meeting Ryan.'

'Arabella? You didn't tell me what Ari was short for,' Ryan said. 'I like it. It suits you.'

'It does, doesn't it?' Julia said, her smile widening. 'Named after a strong, successful woman. She's rising to be even stronger and more successful than her namesake.'

Ari blushed. 'Enough of that. Now, would you like wine, Mum? Flo and I are about to get the drinks, and Dad's going to serve up the meat in a minute.'

'Champagne, please, dear,' Julia said. 'There are two bottles in the fridge and six flutes chilling. We'll all need a glass. I have a few announcements to make.'

Ari started at her mother. 'Good or bad?'

Julia laughed. 'Does champagne spell bad news?'

'Honestly,' Ari said, as Ryan followed her inside to help organise the drinks, 'I'd rather stay away from any news right now.'

* * *

A few minutes later, they were seated around the large outdoor table. Much to Ari's amusement, Julia had decorated a small table for Della and Kayden at the back of the garden so that they could have their own space. 'Our conversation will bore them,' Julia said. 'Let them have some fun. I hope you don't mind, Flo, but I bought some lemonade and some of those potato chips Kayden loves. I thought Della might enjoy them too.'

Flo gaped in disbelief. 'But you always insist he sits with us and you never allow him anything unhealthy.'

Ari stifled a laugh. It was true, but unlike Flo to be so direct.

'Well, I thought it could be the start of my loosening up a bit with Kayden,' Julia said. 'I've been doing a lot of thinking since getting home, and I don't want to repeat the mistakes I made with you girls. Dad suggested that making him feel special might be the first step in softening a bit.'

Flo nodded, and Ari could imagine her wondering how long this new Julia would last.

'Now, before we eat,' Julia said, tapping her champagne flute with the edge of a spoon, 'I have a few things I'd like to say.' All eyes turned to her. 'Firstly, I do want to apologise to you all. While I know that Scott Cohen is responsible for a lot of the recent work-related issues and, of course, for the awful lies he told, he wasn't responsible for me prioritising my work over family in the way I have done for years. In the days before the accident, I'd come to realise this and come to realise that I wanted more.'

'More?' Ari said.

Julia nodded. 'I sent in my letter of resignation yesterday. I'm moving back to Melbourne permanently. I'll need to go back to Canberra, of course, and pack up the house and say my goodbyes. Bridie, my neighbour, will be a little disappointed, but otherwise, I doubt it will have much impact on anyone. It's time to enter the next chapter, which for me equals retirement.'

'Really?' Flo said, her shocked expression mirroring Ari's thoughts. 'But you love your work. It's what you live for.'

'Lived for, perhaps,' Julia said. 'I've been foolish, Florence. I've spent so many years controlling every movement I make.' She had the good grace to blush. 'And many that you all make. It's time to stop and look at my reasons for that. Unpack them for want of a better word with the help of a professional.'

'Professional?'

'Yes, Florence, a shrink. Gigi, for one, thinks it's past its due time. Don't you, Mum?'

Gigi nodded and sipped her champagne.

'What about Project Enigma?' Ari asked. 'I thought it was commercially viable, and you had investors interested.'

'The only part in Enigma that Scott Cohen played was trying to make money from it via investors whom I believe he hoped would buy the rights to the research,' Julia said. 'If he hadn't been involved, I might have been interested in discussing what I'd discovered with an external party with a view to taking the research further and seriously working on the applications it could have, but considering all that went on, I will be requesting that all my journals in Canberra be destroyed. They contain the relevant data.'

'Hold on,' Ari said. 'Isn't it something that could benefit science? Can you destroy it all?'

'Arabella, I was honest with you the day I assured you that Project Enigma was not based on my studies of you and Florence. But it was based on studies of personnel who work for Strategic Intelligence. These were unauthorised studies and often an extension of things that my studies of your and Florence's progress and achievements prompted me to consider. While extremely interesting and potentially powerful to be used by intelligence in negotiation situations and other areas, I've decided that it wasn't necessarily ethical, and I think it's time to walk away from it.'

Ryan squeezed Ari's knee under the table as the family digested this news.

'Which takes me to my next apology,' Julia said. She hesitated and turned her focus to Ryan. 'Before I start, I probably owe you one too. This isn't a normal lunch at our house, so it's a shame this is your first introduction to us.'

Ryan smiled. 'It's not my first introduction to learning about your family, if it's any consolation. I first spent time with Ari on her own the day she found out the news about Flo and Ben.' He shot a look across the table that told Flo and Ben in no uncertain terms what he thought of that news. 'Then, of course, the Scott Cohen situation arose. It's been interesting, to say the least. I'm glad that my first time meeting you all is when a lot of the issues have been resolved and when Ari's been big enough to forgive some of you.' He looked pointedly at Flo and Ben again as he said this. 'I'm not sure I'd be big enough to rise above some of what I've learned in the last few weeks, so I'm grateful to have been able to witness Ari's strength in doing that. The fact that she's also been able to forgive you, Julia, for the manipulation of her life, shows me the depth of strength she possesses.'

Ari lowered her eyes, not willing to look at any of the family. She could imagine the looks on Ben and Flo's faces, and her mother's. She certainly hadn't expected Ryan to stand up for her in the way he had, but she couldn't say she wasn't pleased. To have someone next to her who had her back was something she hadn't experienced in a long time.

'I'd like to second that,' Gigi said. 'The ability to rise above circumstances is an exceptional skill, and I've seen many of you around the table do this during the last few weeks. Ari, of course, has had a lot to deal with, but then so has Ben, learning he had a son and had missed out on time with him.' She turned to Flo. 'I'm not having a go at you; in fact, you've displayed incredible courage with Kayden's medical issues and saving your mother's life after she was attacked by that terrible man. And, of course, Mike, you showed the most incredible strength in not believing Cohen and standing by Julia. If anyone around the table wants to know what love looks like, it's what your father displayed over the last few weeks.' She turned to Julia. 'To not leave anyone out, what you're doing now shows me that you're ready to do the work that will show the girls how much they mean to you. It takes a lot of integrity to stand here and apologise.'

'Thank you,' Julia said. 'It was where my next apology was going.' She focused on Ari and Flo. 'I didn't set out to control either of you, but I thought that if I could help steer you in the right direction it would protect you from failure and heartache. However, I can see that control is what I've done for years. I want you both to know that I will do my best to encourage you moving forward. I won't be planning anything for either of you, but I'm always here if you want to talk through a problem or feel my advice could be useful.'

She raised her champagne flute. 'That's all for now. I'm guessing that once I start seeing this shrink, there might be many more apologies owed, but let's not waste them all today.' She smiled, a glint in her eyes. 'I'm sure the shock of me apologising more regularly and lightening up where I can...' her gaze shifted to Della and Kayden at this point '...will give you plenty to laugh about moving forward.'

They all raised their glasses.

45

Ari helped her father clear away the dishes while Ryan and Ben started up a game of hide-and-seek with Della and Kayden, and Flo sat talking with Gigi and their mother.

'There are some big changes coming up for you,' she said, opening the dishwasher and starting to load the dishes. 'How do you feel about having Mum back full-time?'

'It'll be an adjustment,' Mike said, 'but I'm looking forward to it. We're still fit and active, and it gives us time to think about travelling and looking at what other hobbies we might enjoy together. I'm expecting the changes will be harder on your mum than me, but that's okay. We'll take it one day at a time. I can always escape to the golf course when I need some time to myself.'

'You're so good to her,' Ari said, turning and giving her dad a hug. 'And to me and Flo, too. I don't know if I've ever said it to you before but thank you. I can't imagine what our childhoods would have been like if it had been you who was gone every other week. You made us feel so loved and secure.'

Mike squeezed her. 'Hopefully, that young man out there is

making you feel the same way. Standing up to Mum like that.' He raised an eyebrow. 'I like him already.'

Ari laughed. 'I should probably go and rescue him.' She looked out the window to where he appeared deep in conversation with Della. 'She's a little pocket rocket. Kayden mentioned Mum offered to take them to the zoo. Will she spend time with you and Mum too?'

'We hope so,' Mike said.

'Ben would like her to.' They turned as Flo entered the kitchen carrying an empty plate. 'Kayden and Della have become insepa-rable. When he comes home to be with me, she's getting quite upset. She can't work out why, if they are brother and sister, they can't always be together like a normal family.'

'That's tough,' Ari said. 'Being so little, I guess everything's quite black and white for her.'

Flo nodded. 'When Kayden was talking about his Grandma and Grandpa, she was fairly insistent that they should be her grandparents too. After all, they're sharing Ben's parents. I mentioned it to Mum, expecting her to be negative, and she was quite the opposite. You know, I'm beginning to wonder if that knock on the head was something she needed. She's certainly a nicer person since. I can only hope the new personality doesn't wear off. Anyway, she wants Della to consider her another Grandma, and she's been told she can come any time Kayden does.'

'We got ourselves a new grandchild without anyone needing to go into labour,' Mike said with a laugh. 'It's a bonus for us, Flo, so don't give it another thought. And to be honest, I think she's going to give your mother a run for her money. Did you hear her tell Julia that she wasn't to call her Delilah? That she would only answer to Della.'

'What did Mum say?'

'That she likes to call everyone by their full name and has never used nicknames. To which Della replied, "I love Kaydey and I hoped you'd be my grandma too, but if you can't say my name then that's okay, you don't have to be my grandma."'

Ari laughed. 'Mum wouldn't have liked that. Although, she was calling her Della earlier so it must have had an impact.'

'It did. She pulled Della to her and hugged her and told her that standing up for herself was very important and her mother must have been a wonderful woman to have instilled that in her at such a young age.'

'Wow, she's really making an effort, isn't she?' Flo said.

'She is,' Mike said. 'And Della might only be four, but she has *leader* written all over her. Look at her.'

They turned and looked to where Della appeared to be dishing out instructions for the next game she wanted to play.

'It looks like it has worked out for everyone,' Ari said. 'I'm glad for Ben's sake that he's involved with Kayden. And for Kayden, too.' She smiled at Flo. 'I'll get used to it all eventually.'

Flo reached across and hugged her. 'You've always been the best. I am lucky.'

'We can *tackle anything*,' Ari said squeezing her tight. 'The last few weeks have proven that.'

'You can *take a chance on me*,' Flo said, her eyes noticeably watery as they pulled apart.

Ari smiled. 'Whatever happens, *knowing me, knowing you*, we'll always have each other, Flo.'

Flo squeezed her hand and smiled. 'I love you, Ari. Even with the corny Abba-ing as Kayden calls it.'

They fell silent momentarily, and Ari knew the relief she was feeling that she had her sister back would be mirrored in Flo's emotions.

'Hey, whatever happened about you needing to move?' Ari

suddenly asked, breaking the silence. 'You had sixty days' notice, but that was weeks ago. Did you find anywhere?'

Flo's face clouded over. 'With everything going on, I haven't had time to look. I'll be getting online tomorrow to see what's available.'

'The spare rooms are here for you and Kayden,' Mike said. 'Whether it's for a few weeks or months, you know it's there as a fallback.'

'Thanks, Dad. Now, we should get back outside. Rescue Gigi from Mum and see whether Ryan and Ben need a hand with the kids.'

* * *

Ari laughed as Della chased Ryan from one end of the garden to the other. Kayden was sitting with Gigi, having a rest as his stomach was still sore from the operation.

'I like him,' Ben said, coming up beside her. 'I know I have no right to comment, but seeing the way he was looking at you at lunch and how he made sure both Flo and I knew what he thought of our behaviour was impressive. I'm not sure I would have had the guts to make my feelings that clear, and to tell Julia off too.'

'You're right – he is impressive,' Ari said. 'I haven't known him that long, but I've learned a lot from him in that time. I thought it might be a bit weird with you both here.'

'The whole thing's weird,' Ben said and laughed. 'But, good weird.' He pushed the hair from his face. 'You've got no idea how much Della's changed in the past few weeks. She still has her moments when she's sad about Carrie, but most of the time, she's excited that she's going to see Kayden. She loves Flo too, which is good as we're probably going to be around each other a fair bit.'

'I'm glad it's working out.' Ari realised she meant the words as she said them.

'There's something I wanted to ask you,' Ben said. 'Before I speak to Flo about it. It's just Mum had an idea that could work out well for all of us.'

Ari nodded, waiting for him to share the details.

'As you know, Della and I have been living with Mum and Dad since we got home. That's temporary, of course, while I find something else. But now, with Kayden in the picture, I want to make sure I'm close to where he is, too. With Flo needing to move, that could be anywhere.'

Ari swallowed. 'Please tell me you're not about to suggest you and Flo move in together. I'm doing my best with all of this, but there's only so much I can take.'

'No!' Ben said. 'Well, not exactly. The thing is there's a great investment opportunity coming up in Mont Albert. It's not too far from where Dell and I are or where Flo is. It's a block that contains two townhouses. I was thinking that if I bought them both, I could rent one to Flo and live in the other one, or she might want to buy one if she's able to. That way, we could set up a bedroom with two beds in each house and the kids could come and go between us. It'd be perfect when Flo's working shifts, and, I think I'm going to have some travel coming up, so rather than Dell going to Mum and Dad's, she might be able to stay with Kayden and Flo.' He held up his hands. 'I haven't spoken to Flo about any of this. I thought I'd run it by you first.'

Ari stared at him. How *did* she feel about this? If they were living in such close proximity, was it likely they'd end up together? It was a possibility.

'What are you thinking?'

Ari hesitated. Part of her wondered if she should be the one to stand in the way of Flo and Ben if they were interested in each other, but another part of her realised she needed to say what was on her mind. 'That I'm not sure if I'd be okay if you and Flo eventually ended up together.'

'I wouldn't either,' Ben said. 'Look, don't get me wrong; on paper, if you remove the lies and deception, we're good friends, and we share a kid... But life's not on paper. I didn't intend for you to overhear what I said about Carrie that day, and I'm not saying this now to hurt you, but what I experienced with Carrie was an off-the-charts kind of love. I can't imagine ever experiencing it again, but I'm also not willing to settle for anything less. When Flo and I got together that night, it was two things. One, she's the spitting image of you and I was missing you like crazy, and two, being with Flo is like being with a friend you'd happily hang out with in your PJs on a Friday night. Not a woman you wanted to dress to the nines and take dancing in a grand palace in France.'

Ari couldn't help but smile. 'I didn't realise that was one of your fantasies.'

'You know what I mean, though. Flo was comfortable, Carrie was passionate and loving, and... I can't describe it. Flo and I will be friends and live close by, but not in the same house. It'll give us the chance to date other people and the kids the chance to grow up like real siblings. That's if Flo agrees to give this a go.'

Ari nodded. 'It sounds like you've given it a lot of thought. Go for it. And Ben, thank you.'

'For what?'

'For asking me if it was okay rather than telling me that was what you were doing.'

Ben smiled. 'And I appreciate the strength you're showing that Ryan spoke about so well earlier. Ar, I hope you've found your Carrie.'

* * *

'That was something else,' Ryan said as Ari turned the car out onto Toorak Road in the direction of Melbourne city.

Ari laughed. 'Never a dull moment around the Hudsons.'

'I found myself tearing up when Ben and Flo told the kids about the new living arrangements. Seeing Della hug Kayden like that was so adorable.' He rested a hand on her knee. 'I never thought I wanted kids until that moment, to be honest.'

'At this stage, and our age, it might be settling for being Uncle Ryan to those two,' Ari said.

'Sounds good to me.' They travelled a little further in a comfortable silence before Ryan spoke again. 'I thought you were going to tell them our news.'

'I told Gigi,' Ari said, 'but there seemed to be so many other things going on that I didn't want to overshadow Mum's apologies or Ben's news about the new living arrangements for him and Flo. I'll tell them all later in the week.'

'How did Gigi take the news?'

'She was great,' Ari said, smiling as she thought back to her conversation with her grandmother.

* * *

'You're going to quit?'

Ari nodded. 'Originally, I was going to take a leave of absence and keep my options open, but I decided that I didn't want to do that. I want to do something exciting without every move being mapped out. I'll worry about work when we return and when I'm ready. It wouldn't surprise me if I walked away from law altogether. But I'll think about that when it's relevant.'

Gigi nodded. 'I'll miss you. Make sure you don't go for too long, or I might be dead by the time you return. I am nearly two hundred, don't forget.'

Ari had squeezed her grandmother's hand. 'I'll miss you too. But we can Zoom or call each other. I'm sure you'll be sick of seeing me so often.'

'Where are you going to go first?'

'Ryan wants to show me his favourite parts of Thailand, and then we'll probably go on to Europe. We haven't planned it all out yet, but we'll be going around the world and probably taking a year at least to do it.'

'Do you think you know each other well enough to commit to such a big trip?'

Ari shrugged. 'The worst-case scenario is that we don't enjoy travelling together and will either go our own ways or come home.'

Gigi looked over to where Ryan was chatting with Julia. 'I have a feeling this one won't let you down. There's something about him that feels like he's a keeper. I'm so happy for you, Ari. Your grandfather used to say, "Life flourishes on the wings of adventure." I hope you find that's true.'

'I'm sorry you didn't get to finish your adventures with him,' Ari said.

'Me too, love. Me too.'

* * *

'How do you think the rest of them will take it?' Ryan asked, breaking into her thoughts.

'I think Mum will have a heart attack initially that I'm doing something outside of her control, but then she will explain to us that this will be good for her therapy to see if she can handle it.' Ari laughed. 'Dad will be fine. He liked you, and Flo... she'll miss me. But she has a new life to get used to with Ben and Della, and we'll keep in touch while we're away.'

'A bit of distance might be good for you,' Ryan said.

Ari stopped at a red light. 'I think it will be too. Give me a chance to miss them all and come back ready to be part of the slightly larger family.'

Ryan leaned across and kissed her lightly on the lips. 'Hopefully, after we travel, you'll want me as part of that larger family.'

Ari returned his kiss, a warmth spreading through her as she realised that she hoped that would be what the next twelve months brought. A time to laugh, relax and love with Ryan by her side. Her feelings for this man beside her were different from anything she'd experienced before. Maybe Ben was right. That you only knew the brilliance of true love when you were lucky enough to experience it. The one thing Ari knew for sure, with everything that had transpired, coming out this end of it, she was feeling lucky. Lucky enough to believe that Ryan might turn out to be her Carrie.

EPILOGUE

Julia rolled her eyes as another Abba song played. It was the girls' thirty-seventh birthday, and even after twenty years of hearing them blast out the classic songs, she could never understand this obsession with Abba. But the eye-roll quickly morphed into laughter and pride as she watched Ari swing Flo around the dance floor. Anyone watching would think they were a couple who'd taken dance classes to be perfectly choreographed to 'Dancing Queen'. Their friends seemed to agree as they whooped and clapped.

'Another champagne?' Mike held up the bottle of Mumm they'd been enjoying.

'Look at them,' Julia said, as Mike refilled both her and Gigi's glasses. 'They're having a ball.'

Mike smiled as he turned to watch his daughters. 'They're not the only ones. Della and Kayden are doing their best to copy them.'

'Not quite as elegant,' Gigi said as Kayden dropped Della's hands and fell onto his bottom, 'but they're certainly having fun. If I wasn't nearing six hundred, I'd consider getting out there myself.'

'I'd be happy to twirl you around the dance floor,' Mike said. 'I heard Ari tell Flo she'd organised for the DJ to play *a lot* of Abba. Something about them being able to *tackle anything* when they had each other, and they had Abba.' He raised an eyebrow in question.

Gigi frowned. 'I'm not sure where that all comes from, and while I have to admit, I do love Abba, I'm just relieved that they're friends again. More than friends – look at that twin bond they have.'

The three of them turned their attention to Ari and Flo who were laughing hysterically with Ryan who'd joined them and was now dancing holding one hand of each of them.

'I'd argue it isn't a twin bond,' Julia said. 'Maybe a sibling bond. Look at Kayden and Della. They're as close, if not closer than Ari and Flo were at any age.' And they were, she reflected. She'd always assumed the closeness of her girls was due to the fact they were identical twins. But having observed Kayden and Della over the last twelve months, she wasn't sure that twins had anything to do with it. Was it being related by blood, or was it just that they loved each other? She was itching to pick up a pen to record her thoughts... but she didn't.

Instead, Julia picked up her champagne flute and raised it in the air. 'Thank you.'

'For what?' Gigi asked, the surprise on her face mirrored by both Mike and Heather who sat either side of her.

'For making me realise what's important. I know it's taken far too long, and I'll probably regret forever how I tried to control my girls' lives, but the family gatherings we've had over the last twelve months have brought something different to my relationships with Flo, and now Ari and Ryan are back I'm hoping our relationship will improve too. I know I haven't completely dropped my need to control things, but I'm working on it.'

Gigi laughed. 'Are you by any chance referring to Della's fifth birthday party? While the pony, magician and jumping castle were amazing, and I know Ben and Flo appreciated your generosity, they were perhaps a bit over the top.'

Julia smiled. 'They were the three things the girls always asked for when they were kids and I said no, they were too extravagant.'

'Della loved it,' Gigi said. 'But yes, you've certainly set the bar high for subsequent years.'

'That's okay. I'll deal with it next year. But overall, I'm doing better. I hardly flinched when Flo turned down the nurse manager role she was offered and announced she was going back to medical school part-time. Mind you, that's probably more to do with the fact that she's got Ben helping her to co-parent, so the timing is perfect. But the fact that Ari and Ryan travelled for close to a year, and not only did I have no control but also had to wait for their random updates was hard to start with, but as time passed, I just loved hearing from them and realised that I relaxed between calls. I didn't *need* to know what they were doing, I just wanted to hear that they were safe, and they were happy.'

'I think he might be the one,' Gigi said.

Mike nodded. 'Let's hope so. I have to say I like him.'

'Really,' Julia said, 'even though he doesn't play golf?'

Mike laughed. 'I've got Ben for that. I'm officially allowed to be friends with him because of Kayden so I couldn't ask for a better situation. And Ari's fine with it. She and Ben seem to get along well still. As complicated as everything has been, it appears our family works well when we can officially be classified as dysfunctional.'

Julia erupted with laughter, causing them all to smile. 'I think that should be my job title: Julia Hudson, Chief Executive of Dysfunction.'

Gigi squeezed her hand. 'You're anything but. I'm so proud

you're my daughter. What sets you apart is your ability to observe a situation and determine what would be best for it. You've done it for your work for years and you've done it for the girls for years. And most importantly you've been able to reassess and do it over the past year. Our family is closer than it's ever been, and we've added Ben, Della and Ryan to the clan. I honestly don't think we could ask for more.'

A lump rose in Julia's throat. She'd spent time going through the journals she'd started writing over thirty years ago. The entries started the day Arabella fell from the swing when she was four. It wasn't hard to see how obsessed with protecting them she'd become, and while a part of her would argue that she was only looking out for her girls, the rational part of her knew she'd taken it too far. Now, her priority when it came to the girls, to Mike, to Gigi and to Kayden and Della, was to ensure she not only loved them, but that they knew it as well. Her words, and more importantly, her actions, reflected this.

She knew she still messed up at times, but the difference now, was she was *trying* to do the best for everyone. And for the rest of her life this would become her mantra. She wouldn't dictate or manipulate, she'd encourage, advise if asked, and ultimately be there for her family and most importantly, her daughters.

She lifted her champagne flute to her lips, her eyes focused on the dance floor and the fun her children and grandchildren were having. She'd been given a second chance, and with this, she'd ensure her family knew, with no documented studies and no strings attached, how much she loved them.

ACKNOWLEDGEMENTS

I would like to express my gratitude to the early readers of *A Mother's Betrayal*, whose invaluable feedback helped shape this story into what it is today. Special thanks to Judy and Ray for their insightful comments and to Maggie and Judy who also dedicated time to proofreading the final, edited, version of the manuscript.

Thank you to Cathy Guy for sharing her comprehensive knowledge of the inner workings of an ICU, adding authenticity to the medical aspects portrayed in this story. My heart goes out to Brian, Cathy, Zachary and Natalie that this knowledge was gained through far too many ICU admissions.

Sincere thanks to Janine Garrett for providing advice on current medical administrative practices, including insights into modern communication methods such as texts and messaging systems. Your contributions enriched the narrative and added a layer of realism to the story.

To the publishing team at Boldwood, thank you for your dedication, professionalism, and tireless efforts to bring this story to life in various formats. A special thank you to Isobel Akenhead for her exceptional developmental editing skills and keen attention to detail. Your insights and guidance have greatly enhanced the quality of this manuscript.

Lastly, to all those who have supported me along this journey, thank you for purchasing my books, leaving reviews and continuing to inspire me to pursue my passion for storytelling.

ABOUT THE AUTHOR

Louise Guy bestselling author of seven novels, blends family and friendship themes with unique twists and intrigue. Her characters captivate readers, drawing them deeply into their compelling stories and struggles. Originally from Melbourne, a trip around Australia led Louise and her husband to Queensland's stunning Sunshine Coast, where they now live with their two sons, gorgeous fluff ball of a cat and an abundance of visiting wildlife.

Sign up to Louise Guy's mailing list for news, competitions and update on future books.

Follow Louise on social media:

facebook.com/louiseguyauthor

bookbub.com/authors/louise-guy

ALSO BY LOUISE GUY

My Sister's Baby

A Family's Trust

A Mother's Betrayal

Boldwood

Boldwood Books is an award-winning fiction publishing company seeking out the best stories from around the world.

Find out more at www.boldwoodbooks.com

Join our reader community for brilliant books, competitions and offers!

Follow us
@BoldwoodBooks
@TheBoldBookClub

Sign up to our weekly deals newsletter

https://bit.ly/BoldwoodBNewsletter